Stephanie Theobald

Stephanie Theobald is the author of two other acclaimed novels, *Biche* and *Sucking Shrimp*. She is also a journalist, travelling around the world interviewing oddballs and writing about modern party tribes for a variety of national magazines and newspapers, including the *Observer* and the *Financial Times*.

STEPHANIE THEOBALD

TRIX

SCEPTRE

Copyright © 2004 by Stephanie Theobald

First published in Great Britain in 2004 by Hodder and Stoughton
A division of Hodder Headline

The right of Stephanie Theobald to be identified as the Author of the Work has been
asserted by her in accordance with the Copyright, Designs and Patents Act 1988.

A Sceptre Paperback

1 3 5 7 9 10 8 6 4 2

A CIP catalogue record for this title is
available from the British Library.

ISBN 0 340 82391 7

Typeset in Monotype Sabon by
Palimpsest Book Production Limited
Polmont, Stirlingshire

Printed and bound in Great Britain by
Mackays of Chatham plc, Chatham, Kent

Hodder Headline's policy is to use papers that are natural, renewable
and recyclable products and made from wood grown in sustainable
forests. The logging and manufacturing processes are expected to
conform to the environmental regulations of the country of origin

Hodder and Stoughton Ltd
A division of Hodder Headline
338 Euston Road
London NW1 3BH

I dedicate this book to artist, muse, fellow traveller and shining light, Kristen Tedder who taught me that life is either a daring adventure or nothing.

M x P

ACKNOWLEDGEMENTS

Thanks to: the Interstate Route 10; the staff of the Waffle House in Biloxi, Mississippi; all the matriarchs I met in Glenwood, New Mexico; fifties radio star comedienne Aunt Karen (aka Billy Ione); Courtney Love for pissing people off; the strippers at the 'Loose' night in Soho; Leigh Bowery and Minty for 'Useless Man'; Clare Nobbs my Scarborough friend; Karin Nastie Nassif, my California dialogue coach; Alison Owing's *Hey Waitress!: The USA from the Other Side of the Tray*; my agent Mary Pachnos; my publicist Jocasta Brownlee who is always a breath of fresh air and to Philippa Pride my editor for being easy on the eye and ear when in a hungover state.

CHAPTER ONE

The First Chapter . . .

There has been nothing but white for days. At the Bloated Goat diner everything is white: white gravy, white grits, white sausage, women with white hair and white faces saying white things. 'Don't you worry about crying,' says the waitress, to a sobbing girl at the counter. 'We're all women here. We have a right!'

The only thing not white is the ocean. Back in Biloxi the ocean was black and red and yellow and hot as bathwater. It was like the testicles of a wife-batterer which had been trapped too long inside a sweaty jockstrap. When you plunged into its steamy, treacly depths the salt stung your skin and plastic bags kept floating by that, on closer inspection, turned out to be jellyfish. It was perfect.

Back in Florida, in Panama City, the water was also as hot as bathwater, but it seemed as though the spell was going to be broken: the water looked beautiful and blue, and was covered with sun angels doing tap dances. Luckily it was only an appearance. It was fooling you. It refreshed only for a split second and then you were back burning in hell again. Within seconds of leaving the water, globules of sweat were trickling down the small of your back making your body feel like it was crawling with lice.

I arrived in America a week ago, but the best bit was hitting the South where the only sounds are of tobacco spit sizzling on Tarmac hot enough to melt your skin and the only people are gigantic prehistoric blobs who never tan and whose eyes have turned to red gashes from the endless glare of the sun. Everything is matted and choked, and only limp and squelchy things can grow – eels and jellyfish and white swamp alligators and grey

1

Southern prawns they call 'shrimp' that make a squeaky sound like crunching through a maggot when you bite into their gigantic bland bodies. On the motel TV in Biloxi, it said that seafood in the South was getting fatter. 'The oysters are amazing!' a man interviewed in a restaurant exclaimed. 'Hell! You can get three mouthfuls out of 'em!'

There's something rather disgusting about big seafood, I always think. It reminds me of an inscription on a building here in New Orleans that says, 'Dei Parae Virginis Sine Labe Concepta.' Desperate Virgin Labia Concepts.

So I popped out and bought half a dozen of the oysters and took them back to my Biloxi motel room where I was delighted to discover that they were swollen and creamy as post-flu catarrh. The motel in Biloxi was my favourite so far. Sea Spray Inn, it was called. I opened a chipped magnolia door and found myself in a room with fluorescent strip-lighting, walls sticky with nicotine and a couple of cockroaches still squirming on a soil-brown carpet. The bathroom was fashioned from plastic marble and there was a non-specific oxblood blob on the door with an eyelash stuck in it. The sound of an electric chair turned out to be a furred-up air-conditioning box that phutted and fizzed on to grey curtains made from the fabric of bed-wetting sheets and patterned with sickly flowers that looked as though they'd started out as star-gazer lilies, then been dragged backwards through the sewage-laden waters of the stinking Mississippi.

I'm an expert on stinking motels now. There's more than just one stink to an American motel room. It's always a surprise. Before they give you the key, the desk person always asks you whether you want a smoking or a non-smoking room. What they should ask is if you want a room smelling of chain-smoking squaddies and hookers or if maybe you'd like one smelling of incontinent old people or an overdose of roach spray. Roach spray is plain unimaginative. It's what makes roaches squirm on carpets. Since I've been in America I have become a firm believer in the Roach Motel – something we were never lucky enough to have at the Sceptre. Roach Motels have two garage-style cardboard doors which the cockroaches enter through, enticed by smells they can't resist – putrid cabbage, dirty underwear, that sort of thing – in the same way that the human nose can suss out an imminent good time via smells of flat cider, patchouli oil and freshly washed female hair as they walk in at the front door to a party. There's something nice about cockroaches having somewhere designed especially for them, just as hamsters have cages and birds have tables.

Homes are very important.

Sometimes you see the roaches sprucing themselves up at the gates to the Motel. They pass their spiny legs over their faces (the hairs on their legs act as noses) preparing for the party thrills they expect to find inside: the mystery guests, the air-guitar playing, the endless games of Twister – imagine, with six legs! And then, when they enter, they discover that the floor is sticky with poison that crawls up into their legs, like green ink up the stem of a carnation, proving the truthfulness of the guarantee on the side of the box: 'They check in but they don't check out.'

I wonder, once inside, do they realise that there's no going back? Do they see piles of black corpses and hear wails of pain as the green poison creeps up into their bodies promising a slow, hideous death? Or do they have a bit of time to enjoy themselves before they feel the urge to lie down and take forty winks? Do they cruise through to the back of the party, dazzled by the bright disco lights (cockroaches can't see in red light, but see in green light very well), checking out the talent as they go and making a bee-line for the drinks cabinet?

They said in Biloxi not to come to New Orleans.

'You gotta watch out for them city folk,' the short order cook at the Waffle House warned me. He was wearing a badge saying, 'Team member since 1993'. 'I was there with my wife one time and this big ass black guy comes up to us, says, "Bet you a dollar I can guess where you bought your shoes."'

The waitress, whose lapel said to ask her about flavoured syrups, raised her eyebrows. She said, 'Not that old shoe thing again, Eric.'

Eric ignored her. 'So my wife – she's the biggest sucker you ever met in your life – my wife says, "OK, then, bet you a dollar. Where did I buy my shoes?" Hot damn! What does the guy reply? He goes, "Well, ma'am, you're wearing 'em!"'

Eric narrowed his eyes and scratched a cheek of his Homer Simpson arse with the griddle scraper. He stared at a notice above the door that read, 'If you believe in credit, lend me 5 bucks' and muttered, 'What's it again, Donna? Not "I can guess where you bought your shoes"? Something like that. And you're supposed to reply, "OK, go on, then," and then they say something all cute like, "They're on your feet" . . . and then you lose your money.'

He put the scraper on the work surface, put his hands on his hips and said, 'Now, what in hell is that thing they say?'

Donna came over to refill my coffee mug. 'Don't you mind him, hon,' she said, with a smile. 'He's just a big ol' stick-in-the-mud.'

I'm a bit of a stick-in-the-mud myself. That's why I came to America. To find inspiration. But already I've been breaking the rules, and breaking rules doesn't sit easily with me. For instance, Donna and Eric were the only people I talked to yesterday and that's not my rule. My rule is to talk to at least five people every day so my courage doesn't wizen up, like the muscles of a runner who doesn't exercise enough.

In some ways I've got no excuse because the first instinct of Americans is to be friendly. 'Hi, there! Where y'all from?' is what they like to say to complete strangers. Whether this comes from a compulsive need to make friends wherever they go or whether it harks back to the time of the Wild West pioneers – when you had to filter out the goodies from the baddies in the flash of an eye unless you wanted a bullet in your back – I'm

4

not sure. The problem is that my conversations are never very satisfying. Most of the people I get to talk to are the better-safe-than-sorry crowd – the sexless chubbies in pastel T-shirts, ironed denim shorts with hems, white cotton socks and white trainers, who carry lightweight cagoules in little bags in case it rains. Then there's the fact that they can never understand my accent. When I tell them I'm from Scarborough, they say something like, 'Scarboro? Sure I've heard of Scarboro. Every American knows Simon and Garfunkel.' And then they'll say something like, 'Parsley, sage and thyme, right?' or 'So, hon, will you be a true love of mine?'

I don't like to break it to them. About what Scarborough Fair's like now: in November, opposite the coach car park by Hope Street – no fancy herbs these days, although you can win a gold-fish with fungus on in a plastic bag, or eat a hot dog made from pig's eyeballs, or meet some dodgy bloke who'll give you a free ride on the waltzers if you go back to his caravan afterwards.

I dare say I should broaden my horizons beyond diners but I do like diners. They make you feel at home. You always know what to expect: the salt and pepper cruets always in the same place, the sugar shakers, the spotlessly clean bottles of Heinz ketchup, the black plastic boxes filled with pink Sweet and Lo sachets, the stools at the counter. When you perch on the counter stools it's like sitting on a high chair. You can kid yourself that you've got friends to talk to, that you're not lonely at all.

Best of all about diners are the waitresses. They're regular as clockwork (within two minutes of sitting down they'll have provided you with iced water, a menu and a cheery 'Hi, there!') yet they manage to remain mysterious at the same time. They have old souls, like Red Indian chiefs who, when you ask them a question, never answer it directly. Loni from the Bloated Goat looks like she could sit you down and sort your life out. (On one of her breasts it says, 'Hi, I'm Loni,' on the other it says, 'Satisfaction is our reputation'.) Earlier, she put a sun-damaged hand on the sobbing girl's arm and soothed, 'Shana, baby, when

5

life throws you lemons, make lemonade,' and when that didn't work she said, 'It's OK. Ruby Rose'll be here soon.'

I sneak a peek at Loni as she wallops a lump of grits on to the side of what appears to be the alligator-sausage breakfast ($8.99 plus tax). There's something about her that combines the world-weary and the sexually advanced. Whatever the mystery of the diner waitress, it's the best kind of mystery because you're not sure how to get to it. To get *at* it. The knowledge just hangs there, dangling on a golden thread – sweet and cool as an evening breeze in a wasteland of parched throats and sweaty skin.

You have to be over forty for the magic to work, and Loni fits the bill perfectly. She has proper diner-waitress flesh (like well-roasted meat that comes easily off the bone) and diner-waitress hair (like a poodle – all long and straggly down the sides and short and bouffant on top). When she smiles, you can see the ghosts of the other smiles, the thousands of other smiles she must have pasted on a thousand times before. That makes the smile better somehow. An old-wine smile.

I like diners and waitresses so much that I've decided to write an article called 'Breakfast in America' for the *Scarborough Evening Post* where I've been trying my hand at a spot of free-lancing. I've attended a number of journalism-related night classes at the Scarborough YMCA (or 't'Y' as it's known locally). The teachers all told us to limber up by writing about topics we're familiar with, and what I'm familiar with is waitressing. It was my friend Acid Sarah got me into the game. We started off with Saturday jobs in the Harbour Bar – Scarborough's famous ice-cream parlour from the 1950s with walls covered in old-fashioned adverts ('Eat ice-cream for good health') and wait-resses wearing yellow dinner-lady uniforms. The next summer we progressed to chambermaiding at the Maples Guest House where the landlady was an old trout whose life revolved around Glasgow fortnight – the couple of weeks when a load of beer-bellied Scots comes to town to try to find sex. Then, when we were in our early twenties, Acid Sarah got us jobs as silver-service waitresses at the Sceptre – one of the finest hotels in Scabs. The Sceptre overlooks the sea on the Queen Mary Esplanade and they've got autographed photos of Margaret Thatcher and the manager of Scarborough Football Club framed on the wall behind reception. Nothing's changed since the early days: the head waiter, Mr Spago, still snogs the older waitresses in the broom cupboard after evening service, and he's still a stickler for proper silverware usage. (Queen's Best is for weddings in the Imperial Lounge, Crown Silver is for accountant conferences in the banquet room and 't'crap' is for ordinary guests – consisting of odds and ends begged and borrowed from across town and engraved with various hotel logos, including the Butlins Grand situated across from the multi-storey car park.)

Of course, 'waiting tables', as they call it in America, is very different from waitressing in England. There's none of this skiving off on the Saturday morning after the Friday night before. There's no staggering sulkily up to tables, chewing gum and mumbling, 'Yeah, what d'you want, then?' like some of them do at the Sceptre. They wouldn't make it through the day in America, and over here you can't just go on the dole like you can in England. Hence what I've just written in my exercise book:

> When you get to be forty in America you have to be either a hooker or a waitress.

I like the look of this sentence although I'm not entirely sure what it means. I'm wondering whether to scribble it out or not, and as I'm thinking I'm playing with my macramé bracelet – made from two lengths of leather thong twisted into a series of square knots, laced with a few beads and secured with a toggle clasp. You could say that my bracelet (a memento from another night class) works as a sort of lucky charm. I fiddle with the knots and they help me think. The knots feel safe and orderly, I suppose. Knots make sense.

I jump when I hear a voice saying, 'C'mon, now, babe, pass

your plate over' – in New Orleans, they address you as 'baby' or 'babe' even if you're a complete stranger – and I look up to see Loni and her weary smile. Nobody seems to mind in the USA if you don't clear your plate and, to be honest, this does bother me rather. I wonder if Loni will remark on my perfectly empty plate of jambalaya omelette ($7.99 plus $1.25 tax). I blush as I pass it over but she doesn't say anything. She seems too concerned by the sobbing girl at the counter. 'C'mon, Shana,' she soothes. 'Ruby Rose'll be here any minute now.'

I pinch my bracelet knots again, resolving to speak to the sobbing girl. She's a good candidate because there's something I don't understand about her, and picking up clues and signs is an essential part of being a journalist. Shana's blonde hair, for instance, is up in an impressive chignon yet she's wearing a tatty pink tracksuit. I'm trying to work out why she'd have such a posh hair-do and yet be wearing such an unspectacular outfit when suddenly there's a bang, the door swings open, and everything stops being white.

At first, all you see is a pair of big black eyes. Then the breasts – large and tanned – spilling over the top of an amber-coloured corset dripping with coloured bugle beads and pieces of crystal chandelier. A hush descends on the Bloated Goat and when she finally plunges into the room all that can be heard is the rattle of glass baubles in the snake of hair coiled on top of her head, the swish of beads and the *click, click, click* of stiletto heels on concrete.

She struts towards the counter like an enormous lion who's just had a good feed. She must be six foot and fifteen stone, but this only registers after a while since her flesh is being worked and flaunted to its maximum potential. She exaggerates parts of her body that the less observant might not have noticed: a muscular shoulder here, a well-turned ankle (with diamanté chain) there. Her jewels spark, her nostrils flare, her temples tilt to angles conducive to the light, her eyelids drop slowly down as a show of approval to a lucky onlooker.

Everyone's gaze is pulled into her slipstream – everyone's, that is, apart from the sobbing girl's. She's turned back to the counter once more and sends tears shooting furiously into her glass of iced tea.

There's an almighty crunching sound, as if a shovelful of gravel's been dumped on the floor. Then the sound of hot liquid being poured faster and faster from a bottomless vessel. It's her. The lion woman. Laughing. Laughing and laughing as she tumbles down the three steps that descend to the Bloated Goat counter like a victim pushed from a liferaft in a school-play production of *Mutiny on the Bounty*. She flails this way and that, she throws herself around – snatching at steps, grabbing bar-stool legs, feigning broken bones, roaring, shrieking. And the melodrama doesn't stop when she finally rolls to the counter because she lies there, stroking her forehead like a damsel in distress. It seems to work. A group of over-excited tourists gathers round her, dangling hands above her collapsed body, saying things like 'Let me help you!' and 'Oh, boy!' and 'You OK?' and 'Not again, Ruby Rose!' (this from Loni). Even I leave my stool and edge over to see what will happen next.

But she slaps us all away. The only hand she's interested in is the one belonging to the sobbing girl who finally leaps up from her stool, girded into action by the sight of the charismatic ham actress lying at her feet.

'Ruby Rose! Oh, my gosh! You OK?'

'Sure I'm OK, babe,' Ruby Rose drawls. She props herself up.

'I thought you broke your neck!'

'Don't worry about my neck,' she says, rubbing the back of her head. 'Nobody breaks bones better than I do.' Her American accent is crisp and fast.

'Are you hurt, though?' Shana asks, taking both of Ruby Rose's hands and heaving her to her feet.

Once she's standing, Ruby Rose pulls two of the counter stools together and levers herself upwards, giving her bum cheeks one seat each. 'Hurt?' she says, massaging the small of her back. 'Sure I'm hurt. You wouldn't even have said hello unless I'd done one of my entrances.' She makes a hiccup of laughter.

'I'm sorry!' Shana starts to well up again. 'I'm just having a bad day . . .'

'*You*'re having a bad day?'

'What happened?' Shana looks concerned.

'Mr Eggmont never told me about his family.'

'His family?'

'These two older aunts of his offered to drive me to the chapel of rest. We got stuck in traffic for three hours as I was tripping off my ass on acid to a radio backdrop of "Tiny Bubbles" by Henry Mancini.'

'Oh, man!'

Ruby Rose shrugs. 'I guess it was kind of interesting. The aunts were going on about how the traffic jam was the fault of the Russians – Communism and shit – and I was kind of vibing on it, you know? I mean, I could kind of understand what they were saying. But then we finally get to the church and I can see the blood going around the body of Jesus on the cross and I can't stop laughing and everyone keeps turning round to see what's wrong. And then the priest turns out to be this Californian surfer dude with long, curly blond hair going, "So, like, we're all gathered here today . . ."'

'Funerals always scare me,' Shana says, her lower lip wobbling.

'I love a funeral,' Ruby Rose announces, crossing her legs and turning her right ankle from side to side – admiring the shiny black stiletto on her foot.

'You love funerals?'

'You should have seen the shoes.'

'The shoes?'

'Stiletto heels on marble?'

'Huh?'

'People always wear great footwear at funerals. You ever notice that? *Tap tap tap* down the aisle?' A shiver passes through her.

'You like funerals?' Shana looks as if she might start crying again.

'Sure. Coffins, heels, death. How sexy is that?'

'Sexy?' Shana looks at Ruby Rose suspiciously.

'Yeah. Did you ever see the lining of a coffin? Purple and crimson? In satin? I mean, hello? If death's so sad why isn't the lining made of towelling?'

Ruby Rose gets up from her counter stools and reaches down to retrieve a large gold bag she seems to have dropped in the kerfuffle of her entrance. As she rummages around inside, a couple of crumpled twenty-dollar bills fly up and drop to the floor. She picks them up and scrunches them back into the bag before pulling out a selection of Tupperware containers filled with brightly coloured liquids.

Shana starts snivelling again. She wipes her eyes with the back of her hand and reads the labels on each container as Ruby Rose puts them on the counter. 'Blue Crack, Peach Colada, Cajun Storm, Jungle Juice . . .' A strangulated moan rises from the bottom of her lungs. 'Do you think Mr Eggmont'd mind?' She quails. 'I mean, about us having daiquiris and margaritas at his wake?'

'"Would you like a carburettor or a diamanté butt plug for your birthday?"' Ruby Rose sighs, producing a Jack Daniel's bottle and unscrewing the top.

'Yeah, I remember you askin' him that.' Shana chucks some blue drink into her nearly empty iced tea glass. 'Funny, huh? He sure needed a new carburettor.'

I recognise the drinks as the frozen cocktails you get from machines in the saloon bars on Bourbon Street. The whole of Bourbon Street seems to be filled with frozen alcohol spinning round and round on its head. I went into one saloon there and soon left because my Pineapple Colada was like thick, cold soup (although I did like seeing a baby cockroach – the light-brown *Blattella germanica* – scuttling along a bar, taking refuge behind a small, fold-over sign saying, 'No Shoes, No Shirt, No Service').

'You be careful who sees that stuff, Ruby Rose,' Loni whispers, passing over some more glasses. 'You know what the police are like round here. Wake or no wake.'

Ruby Rose shrugs. 'Present for Mr Eggmont from Café Risqué.'

Loni makes one of her weary smiles. She asks Ruby Rose if she wants her usual, and when Ruby Rose flashes her a smile, she is handed a jug of fizzy stuff the colour of the ocean in Biloxi. 'Thanks, hon,' she says to Loni. 'And don't worry about these guys getting drunk and disorderly. You'd have to drink a truckload of this stuff to get messy.'

'I guess.'

'Yeah, and by that time they'd be frozen solid as a sheet of steel.'

'Stop talking 'bout death!' Shana erupts. 'I can't take no more death!'

'Come on, baby.' Ruby Rose laughs. 'No more tears. We got too much condensation round these parts as it is.'

She pours a slug of Jack Daniel's into her glass, followed by some of the yellowy brown liquid. 'Damn climate,' she says. 'God's punishment for country music.' She takes a swig and bangs the glass down on the counter, panting, 'Jack Daniel's and root beer: best drink in the world.'

The door suddenly swings open and the Bloated Goat fills with a procession of toreadors, devils, clowns and some more girls in tracksuits and chignons with strings of beads round their necks in the shape of monkeys and ghosts. There are also a few Diana Rosses, a couple of Bette Midlers and one couple who stick out of the crowd – a commercial airline pilot linking arms with a nun. (I note in my exercise book that I presume they are in fancy dress since in real life you never see an airline pilot being friends with a nun.)

'Fan-taaaaastic,' Ruby Rose says, watching what I'm guessing is Mr Eggmont's funeral cortège pour in through the door. 'Any excuse to dress up, huh, Danny?' she says to a black ram in a rhinestone thong with plastic horns over his ears and black platform hoofs who's sucking his teeth and reeking of tangy aftershave.

A group of Louis XVI types in gold brocade coats, powdered wigs with jagged stripes of blue down the sides of their necks (to represent severed nerve endings, I'd say) come to the bar to pick up their drinks. Ruby Rose pats one on the back, saying, 'Don't you be making off with that jacket now, Howie. That belongs in my drag bag.'

A young man, with a gym-toned body, wearing just a white vest, tight jeans and flip-flops comes over to greet her. 'Hey, babe. I've got a meeting with a gardener later on. I think you might be interested in sampling some of his produce . . .'

'Bet I'll *love* that gardener.' She grins, adding, 'Your flowers looked bee-oo-ti-ful at the chapel of rest, Slick. You should be proud of yourself.'

'Thanks, Ruby Rose.'

'I *loved* the corset.'

'You liked that?' Slick looks pleased. 'I did my best. Funerals give you more chance to be experimental than weddings, but I thought a corset was about as dirty as I could get. You know what I'm saying?'

'I know what you're saying.'

They both make secret smiles.

'I made it with moss. You should see my teddy bears in moss and chicken wire.' He takes a glass of khaki-coloured liquid that Ruby Rose is holding out to him. 'Good thing about moss is that it never dies.'

'Lucky moss.'

'Yeah. It beats all that macramé flowerpot-holder shit.'

'I don't know about that,' Ruby Rose says, turning and looking at my wrist. 'Some of those knots are cute. What do you say, Peach?'

Suddenly I'm a cockroach tipped up on its back. I glare help-lessly at the offending item on my wrist, knowing I have to say something but not knowing if I should say '*mac*-ramé,' like Slick just pronounced it or if I should say 'macr*aaaaaa*-mé' like we were taught in class.

There you are. Spontaneity. The unexpected. Hopeless. I am. At it. I'm not much cop as a waitress, actually. I might be in my thirties now but customers at the Sceptre scare me most of the time.

'More mash, sir?'

'Aye, lass. I'm a growing boy!'

'Gosh . . .'

It's like being in an amateur dramatic show. The stage fright. The first table of the day is the worst. You'll be about to go out and you're wondering if your mask is good enough. I make myself do it, though. I force myself. I've always tried to be plucky even though it's never come naturally.

I look down at the maple-syrup jug on Loni's counter and force myself to gabble something about how my bracelet came out of a night class I did back in Scarborough. 'I've done a lot of night school, you see. Greek mythology, for instance.' I swallow. 'British narrative verse of the nineteenth century, too. And embroidery. I've done embroidery as well: herbs in Elizabethan needlework, characteristics of Assisi sewing, heraldry and ecclesiastical techniques . . . I gave it up, though. Boring, it was. The teacher suggested macramé . . .'

Shit, I've said it. I've said it wrong. Slick and the Ruby Rose woman are both looking at me as if I've just landed from outer space. Ruby Rose's eyes are gleaming. 'Macr*aaaaaa*-mé, huh?' she says, coming over to perch herself on the two stools next to mine. 'Go on, Peach. I want to know all about your night classes.'

I don't know if she's taking the piss. She's certainly unnerving me. Why is she giving me her undivided attention? 'Well,' I go on, standing up from my stool and picking up the red check lumberjack shirt that's been covering it, 'I suppose I find tying knots quite relaxing, you know . . .' I slip on the shirt so that it covers up my wrists (and my vintage The Cult T-shirt – in case that's wrong too). 'Apparently sailors used to do it at sea . . .' I flinch. 'Knot work, I mean. They used to do that at sea. It's why they call ma – it's why they call it "the sailor's craft" . . .'

I turn to look at her, hoping she'll let me stop now. But she just stares into my eyes and that sends me back to my blurry reflection in the chrome of the countertop. 'Life-belts they made.' It's getting painful now. 'Rope-ladders and shoes and handcuffs—'

'Handcuffs, huh?' she finally breaks in, her voice dripping with innuendo. 'Sailors doing it at sea with handcuffs, huh?'

She turns to Slick. 'We love a sailor, don't we, Slick?'

Slick nods like he really means it. 'There's something romantic about a sailor,' he says.

'Yeah,' Ruby Rose agrees. 'Better than soldiers or airmen. Soldiers smell of sweaty mechanic oil and airmen smell of airplane food.'

She takes another swig from her glass, then tops it up from the Jack Daniel's bottle. 'Sailors have slept with each other too, right? They've been there. To that same sex place.'

I can feel another blush coming on so I rush in with, 'They say that's where the phrase "spinning a yarn" comes from. You know – from when sailors sat on their ships undoing the rope and making it into ma—'

'Into what?' The corners of her mouth are twitching.

'Into "*mac*-ramé",' I say slowly.

She makes a guffaw that is neither old nor new wine but, rather, some kind of bootleg liquor. Then she pats me on the back. 'Pour the girl a drink, Loni. I think she just joined the club.'

I'm not sure what club it is I've just joined but I'm not unhappy about my new membership as I sit on my stool, sipping at my Blue Crack (about ten times more potent than the stuff on Bourbon Street). Ruby Rose wants to know what I've been writing in my exercise book. 'Looks like you're spinning yarns yourself,' she says. I tell her that I don't think I'm much good at spinning yarns. I tell her that I'm having trouble reading Shana, and that I shouldn't be having trouble because reading things is supposed to be my job.

'What's your job?' she wants to know.

'I'm trying to be a writer.'

'What kind of things do you write?'

'Oh, journalism stuff. Freelance. It started out as another night class and then I met someone. She works on the *Scarborough Evening Post*. It's easier if you know someone. I wrote a piece about cockroaches. I'm doing breakfast at the moment. "Breakfast in America".'

I tell her how I'm in the US from England on a three-week fly-drive. I explain how I started my research in Florida three days ago, with orange juice and pancakes, and then how the further south I drove, the whiter things became: grits (like semolina, tasting of porridge), biscuits and gravy (scone things covered in thick, salty béchamel sauce) and now alligator sausage and jambalaya omelette.

'I wanted to be a writer once,' she says.

'What do you write?'

She reaches into her gold bag and pulls out a book. It has a raspberry-coloured cover embroidered with black silk flowers and it's held shut with a thin piece of green and yellow cord attached to the spine. When she unties the flimsy slip-knot, she opens the book to reveal page after page of thick, creamy paper – all of it blank. Some of the pages are ripped and look as if they've been singed round the edges.

'Where are the words?'

'I burned them all.'

'You burn what you write?'

'Yeah. I burn words.'

'Why?'

'I figure there's no point in keeping them once you've said them. And, anyway, burning gives them added significance.'

'Gosh.'

'I figure that burnt words are even more dramatic than a message in a bottle washed up on a beach.'

She slams the floral notebook shut, wraps the cord round it again and returns it to her bag. 'I guess you have sex with lots of different people, huh?'

'Sorry?'

'That's what writers do, isn't it?'

'Probably they're supposed to,' I mumble.

She laughs. She's quick. She gets me. She pokes at my exercise book, and before I can stop her she's swooped it up and she's reading today's grand entry:

When you get to be forty in America you have to be either a hooker or a waitress.

I try to grab it but she's leaning towards Loni, going, 'Hey, the Brit says waitresses and hookers are all the same!'

'Hookers have it better than waitresses,' Loni says, with a frown. 'At least if you're a hooker you get paid first!'

'She's right,' Ruby Rose says. 'If a hooker gives up her goods and her customer walks out, she's literally fucked. As a waitress, though, you work your butt off in the hope of a tip at the end.'

She fills her empty glass with some more root beer, then sloshes in a large tot from the Jack Daniel's bottle. 'You've got a point, though,' she says, turning to me. 'Waiting tables and hooking are both power trips. They're both about manipulation: "No, sir, you don't just want bacon, how about a little sausage too?"'

'The more items, the bigger the bill,' Loni says, refilling my coffee mug.

'The bigger the tip!' Ruby Rose adds. 'Don't forget, Peach: ten per cent when the service sucked, fifteen per cent if it's been fine and twenty per cent if you want to get in with the waitress.'

'Except if you're Ruby Rose,' Loni adds, 'in which case you leave a tip big enough for the waitress to be able to live on steak and lobster all week.'

Ruby Rose smiles. 'The bottom line,' she says, 'is that to be a waitress or a hooker you need big-ass doors in your head.'

'What kind of doors?' I want to know.

'Doors to distance you. You have to be able to cut yourself off. You have to remember that you can walk out of the door into the next room when you're finished.'

'Don't know if I have those kind of doors.'

'I guess you need a crazy old house in your head.'

'Don't know if I have that house.'

'A shitty childhood helps.' She picks up the glass and proposes a toast: 'To burning words and shutting doors!'

When she's polished off another Jack Daniel's and root beer, she wants to know what my problem was in reading Shana. I tell her that I couldn't work out why Shana was wearing a track-suit with a chignon hair-do – that I still can't.

'And no socks,' she points out.

'You see, I didn't even notice that . . .'

'Well, Peach,' she says warmly, 'don't beat yourself up. A track-suit and a chignon's a tricky one. You're like, "If she has fancy hair why not a fancy outfit?"'

'Exactly.'

'OK, so Shana's a dancer. An exotic dancer at the Café Risqué.' She glances quickly to make sure Shana's not watching, then silently mouths the word, 'stripper'. 'She's wearing a tracksuit with her hair all fancy because she's due for a shift, and if you're a stripper you can't afford to get pressure marks on your skin – hence no socks and no tight jeans. Also, you should have noticed that she doesn't mind people staring at her all the time. If you're a stripper you're used to people looking at you. It's your job.'

'I suppose it's quite degrading work.'

'Degrading!' Ruby Rose nearly chokes. 'Oh, my!' Her breasts wobble recklessly in her corset. 'And what else do you consider to be degrading, Miss Macr*aaaaa*-mé?'

'You know,' I mumble, 'pornography and stuff.'

'Really?' she drawls. 'I've whipped more butts in rooms with Bibles than in rooms with porn mags.'

A jolt goes through me. I smell her then. Her body sends off the odour of sour plums and cold cement and the unmistakable waft of marijuana.

Shana staggers back over, her cheeks veiled in a waxy crust of dried tears. Ruby Rose squeezes her shoulder. 'How you feeling, babe?'

'Had some jerks in last night,' Shana slurs, pouring herself another glass of Blue Crack. 'One of them touched me. I got so fucking pissed off. I go, "You got a girlfriend? Your girlfriend's body hot as this? Don't you touch me, motherfucker . . ."'

'You think you got it tough, baby,' Ruby Rose says. 'I was on the panel to judge that amateur stripper contest at the Risqué last week. Man! Some of those chicks were flapping around! I'm, like, "I don't want to see all your lunch hanging out! You never heard of tucking up?"'

'They was showing *pink*?' Shana seems astonished.

'They were.' Ruby Rose nods, her eyebrows raised. 'Girl takes care of her hair, she should take care of her pussy too.'

'Exactly.'

'I wouldn't have minded if they'd been rosebuds.'

'Rosebuds!'

'Yeah, but they weren't. I felt bad for some of them. Lips like butterfly wings . . .'

'Butterfly wings!' Shana shrieks, and has to steady herself on the counter.

We watch her stagger back to the crowd of revellers, then Ruby Rose turns to me and confides, 'Excellent shoes in that contest, actually. Really deep-cut toe cleavage.'

I think she's being serious. 'What exactly do you like about high heels?'

'The sound? I don't know. Everything. There are pictures of me in diapers and high heels, sliding around the house.' She adds that her first ever memory was a pair of high-heeled shoes. 'I remember peeking out from under a table at this woman in shiny stilettos.'

'Who did they belong to?'

'Who knows? Sure stuck in my mind, though.'

'Apparently there's a shoe trick that people in New Orleans say to fool the tourists,' I tell her.

'There is?' Her eyes wander distractedly around the bar.

'Yes. A man in the Waffle House in Biloxi said so. And you lose a dollar if you don't get it right.'

She turns back to me, licking her lips – sort of playing around with them.

'How cute are you.' Her voice is rich. It makes me cross my arms in front of my chest. 'You're so sweet,' she says. 'You're like an angel.'

I feel a bit dizzy with the Blue Crack. Before I know it, I've said, 'You're so evil. You're like a devil.'

I realise immediately this is an inappropriate thing to say because the glow in her face disappears and something strange happens to her eyes. The change is very small, almost unnoticeable. It's like the twitch made by very fresh oysters when you squeeze lemon juice on their edges. The liquid black goes harder and tighter. It all happens in a split second. And then the eyes don't look evil any more. They look afraid. As if there's something she's terribly afraid of.

Slick comes up and bellows, in an exaggerated Southern accent, 'Care to buy some candy to help out the Ministry?'

For a few seconds, Ruby Rose seems not to notice him. And then she murmurs, 'What?'

'Care to buy some candy to help out the Ministry?' Slick says again, pointing flamboyantly to his pocket.

That's when she shudders back into life. 'Candy?' She looks at him with fake disdain. 'You offering me candy, boy?'

Slick motions to the open street and she raises herself up from her stools. She picks up her gold bag, delves into it for a ludicrously large tip – fifty dollars – and prepares to leave. 'Pleasure meeting you,' she says, shaking my hand and not meeting my eye.

I can't believe it. She's turned into a stranger, into one of the stupid cagoule brigade. I watch her follow Slick to the door and then I turn back to the counter, cradling my disgusting blue drink and listening to the *click, click, click* of stiletto heels on concrete fading into the distance.

They don't fade away completely. They just stop. I turn round and there she is in the doorway, staring at me. She checks out my body for what feels like an endless moment until she finally arrives at my training shoes. 'Nice sneakers,' she goes. 'Bet I know where you got them.'

'From Scarborough!' I say it with ridiculous enthusiasm.

'No, you didn't,' she shoots.

The hairs stand up on the back of my neck.

'I'll tell you where you got your shoes,' she says, slowly. 'You got your shoes at the end of your feet.'

The black diamonds are back in her eyes. 'That'll be a dollar, please, ma'am.'

The door opens, and there's a blinding dazzle as the outside world comes to get her. For a few seconds there's a shimmer of amber and emerald on the wall as the sun pierces through the treasure chest in her hair. Then everything is white.

CHAPTER TWO

Munchies

I think America might be bringing me back to life. Everything in America is intense. Even sweets are intense. My favourite thing is Big Red, a brand of cinnamon chewing-gum available in every gas station with such a brutal flavour that it paralyses the veins under your tongue and feels like a wasp sting gradually seeping into your blood.

American gas stations are almost as good as American diners on the making-you-feel-at-home front. What harm could possibly come to you, you think, in a place filled with such a sensory overload of brightly coloured junk food? Sugar-laden air-dried meat, called jerky, bright orange Cheet-Os with wrappers showing a cheetah pulling a lever going from 'cheesy', 'very cheesy' to 'disgustingly cheesy', Hostess Cup Cakes, Ding Dongs, Krispy Kremes, Twinkies (with red love hearts on the Cellophane), Reese's Peanut Butter Cups, Tootsie Roll, Life Savers and a variety of Hershey products all printed in that trusty, squat American typeface.

It feels as though there should be bells chiming gently as you walk into an American gas station, like in Mr Benn when he walked out of the changing room, through the curtains and into his new life. Gas stations make you feel at home while simultaneously transporting you to another world: you fill your car with petrol, you walk over the burning Tarmac of the forecourt and then you plunge into the gas-station shop, like diving into the ocean – a proper cool ocean. One minute you're gasping out in the scorching sun, and the next you're in a big, chilled room filled with the sound of mammoth fridges slamming shut like safes and women at the cash desk saying, 'Mm-hmmmm?' (a less energy-consuming way of saying, 'You're welcome,' in a very hot climate).

Keeping cool is very important in America and gas stations are a godsend in this respect. They have soda fountains, ice packs, walls lined with fridges stocking chilled drinks cans, two-dollar polystyrene coolers that can be filled with ice, then taken to your car and used as portable refrigerators.

Back in Scarborough, Mother and I used to drink hot tea on hot afternoons because, as she pointed out, it cools you down. On hot afternoons in America what you do is drink iced tea from a bucket-sized cup that you can pick up from the soda fountain along with several shovelfuls of ice from the nearby ice machine and a straw – or many straws, if you so choose – and then afterwards you throw everything away willy-nilly.

I was shocked by all the waste to start with.

Nobody has special drawers in America for once- or twice-used straws or for pieces of silver foil, smoothed wrinkle-free with a careful thumbnail and folded neatly away for later use like strips of gold leaf. Pale green foil from peppermint cream chocolate bars, silvery pinky scraps from Easter-egg wrappings, small blue squares from a quarter of Everton toffees pitted with tiny nicks – the result of damage when peeling off the top layer of Cellophane. A scrap of Bacofoil with crumbs clinging to it from its last outing to the cricket pitch or South Bay beach, where it held egg-and-cress sandwiches or something with pilchards in. Never shop-bought picnic food.

There's a story in this week's *National Enquirer* about Jimmy Carter leaving a big tip in a diner and then asking the waitress for a doggie-bag. The waitress in the article seemed to think that such a request was beneath an ex-president, but I think more people should take a leaf out of his book because the waste in America is never-ending. Take the 'nutritional triangle', for instance. On the side of every box of processed food you buy there's this pointless diagram called the 'nutritional triangle', with rice and pulses at the bottom, fruit and veg in the middle

– three to five pieces a day, etc. – and at the top, in the tiny tip of the pyramid, there's the place for fats and junk food. Well, that's a waste of cardboard and ink for a start. Judging by the size of them, nobody in America is taking a blind bit of notice of the 'nutritional triangle'.

Then there are the drinks. The smallest drink you can buy in the gas stations is 'medium', which is, in my book, 'huge'. Then the cups get filled up with huge rocks of ice so the contents go flat really quickly and you have to buy another because it's so cheap anyway. Only I don't. I stay with it all day, drinking it even when it's warm and flat and watery. I hate waste. Still, I don't deny that America has opened my mind to some new truths. The one about hot tea cooling you down, for instance. Hot tea doesn't cool you down at all. It just makes you really sweaty when you're drinking it so that afterwards no wonder you feel cooler. It's a typical case of British masochism: of going through hell and high water so that anything feels better in comparison. Like Mother telling me not to put my jacket on in the house because I wouldn't 'feel the benefit' when I went out. Whereas what we should have done was turn the central heating on because we weren't *that* poor and Mother's school-secretary wages weren't *that* low.

Not that I've gone completely mad in the land of plenty. You enjoy things better if you have a structure, I always find. Hence my daily research on breakfast in America. Hence my plan today to go to an American supermarket, purchase one of the polystyrene coolers (I imagine they'll be cheaper in a supermarket) and fill it with couple of ice bags. Not for soft drinks. I can live perfectly well on warmish watery Diet Coke from the gas stations. No, I want to stock up with some decent provisions. Fruit and veg and brown bread, mainly.

Except that when I enter a vast hangar of a supermarket called Winn Dixie, I find myself wandering round with this big grin on my face, not concentrating on fruit and veg at all. I'm thinking about black stilettos and toe cleavage – about how the front of her black-patent shoe brushed the part of her foot where the toe cracks began, like a very low-cut bikini bottom. I try to force myself back into reality by thinking about cockroaches – my first story for the *Scarborough Evening Post* about the problem of roaches in hotels: 'Unwelcome Guests Check In For Summer'. I thought at the time that it was one of those 'sign' things that people like Acid Sarah talk about. I thought, Bloody hell, Mo Snow, maybe you're a bit like a cockroach yourself – devious and not terribly attractive yet extremely hardy. (A roach doesn't even need a head to survive: you can cut its head off and it'll live for a week – it only dies because it can't get water into its body.)

Now, of course, I'm worried that I'm not being hardy enough: I keep thinking about that Ruby Rose character. Last night, as I lay on my bed, feeling the knots on my bracelet like a makeshift rosary, I started thinking about her again. It wasn't a sexual thing. It wasn't a tickle in my tummy – it was more of an itch on my nose. I didn't want to have her, I wanted to be her, to have her charisma. And then Gary wafted into my mind and I remembered how sweet he was to me. How we'd fall asleep and I'd feel proud to be lying next to him. How he'd hold me tight and nuzzle drowsily into the back of my neck. 'Nice,' he'd whisper, in his strawberry breath. 'Like being on a toboggan.' And before I fell into a deep sleep, the corners of my mouth would turn upwards in a lazy smile as I imagined Gary and me scooting together down a snowy hill under the frosty sparkle of a clear blue sky.

But when I finally fell into a deep sleep, Gary didn't come into it. I was in this dark room – a cabaret somewhere, filled with gents in top hats and monocles and ladies in furs and diamonds. Ruby Rose was on stage under the spotlight and I was proud of her. She was saying something to the audience – I couldn't quite hear what, but I felt excited because I knew that, by the time she'd finished, everyone in the room would be charmed, everyone would be under her spell. And, sure enough, when she'd finished speaking, the ladies and gentlemen uttered a long, hushed '*Aaaaaaaaah*' that wafted warmly on to the velvety air of the dark room. And then I woke up and the itch on my nose was travelling all around my body.

So here I am, wandering round this huge supermarket in New Orleans, getting flashbacks of toe cleavage and high heels, and I'm only brought out of my daze by the sight of a supermarket trolley loaded with a stack of root-beer crates and a pile of very large milk cartons. There's something striking about the trolley. Maybe something about the brown and orange of the cans contrasted with the pea-green of the milk cartons. Whatever it is, I stand there in a sort of stupor, gazing at the cart, until I become aware of Jesus with blood trickling down his cheeks and a camp 'Oh, no, not the flaming thorns again!' expression on his face. Then I see the leather jacket. Jesus is a picture, painted on the back of a black leather jacket and the leather arms are attached to the bar of the interesting trolley.

An old lady appears out of nowhere. She looks like one of the extras from *Rosemary's Baby* – one of the Satan worshippers. I've seen quite a few of them during my week in America. There's always something just a bit odd about the *Rosemary's Baby* ladies – their face powder's cracking like in an old oil painting or they've got gashes of blue eyeshadow or weird things in their hair from the olden days.

'Well, I'll be!' the old lady goes, coming to an abrupt halt next to the Jesus. (Her skin is thin and peeling – like orange *papier-mâché* coming undone.) She squints at a sign saying, 'A&W root beer. Only $2 a case!' and exclaims, 'Now isn't that a thing!'

Leather-jacket Jesus swivels round and turns out to be none other than the Ruby Rose woman from the Bloated Goat! 'You should try root beer with milk,' she tells the old lady. 'It combines the sweet and the savoury thing. Combines the sparkly, creamy thing with the chewy, crunchy thing.'

'Riiiight.' The old lady nods as if she knows exactly what Ruby Rose is talking about.

'I was going to do dill pickles,' Ruby Rose goes on, 'but the colour just wasn't doing it for me today.'

'Can't eat 'em with root beer,' the old lady agrees. 'Too vinegary.'

'Exactly,' Ruby Rose says. 'Too vinegary. Too sour-mouth acid-sting. Bad combination. Have to have Reese's Peanut Butter Cups for it to work properly.'

The old lady nods. 'One time I had French fries dipped in a strawberry shake. Real hot fries and real cold shake. The salt and the sugar.' She shivers. 'Hate it when I burn the roof of my mouth.'

The old lady seems to think that Ruby Rose and I know each other. She asks us if we'll lift a couple of crates of the root beer into her trolley. I say I'll be happy to oblige, and when she hears my accent she says, 'My upstairs neighbours are moving to London. It's a place called Scotland.'

Ruby Rose and I put the root beer in her trolley and the old lady thanks us and starts to move away. Then she stops suddenly, her head flicking in the direction of the bread and cakes aisle. 'Goodness,' she exclaims in delight. 'What a marvellous ass that young man has!'

Ruby Rose watches the *Rosemary's Baby* lady vanish into the distance. 'She's having a great old time.' She smiles, explaining that, in America, men have bars to socialise in while women have supermarkets.

Ruby Rose obviously has bars, though. She looks rather out of place in Winn Dixie – like a Hostess double-fudge-chunk brownie in a health-food shop. Aside from the Jesus leather jacket, she's wearing a gold lamé halterneck top, a leather skirt with zips pulled daringly high at the sides, cream high-heeled shoes and cotton bobby socks with pompoms on the heels. She's still carrying the gold bag, which, I note today, has a yellowish blotch down the front that might well be milkshake.

She doesn't seem surprised to see me. She turns away from the root-beer promotion back to a shelf of Slimfast (stacked next to a shelf of banana and chocolate Hostess Mini Muffins).

'Slimfast and marijuana,' she says, picking up some of the cans. 'I live off the stuff.' Her movement whips up a wind of sour plums and stale weed. She starts wheeling her trolley slowly down the aisle and I follow her, watching her breasts bob recklessly up and down as she glides primly past bottles of Californian red the size of church bells.

'They're pretty strict about marijuana round here, aren't they?' I say, trying to sound casual.

'Don't worry. I trust you.'

'Why do you trust me?'

'I'm like you, Peachy. Reading people's part of my business.'

And that's the point. I want to know what her business is but I don't dare ask directly. She seems to be able to read my mind, though, because she looks at me sharply and drawls, 'Something bothering you?'

I think it must be the way she's looking at me. I can't help smirking. I stand there in Winn Dixie, New Orleans, twitching and blushing in my red checked lumberjack shirt and my probably wrong-brand jeans and training shoes and she's going, 'You're such a geek.' But there's a twinkle in her eyes and immediately I like the word 'geek'.

When I stammer out something about how I'm looking for healthy food, she wrinkles her nose. 'Healthy,' she says. 'I wouldn't know about that. Now, if it was munchies you were after I could help you out big-time.'

So, of course, the next thing I know, we're standing in an aisle specialising in fast-food cheese. Next to a jar of something called Cheez Whiz ('Cheezy. And darn proud of it'). She picks up a metal canister called, Easy Cheese ('Real cheese!') and snaps open the top. She presses the nozzle and begins spraying a bright orange worm on to one of the Cheez-It biscuits she already has in her trolley ('Seize the cheese!').

I'm laughing. I can't believe it. Spray-on food! Food designed to be played with! I tell Ruby Rose that when I was a kid and

Mother made me lunch – say, fish fingers, baked beans and boiled potatoes – I used to mash everything together and make a house on my plate.

Ruby Rose looks puzzled. 'You made houses out of food?'

'Didn't you?'

'Wouldn't have had enough food to make a shed when I was a kid. I was starving during the first part of my childhood and more interested in laxatives during the second part.'

'Laxatives?'

'My record was one hour between ingestion and expulsion.'

'Really?'

'Senna. Bulimics swear by it.'

'Gosh.'

She asks me to tell her more about my house thing.

I'm not sure if it's a wise idea to tell her about my obsession with houses and homes: holes, burrows, nests, cages, Roach Motels, cuckoo clocks, empty TV boxes, Wendy houses, tree-houses, dolls' houses, wigwams and sandcastles, stacked-up tyres, hay bales, the gap down the back of the radiator, big fluffy clouds, the cabins of parked heavy-goods vehicles – especially the ones with a bedroom section hidden behind a drawn curtain.

So I don't tell her everything. I just tell her about my hamster thing. About how, when I was seven years old, I wrote to *Jim'll Fix It* to ask if I could be a hamster for the day. I wanted to live in a cage, sleep in a metal box filled with ripped-up-paper straw, run around on a wheel and drink from the upside-down bottle strapped on to the metal bars with a rubber band and two safety clips (except there'd be lemonade inside instead of water).

'Jim never wrote back,' I tell her. 'Probably my place was taken by some child who wanted to be an air hostess for the day or play a flute in the Smurf orchestra.'

'Wow,' she says. 'You *are* a kook.'

Luckily, she doesn't see me blush because she stops the trolley and picks up a jar of something called Miracle Whip. Miracle Whip is like salad cream with lots of sugar in, she tells me.

Apparently you spread it on a slice of white bread, then place a ready-cut slice of bland Swiss cheese on top and you have what she calls a 'white-trash sandwich'. The experience is all about sweetness and texture (flabby).

'You can't eat the handles, though,' she says, tossing the jar into the cart.

'Handles?'

'Work it out,' she goes. But I can't, because I can't tell if she's talking on a normal level or if it's some special American code word for stripper competitions or something. Then we're in the spray-on cream area. She says that the best thing to do with spray-on cream is to leave it in the fridge for a few days so that all the 'cream' (made from corn-syrup solids) sinks to the bottom of the can and when you press the nozzle a load of gas shoots out and you get hit with a 'high'.

She picks up a canister, opens it and squirts a pirouette of white foam over her tongue. 'Feels like walking on cold marble on a hot day with bare feet,' she says dreamily, kicking off her stilettos and peeling off the bobby socks – throwing them into the trolley. She slowly brings her tongue to the roof of her mouth and, as the cream and the flesh collide, her eyes close and an expression of bliss passes over her face.

I'm appalled and fascinated at the same time. I wonder if anyone ever dared tell her off in her life.

She opens her eyes again and stares straight at me. 'Love multiple sensations,' she says. 'Even better on a hot day is to walk barefoot through confetti scattered on cold marble. Feels like thousands of bits of electricity all shooting up into your head.'

I almost snap at her: 'Do you always eat this kind of food?'

'Honey, I come from a family that couldn't function unless food came out of packets.' She puts the lid back on the cream. 'Raw Pilsbury cookie dough and cable TV,' she says. 'That was my childhood.'

We arrive at the checkout and while we're waiting in line, she pulls out that week's *Explorer* from the news-stand and starts flicking through. 'Shut up!' she exclaims. 'Pig's feet diet!'

'Pig's feet, did you say?' The checkout woman's face appears over the root-beer crates.

'Shut up!' Ruby Rose exclaims again, in a manner that seems to be the American equivalent of 'Well, blow me down!' 'Shut up! It says here you should eat pig guts too.'

She throws the *Explorer* on to the conveyor-belt to add to the shopping. 'Releases serotonin, I guess.'

'What's that "sero" stuff?' a black boy, with a lazy eye, packing the bags wants to know.

'Serotonin,' Ruby Rose tells him. 'It's the feel-good chemical you get when you've done a good workout.'

The boy looks blank. His bottom lip droops like there's a weight attached to it and his eyes flicker to Ruby Rose's breasts. 'Where you heading to today, ma'am?' he asks them.

She seems to hesitate, as if she's not quite sure where she's going. So I offer to give her a lift back to her house. She looks at me, suspicion in her eyes, and then, finally, she shrugs. 'Sure! Guess it beats sticking round here picking my ass.'

She insists on paying for the munchies shopping as well as the two polystyrene coolers ($1.50 each) and the four packs of ice I've picked up. She digs into her bag and hands the checkout woman a handful of crumpled bills. Then we pass out of the cool chamber of Winn Dixie and suddenly find ourselves in the car park, being fried alive under the glassy blue sky with a huge poster looming down at us saying, 'Jesus loves you . . . today!'

Ruby Rose is still engrossed in the *Explorer*, and while she settles herself into the passenger seat, poring over the pages, I load the shopping into the back of the car. When she's had her fill of the trashy newspaper, she throws it on to the window-ledge, removes a pink plastic Power Puff Girl cup from her bag, puts some lumps of ice inside, half fills it with root beer, then tops it up from her Jack Daniel's bottle. Her eyes scan the car park for security.

'You can get fined a thousand dollars for the consumption of liquor in a stationary vehicle,' she explains, tips her head back and drinks. (I like the word 'liquor' as opposed to 'alcohol' just as I like the American 'hooker' as opposed to 'prostitute' because it sounds dirty.) She offers me the cup but I turn it down. I tell her I just want to tidy up a bit. 'Whatever.' She picks up the *Explorer* and flicks through the pages again.

Of course, I'm not tidying up at all. I'm worrying about how long four large cartons of milk are going to last in the back of the car without spoiling, and then I look up and see the back of her head moving, and I realise she's checking out the car. This makes me very nervous because I know that, any minute now, she's going to find my sandwich. My sandwich of shame. Fine for me to see but absolutely not fine for anyone else.

She sees it. My lucky Marks & Spencer's plastic bag with the makeshift sandwich inside. She picks it up. She looks inside. She jumps in her seat with a little shriek. The bag drops to the floor. 'What in hell is that?' she shouts, swivelling round. Her face veers between humour and horror. 'You brought your hamster with you?'

Oh, no. Now I'm mortified. She definitely won't appreciate the concept of the home-made sandwiches. Tentatively, she picks up the bag from the floor. Slowly, she pulls out the contents. 'Oh . . . my . . . God.' She examines the sweating slice of greyish ham and the shards of withered iceberg lettuce poking out of one side of a rock-hard roll.

'You were going to eat this?' she says, looking incredulously in the rear-view mirror.

Bloody, bloody, bloody hell.

'Gosh . . . Just some stuff I picked up from a gas station. The lettuce was left over from a burrito in Taco Bell.'

'Left . . . over?' She mouths the words as if she's never said them before.

'I've always had packed lunch,' I gabble. 'It helps me . . . pace myself. You know. It's good discipline. I drive all morning and

I look at it and I know that by two o'clock I'll be able to eat it.'

'Are you serious?'

'Yes. Even if I'm hungry at one, I'll make myself wait until two.'

'You are something else,' she says, as I slam the back of the car and take my place in the driving seat. 'You could get sandwiches cheaper and fresher in any gas station,' she says, still puzzled.

I can feel a surge of something like power creeping up. She's obviously never met anyone like me before. 'Yes,' I inform her. 'But there's about ten of them in one pack and each one's the size of China.'

She doesn't seem to be listening. 'And your soda,' she says, picking up my Burger King cup as if she's in pain. 'You don't even have it on ice?'

I tell her that if I have the air-conditioning on – as I normally do – then the ambient temperature in the car takes care of that problem.

'Tepid Diet Coke?'

'You should see my laundry concept.' I'm past caring now.

'I can't wait.'

'Well, I do my washing every night in the motels. In the sink.'

'Yeah?' she says, warily.

'Actually, you have to wait until your T-shirt gets all greasy and sticky so that it feels like a piece of tight-fitting mackerel skin against your body—'

'Mackerel skin?'

'Yes, and then you wash it. And you're revived. It's good. Life seems perfect again. In a way that it wouldn't if you just had it clean all the time.'

'Yeah?'

'Yeah. And the thing is, I really enjoy it. Hand-washing is like panhandling for gold.'

'Run that by me?'

'It's satisfying. To do stuff manually? You're stirring round

33

this murky soup and you're looking at a day's worth or a week's worth of dead skin cells and sand and grease from diner break-fasts and that.'

'I guess . . .'

'By looking into the soup you can see that your life has some substance to it. That's you in that soup. You are the soup!'

'And so you don't have any substance if you take your stuff to the laundry?'

'Not the same.'

'Only costs sixty cents a pound.'

'I suppose I am quite set in my ways.'

'My God,' she says, her face lighting up. 'You could start up a whole new school of SM practice! The disgusting sandwich you're only allowed to eat if you've been good! Clothing made from sushi leftovers that you have to wash in a motel sink! And finally, ladies and gentlemen, roll up for the hamster cage! Abandon your slings and your butt plugs and step up to the treadmill! Suck that rodent bottle!'

She starts to giggle and I snatch the sandwich from her hand. I press the automatic window button and prepare to throw the bloody thing into the car park. I'm an idiot. I don't have any power at all. She's just laughing at me. I knew I should have kept my mouth shut. Trust me to pick up some weird American in a supermarket and then have her insult me in my own car. She's right as well. I might have come to America to discover myself and what am I doing? Just bringing my nerdy old Scabs habits with me. I'm a thirty-one-year-old boring bastard who watches the sunset and goes, 'Gosh,' to herself – 'Gosh,' that's what I heard myself saying the other day as I drove through this beautiful old plantation town as the sun melted into a shim-mering estuary with swans and pink flamingos but I was too uptight to know what to do when confronted by something different . . .

She watches me throttling the stinky old roll by the neck, preparing to throw it out of the window. The Marks & Spencer's bag is flapping in the air-conditioner and making a right old din – just to highlight my shame even further – and then, suddenly, she grabs my arm. 'Oh, no! I'm sorry!' she says. She sounds worried. 'I didn't mean to make fun of you. I *love* your packed lunch.'

She takes the bag carefully from my hands and lays it down on the dashboard with the gentleness of someone handling a newborn baby. She sits back in her seat and looks at it for a while. Then she turns round and looks at the back of the car – at the array of T-shirts steaming dry on the seat. 'Your gold leaf,' she says quietly. When she sees my Primus stove she flinches slightly. She picks it up. She examines it. She twists the knob of the calor gas attachment. She smells the escaping gas. Sulphur it is, she tells me. I wouldn't know, I tell her. We didn't do science at the convent. The nuns thought science was unladylike. She doesn't smile. She's somewhere else. I hope that she won't suss about the hot-tea thing. She'd probably think that was really ridiculous. Hot tea on a hot day. She wouldn't get that at all.

'Sulphur,' she says again. 'Lakes of burning sulphur.' She looks at the stove as if she's trying to understand something.

'Sorry?'

'It's a safety measure.'

'What is?'

'The peppery, eggy smell. Sulphur. They put it there so you don't leave the gas on and kill yourself.'

'Gosh.'

And all the time I'm thinking, Well, well, well. What a turn-up for the books. A fifteen-stone spliff-smoking vagina judge from New Orleans taking an interest in my humble Primus stove. Then her eyes turn to the crumpled Marks & Spencer's bag. I'm not sure what's going on. I try to gauge the state of play from the corner of my eye. From a faint twitch in her right shoulder I sense that she's thinking. Or maybe it's more of a decision-making kind of twitch. Then it seems that the moment of doubt is past. Her mind's made up. She turns to me, her eyes fizzling.

She says, 'You want to come out on a picnic with me, baby?'

And in spite of the sweltering heat and the sound of revving cars and the smell of the grey-ham sandwich, the moment feels like the hushed sound in my dream, the cabaret dream, the golden sound of relief and admiration: '*Aaaaaaaah.*'

'Where to?'

'California.'

'Oh.'

That's where she's from, she tells me. She says I'd like it. She says that whereas the Gulf of Mexico is like swimming in the bosom of a big old buttery whore, the Pacific is completely different. 'It's more like a Californian teenage boy,' she says, starting to do up her seat-belt. 'All sporty and clean living with beautiful blue eyes.'

The click of the seat-belt makes me feel strange. I can't help but think about my plan. About how I was supposed to be doing America on my own, to get over Gary, to find solitude, to conquer solitude and come out stronger on the other side. Or something. And then there's my breakfast story. 'The thing is, I'm working on my "Breakfast in America" article . . .'

'So?'

'So, I can't just go gallivanting all over America . . .'

Ruby Rose presses a finger to her lips. 'Research, girlfriend,' she whispers.

'Sorry?'

'You're not just going to write about breakfast in Florida and New Orleans, are you?'

'I suppose not.'

'You know what they eat for breakfast in California?'

'Egg-white omelette filled with low-fat cottage cheese – so I've read.'

Ruby Rose raises one eyebrow in dramatic fashion. 'Only weight-lifters eat that low-fat shit. Most Californians have coffee for breakfast.'

'Oh.'

'In fact, you should talk to my old waitress friend, Leah,' she says, settling into the seat. 'She's in Venice Beach now. That's in LA. She lives near this cool lingerie store called Flambée . . .'

'Gosh . . .'

'Of course,' she adds, picking up the *Explorer* from the ledge, 'New Mexican breakfasts are the most important of all.'

'I suppose food varies from state to state.'

'You bet! You think New Mexicans would go near a fucking grit? No way! Everything's hot in New Mexico – people there have red blood flowing in their veins.'

She opens the *Explorer* and begins to flick. 'Not like Louisiana. Louisiana feels like a plate of something someone left under the bed and it got all funky.'

'You know New Mexico well, then?'

She looks slightly taken aback. 'Never been there, no.' She slaps the paper shut and throws it into her bag. 'But you know what?'

'What?'

'How about we head there now?' She wriggles out of her Jesus leather jacket and throws it into the back of the car. 'California with a New Mexican chaser!'

I can't help smiling at the thought.

'Yes, sir. It's going to be a trip that smells of neon and hot pomegranates and sunsets. There's a special smell to sunsets, don't you find?' She leans over and takes a red and yellow cardboard box from her bag. 'Now, shut the door, close the windows and turn up the air-con. Feels like there's hot eels slipping round inside my clothes!'

I can see some writing on the side of the box. It says, 'They check in but they don't check out.'

My hands flop into my lap. 'A Roach Motel?'

'Yeah, it's a great home, actually.' She opens it up and the unmistakable scent of marijuana wafts out. 'Roach Motel,' she says, taking out a half-smoked joint. 'Get it?'

She hunts round in her bag for a lighter, telling me that she likes homes too. 'I have an ideal home, actually,' she says, 'but it's in my head.'

'Really?'

'Yeah. It's a giant's house. It's designed to be big so it makes you feel thin. And all the walls are curved and there are no edges or spikes so you never feel unloved.'

'Sounds nice.'

She locates a lighter and lights the joint. 'It is nice. Most of the time.' She inhales and blows out a line of thick yellow smoke. 'Thing is,' she wheezes, 'I've been getting this recurring dream. I'm in my dream house but there are always strange people in my bedroom doing weird stuff. And the rooms are always messing with me.'

She picks up the Roach Motel and inspects it. 'They're cute, huh? I like the little garage doors the roaches have to go through first.'

'Garage doors?' Ruby Rose can see a house in a cardboard box. It makes my body buzz.

She frowns and says, 'Oh, my God. I'm so bad-mannered. I mean, you don't mind me smoking, do you?'

But by that time I've decided.

CHAPTER THREE

Haunted House

Next to Ruby Rose's bed there is a can of A&W root beer, some chopsticks, some joint butts, several remote controls, some ripped pages from a Bible, a copy of the *National Enquirer*, a Donna Summer greatest-hits CD, a half-full jar of Miracle Whip, a blue and yellow box of Advil painkillers, a Converse training shoe serving as an ashtray, a white biro with a black Sheraton logo, a lighter, several lighters, a fifty-dollar bill, four twenty-dollar bills, a tipped-up bottle of mineral water and a plastic bag of grass.

Ruby Rose surveys the bedroom and drawls, 'Get me out of this shit-hole.'

Her eyes rest on a long black canvas bag lying next to the TV. The bag is open and already has items spilling from it, including a froth of red tulle and a silver peep-toe shoe with a Perspex platform heel. 'Mind you,' she says, 'I'm not saying I don't like flea-pits. Fantastic hotels just remind me of being with people you don't really want to have sex with.'

She doesn't say why she is living in a motel room when she has apparently been a resident in New Orleans for three years.

'Now, there's another place to live,' she says, going over to sit on the bed. 'A flea-pit.' She kicks off the cream stilettos. 'Prefer a boat, though.'

'Sorry?'

'A bed boat.'

'You've lost me.'

She pats the orange eiderdown. 'These beds are too small. I need a California King.'

'What's that?'

'The biggest beds you can get. When I was growing up my friend Marnie had one. We used to have parties on it. Called it the boat.'

'That's nice.'

'Yeah. Always wanted to live in a boat. There was this marina I loved to go to as a kid in California. I liked to listen to the clanking of the mast tops. A funny noise. Like a line of tin cans strung together on a string.'

'I've never noticed that before.'

'It's one of my favourite sounds. Mysterious by night, though. You can't tell if it's the wind or if someone's there.'

Suddenly Scarborough floods into the room. There's a dinner party and that wanker Duncan is talking to Gary about a man who built himself a ship's cabin to slot into the middle of his house so he could enjoy the sensations of a long sea voyage without ever having to leave home. 'A friend of my husband's,' I tell her, 'he was always going on about this nineteenth-century French writer who wanted to turn his house into a ship and –'

'– fill it with charts and compasses and binoculars and fishing-rods. "A substitute for the vulgar reality of actual experience." Huyssmans.'

I can't believe I've heard correctly. Weees-mans, she said. 'You know that author?'

'That old faggot? Sure. I kind of get his vibe, though. What's that line again? "To drain the cup of sensuality to its last and bitterest dregs." I like that.'

'How do you know about him?'

'Put it down to my deprived childhood,' she says, deadpan.

A cockroach scuttles under a dirty sock and I tell her about Gary's friend, Duncan. 'He went around saying things like, "The realisation of ideas in art is like pouring pesticide on one's dreams."'

Ruby Rose gets up from the bed and goes over to the wardrobe. 'I wish someone would pour pesticide on my dreams,' she says. 'Uproot the fuckers.'

She glares at the clothes hanging on the rail, suddenly shouting, 'Fags!' Apparently a 'drag infestation' has happened, which means that she gave her room key to a bunch of drag queens from the Café Risqué so they could borrow clothes for Mr Eggmont's wake and now they've cleaned her out.

They don't appear to have taken everything, though. She yanks out a handful of pink feathers followed by a leather belt studded with bullets, saying 'My wardrobe's very Rita-Hayworth-comes-to-the-twenty-first-century-and-takes-an-ecstasy-tab.'

She throws the boa and the belt into the black bag, followed by the amber-coloured corset, a pair of ripped fishnets, a plastic doll's head with fangs ('Devil Barbie'), a plastic doll's body with intestines protruding from the neck, a pink gingham Little Bo Peep dress, a white doctor's coat, a pink fake-fur coat, two miniature pink cones with tassels on the end ('titty tassels'), a blue pinstripe rubber skirt, an old lady's nightdress in bobbly lime-green nylon, a body harness made from gold-coloured chains and studded with coloured stones, a pair of pink rubber gloves, a black leather catsuit and a *papier-mâché* codpiece with red spots.

'Apparently I'm a female impersonator,' she says, chucking her wardrobe into the drag bag. 'Ruby Rose is my stage name. College kids interview me for their Ph.D.s on post-feminism.' She stops and holds a leather military cap up to the light (East German, she tells me). 'I freak the promoters out, though. They're expecting all that Diana Ross-Judy Garland tranny shit and I give them my Doris Day-Courtney Love schizophrenic striptease.'

She pulls on a blonde wig, strikes a pose and, suddenly, there before me is a mumsy Doris Day – frightening in itself but made all the more uncanny by Ruby Rose's black eyes, which flash like razor blades.

She yanks off the wig, throws herself down on the bed, lifts both legs into the air and peels off the bobby socks as if they're sexy stockings. I'm not sure if this is instinctive or if she's aware I'm observing her (I am).

She announces that she's going to take a shower. A few minutes later, the water is turned on and a voice emerges from the bathroom: 'Those male-female impersonators,' it shouts, 'they have an easy time, man. They can show their tits till the cows come home. Me, I flash mine, the promoter calls me a freak and claims I'm going to lose him his licence.'

'So you are a feminist, then?'

'That's what the college kids tell me. Me, I try not to think too much.'

The water stops and there's the sound of a shower curtain being ripped back. The cockroach surfaces from the sock.

She comes back into the room draped in two towels, one over her hair and one around her body. 'Thing is, not many women can pull off being a woman. That's where the drag queens come in.'

She goes to the bottom of the bed and picks up a tattered cream dress with elaborate spaghetti straps over the shoulder and beige-sequined fringing around the bottom. She turns and holds it up to the window, telling me that it's her wedding dress. 'Baby-pig skin,' she says. 'Funny.'

'Why funny?'

'My ex-husband was Jewish.' She scratches one of her large buttocks. 'This isn't the actual wedding dress. This is the wedding dress redesigned into an evening gown for the Golden Globes. Bad idea.'

'Oh?'

'It's very tight at the back. I'd been sunbathing all day and my ass was red. We had to sit at the table for hours.'

'Poor you.'

'Yeah. It was really impractical for getting up and down for coke trips to the bathroom.'

When I ask her what coke's like – that I've never done any drugs apart from a few puffs on a joint once that sent me to sleep – she sighs and says, 'My husband used to say that coke feels like the adrenaline rush you get when you lose a lot of money.' She pushes the dress into the drag bag. 'As opposed to the rush you feel when you make it.'

'Do you still take coke?'

Irritation crosses her face. 'Give me a break. I haven't touched the stuff in three months.'

I tell her about Gary. 'I had a husband too,' I tell her, 'but he died last year.'

Her reaction's strange. She doesn't say, 'Oh, I'm sorry. How terrible for you,' like all the others do. She just says, 'Fucking death. I'm so sick of people dying.' Then she reaches into the drag bag and pulls out a folded envelope with 'Cocaine' written in large black letters on the front. She squeezes the package. 'Sweet and Lo,' she says, chucking it at me. Then she throws over a plastic jar with the word 'Valium' scrawled on the front in large pink letters. When I open it up there are peppermint Tic Tacs inside.

'Props,' she goes. 'For the Doris Day-Courtney Love schizophrenic striptease.'

She looks at the drag bag. 'You know, man, why am I taking that stupid dress with me anyway?'

'Maybe it has sentimental value for you.'

'Sentimental!' she snorts. 'He was sweet but I'd never have married him if he'd been poor. I was eighteen at the time. My mother always used to tell me, "A man can never love a woman as much as she needs so he might as well compensate with money."'

'That's one way of looking at it.'

'The only way. I'm thirty-three now and I still agree with my mother. And, believe me, that's a rare occurrence.'

She decides against packing the ex-wedding dress. 'I had some weird dreams last night,' she says, hauling it out of the bag. 'That house in my head – you know, the one I was telling you about?'

I nod.

'Man, you should have seen it! The bed was all squashy and

there was damp fur in it. Like cat hair. And the bed wasn't even in my room. It was over by the transportation dock.'

'There's a dock in your dream house?'

'Yeah.' She sighs. 'See, my house isn't just a house. It's a whole world. There's the house and then there are beaches and a huge K-Mart kind of place . . .'

'K-Mart?'

'An American superstore. The other night I flew up in the ceiling. There was this man in a black cloak who was chasing me. There's a transport place too. But you can't tell if it's a train station or a boat dock or an airport. It's all of them. There's just this waiting room.'

'And are you usually missing something there?'

'Usually.'

Into the space left in the drag bag by the wedding dress she chucks some jars and tubs of cosmetics, some false eyelashes and some strings of beads. When the zip is finally closed, she stands up and pronounces herself to be 'just one big haunted house'.

Doing a U-turn in America is called 'flipping a bitch'. This I learn because Ruby Rose does several of them in an attempt to find the 10 – the highway that will take us all the way to California. Every time she does one, the Mardi Gras skeletons she's hung on the dashboard swing on their bead branches and head-bang the controls.

When we find the right road, she makes a big, American-style whoop and says, 'Man! Am I glad to see the back of New Orleans! That place feels like swimming around in the belly-button of a fat man!'

She has chosen to drive my rent-a-car although she moans sporadically about it. (It's not a car, she tells me. It's a 'sports utility vehicle' or an SUV. All cars of the Range Rover variety are known as sports utility vehicles.)

'It's like driving middle-aged spread,' she complains.

'It's comfortable and safe, though,' I suggest.

'Yeah, "comfortable and safe",' she says grimly. 'That's what America's all about. Never be lost, never be unsafe, never not be free.'

She seems to be enjoying the ride, though. It's chucking it down with rain and we're being hemmed in by a series of CBing truck drivers who come up level to us, peer down lasciviously from their gleaming chrome cabins, then accelerate off, swerving viciously in front of us. This doesn't faze Ruby Rose. She drives as if she's on a game in an amusement arcade, breaking out every so often in a dambuster laugh – all whooshing and indecorous and unladylike. The Mardi Gras skeletons hanging from the dashboard are having a wild old time and a bag of Reese's Peanut Butter Cups she purchased at an earlier gas station gets hurled all over the floor.

When she gets tired, she turns on a thing called 'cruise control'. American cars are simple enough to drive anyway because they're all automatic, but cruise control means that, without even putting your foot on the accelerator, the car maintains the same speed as if there's an invisible robot driving. Cruise control can get boring, however, and when this happens Ruby Rose steers with her knees. She tells me not to worry about this position. Everyone does it, she says. And sure enough we are overtaken by a girl with a bouffant poodle hair-do. 'Look at that chick!' she goes, puffing away on her joint. 'She's driving with her knees, talking on her cellphone, doing her hair and clocking eighty-five! You go, girl!' (It turns out that Ruby Rose chainsmokes joints – not just the hash things that Acid Sarah's into, but pure grass unadulterated by tobacco that drapes the air in a sweet yellow fog.)

Then the rain stops and the sun comes out and huge insects start flying into the windscreen. Ruby Rose makes that special American sound that means 'yuk' and comes out as 'Eeeee-yew!'.

'Eeeeee-yew!' she squeals. 'Check out the big-ass bugs!'

The spectacle is quite biblical: not only is the sunset an uncanny shade of green and pale yellow and the windscreen smeared sepia with the bodies of splatted insects the size of locusts, but we are, to boot, in full-on Bible belt. We drive past a series of churches the size of shopping malls all interspaced with billowing American flags. I see one drive-in church and one bright purple construction that might be a furniture warehouse except that it advertises itself with a huge sign proclaiming, 'World of Faith', instead of 'World of Settees'. And then some mad religious song comes on the radio – a group of singers with thick rasta accents going on about how Satan is an evil charmer, hunting for a soul to harm. Every time the chorus comes round Ruby Rose and I burst out laughing:

> *'Shut dee door, keep out dee devil!*
> *Keep dee devil out in dee night!*
> *Shut dee Door, keep out dee devil!*
> *Light dee Candle ev'ryt'ing all right!'*

We sing along:

> *'Shut dee door, keep out dee devil!*
> *Keep dee devil out in dee night!*
> *Shut dee Door, keep out dee devil!*
> *Light dee Candle ev'ryt'ing all right!'*

'My babysitter, Reba, would have liked that song,' she says. 'She said I was the devil's child. She used to pour Tabasco sauce down my throat.'

'Bloody hell. Very *Oranges Are Not the Only Fruit*.'

'Yeah, it was kind of like that. Only it was sunny outside and it was modern.'

'Didn't you tell your mum?'

She snorts. 'My mother! She'd have agreed with her.'

She offers me a puff of the joint but I shake my head. 'Both of them,' she goes on, indignant, 'both my mom and Reba the babysitter used to get me doing housework the minute I walked in the door. At my mom's house we had this chart stuck up on the wall at home: floor-waxing, vacuum-cleaning, clothes-washing . . .'

'"The devil makes work for idle hands,"' I offer.

'That's what Reba used to say,' she goes. 'I've often been type-cast. Take my breasts. People look at me and they think I have this huge rack, whereas if you look properly you'll see that I don't have big breasts at all. I just look like the kind of woman who *would* have big breasts.'

I look at her front and see that she's right. Her breasts aren't that big. I must have perceived them as big because I've only ever seen them in something tight and plunging. That's what gives them the 'reckless' dimension. Although I reckon it's her nipples that are the real point of interest. They stick out all the time. They're erect constantly.

'When I was nine years old,' she says, 'I was suspended from school in Santa Monica for being lewd.'

'And were you being lewd?'

'Lewd! I was just sitting on a boy's knee. I didn't know what "lewd" meant. I thought I was just being comfortable.'

We pass a store called Gun and Pawn.

'Then, when I was ten, I was the best at reading in the whole of my class. I was so good that my English teacher chose me to play Jesus in the school play.'

'What happened?'

'I'd never seen a script before. First day of rehearsals, I erro-neously read out the name of my character along with the lines that followed after the colon. "Jesus!" I exclaimed, in the tone I was used to hearing between my mom and her boyfriends. "Jesus! Peace be with you!" Later in the week, still in shock from the Jesus mistake and in a moment of freak dyslexia, I misread "breast" for "beast" in chapter three of *Robinson Crusoe* and got hauled up again in front of the principal.'

She makes a hiccup of laughter and the SUV veers towards the hard shoulder.

'My teachers were all right to me,' I tell her. 'I think it was because my dad died.'

'Yeah?'

She doesn't ask for any information.

'He died just after I was born. His surname was Snow. My husband Gary's surname was Baroclough. I was Mo Baroclough for a while, but now I've gone back to Snow. Mo, though. Never Maureen.'

I'm still waiting for her to say some condolency thing about my dad or Gary but she doesn't. As far as she knows, Gary and my dad might both have died in terrible circumstances. She doesn't take her cue though. She just chuckles. 'Mo Snow!' And then she says, 'My name's Billie Harrison.'

She says it, just like that. Without any build-up or anything. I feel out the name 'Billie' in my mind: touching it, prodding it, checking out the shape, wondering how come I'm privileged to have been informed of the non-stage name. Hoping that what I think is right. It's as if she's just stripped a layer of skin off me. It isn't painful, though. There's something refreshing about it. Like bathing my face in a meadow of cool grass on a sticky day in Louisiana. It's like seeing her in a flash – in the time before she grew up, suddenly a child again. Ruby Rose has told me her name. Her real name that, I can tell, she hardly reveals to anyone.

'Why Ruby Rose?'

'All famous people have two names,' she says.

I do a double-take and see that there's a glint in her eye.

'What's the real story?'

'You telling me I'm not famous!' she exclaims in mock indignation, moving out of cruise control and into video-arcade mode. She looks at me and smiles. 'OK, babe, here's the scoop. If you're a performer, you get your first name from your first pet's name – my cat, Ruby – and the second name from the first street you lived in.'

We pass another Gun and Pawn and she tells me how her black

cat Ruby had white markings down her front like a *décolleté*. 'She reminded me of a bordello keeper,' she says. She draws on the joint, looking pensive. I think she's a bit surprised, too, that Billie Harrison just popped out like that. She starts talking about animals. About how she loved animals when she was a child. Especially riding them.

'What sort of animals?'

'Anything.'

'Anything?'

'Sure. I tried a goat once. It was too little, though.'

'What happened?'

'Fell over.' She lights another joint. 'In general, farmyard animals are too small. And don't even think of trying a cow. Cows are definitely not meant for riding.'

'What happened when you tried?'

'Bucked me off.'

I tell her she must have been pretty bruised as a kid and she tells me she liked it. She liked to break bones. 'Crashing and bucking and breaking. I loved all that.' She blows a line of yellow smoke-rings. 'Most years I broke at least two bones in my body. Some years I broke three. Broke my right tibia – that's the bottom of your leg – I broke my right patella and something in my finger called a metatarsal. A patella's in your knee. It makes a big crunchy sound when it goes.

'Ostriches are soft,' she continues. 'Could've ridden an ostrich once. Gotta draw the line somewhere, though. Straddling poultry. Gross me out.'

She is enveloped now in a cloud of thick yellow smoke. 'If it's soft you're looking for, then llamas are your ride. They're real soft. Alpaca belly fur. Imagine that.' She looks me straight in the eye. 'You gotta be careful, though.' She smiles. 'They're not very comfortable. They run. Bumpy. Still' – she slaps her knee, which is then gripping the steering-wheel – 'more pain, more pleasure. Get the picture?'

And that's the frustrating thing: I'm trying to get the picture but I can't. She takes a big drag on the joint. 'Fireworks, roller-coasters, diving in cold oceans, electro-convulsive therapy . . .'

'Electro-convulsive therapy?'

She nods. 'Scary things are easier to handle than other stuff.'

'Stuff like what?'

'Oh, you know . . . words.'

'Words?'

'Yeah. Words have gotten me into trouble over the years.'

'And that's why you burn them?'

'Did I tell you that?'

'You told me in the Bloated Goat.'

She narrows her eyes. A row of wispy yellow clouds bobs along in front of our faces. 'Whatever. I love to watch words rise up into the air in orange tongues of fire with blue hearts, then see them turn into the thinnest of black tissue paper and crumble into nothing.'

'Gosh.'

She heaves a deep sigh. 'Words have often betrayed me in my life.' She offers me the joint again and I decline.

'Betrayed you?'

'That's what I said.'

'How did they betray you?'

But she's distracted now. She glances in the rear-view mirror. 'Fuckin' A,' she shouts, with glee in her voice. 'It's those goddam truckers again.'

I can only sit there and enjoy the thrill that's lodged in my stomach like two weeks' worth of calor gas trapped in one tiny canister. I feel like I've been going around with blinkers on all thirty-one years of my life and now I'm starting to see things out of the corners of my eye. Even when I'm not looking, things flash into my head – half-thought-out notions and semi-formed ideas. It's funny how someone can bring out a new side in you – a side you didn't know you had. Well, maybe you did know you had it but you only saw it very occasionally, like a mirage on the horizon.

The urge to change my life's been brewing for a while now. Since Gary died. Before then it would sometimes occur to me that I was becoming a bit of a drifter, that I should do something 'proper' with my life other than waitressing at the Sceptre and dabbling in further education. One time I did a TEFL course and taught English to a bunch of French kids but they terrified me. A couple of years later I got a librarian-and-information-studies certificate from Scarborough Poly because I believed that librarianship would be all about putting books back in alphabetical order and hissing, 'Ssssssh!' every now and then. But it turned out that there's a fair amount of human contact these days – training up stroppy pensioners for the Internet and so on – so I went back to the Sceptre. I always ended up back at the Sceptre. I was happy keeping things small: night classes, waitressing, Gary.

But something changed after Gary. An itch set in. The day came when the mourning stopped and I became aware of a feeling of warmth. Not a nice homely warmth but a stifling cocoon warmth – the feeling of desperately needing to stretch your mind and soul like you need to stretch your legs when you've been sitting in one place for a very long time.

'You can call me Billie, if you want,' she says suddenly. 'I thought Billie had gone for ever. But you seem to have brought her back to life.'

A rush shoots through me. From the corner of my eye I see her knees driving the car, the diamanté chain glinting on her ankle. There are thick black hairs growing out of her calves. Like flies' legs sticking out from under her skin.

CHAPTER FOUR

Fire?

At seven o'clock we agree that it's time to pull over for the night. We're about three-quarters of the way through Louisiana and we see a sign for a town called Ione followed by a cliché-perfect sunset, which is the logo for the Cosy Inn.

I leave Billie at the car, faffing around with the drag bag, while I go to the reception area. There is a sign on the desk saying, 'Every day is a bank account and time is our currency!' and a young man whose eyes suggest that he's drunk a lot of coffee.

'Hey there!' he booms, in a high-pitched yell. 'How are we DOOOOOO-ING today?'

When I tell him I'm very well, thank you, he says, 'Hey there! Sounds like you're from out of town!'

'Scarborough in England,' I mumble.

'Scarboro? As in Simon and Garfunkel?'

I shuffle my feet.

'And will you be a true love of mine?'

I shuffle my feet some more.

'What's your name, Scarboro girl?'

'Mo,' I say.

'Mo!' he ejaculates. 'Hi, Mo, I'm Freddy, and I know you're going to love it here!'

I have a quick glance round. It's posher than any of the motels I've been to yet. It looks a bit like a private hospital with blue carpet, like the one at Heathrow. Suddenly it strikes me that I might have to share a bed with this Billie woman. This complete stranger. I wonder what'll happen if it's not a California King bed and our skin brushes in the night by mistake. What happens if she starts telling one of her llama-fur stories and she's had a bit to drink? She's three times the size of me, I wouldn't be able to do anything about it.

I normally sleep with nothing on but I think I'll keep my T-shirt on tonight. (Apart from anything else, my taste in baggy T-shirts hides my annoyingly large 'rack', as she'd call it.) I'd also better wear underwear. I don't want to be caught out as an elephant's ear even though I'm not. I don't think I am.

I'm wondering if they automatically give you separate beds when I see a sign saying, 'Free Soda', and, on a coffee-table by a communal TV area, a bowl of tortilla chips and tomato dip. They wouldn't leave that out unless it was free. Free food. I might have to share a bed but at least we won't have to buy anything to eat tonight.

'Boo!' Freddy exclaims, leaping up behind me and grabbing my arm. I jump. 'Hey there, Mo. Don't get scared now! It's your lucky night! I can offer you a double room for thirty dollars, breakfast included!'

'Great.'

'And you know what I'm thinking!'

'What?'

'I'm not even going to charge you any tax!'

'Fantastic,' I mumble, handing over my passport.

'Smoking or non-smoking, Mo?'

'Non-smoking,' I say automatically, and then I remember about her. I hope she doesn't mean to smoke joints in our room. Bloody hell, maybe she's going to do cocaine and then what's going to happen? Police and all sorts. In America, they fling you in jail for not saying, 'How you doing?'.

'Thirty-one, huh?' he shoots, glaring into my passport. 'You're sure holding up well!'

It's a relief to go out to the car and fetch my overnight bag. I'm pretty organised on the luggage front. During the past week, my motel routine has been to bring in only what I'll need for the night. Billie, on the other hand, feels the need to lug in the whole of the drag bag. I'm not going to offer to help. She must learn from her mistakes. But, of course, she doesn't have to learn from her mistakes because Freddy jumps up from the computer keyboard the minute we come in the door. 'Hey there!' he says to her. 'Is that a dead body you have in there?'

Billie gives him a piece of prime eye contact and says, 'It's more of a treasure chest, hon.'

Immediately, Freddy darts round to the other side of the desk and grabs hold of the bag's handles. 'Allow me, ma'am,' he says.

She sucks Freddy up in a glance.

When we get to our room he opens the door, using a card logoed with the Cosy Inn sign. He hands it to Billie, saying, 'You just holler now if you need anything, you hear?' He flashes her another of his manic Moonie smiles and adds, 'I'm only half way through a forty-eight-hour shift!'

Billie closes the door in his face.

'That guy would be so easy to turn,' she groans, collapsing face down on one of the beds. (There are two beds.)

'Turn?' I say, taking out my contact lenses and focusing on the vague mound of her huge bum. But she doesn't answer. She puts the TV on, propping her chin up with a hand and waggling her tanned legs in the air as she flicks over the channels.

'*Touch the screen and be cured of arthritis!*'

'*Lose weight now and feel great with maximum strength Xtreme Lean!*'

I've never been one for TV, although Mother and I did like a good disaster movie. *The Poseidon Adventure* (Shelley Winters doing a heroic underwater swim), *Rollercoaster* (the suspense of getting the bomb off the track in time), *Towering Inferno* (renegade fireman Steve McQueen dangling women to safety in a swivel chair hung with secretaries' tights). As she flicks over more channels, I watch the bum again, this time from the view in the mirrored headboard of her bed. She catches me looking.

'Shall we have a walk round, then?' I say quickly.

'Peachy' – her arms dangle to the floor and she pulls the gold bag towards her – 'you have to realise, I don't do *anything* without a little smoke.'

Then I remember about the room policy: no smoking. I tell her about this. She smiles and says that a fire would give Freddy something to do.

So I let her smoke and at one point I see her absentmindedly flick her ash on the floor as she watches a TV programme about a man who can train wild animals just by the power of eye contact and voice. *'Watch the ears!'* he keeps saying, about a horse that's trotting round in circles on a leash. I'm gobsmacked that she's just flicked ash on the carpet. Unbelievable. But I don't want to come across as a nag. So I say, 'Shall I get you an ashtray?'

'Yeah, right,' she says impatiently to the TV. 'Instead of whipping him into submission you just fuck with his head.'

And then the smoke alarm goes off and someone starts knocking at the door and, of course, it's Freddy. Billie goes to the door, saying, 'Leave him to me.'

'Wow!' he pants, when she's opened the door. 'Sounds like you guys are having fun!'

'No kidding.'

'The . . . uh . . . that's the smoke alarm.'

'No worries, babe,' Billie drawls. She goes over to the alarm, located on the ceiling above the desk. She takes a stiletto from the drag bag, climbs on to the desk and gives the alarm a monumental thwack with the heel.

It stops.

Freddy's eyes bulge. 'Wow! You're sure a lady who . . . Smells kind of funky in here too!'

Billie looks at Freddy with thinly disguised boredom. 'Are you on amphetamines?' she says.

Freddy's eyes get bigger and more speedy. 'Amphetamines! Wow! No way! I don't even drink coffee! It makes me sick to the stomach!'

Billie puts her joint back into her mouth. 'I think the keyboard of your computer's smeared with amphetamines,' she says, returning to her place on the bed. 'I think they soak into your skin as you type.'

At this, Freddy starts flinging himself around in hysterics, saying, 'That's so funny! So hilarious! Oh, my God!'

And then all the lights go out and Freddy shouts excitedly: 'Blackout! Never happened at the Cosy Inn in my memory!' He closes the door and scurries down the corridor.

Now that there's no TV, the only sounds in the room are of Billie sniffing. (She's been sniffing all day. It's not a cold, apparently. It's 'disco damage', she tells me, without elaborating.) I decide to mention that I have some night-light candles with me, tucked away in one of the emergency pockets of my rucksack. This perks her up. She says that candles would be a great idea. So I go to the car and when I return to the room there's a smell of Mexican food and everything is black – apart from two shards of burning paper floating in the air above Billie's bed. I shut the door and there's another burst of fire as a match is struck. It touches a strip of paper dangling down under her wrist and the flame-heavy bottom slinks from side to side like a piece of orange seaweed under water.

I'm not sure if I'm more disturbed that Billie seems to be setting our room on fire or that she's ordered in Mexican food when we could have dined quite happily on the free crisps and dip in the lobby. I don't want her to think I'm cheap, though, so I ask her what she's doing with the matches. She doesn't take any notice. She tears out a strip of paper from her floral notebook and sets it alight. She controls it perfectly. When the flames start crawling towards her fingers she twists the paper to an upward position to slow the burn and when she wants it to burn faster she dips the paper under her wrist. When there's only a thumb's worth of unburned paper remaining she lets go of it in a dainty, confident move. The charred scrap floats down on to the bed – a writhing tail of scaly grey ash edged with a tiny red filament, like the wire on a toaster.

'Sometimes, if you get food on the edge, that bit's greasy and it doesn't burn,' she says, watching the paper convulse in and out until it dies.

'Look here . . .'

'Pretty, huh?' she says dreamily.

'You'll set the bloody fire alarm off!'

'I've already broken the alarm.'

Another match is struck. The blackness shrinks back to reveal a bottle of Jack Daniel's and a brown and orange can. An ear of flame appears from a hand on the bed.

'Are you mad?'

'So I've been told,' she says, with a ripple of laughter.

The woman's totally out of control! This is just the sort of thing you read about in the papers: picking up wacky people in America and them turning out to be complete nutters. Bloody hell. I wish I had a bit of string or something on me. A few alternating square knots might put me back on an even keel. You know where you are with macramé: there are no surprises in a knot.

'Once, I set fire to three acres of hillside,' she says, taking a swig from the Jack Daniel's bottle and slashing another match. 'A proper bomb needs plutonium but you can do a pretty good job by mixing straw and manure and cooking it and putting it in a tube with a fuse in the middle.'

I just cross my arms now and let her get on with it. It's not my country anyway – let her burn the whole bloody place down for all I care.

'I got on well with the science teacher, Mr Harper. He taught me about tennis-ball guns. You need a tennis-ball can with a tiny hole stabbed in the bottom. You pour a small amount of gasoline into the can, you swish it around, you pour it out and then you send in the tennis ball. You light the match, you stick it through the hole and the ball shoots out with a huge bang. It can go as long as eight seconds before it lands.'

'Great.' I hope she notes the sarcasm in my voice.

'I didn't get caught either,' she slurs, pointing her toes like a slutty ballerina and once again removing her socks as if she's removing silk stockings (like that training some girls have to be feminine at all times). 'Well, not really. It was on the news that there'd been this huge bush fire. Everyone was talking about it. And then I come home stinking of smoke and gasoline and I'm, like, "Fire? What are you talking about, fire?"'

She giggles, leaning over to my bed. She strikes another match, grabs the bag of night-light candles and, with an unsteady hand, starts to light some. She's about to throw the dead match on the floor but she catches my eye, does a huffy little pout and puts it in the ashtray. 'Sorry.' She shrugs. 'I get a bit over-excited sometimes.'

I don't say anything. Actually, I'm quite enjoying the show now.

'Here, have some food, it's good,' she says, trying to win me back.

I nibble at a burrito (a flour tortilla stuffed with chicken, refried beans, cheese, iceberg lettuce and guacamole), wondering if I can save some of it for lunch tomorrow. If the room hasn't burned down by then. She seems better now, though. She's just fiddling with a dead match, dipping it in and out of one of the candle flames. Then she says, 'My second ever memory was of walking down the hall wondering how I would explain to my parents that my bed was on fire.'

Her voice is calmer.

'Even at the age of five I knew that fires were caused by something and I knew that this particular fire had been caused by me sitting under my bed playing with a box of matches on some loose-hanging gauze until, all of a sudden, the mattress went up like a torch. As I speed-walked down the hall, getting closer and closer to the door of the TV room where my parents sat at night, I wondered if it would be OK to say that I was in bed when, out of the blue, it just caught fire. By the time I got to the TV room I was a blubbering, incoherent, five-year-old nervous wreck but, as it turned out, this proved to be a pretty good way of handling the situation. I stood there howling, "My bed's on fire! My bed's on fire!" as I watched shock overtake my mother's face and my father rise from his armchair and proceed stoically down the hall. I remember turning on some hammy histrionics of the "I don't know how it happened! I don't know what's going on!" variety as a huge whoosh of excitement rushed through me. I watched Dad – who was still living with us at that point – carry the flaming mattress out of my bedroom as if it was just another crate of the Wonderbread he apparently carted round the factory every day of his life. He took the mattress to the backyard and hosed it down as Mom held me back by the shoulders from the black smoke. And this weird euphoria came over me. I guess it was realising that I'd done something really bad this time.'

She picks up the floral notebook. 'We got the bad babysitter because of a fire I lit,' she says, opening the book and starting to write. 'It wasn't even a good fire. It was an oven fire.'

'What happened?' She's got me interested now.

'I was sneaking a ready-cooked lasagne into the oven. I was about eight. I was always starving. The oven was filled with fat because Mom never cleaned it.' She looks up. 'Or probably I was supposed to clean it. Anyway, it caught on fire and Janey, the cool hippie babysitter, was upstairs making out with her boyfriend.'

'Did you get hurt?'

'No. The hippie babysitter got fired.' She stops writing. 'The firemen came and I liked that. Firemen look after you. Like waitresses.'

She tears a strip of paper from the page, explaining, 'You have to write until all the words come out and you can't breathe any more and then you rip off the piece of paper and burn it. Sometimes, if you have a lot to say, you scribble off five pages and then you rip it all out, put it in the sink and make a bonfire.'

She slashes a match and stares at the flame for a few seconds before setting light to the paper – from the middle this time. She wafts it expertly to and fro, watching pinky grey snowflakes fall on to the bed.

'When I was a kid,' she says quietly, 'I'd burn letters to my best friend at school, burn song lyrics that I thought particularly moving, burn secret help messages to my waitress friend, Leah. As you can see, I still burn words. Sometimes, after a shitty day, I strike a match and toss the lit piece of paper out of my motel window. Sometimes it doesn't rise up into the air in tongues of fire at all. Sometimes a gust of wind blows it back and it catches on my top and singes it and I have to stamp the stupid bit of paper out. Then I really hate words, I despise the fucking things. That's the typical sort of thing that words do, don't you think? They ruin everything.'

The pen glides again over the thick, creamy pages of the notebook. It's quicker this time and she seems to write more down. When I ask her what the point of burning words is, she says that it gets rid of nasty thoughts.

'Can it really get rid of them, though?'

She strikes another match. 'It helps a bit.' She watches, transfixed, as the new strip begins to burn.

I'm still wondering how she got betrayed by words. And what pain she has to get rid of. I wonder what she wrote that was so terrible. She lets the flaming paper float up into the air. It doesn't burn completely.

'You see?' she says. 'There was a burrito pawprint.' When the black crisp lands on my bed, you can still see a couple of words: 'purple' and something that starts 'Lea' – presumably her waitress friend, Leah.

'You see, Mo, the words that stay could be the important ones,' she says.

But I'm not really listening any more. I'm trying to piece things together: if setting her mattress on fire was her second memory and the sighting of a pair of stilettos was the first – as she told me in the Bloated Goat – then what is the connection between the two incidents? Was there a big time lapse between the two memories, for instance? But when I ask her this she just looks irritated. So I go for safer ground. I tell her that maybe she should give words another chance. That maybe she should start writing again and not burning her work now that she's grown-up. 'After all,' I reassure her, 'keeping a diary on a road trip's a normal thing.'

She takes an angry slurp of her Jack Daniel's and then the electricity comes back on, which is just as well. It turns out that Billie can only sleep with the TV on in the background. I am woken at intervals throughout the night by different voices urging me to buy a variety of things: an *'heirloom doll in tribute to John-John Kennedy'*, a *'facelift in a bottle'* and a never-ending line of weight-loss products (*'Have you ever wondered why sea animals never get fat?'*). I also get first-hand knowledge of Billie's disco damage. She grunts and snores and sniffs and twitches her way throughout the night.

CHAPTER FIVE

Shirley Temple

'Eggs up!'
  'Eggs over!'
  'Eggs poached!'
  'Wholewheat toast!'
  'White toast!'
  'Sourdough toast!'
  'Hold the toast!'
At Daddy Ray's a variety of voices ricochets around the kitchen hatch, among them a cheery request for 'Two eggs on a raft and wreck it!'

The speaker is our breakfast waitress, Peggy, a mature lady who resembles an old rag doll coming apart at the seams. Within no time of our sitting down at a table, Peggy had handed me the menu ('Daddy Ray's: the Taj Mahal of American Diners') and suggested I try the LYB – consisting of two eggs, bacon or sausage, grits, gravy, hash browns, Belgian waffle or short stack and toast or biscuits. That sounded a little heavy (LYB stands for 'Loosen Your Belt') after the palaver of the first half of this morning so I've gone instead for scrambled eggs on toast, which, as Peggy explained, is known as 'eggs on a raft and wreck it'.

Peggy has been very helpful with my 'Breakfast in America' research. 'Honey,' she confided, when I'd taken down a page of notes, 'I love to help people out. Sometimes tourists send me postcards to Daddy Ray's. They've went back home, they done sit down and took time to write me. I feel good when I know I made people feel happy inside.'

Peggy soon makes Billie exceedingly happy. When she appears again from in front of a sign that reads, 'We are not gourmey.

We can't even spell it!', she's carrying my eggs and also an oil-barrel-sized glass of fizzy pink liquid stuffed with umbrellas, cherries, swizzle sticks and something that looks like bunting. 'Shirley Temple!' Billie exclaims, telling me that a Shirley Temple is normally something you only get when you're a kid and you go into a bar with your parents.

Peggy informs me that the drink consists of 7-Up mixed with grenadine syrup (made from pomegranates) and topped with maraschino cherries. She's about to say something else when a man hollers at her from across the crowded restaurant: 'Hey, Chicken Legs! Bring me a coffee and make it snappy!'

'What a jerk,' Billie mutters, with a scowl, but Peggy isn't flustered.

'Daddy Ray,' she says, under her breath. 'He told me thirty-odd year ago when I started, "Peggy," he said, "don't you stoop so low to be like them. Smile, say you're sorry and walk away."' She wipes her hands down her apron. 'Best teacher I ever had.'

When she leaves to attend to the man, Billie, who still looks annoyed, starts spitting maraschino cherry stones out of her mouth. Not only the stones but also the stalks, which, when they land on the table, somehow end up knotted.

'Mom used to take me and my brother to this cool jazz club after she finished work,' she says, brightening up. 'A real dive. She'd get her date to buy us Shirley Temples.'

'Sounds fun.'

'Yeah, she taught us to tie the cherry stalks into a knot with our tongue.'

'Good trick.'

'Yeah, it was,' Billie says, tossing another cherry into her mouth. 'It got us to shut up.'

'Really?'

'You can't talk while you're tying a cherry stalk into a knot, right?'

She makes a funny twitch movement with her mouth then sticks her tongue out, revealing another perfectly tied stalk. She puts it, still wet, on the palm of my hand. 'What do you say, Miss Macramé?' she goes, with a wink. 'Bet you never made a bracelet out of cherry knots.'

The stalk tickles my palm. It's not an unpleasant sensation. It seems to travel through my body – in a long, burning circuit – from my palm to the back pocket of my jeans where I hid the piece of paper I rescued from the sink this morning at the Cosy Inn. The feeling only stops when Billie picks up her gold bag, stands up and announces that she's going to ask Peggy for some more cherries.

I'm impressed by Billie's trick, although after this morning nothing would surprise me about her. The exact order of the morning went something like this: I woke up – or, rather, a man on the Shopping Channel woke me up shortly after dawn, saying, 'Start your collection with the inspiring "Miracle at the Wedding" lacquered sculpture shown here.' And then there was a sniff and a fug of sweet yellow smoke and through the haze a ceramic Jesus appeared on the TV screen, tipping up a jug of water that started out grey at the top and ended up red at the bottom. Then Billie came into view, dressed like Madonna in the 'Like A Virgin' video (cut-offs with ripped fishnets underneath and a white vest with a red cross on it, saying, 'Venice Beach Lifeguard'). She was staring at a page of the *Explorer*, a fat joint protruding from her lips.

She slammed the *Explorer* shut and said, as if we'd only spoken a couple of seconds ago, 'I think that if we drive hard we should be able to make New Mexico in three days.' Then she was on the phone, giving Freddy his orders for the morning. Freddy couldn't believe his luck that he was allowed to be Billie's slave. By the time he'd lugged the drag bag out to the SUV his tan had a grey tinge and he looked as if he was about to explode with excitement. She bade him a final farewell, with 'Any time you want to split those drugs with me, you just let me know, babe,' which set him off in another fit of hysteria.

As she explained how she had been 'working' Freddy ('Tricks

aren't just about sex. Everything's a trick. Getting people to do what you want them to do and making them feel good about themselves at the same time, that's a trick too') I was looking round the pigsty of the SUV. I was already peeved at being woken up so early – and at having checked out of the Cosy Inn without claiming our free breakfast – but when I saw the melted Reese's Peanut Butter Cups, the spilled-over cups of root beer, the clutter of joint butts and stray lighters and the handles (crusts from the white-trash sandwiches, which Billie deems too boring to eat) I got a bit brassed off. I was suddenly annoyed at all her talk of slaves and tricks and 'turning' because I was supposed to be going off on my own into the wilderness to discover myself with no more structure than a story on waffles and bacon and orange juice, and now here I was in a car with a fat girl who could only sleep with the TV on and who lit up joints at seven in the morning . . .

Suddenly she went, 'Faaaaan-tastic' in that long-drawn-out way of hers, so I followed where her eyes were and they were looking at the Wendy's drive-thru opposite the Cosy Inn. She didn't answer when I told her I didn't fancy burgers for break-fast. She started the ignition, put the automatic gear lever into 'forward', slammed her foot on the accelerator and, with a huge screeching swerve, we were out of the Cosy Inn car park, skid-ding over the highway and hurtling up towards the Wendy's drive-thru.

'Forget your burgers, Peach,' she said. 'I'm going to get you something *real* tasty for breakfast!'

The only car on the Wendy's car park was this flash white thing – like one of the ones from *Grease*. The driver looked like the man on the Jack Daniel's bottle – all facial hair and a white Stetson – and his car (with a numberplate saying, 'Jesus Christ Is the Way') was lurching about by the pick-up window as if he was well over the limit. The car kept crashing into the kerb by the loudspeaker where you said your order, then reversing, then going forward, then crashing into the kerb again, then reversing viciously, sending burning up rubber from the tyres before making another dash at the kerb.

So what did Billie do? She only went and parked just to the right of the loudspeaker, next to a sign saying,

Wendy's pick-up window
Our founder,
Our friend,
We love you, Dave

So that when Jack Daniel's made his next ludicrous attempt at a manoeuvre, he nearly smashed right into the back of us.

I couldn't stop myself any longer. 'What the hell are you doing?' I shouted. 'Can't you see he's going to crash into us?'

'Yeah,' she went. 'Rear ending. Automatic penalty.'

'What?'

'You're fully insured, right?'

'Of course, but—'

She craned her neck to see into the rear-view mirror. 'Oh, my God,' she said. 'There's a child in there. This is so totally my lucky day.'

I was just thinking about leaning over and grabbing the wheel from her, shouting something dramatic like 'Give me back my bloody car!' when there was an almighty crunch, the SUV shuddered from side to side and Billie whooped, 'Bull's eye!'

I was speechless. I got out of the car to inspect the damage to the rear lights. With a huge grin on her face, Billie linked her arm through mine and took me over to the now stationary white car. There was the sound of lowering electronic windows, then a waft of adolescent hormones and sweaty nylon mixed with an overwhelming stench of whisky.

As the electric window got further lowered, you could hear Jack Daniel's shouting at the girl, 'No, you can't have a chocolate shake and a quarter-pounder! Whoever heard of a fat thirteen-year-old getting a boyfriend?'

The girl shouted back, like some stroppy wife, 'You're not so cute yourself, fat ass!' and Jack Daniel's hit the wheel in exasperation before turning to us with bleary eyes, slurring, 'You know thirteen-year-old girls? You remember thirteen-going-on-thirty and not a brain in your head?'

His breath was making my eyes water, and Billie took over. She played it calm. 'Nice car you got here, sir,' she says. 'Shame about what happened to ours.'

A cloud fell over the man's face, as if he'd realised he was surrounded by thirteen-year-old girls on every side. He muttered nervously, 'We don't want anyone else involved in this. Right, sugar?' and got out his wallet with a shaking hand.

He must have been really drunk because when we ended up back on the 10 we had an added five thousand dollars in the kitty. Billie spread the notes in front of her face in fan formation. She seemed delighted by the whole affair. 'He was *so* like my fucking stepfather. That was just beautiful.'

She knew I wasn't happy about it, though. 'Come on, Mo,' she coaxed. 'People play supermarket-cart hockey all the time.'

I folded my arms tightly over my chest, muttering about how dishonest the whole thing was. More than that, though, it felt strange – money that ended up in your lap without you having done anything for it. Of course, now that it was over, I secretly quite liked our adventure, but I still played martyr for a bit. I told her I wanted to stop off at a diner for some breakfast research, then get back on the road and drive without stopping through Louisiana until we hit east Texas.

The driving non-stop wasn't the problem. It was the diner. 'A diner!' she exclaimed. 'You make five thousand dollars for doing nothing, and what do you want to do with it? Go sunglasses shopping? Go buy a diamond bracelet? No! You want to go to a diner!'

'Billie . . .'

'I hate fucking diners!'

*　　*　　*

That was the weird bit. The bit that pricked my conscience. The thing is, I know that Billie doesn't hate diners. I know she likes them because I read all about it in the sink of the Cosy Inn this morning. I know more about Billie than she thinks.

Last night, after eating the gratuitous Mexican takeaway, she passed out into her disco-damaged sleep – thinking, presumably, that the bonfire was taking care of the wodge of paper she'd thrown into the sink. And it did, more or less. Except that a couple of pages didn't burn properly. As I was clearing up the mess of the pyromania party while Billie supervised Freddy carting her stuff out to the SUV, I couldn't resist reading the words that remained on the charred pages. I felt slightly dizzy as I held the two singed sheets in my hands, but once I started reading the adrenaline got the better of me. I hadn't had a chance to finish everything because Billie and Freddy came back to the room. But the excerpt stuck in my mind. The style stuck too – how she'd written it as if she was a kid, a kid in a diner called Sambo's with her mother and a brother called Ned.

I'm pleased when Billie gets up to go and fetch more cherries for her Shirley Temple. It gives me a chance to read the story again. I pull the sheets out of my jeans pocket and put them on my lap under the table.

On Wednesday, Thursday and Friday evenings, when Mom comes to pick us up from Reba's after work at the flight school, we go to Sambo's for dinner. Mom has coffee, and me and Ned split a glass of milk and a grilled-cheese sandwich. One day it's a 'girl-cheese' sandwich and one day it's a 'boy-cheese' sandwich. That's what Leah calls it. Leah is cool.

The grilled-cheese sandwich comes with home fries and coleslaw. Ned doesn't like the coleslaw very much but Mom won't let me eat his share. She says he has to eat vegetables because they're good for you. Sometimes me and Ned split the child's Blue Plate Special and Mom has coffee. Ned likes the fried chicken and mashed potatoes with gravy best and I like the BBQ short ribs with Curly Q

Cajun French Fries. We both like the pies. If you sit at the counter on the stools you can see the pies even better. They have them in a glass case and on the inside of the case there's a mirror so you can see the tops of the pies. It's sort of like TV. You can sit at the counter and look at the mirror and see the pies — maybe a peach pie or a cherry pie or a lemon meringue pie.

I like sitting at the counter better than in a booth because then you can see what's going on. You can see the coffee machine spluttering and hissing and you can watch the short order cook making hash browns — squeezing them and tossing them with his knife — and when he makes pancakes he pours the batter on the griddle and it goes all lacy at the edges like when a wave comes up on the seashore. Other things you can see when you sit on the counter stools are the little pots where they keep things like the lettuce and the tomatoes for the burgers and you also get close up to the soda fountains and see the waitresses chatting through the hole in the wall to the cooks in the kitchen.

Sometimes Leah is real nice. If she's walking behind the counter, she'll sneak you a soda or a spare Curly Q Cajun French Fry, which are my favorite. 'Here you go, kiddiewink,' she says. And I say, 'Thanks, Leah. Bitchin'!' (I only use that word with her because normally you get told off when you say it.) Being at the counter is exciting. You can see how everything works and you can't help but jig around on your stool until Mom says, 'Will you just cool it, Billie?' even though there's a sign above the griddle in big red letters that says, 'Pleasing you pleases us!'

We usually aren't allowed to sit at the counter because I don't behave myself, Mom says. The booths are OK, though. You sit at the booth waiting for Leah to come over and take your order and to stop yourself talking you look at Sambo on the walls. There are pictures of Sambo on the walls on pieces of colored plastic with lights behind. Leah said some English lady wrote a book back in the day about him, about a little black boy who has adventures in a hot country. I never read the book but the pictures are cool. My favorite ones are of Sambo getting his butt bitten by the tiger and the one of Sambo getting shut in the laundry basket. And the pancakes, of course. There's a picture of a stack of pancakes that Sambo eats (I've counted 169 of them).

I'd like to have a boyfriend like Sambo. He wears cute shorts, a hat with jewels and purple shoes with crimson soles and crimson lining. I don't think I'd be allowed to play with him, though, because Mom says he's a slave, which I know is something like being a Mexican. I want to talk to Mom about this but she just drinks her coffee and looks out of the window. She drinks a lot of coffee.

Leah is the best waitress I ever met. She always says, 'Hi there, kiddiewinks,' and it makes me and Ned laugh. Then she says, 'So, how was the day in the office?' and that makes us laugh because we've only been to school and then Reba's. Sometimes I tell her some of my jokes, not my rude jokes, like the one about the nuns and the tomato ketchup, but the stupid ones like 'What do witches wear in their hair?' Answer: 'Scar'

The rest of the word has burnt away. I think it should say, 'scarespray'. At least, I remember Mother finding that joke in a cracker last Christmas. I'm just thinking how I'm not sure what to make of Ruby Rose, née Billie Harrison, any more when a rumble of bootleg liquor catches me unawares and there she is, back at the booth. Luckily, she's too excited about the cherry refill Peggy's given her to notice me stuffing the diary excerpt back into my jeans. Even so, my heart's booming away and I know that my face must be bright red. I'm worrying that she's going to suspect something when, out of the blue, a cockroach saves the day. It's scuttling along the floor in the middle of the restaurant, bold as brass. 'That's bad,' I mutter. 'Cockroaches in this day and age. It's not necessary.'

Billie looks at my face and starts laughing. She puts her hand (warm and heavy) on the back of mine. 'You calm down, you hear?' she says gently. 'I won't let any roaches get my Peach.'

'But that's not the point,' I burble on. 'You don't even have to use roach spray, these days – I mean, they could use plaster of paris—'

'Mo,' she chuckles, squeezing my hand, 'did anyone ever tell you you're a freak?'

She says it as though she likes me being a freak. I like her liking me so I carry on with my roach information to make her like me even more: 'An inventive way of killing a roach is to mix a dish of plaster of paris with sugar.'

'What?'

'You have to put a dish of water by the side, of course.'

'Mo!'

'Yes, and then the roach eats the sugary powder and drinks the water and it thinks it's having a feast. But then the water hardens the plaster of paris and the cockroach hardens from the inside out—'

'That's horrible!' Her hand springs off the back of mine. 'You've got to be kind, Mo! It's important to be kind!'

I'm surprised by the strength of her emotion. I'm sorry I've upset her. I want to make it better. But I can't think of anything to say and an awkward silence falls between us. We look over to Peggy, who's at the rude man's table. Somehow, she's managed to calm him down. In fact, without doing anything other than smile and keep her dignity, she's achieved the remarkable feat of making him meek. 'You tried to make me happy and I wouldn't even listen to you,' he's mumbling, head in hands. 'I was so rude it's just pathetic . . .' He slumps lower and lower into his seat, his head sinking into his neck like a tiered cake that's gone rotten. Lower and lower the head sinks – his whole body looks as though it's turned inside out now, as if someone should maybe pull him up by the wisps of hair on top of his head to save him from disappearing altogether.

A smile leaks on to Billie's lips. 'That's something you might want to note for your story,' she says.

'Sorry?'

'About how if your waitress is a dominant or a submissive

then it can make the world of difference to how you enjoy your breakfast.'

'I suppose you're right . . .'

'No, *you*'re right, Mo,' she says, turning back to her Shirley Temple. 'I *do* like coming to diners. And you know why?'

'Why?' I'm meek now.

'Because waitresses are kind. They're like your mother but less fucked up.'

'I . . . suppose.'

'And you're right about what you wrote in the back of your book.' She pokes a cherry with the end of a curly transparent straw.

'Sorry?'

'You're right about hookers being like waitresses.'

'Oh?'

'Sure. Like Peggy says, we might seem like we don't have any power but we sure as hell do.' Some sharpness has entered her voice. 'You never feel out of control, even when you're turning a trick in the back seat of a car. It's like being a nanny. You treat the punter like you're their mother and you'd never pull bravado on your mother because she'd slap that look right off your face. You do the job, then you say, "I don't want you doing this again, you hear? Now get out of my car, you dirty little faggot."'

She pokes the cherry with such ferocity that she sends it hurtling to the depths of the Shirley Temple glass.

CHAPTER SIX

Queens in a Teacup

I was woken this morning by the sound of Billie crying. I sat up and there she was: puffing away on a joint, staring at the TV with tears trickling down her cheeks. I asked her what was wrong and she told me how a hairdresser had just given a woman a makeover. 'It made me cry,' she said. I asked if it had been a bad makeover and she replied that, no, it had been a good one. That the woman had started out with really stringy hair and bad makeup and afterwards she'd been transformed. 'You could tell it made her feel really special.' She sniffed.

My stomach always sinks when an American says 'special'. As it does when they say 'unique' about some new film or fast-food product, or 'I love you' at the end of a telephone chat with a parent or child. The words don't really mean anything. They're over-used. 'I love you' is especially over-used. And when you say it in a non-platonic context it's such a drastic step – like using up your three wishes from the genie all at once. You use them and puffs of smoke explode and sparks fly and you think you're going to vaporise with excitement. And then things settle back into place and you sit there waiting for the next tremor, the next set of fireworks, but there isn't one because all the gunpowder's been used up and there's only damp squibs left. I told Gary I loved him once and that was a washout. What I meant was 'I love security', 'I love hiding away from the world.' For all my home-sweet-home fantasies, I know now that security doesn't exist. I know that security's just a superstition.

As Billie carried on sniffing and squelching and sentimental-ising ('It's important to make people feel special, Mo!'), my eyes focused on the 1970s digital radio alarm – the one mod con in

73

our room (Econo Lodge, Mabeline, east Texas. $29.99 plus tax), which claimed it was ten past six in the morning. It was too early to be cynical. Besides, sometimes the lack of cynicism in America can be a therapeutic thing. A lot of the time when Americans say things it's as if they leave a blank space in their wake, begging to be filled up with some nasty, bitter European retort. But sometimes it's nice to stop and hold yourself back. It can be done. You can be on a city street and make yourself hear the rustling of leaves on the trees and not the police sirens.

'Never mind,' I croaked. 'I'm sure the woman's really chuffed with her new hair-do.'

She nodded. 'Tears are just memories, right?'

'Sorry?'

'I haven't travelled for a while. I'd forgotten.'

'Forgotten what?'

'How the further you move forward, the further back you go in your head.'

She said that our trip had started playing havoc with her dream place. Last night it had turned into a cross between Bourbon Street and the Wild West. There was a flood and an emergency alarm and all these strange people were in her house, telling her to hurry up and get out and Billie was thinking, How dare they tell me to get out of my own house. And who are these people anyway? She said she could see a trickle of water leaking through the ceiling and she could hear messages over the loud speaker about a plane that was about to leave.

'But I didn't want to leave, Mo!' she pleads. 'I didn't want to leave at all.'

I'm not good in situations of high emotion. I'm a bit of an ostrich in that respect. The nearest sand I could think of was breakfast. So I suggested we started the 'Breakfast in America' research early before making inroads to Texas. I said that if we drove steadily, we could be in San Antonio by evening.

Billie tried to smile. She picked up the floral notebook that was lying open on her bed. I noticed then that there was writing

74

inside made with a silver marker pen – presumably the one she'd bought yesterday evening in the gas station just after we crossed the state border from Louisiana into Texas. She looked briefly inside the notebook, then closed it. I expected the usual hold-up as she ripped out the pages and burned them in the sink. But she didn't burn anything. She put the book into her gold bag and jumped up off the bed, announcing that she had a present for me. She held out a white paper napkin with something wrapped inside it. 'Bagels, Mo!' she said, handing me the bundle. 'I wasn't sure which kind you liked so I got you sesame seed, onion, cinnamon and one "everything bagel".' She shrugged shyly. 'I got them from the free breakfast buffet. I know you like to economise and all . . .'

I felt terrible. I mean, this was a typically sweet gesture from Billie yet all I could think of was the floral notebook. How she'd written some words in it – that she hadn't burned – and how I couldn't get at them because they were back in the gold bag under the wraps of the silk cover, knotted away under the green and yellow cord. I would have read them, given half the chance. I definitely would have read them. The fact is, I'm what you might call a liar.

My husband's not dead at all, you see. True, Gary did feel like a bereavement. It was as if the police had come to the front door and said, 'I'm sorry, Mrs Baroclough, but your husband has been killed in a terrible accident and you'll never see him again.' Even worse than the bereavement was the fact that he wasn't even dead. He was still there, swanning around. I'd be coming out of work at the Sceptre and he'd suddenly appear and look down his nose at me like I was a bit of muck on the bottom of his shoe. And then one day he phoned me up out of the blue and invited me out for lunch. I asked him what he wanted. I was used to him by then. I was fed up of giving by then.

'I just want to take you for lunch,' he said. 'Please come.' So I did, and the first thing he said was that he was sorry. 'I'm sorry, Mo,' he said. And this time I think he meant it.

I'm trying to work out what it was that I found so glamorous about Gary. He had an attractive roughness to him, I suppose – that true-chef smell of stale sweat and hotel-kitchen gravy. And then he was old – forty at the time – which, for a twenty-five-year-old was something of a feather in a cap. He didn't act like he was old, though. He was like a playful white boxer dog, all bouncy and skittish and given to chasing his tail round and round in circles. And he had these pale, lithe hands that moved expansively as he talked (one of the first things he ever said to me was 'There's no better way to start the day than with a bacon sandwich and a love letter') and he had uncanny blue eyes that looked like an optician's light was constantly shining into them. Acid Sarah reckoned he reminded her of the dodgy bloke who ran the waltzers at Scarborough Fair, but I didn't care what she said. She was seeing Siamese cats with blue heads coming out of the walls that summer and she left the Sceptre in the middle of the season to drive to Spain in an orange Volkswagen with a boy from the local art school and twelve grams of Mexican mushrooms.

I didn't even mind Gary's petulance. The days when he pouted and announced, at the last minute, that he didn't feel like going to the pub with his fellow sous-chefs – all belching up meatballs and lying about the amounts of sex they'd had. Or when he suddenly declared on the way to the local disco that he didn't want to go there because the local disco was his idea of hell. This was all fine by me: it was just proof of his good taste.

He had ambition too. His dream was to get away from the Sceptre and find a chef job in a proper posh restaurant and he accomplished this when a friend introduced him to the head chef of a new French restaurant in town called Le Bateau Ivre. We were happy then, in a way. His wages went up, I inherited a bit of money and we moved in together.

He threw himself into a self-improvement trip. He started to wear charity-shop velvet dressing-gowns that, he said, made you think of a Dickens character with mutton-chop whiskers who drinks glasses of claret and has a manservant. Then he started to read Oscar Wilde – 'Makes the blokes at work laugh,' he said, his blue eyes shining. He'd come in after a day or a night at Le Bateau Ivre stinking of *moules marinières* and I'd run him a bath perfumed with French scent. He'd lie there, eyes closed, as the smells of garlic and fat floated off his white skin like petals falling away to reveal a new bud.

The only blip on the horizon was that he never made a move on me beyond a few chaste kisses. It didn't bother me too much. He was fulfilling other dreams of mine such as eating in bed without getting told off. Gary loved to eat in bed – no semen ever soiled our sheets but traces of fried steak and chips and chocolate cake with tinned custard used to fill it. When he fell asleep at night, I'd feel proud to be lying next to him. He liked me to sleep with my back to him so that he could clasp me round the waist with his strong arms and whisper, 'Like being on a toboggan!'

I seemed to have found my hamster cage at last – a place of exciting domesticity. One day, I was sitting in the back garden looking into the embers of a barbecue. Some of the charcoal had formed little caves that looked like little red homes. They sort of throbbed in and out and they made a tindery, chinking sound. It was very faint but it reminded me of being at Mass. It reminded me of the creepy section when the priest chimes the tiny set of bells to alert you that bread and wine is being trans-formed into the body and blood of Christ. It's a creepy sound – sort of mysterious – and you're scared and comforted at the same time.

Both me and Gary had been brought up as Catholics, although we weren't religious. We just liked the whole campness of Catholicism: the incense, the stained-glass windows, the bells. I did an embroidery night class for a laugh and made a range of biblical-themed cushions embroidered with scenes from the Stations of the Cross, the Serpent in the Garden of Eden and the Visitation with 'Dei Parae Virginis Sine Labe Conceptae' – 'The virgin mother of God, conceived without sin' – written under-neath in gold silk Holbein stitch.

Gary was fond of those cushions. We'd come home from church and he'd throw me on the *chaise-longue* and make me sprawl out on 'Jesus is scourged and crowned with thorns', but by the time he'd got his zip undone he'd have fizzled out. By this time he knew about my boxer-dog thing and he'd just do some-thing silly, like start barking, and I'd laugh and get overcome with affection for him.

I should have seen it coming.

The runt of a Catholic family with an alcoholic father and an absent stepmother. That was excuse number one. Then there was the jilting thing – he'd nearly got married once and he was jilted days before the ceremony. I said to him that we'd tie the knot and then he'd feel secure. So we got married and afterwards I expected him to open up. But he didn't. The lid just got screwed down even tighter. When I pointed out that we hadn't had sex for over a year, he announced that he was going to stop wanking so that he'd have to concentrate on me. I wasn't sure how to take that. Was he saying that without wanking he'd be so desperate that he'd *have* to fuck me? It didn't work, anyway. He took to turning over in bed at night and mumbling that he needed 'more time'.

This went on for more than four years. I put up with it. It was only sex and, after all, I was still having my domestic epipha-nies all over the shop. At one point he took up Nichiren Daishonin Buddhism because he said it would help him to relax more. I'd be woken up at six in the morning by the sound of '*Nam-Myoho-Renge-Kyo, Nam-Myoho-Renge-Kyo*' chanted over and over again and I didn't even have to open my eyes to know that he was kneeling at the end of the bed in supplication before a milk bottle of red campions and a couple of Cox's orange pippins.

I was glad when the Buddhism stopped and the painting began – even though it did coincide with his starting to come home late from work. When I talked to him about it he'd just woof and kiss me on the nose, telling me not to worry. He said that Duncan, one of the owners of the Bateau Ivre, had promoted him to acting head chef. He said he had to schmooze. It was important for his career, he said.

And then the pictures began to arrive. The walls of the house filled up with these awful paintings – bad execution, bad subject matter, the lot. It started with the back view of a woman in white Laura Ashley doing up her suspenders on a seashore. Then came grotesquely proportioned pictures of the local church, sketches of Venice that resembled grade D O-level art and endless daubings of two-dimensional cats looking out of windows. The worst were the lacklustre still-lifes of fruit that looked as if the paintbrush had barely warmed up. The pomegranates stick in my mind with their neat flesh robbed of all dirtiness, and their glassy seeds like pieces of a complicated jigsaw with all the bits intact.

And then the bum pictures arrived. The first was of a man in swimming trunks walking towards the sea – although the painter had achieved the remarkable feat of making the man look as if he was walking backwards. A whole flood of them ensued: endless paintings of this man with a bum like an over-inflated basketball lying on different vertical towels, sitting on a variety of odd-looking walls, peeping through pathetic attempts at waves.

Soon Gary started spouting all these cringy epigrams. He'd arrive home at two in the morning, and when I went downstairs to say hello, he'd be reclined on the settee, a green carnation in his buttonhole, dipping McCain oven chips into a pot of beluga caviar, saying things like 'When one is tired of caviar one is tired of life.' Finally, he started to talk about his new friends. One of them was the manager of the garden centre, another was a married couple he'd met at his Buddhist group – Edward, the battery-chicken farmer, and his wife, Muriel, the journalist. 'There's Duncan too,' he said quickly.

One Sunday lunchtime I met them all. I'd unexpectedly had

to work a double shift at the Sceptre so I arrived home late. As I crept in quietly through the back door, I could hear the kitchen bursting with raucous male laughter dominated by one languid voice. 'What, pray, is for lunch?' the voice asked.

'Fish, I reckon!' said a thick northern hiss, and the table cracked up laughing.

'Now then!' a woman said, her voice like breaking glass. 'You shut your bloody cakeholes!'

'No! Let's be nasty and vicious!' the languid voice teased.

'Aye! Let's talk about pain,' the northerner piped up. 'Tell us, Duncan, how are the nipples coming on? Still inflamed, are they?'

'I had to take the studs out, Keith,' Duncan replied. 'They went all septic.'

'Nipples oozing with pus,' Keith sniggered. 'A grand look, I must say!'

'Yes,' Duncan drawled. 'I've realised that I have too much class to go grunge.'

'Too much class?'

'Yes, my body has better taste than I do.'

The raucous laughter started up again, followed by 'Duncan, you're a caution!' and 'Duncan, you old trollop,' this one from Gary, my husband.

'I smell an eighteen-year-old in the picture,' Keith said excitedly. 'Can't see any other reason for sticking metal through your flesh.'

'Eighteen-year-olds are so boring, aren't they?' Duncan sighed. 'So clingy.'

'I bet you weren't clingy, Duncan!' Keith roared, banging his fist on the table.

'No,' Duncan announced. 'I wasn't clingy. I was wriggly and slippery as a matter of fact.'

'So, what are you up to these days, then, Duncan?' Keith enquired.

'There is always a lustful frenzy to be expended on a cushion of soft flesh.'

'Oooh, that's a good one!' Keith said.

'Huyssmans.'

'Sounds French. Randy bastard!'

'Yes. Of course, I prefer firm flesh to the soft variety.' He looked at Gary with a flare of the nostrils.

'I bet you do, sunshine!' Keith chortled. 'I know you!'

Duncan sighed dramatically. 'Oh, but do you know me, Keith? Are you too torn between desire and glut, hope and disillusionment?'

'Come again?'

'Put a bloody sock in it,' the woman with the broken-glass voice screeched. 'You two'll be the death of me.'

'And if we are,' Duncan said grandly, 'then, my dear Muriel, you can rest assured that we shall throw you a funeral such as Huyssmans threw in memory of his lost virility.'

'What was that like?' my husband panted.

'The ornamental pond was edged with black basalt and filled with ink, guests were waited on by naked negresses wearing only slippers and silver stockings embroidered with tears and only black food was served.'

'Can't get much better than that, can you?' a man with the timid voice whispered.

'Oh, but you can, Edward, you can,' Duncan asserted. 'There are always new perfumes, larger blossoms, pleasures still untasted . . .'

The obvious truth could no longer be denied. My house was filled with a coven of queens and my husband was the biggest one of all.

I cut short the next round of laughter by making my entrance. Gary's pale face went blotchy pink. 'Oh . . . hello,' he said, standing up. 'We were waiting for you. Everyone . . . this is Maureen.'

The men slumped down in their seats like naughty children. Duncan and Keith smirked and muttered, 'Hello,' under their breath.

The woman with the terrible voice screeched, 'Hello! We've all been dying to meet you!'

'Dying,' echoed Duncan, trying to make the word sound significant. Titters filled the room.

'What would you like to drink, then, Maureen?' Gary said, awkwardly.

Gary never called me Maureen and he never asked me what I wanted to drink. The new gallantry didn't last long. Before I'd had a chance to reply, he turned to Duncan. There was something weird about Duncan's orange, perma-tanned skin. It looked like he was wearing foundation or he'd had plastic surgery. I thought that he looked like a mean, manipulative thug.

Gary said, 'Oh, Duncan! Sorry! Empty glass! What would you like now?'

Duncan looked at Gary, his face radiant with malice. 'Whatever I'm not allowed,' he purred.

Lunch was a nightmare. Gary couldn't stop toadying to Duncan, who, of course, turned out to be the artist – and co-owner of Le Bateau Ivre. Keith from Sheffield, the manager of the garden centre, kept droning on in a series of interminable anecdotes with no punchline that began with sentences such as 'Are you familiar with the geography of southern Cumbria?' I watched with astonishment while he downed his glasses of beer – he only drank beer – as if he were a rat swimming along a sewer. He'd tip his head back to a drastic angle, squidge his eyes up and all you could see through the glass would be a snout and two sharp front teeth burrowing deeper and deeper into his amber effluent.

Edward, the timid chicken farmer, was hard work. He was fifty-four years old with a face like a baby's and a manicured head of ginger-brown hair that gleamed like the plumage on a hen's wing. He thought I looked like a good listener. This often happens to me. I am that person you go up to in the street and ask for directions.

'I mean, fifty-four's not old, is it, Maureen? It makes you think, when you've got friends dying at forty-three. I've got money put aside – you can sleep at night with a bit of money put aside, can't you?'

And then suddenly there's a thump in my ribs from the dishevelled woman with the terrible voice. 'Bloody hell,' she screeched. 'Not droning on, is he? Dull as bloody arseholes my husband!'

She – the wife of Edward – looked like a potato root that had just been pulled up from the ground and still had clumps of soil all over it. She had crispy over-dyed blonde hair with dry sprigs sticking out at various angles, like she'd been pulled backwards through a hedge. As she talked to me – she had an inexhaustible knowledge on topics ranging from scrambling motorbikes and mobile-phone networks to the influence of Mars in relation to Venus in the seventh house – she'd punctuate her sentences with hard slaps on my back. She started off by talking about her horoscopes page for the *Scarborough Evening Post*. How she'd ended up working there part time because the editor was one of Edward's chicken customers. The editor apparently told her that she could do horoscopes or gardening and she said she'd do horoscopes because 'I thought it'd be the least mucky option!'

I looked at her and thought that horoscopes seemed to be making her pretty mucky too. But then I stopped myself being mean. She was, after all, very encouraging about my writing. She said I should come round to her house one day and she'd give me some journalism coaching. Then she winked and asked if I'd been to any of the 'parties' yet.

'Parties?' I said. 'Buddhist parties?'

'No!' She laughed, taking off her glasses and polishing the greasy lenses. 'The special parties.' She confided that someone called James put up the prices last term. 'Tight as bloody arseholes, he is!'

I had no idea what she was talking about. I thought I'd better humour her. 'Do you go often to the parties?' I said.

'Oh, yes,' she said, glugging back her glass of red wine and Coke. 'You have to go at the right times, of course. Away from that lot.' She tossed her head in the direction of the men, who were presently huddled in awe around Duncan as he droned melodically on about the realisation of art being like the pouring of pesticide on one's dreams. Then she whispered to me, 'You've got to give James his due. He's very creative. Some of what he does is stunning.'

She winked. 'They've got some smashing equipment down there. Mink oil and whatnot.' She swigged back the rest of her drink. 'Hammer and tongs we're at it.' She banged the empty glass down on the table. 'Ripped the arse out of the place last week!'

She turned to Keith who was sitting next to her and said, 'Weren't we, Keith? A bit discombobulated afterwards?'

'Could say that, Muriel! Could say that!' As Keith roared with laughter, his mouth – the wet rim of a bowl on a potter's wheel – crumpled and spun out of control as the loose skin above his eyelids flapped around like an old tent about to flop down.

I was discombobulated myself. I had no idea what 'parties' they were talking about.

Keith forced his rat lips to concentrate into a prim little pout. 'I've got my winter warmers and my summer pick and mix, that's all I'm saying,' he said. Then he nudged me in the ribs. 'You should see the sex drive on this one at the parties. Formula One's got nothing on our Muriel!'

Over the next few months Gary's behaviour started becoming more erratic. He'd stroll in at two in the morning, his face red with stubble burn – although he was still protesting it was eczema. I'd hear him fling down his dirty work clothes in the kitchen and then he'd begin his stagger up the stairs until finally he'd burst into the bedroom, claw my arm and belch something nasty to me in whisky-soured breath.

One time he came back and it was strange. He wasn't drunk at all. He was sober and it was only five in the evening. A beautiful warm summer evening. He couldn't settle. He kept pacing up and down the sitting room. Then he'd sit down and watch a

bit of TV, only to stand up again and go over to look distractedly out of the window. Eventually, he turned to me and said,
'You know what Duncan says?'

I didn't move.

'He says that when you feel jaded and boring you should go
back to the vices of your youth.' I opened my eyes and saw his
piercing blue eyes. And it was as if I saw them for the first time.
I saw that they weren't unfathomable at all. They were undoubt-
edly the brightest of blues as they always had been – but I noticed
now that there was nothing else there, just azure ponds with no
obvious signs of life swimming around underneath.

The process had begun. The domestic scales were falling from
my eyes. Crumbs in the bed didn't seem so much fun any more.
Smears of chocolate-cake mix and steak grease was suddenly
just plain unsexy. Then I realised I didn't even know what sexy
was. I thought about what Gary had said, about vices of youth,
and I realised that I didn't have any.

I told him that I knew, that I wanted a divorce.

I'd never seen him look so relieved.

I went through a strange time. It was like a period of
mourning. Then I realised I wasn't mourning the loss of Gary
so much, it was more the loss of my domestic epiphanies. At
least they'd been intense emotions.

I eventually remembered Amanda, my hamster. I was eleven
and I'd come home from school to discover that the brown furry
bundle usually to be found breathing sluggishly under a mound
of paper straw was gone from her cage. She'd got wanderlust,
packed her cheeks with sunflower seeds and hit the road. And
that's the thing. You can be a homely type and still run away
from home. You just have to take your home with you. That's
what they say, isn't it? Your home doesn't have to be a place.
Your home is in your head.

I located Amanda later that night in the lounge, in the bottom
of the settee. Me and Mother had to cut it open with a pair of
scissors. It looked interesting in there. All dark and secret with

wooden bars and metal tubes and hidden nooks and crannies to explore. She'd already unpacked her pouches and found a corner to stash her sunflower seeds. She looked pissed off that she'd been disturbed.

The desire to escape crept up as stealthily as the desire to make a home once had. It came upon me as an itch, a scratch, an intuition. The candle I'd held up to domesticity began to flicker dangerously. I heard the chiming of a tiny set of bells and that chapter of my life came to an end. Mass was over, the candles were snuffed out, the smoke vanished into thin air and the congregation ran whooping from the church, thinking only of eating, drinking and relieving the morning horn.

CHAPTER SEVEN

Leviticus Nasty

Of course, I was the one who took charge of the eating and drinking, while relieving the morning horn was Billie's domain.

This became clear later that morning when, at six thirty, following Billie's tearful start at the Econo Lodge, we left Mabeline and continued our drive into east Texas. We stopped off in a small town called Honduras only a few miles from Mabeline, attracted by an establishment advertising itself as a 'rock 'n' roll lounge-cum-bar-cum-Chinese restaurant'.

The Wing Fat was our most unusual breakfast venue so far. In the 'rock 'n' roll lounge' area there were groups of red leatherette easy chairs shaped like Cadillac seats and screwed into the greasy black floor. By a sign saying, 'Solicitation on the premises is not permitted', there was also a juke-box with a plug upholstered into the wall so it could never be turned off; if nobody fed it any money it played an endless loop of 'The Eye Of The Tiger' and 'Tie A Yellow Ribbon Round The Old Oak Tree'. Not that the people sprawled in the lounge seemed to notice the music: through the fug of smoke all you could see were a few human forms slumped in Cadillac seats listlessly raising beer bottles from table to mouth.

Our waitress told us that the Wing Fat served Chinese food in the evenings but from four a.m. through to eleven a full American breakfast was offered. Not that breakfast was a favourite with her: 'See, the drag about the breakfast shift is the toast,' she mused, hand on hip, tapping her front teeth with a chewed pen. 'You gotta do your own toast here and that stuff's ripe for stealing. We get toast fights sometimes – they can ruin your day. Some of the girls, they mark their toast. Like, they'll tear off one of the corners? And then, if someone goes, "That ain't your toast," you can point to the corner and go, "Sure it is."' She shook her head. 'Oh, yeah, toast is the pits. Big-time.'

She wandered off, summoned away by a black man at a nearby table clicking his fingers, dripping in jewellery and swathed in a *Saturday Night Fever* white suit. She approached the table warily, as if it was filled with a group of bolshy waitresses about to pull her into a toast fight, and then I heard Billie say, 'Now, this is what I call home away from home.'

I put my pen and exercise book down and saw that she, too, was gazing at the black man and his entourage – a group of skinny white women wearing black eyeliner and dragging heavily on cigarettes. 'Pimp and his ladies,' she said. 'You can bet he'll never let them order anything more expensive than him.' I listened as she read the restaurant for me: the large transvestite ('Trucker Trannie') sitting alone at a table, sipping a pink milk-shake and making conversation with an invisible person opposite; the two young men in tight blue jeans, chuckling and digging into eggs and bacon ('Rent-boys just through from a night's work'). She pushed away her empty Jack Daniel's glass, saying that the Wing Fat reminded her of the days she worked in New York: 'The diner graveyard shift when you've done your tricks and you're back and safe and swapping stories of the night's work over steaming cups of coffee.'

The thrill came back to my stomach when she talked about her working days.

'What are you staring at, girl?' she said, eyeing me suspiciously.

'You.'

'Huh?'

'I'll have a Jack Daniel's, too, please.'

That got her. 'Excuse me, Miss Peachy, did I hear you right?'

'Sure did.' I was grinning.

I thought she was going to call me a 'geek' again but her eyes started to gleam and she said, 'What's gotten into you?'

'Let's just say that you're turning out to be a fascinating read.'

She pouted, but I knew she was pleased. 'That's me,' she said, 'a regular old pot-boiler.'

She definitely didn't mind me prying, though. I asked her to tell me some more New York stories and she plunged right in.

'It all started when a friend of mine in the East Village said he could set me up with some cabaret gigs. Of course, the work turned out to be mainly stripping but it felt OK. I was living in this apartment with three gay guys who had some great drag equipment. One of them lent me a leather body harness so I could be Jamie Lee Curtis as the cop in *Steel Blue*. The freaks loved that.'

'Freaks?'

'Not freaks like you,' she said, prodding my arm with her mini Jack Daniel's straw. 'Punters, you call them in England. Suffice it to say that there are three sexes in this world: men, women and punters.'

Our drinks arrived and she raised her fresh glass and chinked it against mine. 'After I'd been stripping for a while, the punters started asking to see me in the back room. I was pretty green to start with, but in the end it wasn't that different from when I was a kid in California. When I'd let the tourists take my photo for money – do little extras for money.'

She took a swig. 'Basically, what made me a good nanny also made me a good stripper. And being a stripper led to turning men.'

She banged the glass down on the table. 'It was fun,' she said. 'It was summer. My room mates were tricking too. "Your freak's arrived," they'd go.'

'Do you remember your first punter?' I tried not to sound too excited.

'Sure.'

'What did he look like?'

'I don't know,' she said, dismissively. 'He looked like a married man.'

'What did you feel like afterwards?'

'Relieved? One of my room mates took a picture of me after-wards. There's two hundred bucks splayed out in front of me, a big grin on my mouth and "Thank fuck!" in my eyes.'

She stared into her glass, stirring the liquid with the paddle of her little fingernail. (The glitter on it, I now noticed, was a tiny piece of diamanté serving as the eye of a Playboy bunny that had been painted on.) 'I soon got over that,' she said, picking up the glass. 'It's a bad space to be in. You have to think you're the bomb or you're toast.'

She downed the rest of her drink and said that she'd like to move over to the lounge area. She murmured that the pimp was starting to annoy her (he was shouting at one of his entourage, telling her that she couldn't have a Cheeseburger Royale – served with coleslaw and fries – she could only have a cheeseburger served with nothing). So we got up and installed ourselves in an empty Cadillac while I prattled on. 'What other kind of customers did you have?' I asked, shoving a piece of Big Red into my mouth.

'Mo,' she sighed, as though I'd disappointed her, 'you have to realise, it's no fun being a hooker. You're just a piece of meat who's being fucked.' A shadow passed over her face, which only lifted when the door of the Wing Fat was kicked open by a boy dressed like a cyber version of the Grim Reaper. She sat up in her seat. 'Turning a dom trick,' she said, under her breath. 'Now *that*'s another matter. It's like being a waitress. It's about reading a psyche.'

The longer she looked at the boy the brighter her face became. He looked like one of those new Marilyn Manson-type goths – you know, the ones who kill nuns and wear glow-in-the-dark jewellery. His eyebrows were pierced with rings, his wrists were bound with strips of tin dangling with metal links, and a network of springs was woven tightly into the hair that hung down his back. There was a loud jangle as he threw himself into the Cadillac seat opposite us.

'Morning, babe,' Billie greeted him. 'Looks like you had a good night.'

The boy looked up and was about to say something rude. When he caught Billie's eye, though, something strange happened: a blush seeped up from his neck into his face, like red ink through blotting paper, highlighting the peeling layer of talcum powder clotted all over his cheeks. He snatched at a joint stub stuffed behind his ear in an attempt to regain his composure. But it was too late. His hands were shaking and the joint tumbled into the lap of his baggy red sweatshirt, which read, 'Ready and Willing to Ignite'.

He was sweet. He couldn't have been older than eighteen.

The corners of Billie's mouth twitched and she excused herself to go to the restroom. While she was gone I couldn't help examining the boy more closely. In America, if you stare at people for too long without prefacing it with a 'How y'all doing?' then it's called 'rubbernecking'. It can be dangerous.

Suddenly he looked up and caught me. I chewed my Big Red gum furiously in the hope that this might put him off whatever it was he intended to do. But it was too late. There was a hiss of 'The Cult suck!' He spat a blob of purple bubble-gum on to the floor, which landed dangerously near my trainers. 'Brother-wolf sister-moon shit,' he sneered, with a curling lip. Instinctively, I folded my arms over the front of my vintage T-shirt. (A going-away present from Acid Sarah, as a matter of fact.) 'My uncle listens to that shit,' he sneered again.

'I see.' I glanced down at the purple blob. 'You must be a Marilyn Manson fan then.'

'Marilyn fucking Manson!' This seemed really the wrong thing to have said. He kicked the edge of my Cadillac seat, sending a current of vibrations running through me. 'Don't categorise me, lady! What's with that fucking accent of yours anyway?'

I didn't think he was so sweet then.

'The Cult! Pussy shit!' he growled, without waiting for an answer. He clicked a lighter and stuck the joint end into the ridiculously large rag of fire it emitted. He took a toke and said, 'So, like, are you one of those English goths?'

'There are a lot of goths in Scarborough,' I said, in a tight voice.

'Scarboro Fair!' he scoffed. 'Simon and Garfunkel pussy shit!'

I tried to chew my Big Red in a nonchalant fashion. Finally, I said, 'Those of us in the know call it Scabs, actually.'

He started choking – first on laughter and then on his joint smoke. He was creased up with laughter and smoke, holding his stomach as if something was hilarious. He could hardly contain himself. '"Scabs, Guns and Peanut Butter"!' he was spluttering, as if I'd just said the most rib-tickling thing in the world. '"Scabs, Guns and Peanut Butter"! "Scabs, Guns and Peanut Butter"!'

I was just about get up and slope off back to the SUV when I felt a warmth next to me and it was Billie. It was as if the world was a black-and-white film and then she brought Technicolor. It felt as if, at any minute, she was going to command all the red Cadillac seats to uproot themselves from the floor and the annoying juke-box to unplug itself from the wall and then she was going to choreograph them all in a big, bouncy, slightly kinky cheer-leader routine and they would do all of this because it was Ruby Rose who commanded it. And that was the point: this wasn't Billie Harrison in the Wing Fat rock 'n' roll lounge: it was the one and only Ruby Rose.

The Marilyn Manson fan froze as she ensconced herself in the Cadillac seat next to him, two enormous glasses of Jack Daniel's and Coke in her hands. '"Scabs, Guns and Peanut Butter",' she exclaimed, squeezing him into a corner. 'I love that song! And what about "Angel With The Scabbed Wings"?'

Through the corner of his eyes he glanced at the colossus next to him. 'Yeah . . . *Antichrist Superstar* album, right?'

Billie passed me one of the Jack Daniel's glasses. '*Antichrist Superstar*! I *love* Marilyn Manson!'

'Yeah.' The boy sniggered, cautiously. 'What do you think of "Cake and Sodomy"? And "The Dope Show"?'

'Oh, I *love* "The Dope Show",' she said, slugging back some liquid. 'Bet I know a drug you never tried, though.'

You could tell the Manson fan was still nervous. He snapped his legs together.

'You eaten pig guts?' she asked him.

'What do you mean?' He tried to sound confident, but ruined it by choking on his smoke.

'Pig guts,' she said. 'Releases serotonin. That's the stuff that—'

'I know what serotonin is,' he growled. 'It's the high you get when you're running or—'

'Or when you've been beaten with a strap.'

The boy made a nervous laugh. 'Pig-gut high?' He puffed hard on his joint and, in an attempt to keep his end up, signalled to the young Asian bartender. 'Yo, Sammy!' he went, waving the joint. 'Got a present for ya. Bunch of new green came in today.' He patted a lump in his back pocket.

'Right on, Spider!' the barman replied, with a wink.

Billie's – or, rather, Ruby Rose's – eyes grew slightly larger.

'Spider, huh?' she said. 'And what is that weird outfit you're wearing, Spider?'

I was expecting him to blow up. But he didn't. He stuttered, 'I don't know . . . cyber, goth, fetish . . .?' He knew instinctively that the last word was a dangerous one.

She didn't say anything for a while and then she said, 'Fetish?'

The final hiss of the word hung in the air of the Wing Fat, mixing with breath of bourbon and pot smoke, whiffs of fried egg and toast and snatches of 'Tie A Yellow Ribbon Round The Old Oak Tree'. At last, she broke the tension.

'You're a little pussy.'

'What . . . what do you mean?'

'D-rings don't spell butch to me.'

'What?' He looked over to me. As if I was going to help him. She wrapped her hands round his wrists then. He was mesmerised. 'These are D-rings,' she teased, pulling at the metal holes. 'You don't have these on unless you want to be tied up.'

Somehow, the boy managed to pull his wrists away. You could see he didn't want to, though. He tried to snap out of it. He waved his skinny joint stub in her face, saying, 'Bet you'd like this kind of drug, huh?'

She wrinkled her nose. 'Oh, babe, you're sweet but that's looking a bit soggy to me.'

His face fell. He reached deep into his jeans pocket and pulled out a bag with 'Dewey's Donuts' written on the front in crumpled blue letters. 'Roll one of your own if you want,' he said eagerly, passing the bag over. Then a look of dismay shot into his puppy eyes. 'Shit! I don't have any papers left.'

'Don't you worry about that,' Billie soothed. She reached into her gold bag and pulled out a twenty-dollar bill, the floral notebook and a Bible. I recognised this Bible as the tan-covered Gideon Bible from our room in the Econo Lodge that morning. The Gideon Bible is a sort of idiots' Bible left in every motel room in America. In the front there are suggestions for pages to turn to in a variety of situations: if you're an alcoholic; if you feel like committing adultery; if you feel like killing yourself. In this particular hour of need, she placed the twenty-dollar bill on top of the floral notebook and filled it with a hefty amount of the grass from the Dewey's Donuts bag. At this point, she usually transferred the rolled-grass cylinder into a Rizla paper (although she uses an American brand called Zig Zag.) This time, though, she picked up the Bible.

'Now, let's see,' she said. 'Something on temptation, I think.' She opened the book and flicked through the pages. 'Here we are. One Corinthians.'

She ripped out a page, tore a perfect rolling paper shape and put the grass on it. She rolled up the page, licked it, lit it and passed it to the Manson fan.

'"But I discipline my body," he chuckled, reading the side of the joint, "and bring it into submission . . ."' He put the joint into his mouth and took a drag from it. 'Phat!' he said, looking at Billie, admiration pasted all over his stoned face.

'Gideon Bible,' Billie said, chucking the Dewey's Donuts bag down on the seat. 'Pages thin as Zig Zags.'

'That's cool.' Spider smiled. He told her he'd have to tell his friend Tank about the Bible trick. 'Me and Tank, we do this thing – we send each other the grossest stuff we can think of, like bloody tampons and scuzzy condoms. Plates with food all mouldy on. We put 'em in each other's mailboxes. Like, with tags on, saying, "I am the God of Fuck," and stuff!'

'Eeee-yew!' She wriggled fetchingly, offering him her Jack Daniel's glass. And then, as he slammed back her drink, she noticed something on his finger. 'Nice ring,' she said, taking hold of his hand and admiring the piece of silver jewellery.

'I bought it myself,' he said, breathless from swallowing. 'First weekend job at college.' He grinned. 'My Significant Ring, I call it.'

Billie smiled. 'You a college boy, then, Spider?'

He looked uneasy. He watched her explore his hand.

'I used to have a fantasy,' she said.

'Yeah?'

'I'd have a house on a hill by a high school and I'd break in virgins.'

He bristled. 'I'm not a virgin! I've done a lot of shit!'

With a single look, Billie silenced him. She said, 'You want to play a game with me, Spider?'

It was either the effects of the Jack Daniel's and root-beer slammer or the feel of Billie's flesh on his fingers, but something odd seemed to be happening to Spider. Life seemed to be both leaving and pouring into him simultaneously. He was either wilting or blossoming. Whatever it was, the fact that he hadn't removed his hand from Billie's suggested that he did want to play whatever it was she had in mind.

She leaned over and whispered in his ear.

His mouth dropped open.

She whispered some more.

His eyes bulged.

By the time she pulled away from him, Spider's groin was starting to inflate.

'W-wow,' he stammered. 'That's illegal in a lot of states, you know . . .'

'Doesn't that just turn you on, Spider?'

He made a dirty laugh.

'You want to play the game then, babe?'

'Sure.' He nodded enthusiastically. 'I got a good imagination.'

'Oh, I know you do, Spider.'

'But, like, isn't it bad for your insides?'

'It certainly is if you don't take that big ring off of your pinkie.'

'Oh.'

'Now, close your eyes and enjoy the ride.'

Spider did as he was told. He closed his eyes, removed his ring and listened to Billie's purr like a parched man listening to a waterfall.

'Mmmmm, Spider,' she said, in a voice dripping with sex, her hand engulfing his. 'Oh, yeah, that's right . . . ooooh, yeah, clench it good . . .'

She'd squeezed Spider's hand into a softly clenched fist. She was stroking it, going, 'Now, doesn't that feel good, Spider?'

Spider's eyelids were flickering, his metal headdress was starting to jangle. Quicker and quicker he breathed.

'Oh, give it to me, Spider . . .' she begged, slowly moving the fist back and forth through the dirty fug of the Wing Fat lounge. 'Can you feel me, baby?'

'Yeaaaaah . . .'

'Soft and silky, huh?'

'Yeaaaaah . . .'

'You feel me inside? Soft as a fur-lined glove . . .'

Back and forth, slowly and rhymically, so slowly and so rhythmically . . .

'F-fur,' Spider moaned. 'Soft as a . . . fur . . .' His tongue was clumsy, words clotted in his throat. He groaned some more, surrendering his pallid fist to Billie's firm grasp. 'Soff and war . . .' he moaned, his head flailing from side to side. His groin moved. His groin swelled some more.

'"The two kidneys and the fat that is on them by the flanks and the fatty lobe attached to the liver above the kidneys, he shall remove."'

'Huh . . .'

'"The fat that covers the entrails and all the fat that is on the entrails, the two kidneys and the fat that is on them by the flanks and the fatty lobes attached to the liver above the kidneys, he shall remove."'

Spider's eyes twitched behind their closed lids. 'Ma'am . . . can you not, like, say stuff . . .'

'Leviticus, Spider!' Billie commanded in stern tones, speeding up the back-and-forth motion. 'And the priest shall burn them on the altar as food, an offering made by fire to the Lord!'

'Wha' . . .'

'"The priest shall bring it all and burn it on the altar, it is a burnt sacrifice, an offering made by fire, a sweet aroma to the Lord"!'

'Oh, my God, ma'am . . .' A dull metal thud of springs clanging against a fake leather seat.

'Blasphemy, Spider! "He shall take from it all the fat of the bull as the sin offering. The fat that covers the entrails," Spider, "and all the fat which is on the entrails." Leviticus, chapter four, verse eight.'

'Whoa, man, this is scary . . . I'm sorry, ma'am, but I don't know if I can—'

'Come on, Spider, feel that chopped-liver handshake!' There was glee in her eyes.

'But—'

'Twist at the same time, Spider, twist and punch.'

'What?'

'Punch and twist!'

'This is gross—'

'But you love gross!'

A roar of Billie butter laughter.

I was clutching the Bible. I was flicking through it. It was all correct. All the quotes. She knew it off by heart. Spider screwed his eyes tighter shut to try to squeeze out whatever horrible images had settled behind them. 'Ma'am,' he pleaded, as Billie punched his fist back and forth inside her, 'this is like . . . freaking me out?' But he couldn't move. He couldn't tear his hand from hers: she had him now. He wanted to run and he didn't want to run and in the meantime he moaned and she roared, she roared and he moaned.

'Waaaa!'

'Better than a scuzzy condom, huh!'

'Ma'am!'

'"The hide of the bull and all its flesh, as well as the head and legs, the inner parts and offal . . ." Chapter four, Leviticus, Spider. Verse eleven!'

And then I couldn't flick through the Bible any more. A fat lot of use the Bible was as I sat there taking in the fantasy fisting scene before me. I thought I felt sick. I thought I wanted to laugh. I thought I wanted to burst with excitement. And then, suddenly, his eyes jacked open. 'Oh, my God,' he was blubbering, 'like, total sea monster . . . sucking me up . . . slippery . . . abortion . . . like, killer liver . . . oh, my God, I can't . . .'

'What's up?' Billie panted. 'Dick getting jealous?'

'Waa . . .'

'Come on, babe. Put that in too!'

'Waaaaaaaaaaaa!'

'Your fist turning pussy on my pussy, Spider?'

It was then that he managed to wrench away his fist, to tear himself away from the car seat.

'Sorry, ma'am,' he muttered, caught up in a jangle of metal. 'I have to go meet someone!'

He made a dash towards the door pursued by shouts of 'Hey, man, what about my green?' (from the bartender) and 'Hey, Spider! Don't let your pinkie get cold!' (from Billie).

She stood up to lob the Significant Ring to him. He turned round too late and it landed on a chrome corner of the pool table with a delicate chime. He stopped and looked at the ring as if he'd never seen it before. Then he glanced at Billie, freezing for a few seconds, before picking it up and speed-walking to the door. Billie blew him a graceful kiss as he tugged at the handle. Then, when he was gone, she flopped back into the Cadillac with a sigh of deep satisfaction. 'If I was a highway robber,' she smiled, patting a bag marked 'Dewey's Donuts' she'd unearthed from down the side of the chair, 'I'd kiss a lady's hand and not steal her wedding ring. That's just mean.'

CHAPTER EIGHT

Food of the Gods

So, I take it all back – what I said about there being nothing left Billie could do to surprise me. After the Wing Fat, it becomes clear that crashing into cars and tying cherry stalks into knots with her tongue is just the tip of the iceberg. I can't help but wonder how much more of the iceberg lies under the water and what shape her 'trick' might take next time.

Maybe I'm just being a killjoy, though. It's not that I don't love being with her or find her company unstimulating – I mean, how nutty is she? I think that I'm feeling rather over-sensitive, thanks to the enormous Jack Daniel's hangover I woke up with this morning. Not that she has one. She woke up in a rollicking good mood, announcing that she wanted to go to K-Mart for something called 'ambrosia' – pronounced 'ambroja'.

It seems a practical idea, in any case. Since New Orleans we've been eating solid junk food: Arby's, Hardee's, Wendy's, Denny's, Long John Silver's, Chuckee Cheese's, Jack in the Box's, Waffle House, Taco Bell, In-Out Burger, McDonald's – not to mention all the breakfast joints we've been to for my story. The novelty of crap has worn off. I need some healthy food – a bit of order in my life.

So it's with a hopeful heart that I pull off the 10 just after San Antonio, Texas, resolving to buy a week's worth of good food and not let myself get distracted by Billie's munchies obsession this time. We enter an enormous supermarket that feels like a cash-and-carry crossed with an immense, ghostly marsh filled with formless miasma and chill spectres. I follow Billie to the 'salad bar' – although there are no signs of salad, as such, just bowls filled with strange, sugary mixes like Miracle Whip and tinned green beans, tuna, macaroni, tinned peas and more Miracle Whip, and something that Billie orders containing tinned tangerine segments, mini marshmallows, desiccated coconut and Cool Whip dressing, which goes by the name of 'ambrosia'.

As she looks into the contents of the tub her eyes well up, and when we walk away from the salad bar she starts pulling mini marshmallows from the tub as if they're tissues to dry her eyes. She explains, 'The day I found out I didn't make it in the cheer-leader try-outs my mother made me a huge bowl of this stuff.'

She sucks a tangerine segment. 'I couldn't try out again,' she says. 'Mom said she couldn't afford it.'

She doesn't expand on this because suddenly there's the sound of a police siren, followed by a dramatic voice over the Tannoy saying, 'Attention, K-Mart shoppers! Attention, K-Mart shoppers! Blue Light Special!' and the chill miasma of the supermarket turns into a rowdy Wild West saloon where an exciting crime has just taken place. A stampede of barnacle-faced *Rosemary's Baby* little old ladies rushes towards a distant flashing blue light.

'You'll like this!' Billie says, snapping back into good humour and pulling me with her into the scrum. 'Blue's a good colour in America. It means that something cheap is about to happen!'

If American supermarkets function as bars for women who never normally get a chance to talk to anyone, then the Blue Light Special is like a fantastic drinking game that puts bingo and Tupperware parties in the shade. Billie and I are pulled along towards the dazzling blue beacon – whizzing and twirling and casting brilliance on to the victim of the hour (today's item: wieners) like rats to the Pied Piper, borne up on a cloud of cama-raderie and creaky whispers of 'I hear it's over near pet food!' and 'I hope stuff's left when we get there!' And then we arrive, and everyone's spirits drop momentarily because the journey is over and we've come to the end of the blue rainbow. Women stare at the hot-dog sausages, cordoned off into the Blue Light area like a dead body with a chalk template squiggled round it. 'Wieners!' a sign says. 'Twelve for a dollar!'

I'm pretty impressed by the gold at the end of the rainbow. These are proper frankfurter sausages – nothing like the rubbishy hot dogs you buy at Scarborough Fair. I make a suggestion.

'If we bought a couple of packs we'd have twenty-four wieners for two dollars. We could live for a week on about five dollars if we bought some bread rolls and some lettuce as well.'

Billie seems uninterested but I go on anyway: 'We could eat wieners for lunch and dinner. We could have four for each meal so we wouldn't be hungry. We could fry them one day on the calor-gas stove then boil them in water the next for hot dogs.'

I add that we should buy a bag of potatoes, too, because then we can have boiled potatoes one day, potato salad another and maybe I can even try out *pommes de terre dauphinoises* at some point. (I tell her that I didn't live with a chef all those years for nothing.)

But Billie just wrinkles her nose.

'Billie!' I say, exasperated. 'You want everything, all of the time, right now!'

'So?'

'I think it's good to wait for things. Food rationing, for instance. I think it's good for you.'

'You do, huh?' She yawns and tells me that I'd love the other American blue thing then: the Blue Plate Special, which is a discounted dish of the day in a diner – similar to the Early Bird Special, only you can order it at any time.

'My mother used to pick me and my brother Ned up from the babysitter's and take us to a diner called Sambo's where we'd split the child's Blue Plate Special.'

There's the familiar doom in her tone when she says the words 'my mother'. I'm wondering why this is – especially since what I read in her notebook the other day doesn't exactly paint her mother as a dragon – when we see a bouncy party of perky white girls approaching us at the helm of a huge shopping trolley.

'Oh-my-God,' Billie gasps. 'Talk about cheer-leaders!'

As the girls park their trolley in front of the wiener Blue Light display, Billie glances into it. Then she takes me aside and reads the situation for me. She explains that these are a bunch of college girls who are shopping for a scarf-and-barf party. In the olden days, she says, girls had slumber parties where they'd hide other girls' bras in the freezer overnight and put girls' hands in bowls of warm water while they were asleep so they'd wet the bed. But gradually these changed into evenings of compulsive scoffing or 'scarfing' followed by 'barfing' or chucking up. K-Mart is a good place for bulimics, apparently, because lots of things come in economy bulk size.

In the girls' trolley there are: six economy packs of Oreo cookies, six of Ding Dongs and six of Twinkies (cheap and plentiful), six boxes of Cheeze-Its (wheat is easier to throw up than potato chips), Granola bars and apples (so you can kid yourself you're being healthy), a dozen frozen pizzas (easy to eat), Nilla wafers (vanilla biscuits that can be mushed up with milk into a sweet pap), twelve cans of bean dip and twelve packets of Fritos (scoop-shaped for ease of use).

Billie says that wieners are good because they're small (bulimics hate to be faced with a full plate) and easy to shove down your throat. The downside is that sometimes chunks of them come out of your nose when you barf, although 'That's nothing compared to what happens when you throw up rice.'

The girls seem pleased with the wiener Blue Light Special. 'So, like, how many should we get?' a girl with Hannibal Lector teeth braces asks. 'Couple of packs each?'

'No, man, like, three packs maybe,' a girl with a black ponytail replies, with a smirk. 'I didn't eat, like, anything yesterday?'

(They all talk in that American teen-speak that sounds as if there's a question mark at the end of everything they say. The lilting intonation makes them appear more democratic – more prepared to listen to others – whereas, in fact, it's just as bullying in intent as the old-fashioned way of speaking.)

'What about getting some root beer and ice-cream?' a girl in a pink jumper suggests timidly.

'What?' the braces girl snaps.

'Well . . . I thought we could maybe make some root-beer floats?'

'Root-beer floats!' The braces girl is incredulous. 'Are you kidding, Maria!' She turns to the others. 'Hey, you guys, Maria wants us to do root-beer floats?'

Six voices chorus, 'Root-beer floats?' in disdain, and six pairs of eyes burn into poor Maria, who looks panic-stricken at the trolley filled with Oreo cookies, corn chips, Twinkies, frozen pizzas and bean dip, wondering what on earth could be the difference between all that and root beer.

The braces girl puts Maria out of her misery. 'Maria!' she barks. 'Liquid is, like, totally absorbed faster than food?'

'Y-yeah?'

'Yeah, so ice-cream and sugar sodas are out. Do you want to digest some calories or something?'

Maria goes pale but then the girl with the black ponytail says, 'Hey, Julie, get off Maria's case. She's new here. And you know what?'

'What?'

'She, like, totally reminded us that we forgot diet soda?'

'Yeah!' another voice trills. 'We didn't get any Diet Coke yet!'

'Diet Coke!' the girls sing in unison. 'Diet Coke!'

'What about chocolate martinis?' Maria does seem a bit of a glutton for punishment.

'What do you mean?' The braces girl looks suspicious.

'Well . . . like, I know it's chocolate, but that's not all. It's chocolate liqueur with vodka and orange vodka. And a pansy?'

'What?'

'You know, like, a flower? It's a Mexican thing?'

The other girls look at each other. Then the black ponytail says, 'Puking up flowers?' She says it again: 'Puking up flowers?' And then, in a eureka! sort of voice she announces, 'Angel barf!'

The college girls love the idea of angel barf. They're all about to set off to the liquor aisle to buy their vodka when they're stopped in their tracks by a voice saying, 'What about devil barf?'

They all turn round and look at Billie with thinly disguised horror. Even if Billie seems to have been a practising bulimic in the past, her size suggests that she isn't one now.

'Devil's got the best tunes and the best barf,' she continues, unfazed.

'The best barf?' the braces girl sneers.

'Yeah, what do you think the devil would throw up?'

Some of the girls start to smirk. 'I don't know, man,' one mumbles. 'Fire and brimstone, I guess.'

'The Hope Diamond?' Maria suggests.

'A bunch of cocaine and a couple of dozen tabs of X!'

They're getting into the swing of it now. They think Billie's quite funny. Billie starts suggesting other things the devil might throw up – empty toothpaste tubes, dentures, horse-chestnut thistles, popcorn and orange juice.

'Popcorn and orange juice?' Maria enquires.

'Hardly any calories in popcorn or orange juice.'

'So?'

'So you can't throw it up if you eat too much.'

'Really?' Wide eyes.

'Sure. Four buckets I scarfed one time. Orange juice swells it up in your stomach.'

'Really?'

'Sure. Feels like you're going to split open.'

'Gross!'

'And then, if you do manage to get any of it up, it scratches on the way out.'

'Ouch!'

'It was the first time I ever got my stomach pumped.'

'Oh, my God!'

The girls are all crowded round Billie now.

'Typical of the devil, right?' she says. 'Barf that you can't barf up.'

There is a mass wrinkling of cute noses. They love Billie now. The black ponytail girl points to a red breakfast-cereal box on a nearby shelf. On the front is a bowl of multi-coloured puffed wheat. 'This'd be cool devil barf,' she says. 'Red and yellow and orange and purple . . .'

'Yeah,' braces girl says. 'Like throwing up Disneyland?'

'Yeah,' Maria says, 'and afterwards you'd have gross purple-haze death breath?'

The girls laugh, but Billie frowns. She looks almost pale. 'You gotta be careful with purple,' she warns, grabbing the trolley and moving off. 'And steer clear of purple frosting.'

The girls look puzzled. I'm puzzled. Billie pushes the trolley off before we get a chance to say goodbye. When we get to the fruit and vegetables section, I force a laugh and ask her what she meant by the purple frosting. She's evasive. 'Long story,' she mumbles, as she examines a pile of pomegranates. 'Forget it.'

But I don't want to forget it. I can see that something's still troubling her so I go for another tack. 'Why do you like the devil so much?'

Her hands freeze on the fruit. 'What?' She looks as though she might start crying.

'Oh,' I backtrack. I hope she's not going to throw a big scene in the supermarket. I wouldn't know what to do about that. 'Oh, I didn't want to upset you. I just meant that . . . well, you bring the devil up a bit. You know, your babysitter trying to get the devil out of you with Tabasco and . . . and all that Bible stuff you were telling the Marilyn Manson fan . . .'

She won't meet my eye.

'. . . and the first time I met you, you went a bit weird when I said you reminded me of the devil.'

'I did?' She goes back to the pomegranates.

'Yes, your eyes went sort of funny.'

She turns to me then, a smile on her face. 'They went funny, huh?'

'Don't you remember? When we met – what, four days ago?'

'To tell you the truth,' she says, opting for two perfect, waxy pomegranates, 'this drive's making me remember a whole bunch of stuff. Nothing recent, though.' She pats the joint tucked into the cleavage of her tight white shirt. 'Short-term memory's kind of shot, if you know what I mean.'

She cheers up more when we get into the car park. She takes one of the pomegranates from the bag and throws it up and down in the air.

'One thing I do remember from back in New Orleans – I told you that our journey would smell of hot pomegranates, right?'

I tell her about Duncan's bad pomegranate paintings in Scarborough, and she smiles. She says that painted fruit should never be clean. 'If I was going to paint fruit,' she says, 'I'd pour water over it. Or I'd wait till it rotted.'

She throws the fruit even higher into the sky as we walk towards the SUV.

'Pomegranates should never be cut evenly,' she declares. 'They should always be torn open.'

As she watches me load the shopping into the back of the car (two packs of wieners, one pack of hot-dog buns, two pounds of potatoes, one tub of mayonnaise, one bunch of mint, one lettuce, some random fresh fruit, two packs of ice, a guidebook to America and a big pack of washing-line – Billie's choice – total cost $23.56) she carries on throwing and catching. 'If you were a miniature person walking in a bunch of pomegranate seeds it'd be like . . .'

'Walking in the mountains,' I suggest. 'Walking in red glaciers!'

'Walking through glassy red clits,' she corrects, and lobs the red fruit up in front of a gigantic poster that says, 'Vasectomy Reversal – Come To Texas And Get Your Balls Back.'

There's a smack and it's clasped back in her hands. She sinks her teeth into the waxy rind, setting a stream of red juice running down her chin. 'Eating a pomegranate is like eating a cock,' she says, wiping her mouth with the back of her hand. 'You can't do it in any seemly way.'

I nod.

'Actually, maybe sucking cock is proof that women are supposed to be submissive to men. You can lick a cunt and it can look quite artistic but with a big cock shoved down your throat . . . I mean, hello?'

'Billie!' She makes me laugh.

She looks embarrassed. 'I'm sorry. God, I come out with the grossest stuff!'

I shake my head. 'I love your gross things.'

She still looks bashful. 'Great story, though, huh?' she says. 'The Greek myth about pomegranates? About the dangers of succumbing to temptations of the flesh?'

There's something about the way she says 'flesh' that makes me turn into a geek again. 'I – I studied Greek mythology at night school. But, yes, I – I can't remember exactly . . .'

'My stepdad loved that story.'

'Remind me how it goes again?'

'Persephone and the pomegranate.'

Somehow she manages to rip the fruit in half with her thumbs. 'Persephone the virgin, snatched up from a spring meadow by the god of the underworld.'

'Sort of a devil figure, wasn't he?'

'Now who's obsessed with the devil?'

All of a sudden, there are sticky fingers on my palm and then a tiny mound of red seeds. Billie smiles at me and I automatically put the seeds into my mouth. Crunching on them feels cool and sweet on this hot, sweaty day in Texas.

'The god of the upper world was going to make the devil release Persephone,' Billie goes on. 'But then the devil tempted her into eating some pomegranate flesh and she got trapped in hell.'

My jaws stop their crunching. I make a stupid laugh. 'I see. I wonder where that leaves me.'

She doesn't answer. She just licks the honeycomb of her pomegranate half, like a kid licking a lollipop. And then she says, 'Personally, I think Persephone liked it down there.'

'Sorry?'

'Down there in hell. I think she liked it. She only had to stay in the underworld for six months anyway.'

'Oh, yes, that's why we have winter, isn't it?'

'So they say, Peachy Peach.' With her nails, she digs out a cluster of ragged seeds. 'They say the earth goes into mourning for her every year when she has to go underground, which is how come we get winter. But I don't think she was doing so much mourning herself.'

'No?'

'No. I think she knew exactly what she was doing when she ate those pomegranate seeds.' She licks her wrist.

'Really?' My voice sounds shaky. I look at my red-stained palm before hurriedly wiping it down the side of my jeans.

'Sure,' she goes on. 'Some flower-gathering virgin let loose in the underworld? I mean, hello? How much fun did she have!'

'Let loose in the underworld . . .' My eyes meet hers.

'Let loose in the underworld.' She holds me in the blackness of her eyes for what seems like an age, and I'm only released when a small smile snakes on to the juicy red lips and suddenly I want to hurt her. I want to rip open a sticky red pomegranate and rub it all over her skin, scratch her with its rough rind then drip hot drops of juice on parts I choose to ease her and irritate her, and she might squirm and beg forgiveness and say, 'Oh, no! Oh, please!' like they do in the porn mags in the changing room at the Sceptre. But instead of grabbing hold of her I find myself laughing. I put both my hands into the pockets of my jeans and I look at my feet and laugh and I don't even know what I'm laughing at. Her laugh comes, too. A hot, sugary laugh, which turns into the chuckle of a kid: all sherbet and ice lolly – watermelon, cherry, banana.

We're being too conspicuous. A man in a camouflage outfit drinking from a brown-paper bag approaches us from a shiny red pick-up truck parked a few metres behind us. He's in his early forties with a shiny shaved head and no lips. His pale face looks like a pig's thigh. 'How y'all doing?' he says, staring at Billie's cleavage with eyes that look both psycho and shy. Another man in a military outfit comes to join him. This one has a face like a pig's trotter. He breaks into a smile.

'Howdy there,' he says, his trotter skin turning rosy as an apple. 'The name's Raymond.'

The pig thigh tells us that he and Raymond are brothers. He himself is called René.

'Are you soldiers, then?' I ask vaguely, still digesting Billie's apparent invitation to take me to hell.

'Soldiers! Hell, no.' Raymond beams. 'We're hunters.'

'What do you want to catch?'

'Mercy!' Raymond exclaims.

'We don't catch,' René snarls. 'We kill.'

'What do you kill?'

Raymond grins. 'Elk,' he says mischievously. 'We're goin' to New Mexico in that there Dodge. Going to kill us some elk and make us some jerky!'

'Elk jerky! Yum!' Billie likes the sound of that.

I ask Raymond how they kill the animals and he says that some people kill them with special laser-directed tracking devices and some use bows and arrows but that he and René don't use either. 'We use muskets!' He smiles proudly. 'You push the gunpowder down like in the olden days, and then . . . boom!' He does an impression of a musket barrel exploding.

'Ouch!' Billie says, as if she's just stubbed her toe.

'We got one of them global positioning systems too,' René says hurriedly. 'Got a real good deal from eBay. It's worth five hundred bucks.'

'And what's a global positioning system, hon?' she asks.

René seems shocked by her question.

'GPS, we call 'em in the trade,' he says. 'It tells you where you are in the world.'

'You know where you are in the world, René?' Billie asks him.

'Sure!' he says. 'Right now we're about twenty-eight degrees north and ninety-eight degrees west.'

'Cool. And where's twenty-eight degrees north and ninety-eight degrees west?'

René looks confused. 'Like I say,' he replies. 'It's . . . at twenty-eight degrees north and ninety-eight degrees west.'

Billie doesn't look very impressed so he invites us over to sit in his Dodge, saying he has beer in a cooler in the back. Billie picks up her Roach Motel and then the two of us walk over to the truck. René hands us both a beer in brown-paper bags without taking his line of vision from an area that hesitates between Billie's cleavage and the joint she's removed from the Roach Motel.

'Where you two ladies headed?' he asks, chewing gum as if it's nasty but pleasurable thoughts.

'California,' Billie says.

'There's some sick people out there, ma'am.' He takes a big slurp at his beer, his eyes still flickering between Billie's breasts and what she's holding in her hand.

'You can say that again, René.'

'We'll escort you if you need. We can take you as far as New Mexico.'

'That's where we're headed,' Raymond chips in. He fishes around in his back pocket and pulls out a grisly-looking ear-plug all black and covered in fluff. He brushes off the top of the plug and puts it into his cheek.

'Chewing tobacco.' Raymond smiles bashfully at me. 'Should have given the stuff up by now, hey, bro?'

René is scowling.

'We was on the unbeatable baseball team, right, bro?' Raymond carries on, beaming. ''Cept we tried some chewing tobacco on the last game of the season and we lost cuz everyone was puking!'

I watch him wiggle his cheeks around, then spit a Cherry Coke-coloured pellet of spit on to the Tarmac. He takes a circular plastic box from his other back pocket and offers some to me. 'Wanna try some?'

But I don't get a chance to try any because René snatches the case from Raymond who flinches and goes back to drinking his beer sheepishly. René continues to burn holes in the joint that Billie is now smoking. Finally he growls, under his breath, 'You in the market for some hoochy-coochy?'

Billie says nothing. She carries on puffing. He thinks she hasn't heard him. So he rephrases the question. 'Cash,' he says. There's a leer on his face.

I watch Billie's face. René watches Billie's face. Billie carries on puffing at her joint. She smokes just long enough for René to start shifting nervously on his feet. Finally she looks up. She gives René what I imagine must be her nanny stare. 'Used to carry a lot of cash, René,' she says, slowly. 'Big wads of cash in my purse. They loved it on Rodeo Drive. I'd go in for a Versace suit and they'd be, like, "Are you famous or something?" In Japan they were all bowing down to me and giving it all the *"watta . . . wanga . . . shimasho . . . sheiseido"* Japanese shit.'

René starts to look worried.

'In London they hold every note up to the light to make sure it's real. Handling real money freaks them out. I know the score, though. Once, my Bond Street bill came to two thousand dollars. I made sure the assistant gave me the five-hundred-dollar discount for cash. Bought him a belt for two hundred with the change. That made him smile. Love to make people smile.'

René looks like he's about to break out in spots. She leans against the side of the Dodge. 'Didn't need the cash anyway,' she says. 'Already had five hundred dollars in my handbag, paper-clipped into a brochure entitled *Excursions in North Devon*. It arrived there following a telephone conversation from a London drugs counsellor named Victoria. Real preppy. Preppy English are the worst. Think they can get you to do anything just cos of their accent. Usually they can. "I know that Tuesday is your day off," she goes, "but it would be spect-aaaac-ularly good if you could meet me in that little lane. Um . . . I'll take ten T-shirts this time . . . er . . . yup. Anyway, I know it's your day off but thanks again ever so much. Lots of love."

'Couldn't say no, though. Call them what you want: T-shirts, envelopes, Evil White Lady, it's still a hundred dollars a packet. That's fifty dollars wholesale. Five hundred dollars' profit for half an hour's work.'

She turns to Raymond. 'Do you like marijuana?' she asks him.

'Marijuana!' Raymond goes, like a kid. 'Yeah!'

'You want a hit?' She waves the smoking joint in front of his eyes

'Yeah!' he says again, as if Billie is offering him a fantastic chocolate bar.

He takes a drag. In his weak blue eyes, clouds begin to bluster past in a huge wind, sending tablecloths flying, washing blowing off lines and unruly canisters, Cheet-O packs and Hershey Bar wrappers scattering across a desolate landscape. 'Shoot! That's strong,' he says, a silly grin soaking into his face. 'Spliffie, right? That's what you guys say in England?'

'You have spliffie when you go hunting?' Billie asks him.

'Yeah! When we shoot the elk we have beer and marijuana afterwards, and then we start over. Boom!' Another spastic explosion of hands and arms.

'How many did you kill so far?' Billie asks.

'Got one in the shoulder a couple of years back,' he says, as René snatches the joint from him.

Billie lets René inhale deeply before she says, 'Consider yourself lucky, René. I can't help being generous.'

She begins to smooth down her top. 'See, the thing about my line of work is that it's all about tainted money. I liken the experience to finding stray money in the street. What do you do with free money that you stumble upon? You go to a bar and you get rid of it as quick as you can. Why? Because it feels like play money. Like unreal money. Free money. Easy come, easy go. Number one: you have to spend it all. Number two: you have to spend it on other people. It's the same thing with my kind of money. One morning when I left my house, there was over forty thousand dollars on my bed in different currencies: sterling, dollars, pesetas, you name it. Maybe there was twenty thousand, maybe ten thousand, who knows? Only thing I'm sure of is my grass bill. One hundred seventy-five dollars a week. Wholesale price, obviously.'

René is just staring dumbly at Billie's breasts with huge, dilated pupils.

Billie turns to me and says, 'You know what, hon, just now I got this overwhelming sensory memory of cold varnish on my face, your hand under my skirt and the smell of burning hot dogs.'

My face catches light. I don't believe it! She's gone too far this time! What on earth is she talking about? René and Raymond want to know more too. 'Your line of work . . .' René stammers. 'You mean . . . you mean you do porn and shit?'

Billie takes the joint back from René's limp fingers. He reddens when he realises he's lost his smoke. 'Women jerk off now, don't they?' His lips turn mean. 'It's all thanks to Madonna, I know it is. Bet you'd do stuff, for money.'

I expect Billie to step up to René and give him a great big wallop across the face. But she doesn't. The Dodge door is open and she goes to sit side-saddle on the driver's seat. She lowers herself slowly on to the beige leather and crosses her legs, languidly. René starts jigging. He's waiting. It seems he can't wait much longer. She makes him wait longer.

Dusk is seeping into the remains of the day, turning the sky into a psychedelic tabby cat. Billie closes her eyes and takes a slow, deep breath, bathing her face in the the last rays of the sun. Everything feels incredibly slow and sleepy: flies buzz in the air, horns wheeze softly, passing shoppers make asinine comments to each other on the way back to their cars:

'They say it strengthens your transversals and your dorsals . . .'

'Everybody in the office hates him, I'm no exception . . .'

'Didn't like the look of that gourmet Monterrey Jack . . .'

Two Texan pig parts in combat outfits, an English girl wearing an overly hot lumberjack shirt, an ex-nanny hustler with quite moderate-sized breasts stuck in a K-Mart car park in the middle of Texas.

And still we all wait for Billie to speak. It feels as if she's never going to speak again. René looks panicky. She gives him the look again: the nanny look. 'No shit, René,' she says at last. 'I like to jerk off.' She smooths down her top again. 'But you know, hon, I always find that you have to get the specifics right. Jerking off's not so cut and dried. You think, Should I suck her pussy and then maybe turn her over and stick my tongue up her asshole and whir my tongue around?'

Billie said 'she'. It definitely was a 'her'. The words sound even more shocking in the wilderness of the K-Mart car park. René and I glance at each other momentarily. His eyes look like they might bulge out of his head. The brown bag in his hand starts to rustle. He stutters, 'You like women, then? You one of those—'

But Billie cuts him off. 'You know, René,' she says, 'I'm not going to tell you lesbian stuff for free. You want information, it's going to cost you.' She stubs the joint out with the Cuban heel of her cowboy boot. 'Forty dollars,' she says.

He glances at me. Only for a split second. He knows the right thing to do. He dives into his back pocket and snatches out two crumpled twenty-dollar bills.

Leisurely, Billie opens the Roach Motel and takes out a fresh joint.

'Come on, then,' René blurts out, in a greasy voice. 'I given you my money. And – and what about them wieners?'

'"They check in but they don't check out,"' Billie reads idly, from the side of the Roach Motel. 'You know, René,' she says, looking up, 'thing about jerking off is that often times you can't pin it down. Often times your mind switches. Specially when you've got a girl on your mind.'

Billie has René's undivided attention.

'You think, Shall I lick inside her asshole like a tongue in an empty tub of Cookie Dough Dynamo, gouging so hard that your tongue roots hurt? And then suddenly, out of nowhere in your fantasy, you see a diamond leash. Bing! goes a little bell in your head, and the picture changes. That cute ass disappears and there you are in the dream house in your head, lying face down, with a leash – a beautiful, sparkling, diamond leash tied around your neck – held by a hand coming from due north and you lying, south, beneath her pussy. You've got one hand on either of her thighs and at the same time you're wondering if you'd be doing this on a bed, or on a yoga mat when suddenly there it comes again – bing! Another change! You get bored of the submission fantasy, you want to do the wet, sticky thing, you want to mould your wet hot pussy with hers in the scissors position, you want to—'

'Son of a hog-rustler!' Raymond wheezes.

'You – you want to what?' René gulps.

'You want me to go on, René?' she says. Of course he wants her to go on. He wants to find out the secret. I'm wondering what it is too. I'm thinking about how you can't eat a pomegranate in a seemly way but you can flick your tongue in an artistic way among a mound of glassy red seeds.

Billie is looking at René in a way that I know means 'money'. I hope he pays up. I want to know about the wieners and the cold varnish too. I wonder if this is some sort of trick, like the New Orleans 'I'll tell you where you got your shoes' con. In any case, I'm pleased when René quickly hands over a couple more dollar bills.

'You know what the sexiest thing in the world is?' she says suddenly.

Raymond is mumbling something about this being a crazy day and René just barks something about diamonds. 'That leash thing. Reckon that diamonds on a leash would be kinda . . .'

Ears are pricked, eyes are salivating.

'Try again, René.'

He hesitates before giving what I think is quite a good answer. 'How about sex in a bedful of dollars?'

116

'Think so, René?'

'Yeah.' He's getting cocky now. 'Sex in a bedful of dollars. Dollars and tequila and a woman with big bazookas.' He smirks. 'Two women with big bazookas!'

Billie gives him an excellent withering look. 'Nice try, René,' she tells him. 'Unfortunately paper cuts are a drag. You don't want paper cuts.'

René looks wounded but Billie has no mercy. 'Come on,' she teases, 'tell me what the horniest thing in the world is.'

'What is it?' René explodes. 'What the fuck is the horniest thing in the world?'

She takes a deep puff of the joint. 'I'm going to tell you any minute now,' she says, exhaling. 'Horniest thing in the world's also the most precious thing in the world.'

'Precious?' René's ears prick up.

'It'll cost.' Billie sighs.

Without a moment's hesitation René digs deep into the pocket of his khaki trousers. Then, fifty dollars in hand, he strains forward in case he might miss the pearls Billie seems about to spill from her mouth.

I twist the knotted leather bracelet round and round on my wrist, I feel the knots, fiddle with the loose ends with nervous fingers. But she makes us wait. She makes us wait to hear the horniest thing in the world.

'So you're with this woman,' she says, finally, looking at me in a way that makes my stomach feel not hungry any more. 'You're sitting in her kitchen. She's not so much into food, she's more into economy and nourishment. She hasn't got much in the way of money. In fact, you have just committed the terrible crime of laughing at her meticulousness, at the painstaking way she does her shopping since every cent she earns is hard come by. Is honestly come by. She even budgets for wieners. Can you believe that? Two packs of twenty-four hot dogs: four for each meal – barbecued one day, grilled the next. Expected lifespan of said wieners, one week. Then there's the potatoes: boiled on Monday, diced on

Tuesday, married on Wednesday, buried on Thursday. Whatever.' She taps the side of her head. 'She's got it all in there.'

René glances at me with a frown. He looks confused. So am I confused. I'm grabbing on to my bracelet knot and I don't intend to let go.

'So, anyway, on this particular day you notice that there are some new arrivals on the kitchen table. Three blank packets of pancake mix.'

'Pancake mix?' René stammers, as if the words are stuck in his throat.

'Yes, René, pancake mix. Except that this particular mix isn't even Aunt Jemima's. There are three individual packs laid out on the wooden table and they're all completely blank. On the back of each is a paragraph of writing in cheap blue pen. The writing is short-hand instructions for how to make the stuff up. "Pour contents into bowl. Stir in three cups of milk. Add egg if desired." The mix is so cheap that the company hasn't even printed the instructions on the back of each packet. She's thrown the box away and she's written the instructions there herself. Man, I laughed at her personalised pancake mix. I thought I was way above those three packets. You have to understand, I'm the kind of person who feeds sushi to her cats, who eats out in restaurants almost every night. Business and pleasure. I don't count pennies. Don't buy pancake mix, don't ration hot dogs for different days of the week.

'But I wasn't laughing for long. She's totally pissed off with me at this point. She slams me down over the edge of the kitchen table, she kicks my legs apart with her feet, sending me falling on to the cold surface of the varnished table top. Chipped varnish. She rips up my skirt, she slaps me gently between my legs until I'm begging her to satisfy me good. Then she does. She shoots her fist up my pussy and she pumps away. Cos you know something, René? No dick in this world is as good as a good fist. Let me tell you something for nothing.' She looks down into her hands. 'In fact . . . let me tell you something for eighty dollars. Let me tell you that a scrunched-up fist, attached to the right loving arm, is as sexy as erotic organs are ever going to get. You hear that, René? You know what I'm saying?'

René doesn't look red any more – he looks green. There's no stopping Billie now, though.

'So, as I'm being thrust over the table with the life being fucked out of my body, the thing in front of me, the object before me is one of those packets of goddam pancake mix. From this angle, and with this incredible sensation inside me, it now seems bigger than the room, bigger than the whole house. That white packet with its scratchy blue pen and its ridiculous cheap instructions looms up like a dramatic installation, like a dramatic installation on fire, like a goddess speaking tongues, like an Andy Warhol painting tap-dancing along the table. It rears up in all its huge significance and laughs in my face for having dared make fun of it. That dumb-ass, cheap-ass pack of pancake mix is my new religion, it shakes the room like an earthquake, it becomes part of me, it comes with me. And that, coupled with the smell of the sausages burning under the grill – the cheap Blue Light Special wieners that have been neglected in the heat of the moment and today is only Monday – all this only adds to the tension I can feel in my woman. I feel her dilemma, her vague *Angst* that smells stronger than the aroma of charred pork. I can feel all that, yet still she carries on with the task, still she overrides all thoughts of the imminent destruction of the sausages as she carries on with her hand, pumping into me, driving into me, killing me into life. You heard of a zipless fuck, have you, René? Well, let me tell you that this wasn't one of those. That afternoon, smelling of cold varnish and burning wieners, I will remember, I swear, until the day I die.'

Billie straightens her skirt, stands up from the Dodge seat and walks back to the SUV.

Half of the notes have blown away by the time we get back on the 10.

CHAPTER NINE

The Midas Touch

There's no stopping her now. The further we travel forward, the further her memories go back. The floodgates are open and random objects start to transport her to places that make her act like a child let loose in a store full of candy or a diner full of pies.

We're breakfasting at Dougal's Smokehouse in Fort Channing, Texas, and Billie is contemplating an apple-pie cabinet. It seems to be like the one in Sambo's that she described in the floral notebook: a stainless-steel box with fluorescent lighting and a slanted mirror on the inside of the roof so that customers can see the tops of the pies without having to stand up.

'They look like a row of unmade beds, don't they?' she says, jigging up and down in her seat. 'Bad lighting. Like a peep-show for pies.'

And I just have to raise my eyebrows for a whole torrent of glittering information to come pouring out.

'I was in this peep-show in Belgium, one time,' she explains, her mouth bulging with refried beans. 'Dirty fuckers, the Belgians. You'd hang out in this common room smelling of hot lights and face powder, and when it was your turn, a bell would ring and you'd go up the creaky wooden staircase to a room with a revolving bed and tiny slats all around for the men to look in through. You'd be dancing on this pink fake fur bed with this apple-pie lighting and a bunch of ninety-year-old men pressing themselves against the windows with poppers up their nostrils shouting at you in Flemish.'

She turns back to the apple-pie cabinet. 'First trick I turned was in a room with a mirror on the ceiling. Reminded me of an apple-pie cabinet. Except there was this guy's back instead of a pie crust.'

Our waitress, Coretta, comes to see if we're enjoying our meal. 'Best breakfast I've had in a week,' Billie says, rewarding her with a succulent smile.

We're eating a traditional Texan breakfast: *chorizo con huevos* (minced hot sausage with scrambled eggs) wrapped in a soft tortilla pancake with a side order of refried beans and hash browns. Apparently, the further west we get the hotter and more Mexican the breakfasts will become. Billie can't eat very spicy food so Coretta said she'd get the cook to put just a tiny amount of *chorizo* in. She asks Billie if it wasn't too harsh on her stomach.

'Not at all,' Billie says. 'It was sweet as our waitress!'

You can see Coretta's pleased. 'Guess you're hot enough without eating spicy food,' she says.

'You got it, Coretta!' Billie says, wiggling her chest as the waitress smiles and traipses off back to the hissing coffee machine.

The minute she's gone, an old man with a stringy neck walks past our table. 'Hi there, baby,' he says to Billie. 'I got some corned-beef hash at home . . .'

Billie raises her eyebrows.

'It's been out all day . . .' He hesitates. 'But it sure is tasty.'

Billie flashes him a smile. 'Thanks, hon,' she blasts, in her hard, fruity, Ruby Rose voice, 'but I guess I've had my fill today.'

We watch him fumble his way to the door, bumping into tables as he goes.

'Do I have "hooker" written on my forehead?' she asks me, a wry smile on her lips.

But I can't answer. I'm thinking about how I'm not the only one to notice the thing that's . . . special about Billie. I can't put my finger on what it is. In fact, there are still so many things I want her to explain and I hope she does soon because the spangly apple dangling in front of me on a frayed golden thread is driving me round the bend.

When we drove back on to the 10 from the car park of K-Mart I was too stunned to mention the wieners and cold-varnish fantasy. I just said, 'Those blokes were pretty funny, weren't they?'

She was tucking into a packet of teriyaki beef jerky. There was grease and glee all over her face. 'Yeah,' she said. 'You can make men feel like they've had sex with you even if they haven't and they keep coming back for that feeling.'

'Really?'

'Sure.' She crammed her mouth with another handful of dried meat. 'I could have turned those guys so easily.'

We don't tell each other everything, of course. She doesn't mention what she meant by the wieners and the cold varnish and I don't mention the Midas touch.

She looks over to the restroom and says, 'Being a dominatrix is like being a nanny. Men just want to be fed and get their ass slapped.'

I grab my coffee mug and try and concentrate on drinking. But the thick, slippery rim of the mug becomes a mouthful of Billie's breasts. I gulp. I start to choke.

The Midas touch I am afflicted with isn't of the everyday variety: everything I touch doesn't turn to gold, it turns to sex. Everything has started taking on carnal connotations from the Reese's Peanut Butter Cups that slither over my tongue like tiny oiled nipples to the rims of coffee mugs. I'm not even safe on the high chairs at diner counters. The chrome edge of the seats reminds me of a lion's muzzle and then I see Billie's lion shoulders strutting along towards me and I want her to maul me.

I don't know what to think about that won't get me restless, yet I don't want to think about non-sexual things. I can't concentrate. My 'Breakfast in America' article's gone right out the window. To be honest, I couldn't care less about *chorizo con huevos* or refried beans because I'm not me any more. I am the suede couch and the body, I am the llama and the saddle. When I wash my clothes in a motel sink, the splashes of dirty water jump up to taunt me. I look down at the bra wrapped around the T-shirt, at my boxer shorts rubbing against my socks, and what I see is a load of filthy clothes having an orgy of dirty sex. There's a persistent tickling in my tummy and an ache in my groin. There's something about her that makes me gnaw my lips – like a chocolate cigarette that you can't suck for very long. You have to crunch it.

Billie clasps my arm with her warm, fleshy hand and asks if she can get me a glass of water. But I've nearly stopped choking by this time so it's all right. Although, of course, it isn't all right at all. She tells me that she's going to the restroom and when she's gone I look round at the sexless tourists in Dougal's Smokehouse and when I see the sweating rings of neck fat it becomes moist flesh, nakedness, a mouth; I look at the restroom sign and I imagine a boudoir, a real room where you go to rest – filled with heavy crimson drapes and velvet couches and lips sucking sticky red flesh and ruby juice running down a chin and dripping on to the *chaise-longue* she's sprawled naked on. 'Turning' is a phrase that she uses often. 'He'd be so easy to turn,' she says, and it sounds like a wallet being turned over and also it sounds like spinning on a merry-go-round or turning someone's key round and round until they're so wound up that they feel teased and utterly restless.

Lying in the sun has something to do with the Midas touch, I'm sure of it. For the past two days we've been taking it easy, driving for only two or three hours a day. Billie has taken to sunbathing naked on the floor of our motel rooms with the windows open and the sun streaming in. I watch her apply endless baby oil to her body (to speed up the tanning process, she says) as I sit in a chair in the shade, all hunched up and pale, with my pussy – as she'd say – fizzling like Space Dust. It's no good trying to concentrate on clinical thoughts. Such as why she has lines of scar tissue all over her brown body like seams of botched stitching. I want to climb up and slither all over her like the tiny people on Gulliver. It must be the heat. It must be. The heat is slippery. My tongue slithers along the rim of the blasted coffee mug, which has now become inner thigh, buttock, armpit. I think of the baby oil. I think of rubbing it into her skin. Of me doing it. Of asking if I could. I'd start with the nipples. Rubbing it in there and then, if she liked it, I'd tell her she couldn't move. She'd have to lie there with the feel of a hot oily hand on hot oily flesh in the most sensitive places, turning her groin to Space Dust. This morning in the motel, she asked me to lie down next to her in the sun and it felt as though invisible threads were connecting us to each other. Me to her, at least. I was her puppet on her string. Every move she made sent a twitch into some part of my body: her left breast moved, it pulled on my clitoris – the two were directly attached; she flexed a leg and my left nipple melted to a puddle of chocolate.

I have already constructed a mental Airfix kit of the sex we would have. It would be a bit grubby, like she is a bit grubby: her nails are dirty from so much joint-rolling and she smells a bit like a fruity ashtray. And like stale tea and raw kidneys and sherbet. At night when she's asleep I roll over in my bed so I can be as close to her bed as possible. I inhale her as much as possible. I like to say goodnight, for instance, because we do a combination of the European farewell greeting (a kiss on both cheeks) and the American one (a weird body hug with no face touching) and I get to inhale her all over again. My head's a disgrace. If you made a slide show from a series of thin strips of my cerebral cortex it'd be a fright. Each strip would be packed with dirty shapes and visions and haphazard body parts all superimposed on top of each other, all waiting to unfold like Chinese flowers at the slightest drop of lubrication. Alcohol, for instance.

Some evenings, as I lie in the bed next to hers, I think about suggesting alcohol – another Jack Daniel's binge, for instance. I think, If we both got very drunk and I said to her, 'What do you really want to do now?' she would say, 'Kiss you,' and we would. It would be as easy as that.

Except that I don't say anything, I just think. I know that my thoughts wouldn't look anything like flowers if they did unfold. They'd look like a pile of legs and torsos and groins and fingers all lumped higgledy-piggledy on top of each other – like the crates of dismantled mannequins you see in shop windows after the January sales. My thoughts would look like porno macramé – which is what my leather bracelet reminds me of, these days. Whenever I pick up Billie's K-Mart washing-line and try to concentrate by doing a stint of the 'sailor's craft', I have to stop immediately because the entwined knots strike me as indecent, like something out of the *Kama Sutra*. I try to sleep to forget, but sleeping in the same room as Billie is precarious on the best of occasions. In fact, as travelling companions, we are completely incompatible: I'm hungry when she's full; I'm hot when she's cold; I want to sleep when she's awake. At night, for instance, Billie likes the air-conditioning off and I like it on. So we both get up throughout the night – one of us turns it on, then the other one gets up half an hour later and turns it off. The air-con rattles and judders when it's on, giving out a stale cool like the inside of a bag of pre-prepared lettuce, and when it's off it's unbearable too – as if someone's blocking up your nostrils.

The night after we met the elk-hunters, things were different. Her disco damage was still there – she was still twitching and belching and jerking – but she wasn't really asleep because every time a silly advert came on the TV she'd giggle.

'*Stop! Don't eat that donut! Call 1-900-Bananas.*'

Giggle.

'*This cardigan's called "Gold" because . . . it's gold!*'

Bolt upright in bed.

'Shut up!'

'*It's got gold sequins and gold buttons . . .*'

We couldn't get to sleep then. We were both giggling, both upright in our beds. It was good to stop pretending to be asleep. When we got bored of the Shopping Channel, we started trampolining on the beds and then she said she wanted to go outside for a drive. It seemed a strange thing to do at three in the morning but I handed her the SUV keys, and as she picked up her gold bag, she made some comment about the smell coming from the polystyrene coolers that I'd brought in from the car – now sloshing around with melted ice water, stray hairs, crystallised lettuce leaves and two packets of wieners that I don't dare to open.

When she'd left the room I realised that she was right. That we'd hardly eaten a thing from the K-Mart spree and now everything had gone to waste. Actually, not everything was totally spoiled. There was one K-Mart carrier-bag with a selection of fresh fruit inside. So I drank a glass of neat Jack Daniel's, listened to a Dido song on MTV, had a cry and an unspectacular wank with a banana and then fell asleep.

I dreamed that Billie was scratching her nails over the flat of my hand and her nails were made of pomegranate seeds. She stared at me with a look that was something between spiteful and hungry, and when I tried to close my hand over hers, she lifted hers away and I couldn't get her. This went on for a while. When she stopped scratching I wanted her to do it again. I wanted her to dig her sharp red nails into my hot damp palm. And then there was a blast of sugary breath and a pile of wet seeds rained into my hand, setting a swarm of butterflies loose in my tummy.

I woke up with a jolt to find the banana on the floor, split and brown. Worse luck, the Midas touch hadn't gone away in the night. We finally got into the car and I saw the second pomegranate we'd bought from K-Mart on the dashboard. It was becoming more and more ripe. It had swelled and darkened and it was full of hundreds of mini clits. You could just imagine the frantic orgy going on inside. Billie drove in silence and I just glared at the bloody thing, thinking that even a piece of fruit was more interesting and devil-may-care than me. If I was a fruit I wouldn't even get to have the playboy life of a banana. I'd be something boring like an apple – an apple dangling on a branch, getting older and older, heavier and heavier and who wants over-ripe fruit? One day it would be too late. I'd drop to the ground

with a splat and I'd look like one of the *Rosemary's Baby* little
old ladies and have to make do with beetles and bird's beaks
and young men's bums spotted in the aisles of supermarkets for
love interest.

And now here we are in a diner in the middle of Texas and everything around me brings torment – from the waitress, whose
charisma is only a shadow of Billie's, to the sign on the counter
saying, 'New York Strip', a kind of fillet steak, apparently, which
only serves to bring on another attack of the Midas touch.

Her bag being gold doesn't help matters. I look over at it,
slumped coquettishly in the middle of the table. And then the
thought comes to me. I know it's a bad thought. I know it's a
bad thing to do because you never know what you're going to
find once you start rifling through other people's possessions.
And yet I know exactly what I'm going to find: the floral notebook. I've been trying to forget about it but I can't forget about
it. I could have been imagining it when I thought I saw a page
of silver writing back in Mabeline but I don't think so. And I
suspect she's been writing in it again these past couple of days.
Not that I've been able to catch her. She's excellent at hiding
stuff, is Billie. She drops a few hints about the devil, a few crumbs
about the mother she supposedly hates but whom she can't stop
talking about. She lays a trail of cloak-and-dagger innuendo
about the colour purple, for heaven's sake, but she never fully
explains anything. It's all part of the Midas touch and it's driving
me mad. I'll just take a quick look. She'll probably tell me about
it later anyway – I read about the Sambo diner and then she told
me about it later.

She probably doesn't mind me reading her notebook.

I'll just have a quick flick.

I pull open the lip of the bag. It's a shock to touch it for the
first time. And even more of a shock to feel the floral book. The
black silk flowers are prickly to the fingertips. I glance round
the restaurant to make sure Coretta's not watching. The skinny

piece of green and yellow string that wraps the book isn't even tied in a proper knot. I bet it'd be a cinch to unravel. It is. It's an even easier cinch to open the floral door of the book itself.

The silky cardboard creaks open like the hinges of a haunted house.

Inside, everything is silver. Some of the paper on the back pages has been torn out and some is brown and charred round the edges. But many of the pages have been filled with her scratchy scrawl in silver letters. She *has* been writing. At the top of the first page it says:

There is never enough food. I am always starving.

Starving! What's *that* about? She eats all day! There's food muck all over my car. I read on with a pounding heart.

Mom says that eight-year-old kids don't need much food, but when I come back from school I've always burned up a ton of calories. Calories are like gas. Food is gas. You need it to be a track runner like I am. A sprinter. I like sprinting. Well, I'd rather be a cheer-leader but that's another story.

So, more of the memoire. Written by a thirty-three-year-old woman from the stance of an eight-year-old. I wonder what it is, this strange diary. A short story? Some form of personal therapy? I wonder why she's doing it and why she's doing it now. There seems to be some stuff about the mother, though:

My mom is beautiful. Everybody thinks she is beautiful. She wears high-heeled shoes shiny as skyscrapers and she flies airplanes. She works as the office manager at the flight school at Burbank airport so she gets free lessons. She says she's going to get her Cessna licence if it kills her. Me and Ned, we don't see her that often but she says we should be glad we've got such a modern mother.

Sometimes when Reba is ill, we get to go visit her at the airport after school. Sometimes there are men in her office crowded round her desk drinking beers. They are pilots, although they don't wear jackets with gold buttons and peaked caps like on TV. They give Mom drinks with ice and lemon in and they say, 'C'mon, CC, gotta keep up with the boys!'

My mom's name is Carrie Clare but she's the only woman in the whole of the flight school so they call her CC, like a guy.

Usually she stops laughing when me and Ned walk in. She looks kind of sore. If the boss is there, he's nice to us, though. He's called Casey and he's eighty years old. Mom says he drinks beer when he flies the planes. Sometimes Casey says to me, 'Hey, Billie, you're shooting up quicker than a beanpole!' I get embarrassed then. Later, I tell Mom that I don't want to be like a stupid tall beanpole when I'm only eight years old. I tell her that it's not fair and she comes out with her catchphrase, 'Life isn't fair, Billie.'

On the noticeboard in Mom's office there is a picture of her patting the fat belly of the plane she flies – a Cessna 172 Skyhawk – and underneath is a quote from Helen Keller. It says, 'Life is either a daring adventure or nothing. Avoiding danger is no safer in the long run than exposure.'

I know Helen Keller was a really cool lady but sometimes I blame her for Reba, for having to go to Reba's. Sometimes I wonder if I'd rather be blind and not go to Reba's. Sometimes I would rather be blind. Although I'd rather Reba was blind. Stealing frosting would be a lot easier if she was blind.

Every day after school when I walk through Reba's front door, I look up to the counter to see what color it is. White is the ideal color because it's easier, although purple and orange are my favourite colors because there's more danger involved.

Reba is a gnarly Mexican woman with fleshy lips and droopy eyes and grey skin. She is our babysitter and also a cake-decorator. She is good at the cake-decorating. She makes bright green cars and orange spaceships and princesses wearing cool prom dresses and birthday cakes with Batman and wedding cakes with couples in love boats decorated with pink and silver roses. They are beautiful cakes.

Me and Ned are never allowed to eat the cakes unless one of

them falls on the floor by accident. When this happens — which is very rare because Reba is the kind of woman who doesn't let cake fall on the floor — she won't ice it up special for us. We just get lumps of it for dessert, all cracked and dented and sometimes with patches of dog hair on it. Reba probably does this as punishment for me being so bad at housework. There shouldn't be any dog hair on the fallen cake because I'm supposed to sweep them all up. Reba says that the devil makes work for idle hands and so she writes me a list of chores to do every week — cooking dinner, waxing the floor, vacuuming. When I tell Mom that it's not fair that Reba makes me do the chores because I have to do the same ones at home, she doesn't do anything about it. Mom always says her thing about how life isn't fair. 'I'm sorry you think it's not fair, Billie,' she goes, taking one of her headache tablets, 'but life *isn't* fair.'

When me and Ned arrive at Reba's house after school, she looks up from her frosting bowl and she says something like, 'Go get out of my hair, you hellcats!'

Reba speaks good English. Her parents were Mexican but she refuses to speak Spanish. Mom says that Reba is trying to better herself. I say that Reba would be better if she was a nicer person and Mom will do a big sigh and tell me to *quieta la boca*, which means 'make your mouth still' in Spanish. This is the first piece of Spanish I ever learned. Mom says it when she wants us to be quiet. Sometimes she says, '*Quieta la boca, chiquitilla*,' which I like better because '*chiquitilla*' sounds like a tickly feather scarf. '*Chiquitilla*' means 'little girl', and when Mom says it, it means she's in a better mood. Sometimes she doesn't even say, '*Quieta la boca*.' She closes her eyes and rubs her head and says, 'Give me a break, Billie, I've been working all day,' or 'I've got a headache, Billie, be nice.'

So I am nice. At Reba's house we have to take our shoes off and I do it, even though it is cold in the house and even though the floor-boards are chipped and the crevasses between them are stuffed with squashed bugs and black lines of grease and tufts of German shep-herd dog hair that are too hard to sweep up.

When Reba tells you to get out of her hair there is a choice of

three things to do. The choice of what to do is: start the chores, go
to the backyard or go to the Bible room. The backyard is gross. It
measures about five feet by five and there are three mangy, stinking
German shepherd dogs licking their balls. That's if you're lucky. If
you're not they'll come up to you and look scary and sniff your
crotch.

The Bible room is a place where there is no TV (Reba doesn't
allow TV in the house because she thinks it's devil's work too). You
have to study the Bible in there because sometimes Reba gives you
tests. The part called Revelation is OK because it tells you stuff that
will happen in the future. The things that scare me the most about
the future are, one, that the earth will get too close to the sun and
burn up, and two, that there'll be a big earthquake one day and
California will fall into the ocean. In Revelation, it says you will
know when the future gets here because a bunch of men on horses
with heads like lions are going to appear over a hill wearing breastplates of fire and sapphire and sulphur. Also in the future there will
be a terrible earthquake when the sun turns black like sackcloth
made of goat hair and the moon turns blood red and the stars fall
from the sky like ripe figs from a tree in the wind and the sky rolls
up like a scroll.

The bit about the future that Reba's interested in is when all the
adulterers and murderers get thrown in a fiery lake of burning sulphur.
Her son, William, says she's obsessed with the kooky stuff from the
Bible. Once, he showed me some funny stuff from the Old Testament
that said how you mustn't 'lie with animals', which William says
means fool around with them. That's gross.

The good thing about the Bible room is that I can sometimes sneak
in my own books, covered in brown wrapping paper like her Gideon
Bibles are. I try to keep up good grades in my English class because
I would like to be Lucille Ball when I grow up. Mom says that Lucille
Ball is the first woman in America to have her own TV production
company. That is a good thing. Mom says that Lucille Ball is independent, which means that she has enough money of her own to do
whatever she wants. Mom says it is very important to be independent.

I like Lucille Ball because she wears high heels and she is funny. She lets people throw cakes on her and rip her clothes off.

One day, I came in from the Bible room and smelt that Reba was out of the house. I always know when she's in the house because she smells of sour milk. She rarely leaves the house without telling you so the frosting is hardly ever left unattended. If you get anywhere near her when she's frosting, she'll growl something like 'Keep your dirty hands off of my things!'

The bowl was purple that day. It was still on the counter with the spoon inside. I was real hungry. I'd done three hours of track that afternoon. I looked to left and right, in front and behind to check there were no enemies around. Then I climbed up on the stool and feasted my eyes on what lay before me: a sponge cake with an edible cheer-leader on top (William would like to see me dance in a dress like that) and a see-through bowl filled with purple frosting.

The bowl wasn't even full. There was only a bit of frosting left in the bottom and on the inside there were just drips, lots of crusty drips with cake crumbs stuck to them. I figured that nobody would care about a bowl filled with gunky dregs. I just dug right on in. My neck was on full alert for Reba's return, but mainly I just wiped my finger along the edge of the bowl – where the drips were – and then I sucked my finger. So sweet and creamy. I swirled the frosting around in my mouth and it was like the best, tastiest, happiest washing-machine in the whole world going on in there. Then I opened my eyes and looked at the cheer-leader girl on the cake. My greatest hope is that one day I'll be a cheer-leader. When I get to Junior High when I'm twelve, I'm going to do the cheer-leading trials, and that's a test of skill and beauty and popularity. They're in September. Tickets are only two dollars. You have to do a cheer dance that a teacher has taught you and then you do your own special cheer dance. You get extra points if you know any gymnastic stuff. At the end, when the judges announce the girls who made it, the ones who didn't start to cry and the girls who made it automatically bond and have a slumber party that night.

Cheer-leaders are like royalty because they get tons of attention.

My mom was a cheer-leader. She had skill and beauty and popularity.

So far, I can do everything except a back flip and that is because I am too tall. I am already five four at eight years old. I worry that I might not get chosen because I am too tall. My dance coach tells me not to worry, but I do. I worry that I'm just a freak. A bean-pole freak.

Anyway, I ate as much of the frosting as I dared and then, when Reba came back, I was in the kitchen, preparing the Hamburger Helper. It was Stroganoff Hamburger Helper that night. My favorite and I was hungry. Dinner started off as usual — Reba saying grace, 'For what we are about to receive . . .' and then she stopped dead. She scraped her chair back and stood up. Her flabby lips dangled to and fro like wet dish towels. Those lips were about to spring into life, I could tell. Wet dish towells sting when they hit your butt. I wondered what was coming.

Ned just carried on eating. Little Ned was only four, he didn't know what was happening. Then it came. Reba growled, 'What have you been doing?'

I didn't know what to do. I put my face close to the Hamburger Helper on my plate. I wished the pasta shells could whisper me something, some answer that'd make her shut up. But they didn't say anything so I just looked at her coming closer and closer, going, 'What you done, girl? What you done?'

The sour-milk smell came out of her mouth and then she grabbed my chin. She has fingers like the wire on a mousetrap. 'Been eating frosting! You been eating my frosting!'

I knew that I had to say no. I couldn't say anything else. If I said, 'Yes,' it'd definitely mean the wooden spoon, but there might be some way out if I said, 'No.'

'No, ma'am!' I said, although I couldn't open my mouth very well because of the mousetrap. Then Reba started off on her Bible stuff, hissing her Bible stuff into my ear like an old witch, 'And the tongue is a fire, a word of iniquity, it defileth the whole body, and setteth on fire the course of nature . . .'

She was squeezing tighter and tighter with her fingers. Soon there might be holes in my cheeks. 'What do you say, girl!'

'Honest, Reba, I never ate no purple frosting!' I say, and off she goes, about my tongue being evil and full of deadly poison, and I'm still doing my best to say that I've been good when Ned ruins it. He's hungry. He wants to eat the Hamburger Helper. You can't blame him, my little kid brother. He's only four. He says, 'What's that purple stuff on your mouth, Billie?'

I give in then. I let the big steel clamp pierce my cheeks. I don't put up any more fight. Part of me is pretty pissed. The only reason I didn't look in the mirror before dinner was that Reba's always telling me vanity is a sin that can end you up in the burning sulphur lake.

I was sick to my stomach, I didn't want any Hamburger Helper then. I was pissed. I wanted to know what the point of trying to be good was because everything I did seemed to be wrong.

And then, the next thing, there's a bottle stuck in my mouth. It all happened in slow motion. It was kind of nice to start with. My chair was jerked back like on a ride at Mystic Mountain and then my head was pulled back. The cold screws were on my chin, pulling my mouth open like I was a baby and some crazy mother was force-feeding me milk. There was a bottle in my mouth, cold, a thin glass neck. It hit my teeth and then I found out that there wasn't any milk in the bottle – there was only Tabasco sauce. Reba was shaking a bottle of Tabasco sauce down my throat. I was choking, spluttering, and to start with I couldn't feel the burning. I could hear Ned chuckle – it must have looked pretty funny – and I could hear Leviticus, going, 'The priest shall bring it all and burn it on the altar, it is a burnt sacrifice, an offering made by fire, a sweet aroma to the Lord!' and only then does my throat start to burn. Tabasco sauce is dribbling out of my nose and I wonder what red booga looks like and I wonder if my tears are red too. I can't see them, I can just feel them pouring down my cheek, all hot and wet like the burning lakes of hell that I'm soon going to be going in and I can't move and I hate them all and I'm already planning

134

to eat some more frosting only next time I won't be stupid, next time I'll wipe my face or maybe I'll only eat white frosting. But right now I hate everything, I hate the frosting and the Tabasco sauce and Reba and God, but I don't hate the devil because Reba keeps telling me that I'm on his team and maybe he's the only one who understands me.

The silver words end. I shut the book, tie the string around the outside and chuck it back into the gold bag. I feel manic, though. Within seconds of finishing the story, my hands are back in the gold bag, rummaging around among her things: the Roach Motel, the *Explorer*, some loose dollar bills, some keys. I can't seem to stop. Now that I've broken into one place I shouldn't have gone, I can only think of trespassing somewhere else. And the trespassing helps – it helps me stop thinking about what I've just read. Somehow I know that Billie didn't make all that up – I know she's trying to set something straight, to understand something. Something I shouldn't know about, somewhere I shouldn't have gone. I grub around in the depths of the gold bag, my palms sweating, my heart thumping, hoping Coretta doesn't twig what I'm up to. And then I see something among the muck at the bottom of the bag that makes my eyes prick.

Underneath three or four heart-shaped stones stuck with bits of gum and marijuana twigs is a dog-eared birthday card showing a cartoon angel girl with wings and a halo. I pick the card up. It looks quite recent. Inside, an even hand has written, 'Happy birthday, Billie. I hope things are fine in New Orleans. Remember, I love you, Mommie.'

The card seems an even deeper trespass than the diary. Tears are still pricking at my eyes and I also feel a bit sick. A bit disgusted at myself. Stop right there, Mo Snow. I dump the gold bag back on the table and grab the copy of the *Explorer* peeking out of the top. I close my eyes, take a deep breath and when I open them, I see the words, 'Gina Gammon's Love Matches'.

The paper is folded over to the lonely-hearts page. Two of the ads are ringed:

> Black man, disabled veteran, minister, divorced, 70, seeking Christian Black lady, Holy-Ghost-filled for marriage, if the Lord wills. Write me.

> Humble, obedient, generous White gentleman, 62, retired sea captain residing in New Mexico, is looking for Black, Filipino, Hispanic or Asian lady with round curvy hips who is aggressive and dominating yet also caring. Handicapped, disfigured, incarcerated welcome.

She's put an exclamation mark in blue pen by the first ad. Not by the second one, though. That has an X beside it. An X, and an underlined phone number in the same blue ink. She's also written the phone number on the front of the newspaper – which I immediately recognise as the *Explorer* she bought from Winn Dixie in New Orleans.

The penny drops. So that's why we're heading for New Mexico! The 'retired sea captain' lives in New Mexico and that's why Billie's been insistent about the place. I wipe the sweat off my top lip, realising that I've gone utterly overboard on the self-induced revelation front. Thanks to my devious rummaging, part of me can't stop seeing flashbacks of an eight-year-old little girl getting Tabasco shoved down her throat by a nutty babysitter while the other part of me – a part I realise I must focus on – is pissed off with bloody Ruby Rose for planning a trick behind my back. The more I think about New Mexico the more furious I get until I don't know what I'm feeling any more – everything is trapped in a burning whirl of disgust and fear and excitement . . .

She appears at the table, her eyes sparkling. I'm so wound up that I can't speak. All I can do is watch as she picks energetically at some scrambled egg remaining on her plate, announcing that 'Waitresses are a lot like kids, actually. They understand

kids because waitresses and kids both get the same shitty treat-
ment. They both get ordered around and told what to do.' She
looks up, licking her fingers. 'You know the diner waitress I was
telling you about from when I was a kid – Leah?'

'I . . .'

'Well.' She sniffs. 'When I went into Sambo's I always knew
that Leah was going to be nice to me. She was like a guardian
angel.' She fiddles with her nostrils, brushing underneath her
nose. 'Yeah, I guess that must be it. In diners I always knew there
was going to be a guardian angel.'

I don't know what it is that makes me do it then, right at the
very moment when she seems to have reached some sort of
contentment. But the bubble of fury suddenly bursts and I slap
the *Explorer* down in front of her, shouting, 'So, are you going
to be a "guardian angel" to the "retired sea captain" when we
get to New Mexico tomorrow?'

And then I realise I'm right because her eye does the twitchy
oyster thing and she snatches the *Explorer* back, saying, 'Thanks,
Mo! Nice to know you've been snooping around in my stuff!'

She starts rubbing furiously at her nostrils and sniffing and
trying to stand up. But I won't let her stand up. I grab her hand,
going, 'What are you then? Asian? And, what, are you handi-
capped or disfigured? Or both?'

That sends her into orbit. Even as I'm saying it, I know I've
ruined everything. She starts shouting, 'Mentally scarred,
unstable, whore, hooker, drug addict, nanny – the whole fucking
nine yards if you want to know!'

That is the sentence that seems to be the deciding factor on
the turning-Dougal's-Smokehouse-into-dead-silence front. The
only sounds in the place now are the never-ending hissing of the
coffee machine and the muffled blare of the TV. But I don't care
about other people any more. I'm struggling to keep my hand
on her arm because I'm scared she's going to leave and that I'm
never going to see her again and I don't want that, I definitely
don't want that. I have to keep her talking. 'What did you bloody

expect?' I say, in a panic. 'Didn't you think I'd twig at some point?'

The thing is, I don't think she really cares about my discovering her rendezvous with the 'retired sea captain'. The fact that I poked around in her bag seems to be the serious crime. (I'm really hoping I didn't leave any greasy fingermarks on the pages of her floral notebook.)

She gets to her feet, grabbing both my arms with her far stronger hands and yelling, 'Steal my private things! Kiss my ass!'

She's wild, she's shaking, her pupils are huge. 'Kiss my humungous fucking ass!' she screams, wiping a hand over her face and leaving a smear of egg and refried beans. 'Steal my private things! Take everything from me! Kiss my fucking ass, you dirty little punter!'

We struggle some more until the tomato-ketchup bottle rolls from the table on to the floor and smashes. She rips free of my hands and slams the table with her fists. It seems as if she's going to crash to the floor herself, but she manages to steady herself by holding on to the table as tears slide down her cheeks. Slowly, she lowers herself to the floor and crouches among the shattered glass, sobbing out a series of jerky words. 'That's what you are, just like the rest – a dirty punter. Rip your fantasy out of me and then fuck off.'

With trembling hands she reaches down to the thick red clots among the fragments of glass. 'You're like all the rest, you just want the details. You'd get a fantastic newspaper article out of that, huh? "Fat girl dominatrix drug-dealing piece of pussy . . ."'

These are the magic words. Coretta the guardian angel appears from thin air. A wrinkly hand appears on Billie's arm. 'Hush now, child.' She pulls Billie up and pushes her gently on to the slidy red seat of our booth. She sits down next to her, simultaneously summoning a Mexican bus-boy. She pats Billie's hand and tells her, 'Diner blood, that's what we call ketchup here.' As Billie watches the bus-boy clear up the mess and feels Coretta's hand on her arm, her breathing calms down and her body relaxes. Coretta even knows how to get rid of the staring customers. 'OK, y'all,' she drawls, turning round to the restaurant. 'There's TV on in the corner if you need a little drama.'

Then they're gone. There's just Billie and her – and me looking in. She passes Billie a napkin. 'C'mon, child, wipe your eyes now.'

Billie breaks into more tears. 'Oh . . .' she cries. 'Oh, Coretta, nobody was that nice to me in such a long time . . .'

'Hush now, honey,' Coretta soothes. 'You know what they say about lemons . . .'

'When life throws you lemons, make lemonade,' Billie answers, in a quivery voice.

Coretta turns to me. 'You take care of your friend now.' She looks deep into me as if she knows every fibre in my body. 'And remember, the first breath is always the deepest.'

She turns to Billie and says the same to her: 'The first breath is always the deepest.' She pats her arm again. 'You just remember that.'

Billie clasps Coretta's hands. 'Thank you,' she says.

Coretta shrugs. 'That's me, sweetheart. Eggs and advice over-easy.'

We watch her walk back to the kitchen hatch where she positions a line of plates expertly on her arm.

'Shit, Mo,' Billie says, slightly alarmed. 'Maybe she really is our guardian angel.'

'What did she mean, "The first breath is always the deepest"?'

Billie turns to me. 'I'm sorry, Mo,' she says. 'I'm feeling a bit tired, I guess. Feeling a bit like a refried bean. Refried and refried and refried until I'm just a mush.'

'A refried bean?'

'Actually, no. Not a refried bean. They're lovely and I don't feel lovely. I'm more of a *tamale* with stuff oozing out of the sides.'

'I . . . I just want to know about you,' I stammer.

'I know,' she says. 'And believe me, Peach, you're getting to know me more than most people have in a long time.'

She makes room for me on the seat and I squeeze in next to her. Without even thinking, I pick up a napkin from the table, lick it and gently dab the smear of egg and refried beans from her cheek. As my fingers touch her skin through the soggy paper, it feels strange. It feels moving somehow. As the napkin slides over her cheek, I see the tiny golden hairs there, I smell the elixir of hot perfumes she exudes. Billie giggles and says I'm tickling her. She says that her mom used to blow cigarette smoke into her ears when she had earache and it was too expensive to go to the doctor's. 'The smoke felt nice,' she says, meeting me in the eyes before making a gauche shrug and staring down at her hands folded neatly in her lap.

I gaze at the paper napkin, now stained pale yellow and purple. More pleasure. More pain.

When we're ready to leave Dougal's Smokehouse, Billie leaves Coretta her customary tip – a bundle of notes the size of a small apple – and we head back to the car. I drive, Billie chats and rolls joints, and there's an incredible restful feeling of warmth and calm between us.

I am travelling across America with a woman I don't even know who is taking me places in my head I've never been before. She reminds me of being a kid – of the naughty thrill of the word 'divorce' when I was a child. She has a stage name and a secret name that she tells nobody. Only me. She is complicated like that. Her eyes are a bit mad, like she's taken acid a lot, as opposed to an ecstasy person or a spliff person – although she is a spliff person too. She likes to put things right and make people happy even though she had a horrible babysitter, and she likes diner waitresses because she is looking for a new mother. She over-tips and she always has something nice to say about the way people look. She likes TV, she has a giggle that is sometimes like bootleg wine and sometimes like sherbet, and sometimes she burns words because words have betrayed her. She has a tendency to call herself and her 'punters' 'freaks'. She is not a freak, though, she is sane. She is like a child and she is also like a backstage pass that says, 'Access all Areas'. She has indecent nipples and reckless breasts – although I know that my Midas touch is a self-induced affliction. I know that I'm focusing on lust because I don't want to focus on love. It would be terrible to fall in love. It would be unthinkable.

And yet, right now, I can't believe that we could ever have argued. At this very moment I can't imagine not being with her. I can't believe I sneaked into her diary. I'm trying to forget it ever happened. I'm refusing to think about a lot of things. I concentrate instead on the 'retired sea captain'.

'Why did you call him up, then, Billie?'

'I don't know.' She sounds genuinely puzzled. 'I saw the advertisement back in the parking lot at Winn Dixie. I thought it was funny. To start with. After that I thought about how I could do with the money. And then you informed me just now that we were going to New Mexico.'

'Are we?'

'We cross the state border tomorrow.'

'But are you going to "turn" him?'

'I called him.'

'What did he sound like?'

'Old.'

'That's a shame.'

'That's very good, actually. I like old men. They're sweet. Well . . . actually I've done some dom stuff with holocaust survivors who were pretty . . . yuk . . . but in general old men are easy to get off.' She puts a new joint in her mouth. 'And they're so grateful. They're, like, "I've got what you want, you've got what I want, let's do it!"'

She pulls the Gideon Bible from her bag with one hand, lighting the joint with the other. 'There was this one old man who was really nice. His favourite thing was severe sensory deprivation. He liked to have buckles and straps bound over his rubber-suited body. He'd have me sit on him so he couldn't move and after a while he'd want me to pee down a funnel and hose that went into his rubber suit.'

'Why did he like that?'

'Oh, you know, it was about letting go. Completely letting go. No more thinking.'

'Was he married?'

'His wife had died of leukaemia.' She starts flicking through the Bible on her lap. 'She'd had it for years. She knew he was seeing somebody. She wanted him to see somebody. He loved her very much.'

'Love!' I don't want her to talk about love.

She smiles. 'You know, you shouldn't be so hard on love. When I was a kid, someone told me that in the Greek translation of the Bible there are twenty-seven different words for love. Then the Bible got translated into English and love got summed up in just one word.'

But talking about love isn't safe. I don't want to know anything about Billie as a kid either. All I want to know about is Ruby Rose.

'Where does the retired sea captain live?'

'His answering-machine said something that sounded like "Carlota". I already checked in the map book and there's a place by that name in south-west New Mexico. Apparently that Apache guy Geronimo used to hunt there.'

'Yeah?'

'It's seven thousand feet up in the mountains,' she says, leafing through more Bible pages. 'An old gold-rush town.'

'Gold . . .'

The land has turned into desert. If Louisiana was squelchy with maggots and body lice then western Texas is a roaring dragon, hissing out dry air on to a harsh red landscape. 'Look at this,' she says, with a laugh, showing me the Gideon's 'Where To Find Help In Time Of Need' page. 'For times of temptation: Matthew five, verse six. For times of depression: Luke nine, verses eight and nine. For times of joy: two Corinthians, verse three.'

She slams the book shut and slumps down in the passenger seat. 'What about times when you're feeling horny? Doesn't say anything about that.'

The Bible and the joints and the steering-wheel and the seats and the whole car and the whole of the Interstate-10 and all the mountains and all the valleys and all the flowers and elk and vultures and snakes and everything in the whole of Texas turns into one big slippery crock of twenty-four-carat gold.

CHAPTER TEN

Lip-smacking, love-biting, thirst-quenching . . .

Van Horn is in the foothills of the Sierra Diablo. It is the place where Central Time becomes Mountain Time. In Van Horn you are literally on the edge of time.

The sky has turned an incredible shade of pink. A silvery purply candy colour, the shade of the inside of a hamster's ear. It bathes everything in the town: the mountains, the State Route 54, the rusty poles with M-O-T-E-L at the top in fluorescent red, the telegraph wires, the dilapidated houses, the straggly row of shops – a dusty 7/11, Verne's body shop, a couple of cheap Mexican restaurants. Thanks to the sky, the man-made things can be forgiven. The bad layout doesn't matter, and even the most banal objects become mysterious in the eerie pink light.

We walk along a dirt track because it sounds as if there's a blue ocean at the end of it. But when we reach the end there's just a bigger road with roaring trucks that honk their horns like express trains when they see us and then roll heavily away.

So we leave the fake ocean and wander back to the motel along a track made of rich red soil pitted with shards of sugary pink marble and baroque plants that coil and swirl and shimmer with a fine dusting of rose flour. The track winds past some shanty houses draped with faded Stars and Stripes where Mexican children with green eyes dance, and dazzling white shapes blow on washing-lines. A dog does a somersault and a ghost with a wispy white ponytail watches us as we walk by so we look him in the eye and say, 'Hi there, how y'all doing?' and he nods sagely, then vanishes into the red dust.

*   *   *

It's scary to let yourself sink into the unknown but it must be done. The yellow snake has transported me to a tranquil place where everything is bathed in a new radiance, giving it a slightly different shape, a subtle new meaning. Nothing is radically different, though. There is nothing to be afraid of because every-thing is pure coincidence: we are only in Van Horn because I was driving and tired and a yellow snake told me to follow a pink cloud.

Soon after we left Dougal's Smokehouse I decided to sink into the unknown. There'd been too much excitement in the day, so when Billie passed me the yellow snake I took it and started to smoke. And as the Sermon on the Mount began to smoulder, I realised that I didn't feel so different. The snake just made me see how tense I'd been before.

Now that we are in Van Horn everything is calm. Here we sit on the motel porch, breathing in the pink desert air. Maybe without the sky, Van Horn wouldn't even exist. When I go into the motel room and take the pieces of sugar-pink marble from my pocket they've turned to dirty old stones, as disappointing as picked wild flowers.

Billie knows what has happened. She appears in the doorway. 'And it was all a dream . . .' she croons.

She gives me a present. 'See?' she says, laying a heart-shaped stone on the flat of my hand. 'There's always love lying around. You just got to look for it.'

I recognise the stone. I've already seen it in her bag. At Coretta's diner. The snake takes care of the guilt. The snake takes care of everything. I giggle and when I look into Billie's eyes they seem sad. I don't want her to be sad. This is fun. Van Horn is fun. I tug her sleeve. I show her the bed. The headboard is made from squares of padded chocolate seamed at the edges. It makes me giggle. There are chocolate rivers scooting down the seams into a chocolate lake. I nudge Billie. I say, 'Look! Chocolate rivers!'

And Billie smiles at last. She nudges me and points to the sink. 'Look!' she says. 'Like a tablet. A big chunky Quaalude!' She likes the sink so much that she nearly starts to cry. 'So clinical.' She sighs. 'So sturdy and medical.' And I know what she means. As safe and sturdy as American typeface on a Hershey Bar, as soothing as a swim in a lake of warm chocolate.

'I like this room,' Billie says. 'And did you see the Pacific Union railway track out back?'

'Maybe that's why the room only cost twenty dollars.'

'I love trains when they come,' she says. 'They shake right through you.'

When we go back outside to the porch, the sunset has almost vanished. Nearly all colour has been sucked out of the day.

'Sunsets are a lesson in living in the present, aren't they?' I say slowly, sitting in one of the chairs. 'You have to appreciate the here and now. The sky might be amazing and you might go and get a beer or something so you'll appreciate it better. And then when you come back it's too late. It's gone.'

Everything is in slow motion. Everything is relaxed and dreamy. A warm, throaty giggle joins the other sounds of dusk – the humming of the telegraph wires, the bumbles from the car park, 'You want a burrito and a Dr Pepper?', 'Dallas Cowboys kicked their ass, yes, siree!', French horns and elephants wailing for their young as the man in the room above scrapes his furniture around.

'You still stoned?' Billie chuckles. 'Man, wish I was a grass virgin.'

She honours me with the first puff of a new joint. I take a deep drag and watch the movements of the frisky snake. I close my eyes and there are shapes in different colours and worms and sparks of electric all darting and dancing and bouncing off each other.

'Do you prefer sunrises or sunsets?' I ask.

The yellow snake slinks over the top of her head. She's wearing a yellow halo, a golden crown. She is King Midas.

'Sunsets have that energy of being old and wise and having seen it all,' she says. 'Don't you think?'

'Yes, like the difference between the beginning of a fire and the end of one.'

She smiles. 'I like you on this stuff.'

'And what do you like best?' I ask. 'The beginning of a fire or the end?'

'End of fire? That's a scary thought. Reminds me of a black hole.'

'A black hole?'

'A star that dies. When I was a kid I was scared that the sun might die one day because that's a star too, right?'

'What does a black hole look like?'

'It looks like a crazy paper spiral spinning out of control. You go in and you never come out.'

'Maybe you could go in and then come out without going the full way down.'

'Can't do that.'

'Why not?'

'That's not the way black holes work.'

'Bet I could find a way out.'

'You could, huh?'

She sounds pleased that I know how to outwit black holes. She chuckles and starts to talk about her dream house. 'It was funny there last night,' she says. 'There were all these new rooms that I'd never seen before. And all these different families who shouldn't have been there. In one room there were two little girls getting confirmed. They were kneeling primly with their tongues out, waiting for the wafer of bread, and there were black velvet dresses and white knee socks hanging on hangers. In another room there were teenage boys doing naughty things – some were on skateboards carving up the floor with their wheels and a skinny woman with blonde hair was shouting at them to do the vacuuming and make their beds and they were throwing matches at her. There was another room filled with amateur painters but they were chefs too. They were giving out plates of wieners to waitresses and one of the waitresses was my mom. She was young.'

'What were you doing in the dream?'

'I was wearing this geeky spaz outfit. Bad secretary, striped nylon polyester, and I kept saying to everyone, "Look at me!" and laughing. I didn't mind lots of people being in my house, though. I thought it was kind of cool. If the husbands and wives didn't get along it didn't matter because you could go and chat with someone else.'

'And did you find your room?'

'Yeah, and when I found it it was even better than usual. There was this huge closet there and the light inside was bright and fresh like the light beside the ocean.'

'How did you know it was your room?'

'Oh, it just felt like a safe feeling. I was, like, "Oh, fantastic! I can sleep now."'

She stretches out in her chair, arms above her head, legs reaching to the very edge of the wooden porch. 'Pity we can't go for a walk in the wilds here,' she says.

'Be freaks in the desert?'

'Yeah, freaks in the desert.'

'We can when we get to New Mexico tomorrow.'

She shakes her head. 'It's OK, we're not going. We'll go straight to California. I'll take you to the beach.'

'No!'

I'm serious about this. I want to see the retired sea captain. I want to turn my life on its head at last. To leave my Mo Snow skin. 'We have to go there,' I say, urgently.

She draws back in her seat. She gets smaller. There's an expression on her face that's unfamiliar to me. I think that maybe she's hurt. I think I've hurt Billie.

But I have to go on. I have to bring Ruby Rose back. Ruby Rose is easier than Billie. Billie's a conundrum. At least you know where you are with Ruby Rose. So I appeal to Ruby Rose. I say: 'If you don't think you can do it, that's OK.' And then her eyes flash.

'What do you mean, if I can do it?' Her Ruby Rose voice returns. She starts to inflate.

'Just thought you might show me what a trick is and then I'll stop pestering you.'

'You will, huh?'

'Yes. I want to see you being Ruby Rose.' I think it will be easier to get Ruby Rose to pick apples than Billie. 'It wouldn't be any big deal doing the trick, would it?' I say, flicking ash to the ground with the tap of a capable index finger. 'I mean, you've done this kind of thing before.'

I raise my eyebrows and hold the joint between two fingers like the way I think a 1950s Hollywood star might. I hardly register it when she repeats my words, 'This kind of thing?' I'm feeling great. I feel much more powerful since I started smoking the yellow snake. In fact, I'm so laid-back that the joint drops to the ground. It falls from my fingers and I smile as I watch it smouldering on the floor of the wooden porch. Then there's the sound of a bottle smashing against brick and I get tipped out of my feather nest. Shattered glass ricochets over the porch and then strands of black hair lash into my eyes as she grabs me by the scruff of the neck, hauls me to my feet and screams in fury, 'Pick that up, you dirty little bitch!' She throws me to the ground and there's the prickle of glass gravel under my palms.

I've been pushed into another story. All of a sudden I'm in the middle of America in the middle of the night in the company of one of those white-trash housewives who live in trailers that you see on TV. And the thing is, I'm not sure if Billie has become possessed or if Billie's putting on Ruby Rose. I feel like an idiot for having dropped the joint. When I lean over to pick it up she steps on my hand. She starts to crush my hand. 'You can wipe that smile right off of your face,' she hisses, as if this is to be my last night on earth – although it still could be a voice that she just got out of the dressing-up box. The topsy-turvy feeling going on in my head could just be part of the 'turning' because I feel like I'm turning round and round and the walls are slippy and there's no telling which way is up.

She's hurting my hand. My hand's really hurting. I'm not sure when the right time would be to start protesting. It's coming. The moment is coming very, very soon. My heart pounds in my chest. 'My . . . hand.'

But she just scoffs. 'You pussy,' she sneers. 'That's nowhere near to pain.'

She releases me then. She takes the foot off my hand. And, of course, then I don't want to go back to the feather nest. I want to be taken down to the ground again. Have my nose rubbed in the dirt. 'Dirty girl, aren't you?' she says, hard as nails.

It's dark now. The sliver of moon in the sky makes me brazen. She's more like the moon than the sun. The moon that swells everything, makes the sea bigger and wilder, brings agitation and makes cups overflow at the brim.

'Yes,' I say, still on my knees, helicopter blades beating in my blood. I tell her that I want to see what else she has in her repertoire.

'Oh, you do, do you?' Her sigh trails off into the dark like a line of smoke-rings.

Then Ruby Rose returns. Ruby Rose gestures with her head to the mess of glass and says, in a voice riddled with contempt, 'You'd better make yourself useful.'

She goes into the room and slams the door shut.

When I've collected all the glass and put it into a neat pile I'm not sure what I should do. If I should go into the room. If I should knock before I go into the room. I wait for Billie to take charge of the situation and sit on the porch, my back against the door, flicking through the Gideon Bible that Billie's left out, along with the Dewey's Donuts bag and her lighter. I rip out a random page, fold it into a taper, click the lighter and watch the flame. When I can't hold it any more I let go, and a rag of black tissue paper floats to the ground and lies there, gasping for life, throbbing like hungry red lips or like slinky maggots gasping up the last draughts of air before turning to pinky cinders soft as face powder.

I hear the music then – coming from a cheap stereo. Crackly Madonna with a throbbing bass. The door opens and she stands there like I've never seen her before: eyes are sparkling like a whole mine of diamonds, nostrils are flaring like a fucked-off dragon. She stands there magnificent in the cheap gold halter-neck snagged under the arms, red nylon hot pants, a pair of scratched peep-toe shoes with Perspex platform heels, a rope of black hair secured to the top of her head with a single black chopstick. She doesn't look like an apple hanging from a branch. She looks like something rotten. A rotting cherry dangling on a threadbare stalk.

She is perfect.

My eyes crawl all over the red nylon hot pants. They waft images at me in tantalising waves: difficult-to-get drugs, vomiting in back alleys, a dead fly in a glass of absinthe, nipple tassels, disco lights, old wine, strippers, dancers, slits and tits and slings, black holes and dying stars, the sexual obsession of a random bare forearm. All these things the hot pants say, but I can't articulate them, can't formulate them properly.

Deeper, deeper, throbbing bass line. She starts moving in front of the wardrobe, hips swaying round and round in a circle as if she's dancing only for the benefit of the person in the mirror, the person known as Ruby Rose. She glances at me, a brief swish of the eye, then back to the mirror to check out the third person in the room – sticky, pungent Ruby Rose.

Deeper, deeper, throbbing bass line. She bends over – plucked red nylon mounds thrust insolently at me – she slides her hands slowly down the backs of her legs. When they reach the ankles she draws her hands back up the front of her legs and slides them through her crotch. Her hands press teasingly over the crack in her arse and then she slides upright, spins round to face me, her hips still swaying, her mouth pouting as if it's waiting for me to place a tasty morsel inside.

She approaches. She moves over my body like a zip, as close as a zip but without touching me. I can smell her breath, her body odour. BO and pill dust and sugary plum perfume. She smells of sour plums and stale armpits and crushed-up aspirins even though she has washed. There's no getting rid of her stain – a whore stain, a dirty whore, a shop-soiled street-walker. She slides over me, slithers over the air slowly, so slowly, like a drip of maple syrup trickling down the lip of a jug. Slow and lazy it oozes its way down and you can't help putting your finger out to lick off the sweet wet drip. But you get your hands slapped if you do. You try again and you get another slap: 'Keep your hands off what you can't afford.' The razor voice carves into you and you can't tell if it's joking or serious, you can't tell if another liquor bottle is going to smash over the wall, over you, and you can't wait for either, you want everything to happen, to want her to want you, to want only you. You don't know her any more: some new person has come to inhabit her body – Ruby Rose has come. The Jezebel street-walker in red nylon hot pants and cheap high heels with scratches and chewing-gum on the sole, who'd fuck you for a dollar and then slap that smile right off your face, look you savagely in the eyes and make you feel like she was the Queen of Sheba, the King of Midas.

Beating, beating, dirty bass. The black chopstick is released from her head and a skein of black hair whips me around the face turning me into an electric clock in a power cut – a clock going backwards. 'Get on the floor, dirty girl!' She commands it as if she's telling me she loves me. So I do, I get on the floor. I have no option. Thank fuck I have no option.

And when I'm on the carpet it's even better. I lie on the carpet, on the cockroach playground, because I know that cockroaches have been here too, squirming and stroking their bodies with their black feelers, their dirty black sweat. I look up into her crotch and a sour wind wafts over me and she's saying, 'Pussy, baby? You want a piece of pussy?'

I am an honorary punter, I am one of the men she turned. This is what has happened in the past. I am privileged.

'Chicken? Piece of chicken, baby?' she taunts, an ankle with a diamanté chain dangling, and I am ready to be gutted, to be skinned and tied and trussed up for the Early Bird Special. I am trussed in state in a restroom strewn with four-poster beds and vermilion wallpaper and silk cushions and tawdry red temptress fruit that waitresses with well-roasted necks suck as I strain at my chains. It makes me wild. I feel sick in my stomach. My thoughts lose coherence.

'Pussy, baby? Piece of pussy, baby?'

She keeps talking about the piece of pussy as if it's something you can eat, like a piece of cake or a slice of Sunday roast. I imagine her slipping off her hot pants to reveal her fat pussy like a sluggish cat or a picked-at joint of Sunday beef that's been hanging around in a hot kitchen for a long time – dangling there above me and me not allowed to touch. Just glimpses and glances and itches, just hot fatty drips falling down on me. I think of worms and rats and the dead birds that you stab with a trowel to see the maggots squirming inside and cockroaches rubbing their dirty legs together. It's dirty and nasty and I moan, I reach up for her, I'm going to die, this is everything, this is what men have, I am the punter, this is the turning. Her eyes sparkle again and the blinkers open for a few seconds. Some things become clear: lip-smacking, love-biting, thirst-quenching, toe-sucking, piss-drinking, tit-tweaking, gut-wrenching, fuck-stenching, ever-pleasing, never-ceasing, harmful harmful harmful girl.

Beat, beat, beat, beat. My body is no longer my own. My head flies back. A big black eye is over me, a big black pussy straddles me, a dark decaying cherry that I am ready to bite – my first and final bite. I thrash under her, she commands me not to move.

I look into her eyes and there's a rumble. A train is coming. It comes distant and faint and then harder and harder until you can feel the vibrations pulsate through your body, harder and harder, and the ghetto-blaster shakes on the desk and the cheap cups rattle on the shelf and chinks of plaster fall down from the ceiling and then it comes into you in an eternal moment, a constant rushing through, a constant taking in, and it could be like death scraping through your scalp, it could be like falling into the black hole, falling deeper and deeper into the black spiral with no exit.

I thrash under her, she commands me not to move. But my eyes disobey for a split second and she's not pleased. She puts a Perspex heel over my face and she won't allow me to lick it.

CHAPTER ELEVEN

Angie's Truck Stop

In Angie's Truck Stop, the *chorizo con huevos* is excellent. Spicy, but not too much. Billie has a flour tortilla with scrambled egg rolled up inside. It is also of a good standard because I have tasted it. Crispy and oily on the outside – a bit crunchy, even – and then soft in the middle. Eating oily hot Mexican food in the middle of a desert is the same idea as drinking hot tea on an English summer's day. My face is sweating even though there's air-conditioning in Angie's Truck Stop to make up for the 103° El Paso desert temperatures outside.

Everything would be perfect if it wasn't for the sour cream.

The Mexican waitress – possibly Angie – keeps forgetting to bring it, even though I've reminded her a couple of times. When she took our order I asked for sour cream on the side and I asked if it could be in one of those white cardboard containers, like mini chefs' hats. Billie likes the mini chefs' hats and I know they have them. All diners have them.

She – Angie herself, maybe – finally brought our two plates over. Billie's came with tomato salsa on the side. It was of a very good standard too. And yet the sour cream wasn't there. It still isn't here. I'm wondering if I should ask for it again.

Albeit I didn't ask for the sour cream until after the order was taken by the putative Angie but, even so, she doesn't seem very on the ball today. Obviously I've never met her before and maybe she's just not a very good waitress but I don't think it's that.

The truth is that everything is strange in Angie's Truck Stop. It feels as if everyone's bones have dissolved. Big bears with red faces and baseball caps sit at tables, gawping at the TV with their mouths open. One has the eyes of someone who was in a terrible car crash and had to have plastic surgery. That's what being a truck driver in America must make you look like. The man is so engrossed in the TV that his fork keeps pronging into his hairy cheek, sending pancake lumps juddering back on to his plate. His breakfasting partner keeps muttering, 'Holy cow,' as if he's waiting for a chef's hat of sour cream too.

In Angie's Truck Stop everything is floppy and wavy. It's as if the leaves of the waitress's pad are made from flour tortillas – big, flappy, elephant-ear tortillas – and Angie's pen is just a twisted-up tea-towel in a pen shape, all steamy hot and clean but not any good for doing any writing with.

When the woman – possibly Angie – took our order, her eyes kept flicking to the TV and then she'd look back down into her waitress pad again. One minute she seemed like a Latino diner waitress should be: efficient, slightly insubordinate and sexy, and the next thing, she'd spun off into some strange world of her own.

Billie rips into the tortilla, her eyes glued to an airport scene on the TV. 'The transportation dock in my dream was an airport last night,' she rattles away, her mouth bursting at the seams. 'I think people were going skiing.'

'Yeah?' I'm not really listening. I've turned to look through the hatch. I think that maybe I'll see a Mexican kitchen boy scooping the sour cream into the chef's hat at any minute.

'Airports are weird, don't you think?'

'I suppose so . . .'

The colour through the kitchen hatch is sepia. There's a woman with a plump face standing in shadow. She is dark. Her dark hair is in a bun. She wears a sleeveless dress.

'When you're standing on a piece of floor at an airport, do you ever wonder about all the things that might have happened on that spot? Like who got their heart broken there or who had a panic-attack there?'

'Never thought that, no.'

'Or maybe someone lost their mom there one time . . .' She can't stop speaking at a hundred miles an hour.

'Maybe . . .'

Billie tussles with her breakfast. 'Maybe some kid waited there to be picked up by his mom. And she never showed. There's nothing worse than your mom never showing.'

'Mmmmm.'

You can hear some Mexican boys running about in the back of the kitchen. Nothing unusual about that.

Maybe it's all right, then. Maybe it's the yellow snake that's making me feel niggled about the sour cream. I'm stoned again. Yesterday, in Van Horn, the sweet yellow snake made me feel strong and safe, made me see the imaginative side of life and the positive side of life. (Billie says there is always a positive side to life.) But today it makes me feel on edge. I swivel back to my plate and Billie starts to tease me about my new grass habit. She's not floppy at all. She's strangely wide awake this morning. She gabbles away about how I'm going to go to hell and she doesn't give me time to reply. She says the lakes of sulphur are the colour of the yellow snake and they smell of sweaty armpits and bad eggs. They smell like Billie, then, I think. Although Billie also exudes cement dust – the crushed-aspirin aroma – which adds to her main perfume of sour plums. Today the smell seems to be seeping through her skin. It's so strong you think that if you poured some water on her there'd be a big fizzling explosion, like when magicians pour potions from test tubes on to the ground and there is a big puff of dry-ice smoke. If you poured potion on Billie's flesh there'd be a big puff and then afterwards you'd be able to see a fizzy paste on her skin like sherbet with water in. There'd be a good excuse to lick her then.

The niggling feeling returns. She's wearing too many clothes this morning. Or, rather, now that she's wearing clothes all I can see is her wet flesh last night at 'the turning'. I try to fend off negative thoughts about the sour cream. I wish it would come, though. It's getting ridiculous. The colour of the walls suddenly looks like sky blue with sour cream swirled into it. It's white as sour cream on the TV, too. Actually, it's snowing on the TV.

There is a man wearing a white T-shirt and chinos and a base-ball cap. He's talking quickly on a mobile phone in front of a big soda fountain of snow. There's another man with his back turned to the screen. He's taking photographs of a snowy mountain, a mountain the shape of a snagged nail. A man in green is wearing a skiing mask. In the heavy snow. There is heavy snow, yet people are wearing T-shirts.

On so many levels, everything is fine in Angie's Truck Stop. And yet it's not. Everything is blurred. I'm not sure if it's pleasantly blurred. I lost my contact lenses last night in the thrill of my own personal cabaret show, so Billie has filled me in about the row of apple pies and pecan pies laid out on the counter – pale and sugared and perfectly round. She says that the stools at the counter are great too. She's wondering if they're still here from the fifties or if they bought them specially. There's a Mexican in a scarlet shirt and with a handlebar moustache like a *Come Dancing* contestant sitting on one of them. He's kicking his legs to and fro on to the wall under the counter, cracking jokes, half in American, half in Spanish. 'Hey, baby, let's roll,' he says, to the Angie woman. '*Dame un* pancakes *con tomates*.'

'Something calming about those stools!' Billie pants, jigging her legs up and down under the table. 'Nice to have something calming.'

So she's noticed the atmosphere, too. It isn't just me.

'Calming?'

'They remind me of the sink in the motel last night,' and she starts firing away with machine-gun-like speed about the white tablet in the Van Horn motel, about how beautiful it was – like a big chunky Quaalude. I think of asking her about bonfires. About why she didn't start a bonfire in the beautiful sink this morning. When I woke up she was sitting in a corner, huddled over her floral notebook, root beer and Jack Daniel's in one hand, pen in the other, and when she saw me she slammed the book shut. There were some crispy curls of charred paper on the floor as well as some strips of paper that hadn't been burned.

She picked these up and stuffed them inside the covers of the floral notebook as if I couldn't see what she was doing but of course I could. I could see that she was closing her notebook and she wasn't setting fire to anything.

But I don't want to think about her diary any more. Best to leave that well alone. So I watch her looking wistfully at her tortilla, jaws grinding. The lack of sour cream is making her nervous too. It really is most irritating. When will it arrive, for heaven's sake? I can't bear the suspense any more so I go to the restroom and when I come back everything is absolutely fine. Angie is at our table, the sour cream is in her hand and everything is shipshape once more.

Then I look up to the TV and one of the most beautiful images I have ever seen in my life flashes across the screen.

A froth of flame explodes in the sky. A stream of sycamore helicopters spins down the sides of a melting metal pillar.

Billie frowns. She turns to the woman we think is Angie and says, 'What the hell is that?'

'Bad, huh?'

'Where is it?'

'New York,' the woman says.

'What happened?'

'Some planes flew into the World Trade Center.'

'Oh, my God.'

'I know, it's crazy.'

'Oh, my God.'

'Can I get you guys anything else?'

But Billie is silent and my heart is still beating with the thrill of it all, so the woman who by now we think definitely must be Angie goes back to the counter. Billie says it again: 'Oh, my God.' She turns to a clean-cut young man wearing a denim shirt. 'So there was a terrorist attack?'

'That's what they're saying.'

'Shit.'

'I flew from Dallas to LA a couple of times on American

Airlines,' he says, with a friendly smile. 'When I went through security they didn't even ask for ID.'

There isn't a mountain any more on the screen. It looks as if King Kong has squashed New York with his foot. There's grey snow falling all over New York. The big bears with the red faces and the baseball caps continue to gawp at the screen.

'The people jumping from the building get me,' the scarlet Mexican says, swinging round on his stool.

'Right,' one of the bears mumbles.

'How bad was it up there that the better option was to jump?' he says, gesturing a scarlet arm at the whirring sycamore keys. He whistles.

The bears stop eating.

A crash of pots and pans erupts from the kitchen, followed by shrieks of laughter from the shadow-faced woman cook and the woman who is possibly Angie. The scarlet Mexican beams as he swivels round to the restaurant. 'Ay! Sorry, folks, another plane just crashed into the restaurant!'

The workers in the kitchen cackle with laughter.

I'm not quite sure what to make of the post-Twin Towers world. I suppose the drugs are much to blame. I've smoked so many joints that I'm not sure what's important and what isn't any more. My stomach knots up with excitement and anxiety when I think about what just happened in New York. I'm not sure if it's scary or corny. When we drive through the last few towns in Texas, there are people at the side of the road holding banners saying, 'America, Land of the Free!' and 'Honk three times for freedom!' The landscape is filled with American flags billowing at half-mast and people hooting their horns and flashing their headlights in the spirit of some kind of solidarity. The radio stations are filled with panic and lack of information. One station says, 'The El Paso authority recommends that nobody take a shower as a precaution against chemical warfare.' The next one says, 'Give blood, hang out a flag and say a prayer . . .' and the next is a phone-in station with a trembling-voiced DJ, who keeps saying, 'America's hurting real bad.'

If something like this had happened in England they'd be playing John Lennon or Elton John, but here they're all tangled up in the religious thing and an obsession with talking about 'freedom'. All the stations are playing 'The Star-Spangled Banner' and 'America, America' and some warbly woman opera singer is trilling, 'My eyes have seen the glory of the coming of the Lord . . .'

Billie switches channels. 'I rather liked that,' I tell her.

'Oh, did you rather like it?' she snaps. 'I fucking hate it. My mother used to play it.'

I've been aware for some time now that the world is a place filled with trip-wires called 'Billie's mother' that I keep stepping on by accident. Of course I'm intrigued by the mother – about how she could have turned Billie over to that babysitter, about what she must be like – and yet since the planes hit the Twin Towers, the situation has become more tricky. The fizzing energy of breakfast has been transformed into a series of unexploded landmines and even when I step on something that appears innocent it explodes in my face. For instance, when we left Angie's Truck Stop, Billie pointed to a phone box by the side of the building. I thought she was pointing to a Mexican boy carrying a crate of lettuces into the back kitchen and I smiled at her. She demanded to know if I was going to call my mother or not and I realised that I hadn't even thought about calling my mother. That the only feeling I was aware of was something like a sick euphoria – like a surge of superiority about being in America at exactly the right time. A historic time. I was thinking of maybe calling Muriel back in Scarborough and trying to sell her a story, although I knew I wouldn't get round to it. Mainly I just kept seeing the beautiful image – the sheet of flame as big as the sky.

Billie said that she couldn't believe I wasn't going to call my mother at a time like this, and as she ranted on all I could think of was the cost of a transatlantic call and that I couldn't imagine speaking to my mother when I was stoned.

'Well . . .' I hesitated. 'Maybe I'll call her later.'

She became furious. 'What do you mean, you'll wait until later?' she yelled. 'Maybe there *will* be no later. Maybe World War Three's about to break out and then everything'll be lost!'

The passion in her voice shocked me. Her face was drenched with sweat, her eyes looked panicked. I thought about asking her why she didn't call *her* mother but then I realised I couldn't deal with the drama of the reply. So I trundled off obediently to make the call.

'Oh, thank God you rang,' Mother said. 'I saw it on TV. Are you all right?'

'No, I've been blown up.'

'Oh, Mo! Everyone's in a right state here.'

'They're having a laugh about it over here.'

'Really?'

'Think it's hilarious.'

'Oh dear. Did you see the people jumping from the tower? Terrible business.'

'Mmmm.'

'When are you coming home?'

'When the body-bag gets here.'

'Oh, Mo, love, don't joke about such things.'

'Sorry.'

'What's the weather like?'

'Hot.'

'Lovely.'

'Just drinking a cup of tea, actually.'

'Really, love? I always think a nice cup of tea cools you down in the hot weather.'

'I know.'

'Funny, you never used to like it.'

'Yeah, well, this old dog's learning new tricks.'

'Lovely. Do keep safe, won't you, Mo?'

I could see her back in Scabs, crossword abandoned for once in her life, eyes glued to the TV, pulling the atlas out to see where exactly El Paso was, calling up her friends from the St John's Ambulance Brigade to tell them I was OK, suggesting that a jumble sale for the families of the victims was the least they could do – patchwork, woven purses, home-made jams with greaseproof tops and rubber bands.

I walked back to the car feeling sick. A sickness like a secret guilt. Like a blister on the roof of your mouth during a lovely meal. When I got into the SUV Billie asked me how it had gone with my mother and I had this urge to tell her that too much love can be as bad as too little. That being smothered in love can turn you into a bad person. A tyrant, a capricious meanie.

But I didn't say anything, and now we drive on in silence towards the New Mexican border and, as we do so, the yellow snake wriggles out of my blood. Billie hasn't lit a joint in a while now and I daren't ask her for any more in case I get it in the neck again. The effect of this gradual sobriety is that my brain starts to feel like a felt-tip pen whose top's been left off overnight and I don't know what to feel about the flashing lights of the newly terrified Americans and the half-mast flags and the anxious excitement that gnaws away in my belly when I think of that image on the TV.

It's weird how you act when you're freaking out. Of course, I start thinking about macramé knots and, before I know it, I've opened my big mouth and said, 'The retired sea captain is probably going to want some fancy ropework.'

The car lurches to one side of the road.

'Oh, my God,' she says, hitting the steering-wheel. 'He'll probably want some kind of kinky Good Ship Lollipop scene. Or I'll have to tie him to the dining-table mizzen mast . . .'

'It's all right,' I mumble. I'm not sure what I'm saying any more. 'Just do a couple of exploding knots.'

'What?' she snaps.

I feel myself blush.

'What the hell's an exploding knot?'

'You know.' I shrug. 'Like a clove hitch or something.'

'No, I don't know.' She glares at me.

I take a deep breath. 'Well, you use a clove hitch to attach a rope to something like a branch. Or a bar.'

'Go on.'

'To keep it from slipping when tension's applied.'

'And what's with the exploding stuff?'

I shrug. 'You know . . .'

'No, I don't know,' she shouts impatiently. 'You keep telling me I know but I don't know!'

'OK!' I wish I'd never begun this. 'I seem to remember that they're called "exploding" knots because they untie easily with one tug.'

'Yeah?' She looks suspicious. 'How come you know all this? That macramé teacher of yours sounds pretty advanced.'

I tell her that it must be remnants of knowledge from my childhood in the Girl Guides. Her face softens. 'The Girl Guides?' she says. 'How cute is that!'

She starts to brighten up. She quizzes me more on knots but I tell her I can't remember anything, that I'm actually hopeless at tying knots, apart from the macramé basics. So she announces that we're going to stop off at an Internet café and download the information. We have to be quick because we've decided to get to a place called Lariat by nightfall – a small town about seven miles from Carlota and about four hours' drive from here. So when we get to a town called Silver City, we go into an Internet shop and she soon locates a Girl Guides of America site with an impressive knot section. By the time we get back on the road, she has a huge wad of A4 printout.

Billie might be impressive at tying cherry stalks into knots with her tongue but she's not a natural with her hands. '"Bowline",' she reads out slowly, from one of the printed sheets as I drive. '"This knot is used to make a non-slip loop in the end of a rope. While it is used for climbing and rescues, a figure-eight loop knot often is best in those situations.'" She starts rifling though the other sheets of paper. 'So where the fuck's the figure-eight loop knot?'

'Maybe you didn't download that.'

She picks up one of the sheets of paper and looks closely at some sketching. 'There's one here called a margarita,' she says. 'Looks kind of squashy and limp, like if you'd drunk a bunch of margaritas.'

She turns to a new page. 'The San Francisco looks pretty funny.' She spends a while trying to make one but ends up throwing lengths of lump-filled K-Mart washing-line to the ground, declaring that she doesn't like the knot anyway. 'Just like San Francisco,' she snarls. 'All anal and tight!'

She picks up a half-empty packet of teriyaki jerky from the back seat and starts to munch.

'My stepdad would bust my ass for trying a knot like that.'

'How do you mean?'

'We used to go sailing with him. Me and my brother. We used to have the knot test before we were allowed to get on the boat. I used to get Ned to do mine.' She tears at a piece of jerky. 'Oh, well, best to look on the bright side, hey, Miss Girl Guide? At least I didn't have to write papers on knots.'

'No?'

'No. Just stuff on French novels. Nineteenth-century, mainly.' She grimaces. 'My stepdad was a fan of French literature. He thought it'd be good for me.'

'And was it?'

'Sure. That time I set fire to three acres of hillside? I started the whole thing with a bunch of Balzac novels. They were way too long, man. Pages of description about someone's nose.'

'You must have liked some of them.'

'Maybe.' She thinks for a while. A smile creeps on to her face. 'One was about this high-class hooker. She was an actress who graduated on to hooking. It was kind of cool, actually.'

She picks up the washing-line from the floor and starts a new knot ('Slip-knot, can't go wrong with that one, right?'). She smiles to herself as she concentrates on the twisted shapes in her hands. 'The book was called *Nana*. I wrote the essay in this really sloppy style to try and piss my stepdad off. He was a fanatic for good grammar . . .'

The line moves more confidently in her hands. 'I wrote stuff like "Nana is this high-class ho' who's like a French version of Rizzo – the leader of the Pink Ladies in *Grease*. Nana's from the nineteenth century, though. She has sex with really ugly guys who are rich and then they give her castles and nice clothes and she gets to party a lot. In France this is called being a courtesan."' She laughs again. 'One time I had to write a paper on this directory of high-class hookers of the *belle-époque*. One group called themselves the Laughing Women. They held a monthly women-only dinner with an orgy afterwards.'

'Sounds fun.' My palms start to sweat on the steering-wheel. I'm not sure if this is more of the Midas touch or just nerves about going into the domain of Billie's childhood – a domain I've already wandered in and still feel guilty about.

'God knows where he got that one from.'

'Any good, was it?'

'Munching each other's commodities.'

'Sorry?'

'That's what they did after dinner.'

I feel my heart pound in my chest. To cover my embarrassment I say, 'Maybe I should have been a hooker.'

It's a ridiculous thing to say because I know I'd have been a hopeless prostitute. But she just holds the completed slip-knot triumphantly in the air and corrects me: 'Courtesan, honey,' she says.

I plough on with my stupid comments. 'Maybe I'm just a poor little whore who wants to be adored!'

'Maybe you're a poor little bore who wants to be a whore,' she drawls back.

By now we've left the 10 and joined a minor road that leads

to Lariat – the 180 – a poorly surfaced track that leads deeper and deeper into the desert. We're well into New Mexico now – a state comprising 17 million acres, according to the guidebook – and the immense space is beginning to feel overwhelming. The red mountains loom up to the skies and the earth stretches out wide as the sea, dotted with names like 'Devil's Elbow' and 'Slaughterhouse Spring' and 'Skeleton Ridge'.

Billie flicks aimlessly through the printout pages. '"A bend is a knot joining two ropes. A hitch is a knot joining a rope to something else. A knot is any lump in a rope . . ." OK,' she says, bored. 'Maybe the Girl Guides aren't as exciting as I thought they'd be.'

She chucks a final ear of jerky into her mouth before throwing the empty bag to the floor (along with some handles, some Reese's Peanut Butter Cup wrappers and some crumpled balls of printout paper). There's a prick on the back of my neck and it's not the Midas touch this time. It's irritation. She's so bloody selfish. I'm aware again of Billie as a complete stranger who is taking over my car, invading my life and littering both up. 'A little bore who wants to be a whore' indeed! I glance at the bright orange Cheet-O crust on the edge of the passenger seat and then I see the complete pig's ear she's made of a lorry knot – a useful knot commonly used for tying one object to another – and I smile. (The restless ghost of the sulphur-coloured snake is much more vicious than the snake itself.) I try to sound bored like her. 'What's the big deal with being a dominatrix, anyway?' I say.

'The drug,' she replies matter-of-factly.

'Cocaine?'

'Not the coke, Geek Girl. Serotonin. Remember the pig's guts diet? Serotonin's the happy juice that naturally gets released with pain? It's a huge rush. A huge wave of everything OK.'

'And what else?' I say stiffly.

'What else?' She laughs her rich laugh. 'Well, let's think . . . How about everything else in this world just going away? Because it does. There's just you and this person, and there's this tremendous . . .' gestures '. . . between you. You're so connected with the person you're aware of the flicker of an eyelash.'

'The flicker of an eyelash?'

'Yeah. And a grain of sand becomes as big as the whole world.'

I swerve to avoid a rattlesnake that darts out from the vicious scrub lining the sides of the road. It squirms on its belly through the film of red flour that covers everything and disappears behind a cactus plant with sticky yellow flowers and spines as big as tiger claws.

'But what about if one of your customers turns psycho?'

'Never happened to me,' she says. 'The important thing is not to get wasted on drugs when you're with a freak. If there's coke involved, the best thing is to blow it off the side of the table, then pretend you're dabbing the remnants on to your gums whereas in fact you're flicking it all on the floor with your hair. The freak won't notice.'

'But what if the freak's on coke?'

'That's OK. Except he won't be able to get a hard-on. He'll be tugging away for ages, trying to get off. Tug, tug, tug.'

I ask her what happens if the pain starts to get out of control.

'Come on!' She laughs. 'You don't get so out of control that your bottom is saying, "No! No!" and you don't hear it or don't process it.'

'I thought you had to say "peanut butter" or something. To mean "stop".' I take my hands off the steering wheel and fold my arms tightly over my lumberjack shirt. 'I mean . . . I read that once on an Internet site.'

She sighs. I know she must find my questions tedious. I like it when she puts on her teacher's air, though: her the teacher and me the tedious pupil. I like it when she stops talking about love and goes back to being Ruby Rose.

'No you don't say, "peanut butter"!' I get a withering look. 'You choose a thing called a safe word before you start.' She turns round and picks up a can of Easy Cheese from the back seat. 'You can say something like "enough", if you want.'

I swerve again. I don't know what she's trying to say. Is she telling me that I can say, 'Enough,' and get out here and now? I don't know if she's trying to be significant or if I'm just being paranoid. I don't know anything any more. My head aches. Where's the bloody joint when you need it? 'But what pleasure do you get when you're doing it for money?'

'Stripper rush,' she says, without hesitation.

And immediately I'm back in the motel room in Van Horn utterly in lust with Ruby Rose. But I walk straight out again because I don't want to go down that path. I want to stop it now. Stop the stupid Midas touch game. People were jumping out of burning towers today, for heaven's sake. It's time to get back to reality. I start rabbiting on about the Sceptre.

'I think I had waitress rush when I used to work in my hotel in Scabs,' I say.

'Yeah? And what did you do when you had it?' She squirts cheese on to her tongue.

'You had to have a few beers at the pub afterwards. You couldn't get to sleep otherwise. How about you?'

'Sometimes I'd make love with some of the gay men who worked with me.'

I blink.

'Why did you do that?'

'A gayboy friend of mine says he likes sleeping with women when he's feeling dirty because it's such a taboo thing to do.'

'Yes, but—'

'I wanted to remember that things can be pure and beautiful.'

'How do you mean?'

'That sex doesn't always have to be something where you work things through because you're so fucked up.'

'Like your dominatrix customers?'

'You know,' she says, ignoring me, 'in a lot of peep-shows I've worked at, the girls used to go bed together.'

'Lesbians, then, were they?' I say, a bit too stroppily.

'It wasn't necessarily a sex thing. Women understand where

other women are coming from emotionally.'

'Platonic orgasms, you mean?'

'What?' She leans forward towards the dashboard and switches on the radio.

'Sounds like fucking to me, Billie.'

She looks at me with barely disguised distaste. She starts to fiddle with the radio dial. 'Being held and made love to is different from fucking.'

'There was flame upon flame upon flame . . .' the radio says.

She tuts and discards another piece of washing-line, lumpy with failed knots.

'The peep-show girls sleeping with other girls – it doesn't mean they're lesbians.'

'Doesn't it? Why don't they just go shopping together if they want company?'

'You don't always feel like shopping.'

'You'll be telling me next that not all married people are heterosexual.'

'What is your hang-up about sex, Mo?' she snaps.

'What do you mean?' I know very well what she means.

'Who fucking cares? is what I mean. Two men holding on to each other for dear life as they fall from a burning tower – do you think they were worrying about looking like fags?'

'I—'

'There are moments beyond love or gender. There are moments about being a human being.'

'Yes, but we're not all falling from burning towers.'

'Oh, you think so?'

The day is becoming more and more unusual.

There is the rumble of the engine, the rattle of the skeletons, the bumping of the pomegranate on the dashboard, Billie's talk of stripper rush and eyelashes and all this is framed by these other-worldly El Greco skies that look how you imagined heaven to be when you were a child. I suddenly start to think about all

170

the people who died today. On the radio they're talking about unofficial estimates of ten thousand casualties. The roar of excitement and anxiety passes through me again and then on the radio I hear a recording of a terrible twisting-metal sound and a woman in a New York street screaming in a wild panic: 'They're jumping out the windows! They're jumping out the windows! I guess they're trying to save themselves . . . I don't know!'

'Fucking knots,' Billie mutters, 'fucking trick, fucking Brit. I could be hanging out at the Bloated Goat by now. Or shaking my ass making a little money,' and I hate her again.

Or maybe I'm just scared. You can get scared in the desert. Your mind becomes like an El Greco painting: hyper-real. That's why the pioneers tried to tame the land. The pioneers were geeky. They pretended they weren't scared. They went round saying, 'How y'all doing?' to suspicious-looking strangers as they gave them a quick once-over, and they gave names like 'Ship Rock' to an eerie immensity of 12-million-year-old volcanic mountain just outside Farmington that the Navajo Indians believed to have been a huge black bird that flew in from the land beyond the setting sun and was petrified to stone.

The pioneers gave up in the end, though. They started giving places scary names like 'Devil's Elbow' and 'Slaughterhouse Spring' and 'Skeleton Ridge' because they finally realised they had to live with their surroundings rather then conquer them. And also because they were shit scared.

Here, in the desert, all your previous life is burned away – K-Mart, Mexican breakfasts, diner stools, root beer, apple pie – everything floats away, everything is sucked up into the powerful skies above. You wonder how much putrid flesh filled this land, how many rotting corpses with twisted mouths and pulpy features lay on the ground covered with red-flour veils and riddled with arrows and gun holes and vulture wounds.

As an English person driving through the New Mexican desert, you have to abandon all thoughts of 'meadow' or 'lawn' or 'stroll' or 'quaint'. There's little to cling to, few places to dig in your hooks, to orientate yourself back to what you know. Take the mountains. The word 'sacred' keeps springing to mind and I don't know anything else that, just from standing in its presence, evokes the word. They've stood here all these years, the mountains. They're more breathtaking than any man-made tower or dome. The shape hasn't been tempered by fashion or politics or ignorance or malice. These mountains ended up looking like carrot tops and Cubist paintings and lions' backs and fat buttocks and Roman noses just by standing still and being whispered at and spat upon by centuries of wind and rain and sun. The clouds blow overhead to protect them from too much harshness.

I wonder why the people in New York were chosen to die today and where they are now. I think that when bad English lawns die they go to New Mexico. They become dusty cacti left to scream out silently as they burn up on rocky mountainsides. Nobody notices them and their only company is a few surly lizards who were smarmy misanthropists in a former life and who've been abandoned to a dusty, desolate place where they can hate themselves to their hearts' content.

'The smell was like burning metal and plastic and sulphur . . .'

Sunset is coming. The sky is taking over: there is an alien spaceship landing in front of us, the Second Coming to the right, a psychedelic heroin trip to the left and behind us, like an intense purple bruise, the devil is coming to get us.

CHAPTER TWELVE

Global Positioning

Billie is already the talk of Lariat. A trick of hers has set the town talking. It involves a penknife and a jammed bathroom door in a motel room. There are only two motels in town. One is very clean and doubles as a Bible camp while the other, the Buffalo, adjacent to the town's gas station and general store, is more ramshackle. Billie says she's not going anywhere near a Bible camp so we choose the Buffalo.

We pull over on a car park with weeds growing through the Tarmac. Sitting on an upturned box is a stray old man with grey stubble, slitty eyes and a gnarled cigar clutched between his teeth. He's seen better days, as has the stray old dog sprawled by his side. We go into the reception area and see plumes of smoke rising over the top of an easy chair positioned in front of a TV set. The back of a fuzzy perm is visible and then, at the sound of our entrance, the perm turns and stands up, and before us is a woman in her early sixties wearing a stripy T-shirt, easy-fit jeans and slippers.

She squints through heavy-rimmed glasses, introduces herself as Vera, then trundles up to a reception desk laden with staplers, pens, phone directories, a fax machine, an overflowing ashtray, empty FedEx packets, reams of knotted telephone flex and an overstuffed letter-holder.

'Now, let's see,' she says, rummaging round. 'Got my guest book here someplace . . .'

I like the look of Vera. She has very bad posture. Her back is hunched and her head looks as if it's sticking out of the front of her chest. She leans towards the door and, still looking down at the chaotic desk, she shouts out, 'Bud, you seen the guest book?'

There's silence, and then a slow 'Huh?', which seems to come from the stray old man outside. Vera shakes her head and takes a final drag on her cigarette. 'Don't know why's I'm asking him,' she says, stubbing out the butt on the rim of the overflowing ashtray and lighting another. 'He barely knows what happened in New York this morning.'

Vera has a good walking style too. She doesn't so much walk as shuffle. She shuffles to the other side of the room, where a scratched wooden table is covered with eggy breakfast plates, a bottle of ketchup and salt and pepper cruets.

She explains that her office is also her house. ('More convenient in some ways and not so in others.') She flips through a heap of magazines stacked against an ancient stereo player but she still can't find the book. She puffs on the cigarette and stares, puzzled, at the part of the wood-panelled wall where two splayed bears and a stag head (or possibly an elk head) are hanging. She narrows her eyes and you can't tell if it's a reaction to what's coming out of the stereo (George Bush intoning, 'There's a saying out west: wanted dead or alive!') or if she suspects that one of the animals might have lifted her guest book. She shuffles back to the front desk, narrowly avoiding the big bunch of dried chillies hanging from one of the fan lights and careful not catch the large Stars and Stripes flag that's laid out over two easy chairs.

'America's hurting real bad,' she says, as she sits down on the chair and opens some drawers in the desk. She scoops around inside but they seem to be filled with more curios and still no guest book. She closes them and says, 'I reckon you're fine here for a couple of nights. We got a few cancellations, I know that much.'

She says that she doesn't have any more rooms with single beds but that the double bed we're getting in room four is 'real comfortable'. Billie signs in as Ruby Rose and Vera hands her a key, advising her that you have to run the water for a while before it gets warm. 'Don't give up, though,' she says cheerily.

Our room is wood-panelled and very dark. It has brown carpet and brown walls and the only point of brightness is the border of gold braid that runs along the bottom of the brown curtains. There is a jolly collection of three souvenir plates hanging on the wall, one marking the wedding of John F. Kennedy and Jacqueline Bouvier, another from the Queen of England's 1977 Silver Jubilee and the third showing some olde-worlde scenes of Silver City surrounded by what might be Native American hiero-glyphs. It takes a while, however, for the décor to register. At first, all I can see is the bed. This is the bed that will hold me and Billie together for the first time yet on our trip. It's defi-nitely not a California King: it's more than usually narrow for an American bed, as a matter of fact. I can hardly believe my luck. I wonder what will happen in it tonight. I know something has to happen in it. We can't go on beating round the bush for much longer. I decide that I love the room. It smells faintly of pine trees and there's even a friendly Roach Motel on the carpet.

The only problem is that we can't get into the bathroom. The lock seems to be jammed. I can't open it, and as Billie has suddenly disappeared for one of her smokes there's no option but to go and fetch Vera.

'Lock, huh?' she says. She shuffles over to our room and tries to force open the bathroom door by turning the handle and pushing hard, but it won't budge. 'Darn thing,' she grunts, her cigarette gripped even tighter between her teeth, her face straining to red. 'Been asking Bud to fix this for years.'

Just as she gives up, Billie walks in. 'What's up?' she says. 'You got trouble there, Vera?'

Vera just grunts so Billie opens her bag and roots around. I'm worried that Vera might smell the marijuana and banish us from the motel or call the police or something, but she just puffs peacefully away on her cigarette and says, 'Looks like you got some useful stuff in that there bag o' yours, Ruby Rose.'

'Sure have, Vera,' Billie replies, still searching. A couple of twenty-dollar bills flutter to the ground and then, finally, she locates what she's looking for: a penknife. She opens out a screwdriver attachment, then goes to the jammed door and sticks the tool into a tiny hole in it. 'My little brother was always locking himself in the bathroom when we were kids,' she murmurs. 'I used to do this all the time.'

There's a click and the door breathes out. Billie pulls it open. 'There you go.' She turns round, beaming. 'Good to know I can still pick a lock.'

Vera takes the cigarette out of her mouth. She holds it for a good fifteen seconds. The wrinkles on her forehead change position and she nods gently in approval. 'Hot damn,' she says. 'You'll have to teach me that one some time soon.' The cigarette returns to her mouth. 'You girls want to come over to the Thunderbird, I'll get y'all a drink on the house.'

At just after four the next afternoon, I meet Billie for a late lunch at the bar opposite the Buffalo called the Thunderbird. Outside there's a canvas sign saying, 'The Thunderbird welcomes hunters to Lariat', and a newly hung American flag flying at half-mast. Inside it's murky. In the front area there's a juke-box, a pool table and a long shelf of Jim Beam bottles in the shape of Elvis statuettes. In the back there's a restaurant dotted with moustachioed men in tight jeans and stiff-brimmed cowboy hats sitting at tables with red-checked cloths.

I'm trying to turn over a new leaf with Billie – trying to stop 'bagging' on her, as they say in America, to be encouraging and obliging. I want to pull her out of the doldrums she seems to have fallen into since yesterday's terrorist attacks. But over lunch she's all cryptic and snappy. When I ask her how her day was (she left very early this morning for another solitary drive in the SUV) she says she doesn't want to talk about it, and when I try to start a conversation (on the back of the menu is a page entitled 'Somethin' To Talk About', with questions such as 'If someone paid you $10,000 would you give up television for a year?', 'Which celebrity would you invite to your party?' and 'What emotion could you do without?') Billie starts acting all long-suffering. She replies that, no, of course she wouldn't give up TV for ten thousand dollars, that for the party she'd have Anne Frank, Anna Nicole Smith and Marlene Dietrich as guests (and then she says that, actually, no, she'd have just Courtney Love). When it comes to the emotion she could most do without, she pushes her fork slowly into the menu's plastic covering, saying, 'Passion.'

It's a relief when our waitress comes over. She's wearing an old-fashioned badge with 'Hi, my name is . . .' on the first line. On the second line a name has been slotted in: Clara. While Billie pores over the menu, Clara and I make friends. She tells me that Lariat is a town of matriarchs and sassy divorcées. That Vera doesn't just own the Buffalo Motel but also the town's four other commercial establishments: the Thunderbird, the gas station, the adjoining general store and a small breakfast joint called Annie Sue's. Clara confides that she waits tables so that she can afford to run her ranch four miles out of Lariat up in the hills, at the beginning of the Barnard Road – the road that's going to take us, in a climb of two thousand feet in seven miles, to the ghost town of Carlota. Clara's ranch consists of eight acres, a trailer home (where her mother lives too) and 'a few horses', she doesn't know the exact number.

'Pretty funny how a homecoming princess ended up living in a trailer,' she says with a tired smile.

At this, Billie perks up. 'You were a homecoming princess?'

'Sure was,' Clara drawls.

'Oh, my God!'

'Senior year.'

'How fantastic! And did you get to wear a great dress?'

Clara squints. 'I guess it was something made of satin,' she says, looking into the distance.

'I bet you felt really special.'

Clara shrugs. 'Don't know about that . . .'

'Oh, come on!'

Clara starts to smile. She nods. 'I guess I did kind of like the attention . . .'

I'm about to ask what on earth a homecoming princess is when, out of the blue, Clara cards us. This means asking for proof-of-age ID when you order a beer. Billie wants a Rolling Rock to go with her chicken burrito and even though I'm thirty-one, Billie is thirty-three, and neither of us looks like we're younger than twenty-one, Clara is stubborn.

When she walks off to another table, Billie rolls her eyes and says, 'Man, she totally reminds me of my mother,' with her usual doomy emphasis on the word 'mother'. Then she picks up the menu and starts reading the 'Somethin' To Talk About' page, signalling, I presume, that I am the one who's been chosen to go back and fetch the passports. This is a bit rich as I didn't even want a beer in the first place. But I don't feel like arguing so I make the trip back to the room. On my way I bump into Vera.

'Where you going in such a hurry?' she asks. When I tell her about the carding she starts chuckling. 'That's Clara, all right! Best waitress in Lariat.'

'Gosh!' I say.

'Pardon me?' she says, squinting at me.

'I mean, that's one way of looking at it . . .'

'You British, right?' She surveys the knotted leather bracelet on my wrist, dubiously.

'Absolutely am!'

She sucks hard on her cigarette. 'Why don't you bring that Ruby Rose friend of yours in for a drink tonight?'

I try not to let the irritation show on my face. Here we go again, I think, another person inviting Billie, praising Billie, bowing down to the wonderful bloody Billie. Do these people have no consideration for my feelings? Don't they realise that I'm equally interesting, albeit slightly less showy about it?

'She's a character, your friend, huh?'

'She certainly is, Vera. Oh, yes, she certainly is.'

'There'll be some characters in the bar tonight that she'd love to write about.'

'Write about?'

'Sure, she likes to write some.'

'She does?'

'Sure. I seen her scribbling away for hours this morning over in Annie Sue's.'

I can feel myself going cold inside.

'Gosh?'

'I was in there jawing away this morning. She was there too. We talked a while.'

'Really?'

'Didn't want to disturb her none. Looked like she was in another world!' She takes the cigarette out of her mouth and chuckles. She starts talking about some of the people who frequent the Thunderbird, only I'm not listening. I can feel this blast of anger rushing through me and I'm trying to keep a lid on it. I've been trying to let the whole diary business of Billie's go, trying not to think about it. I know she needs her secret place and if I'm writing my 'Breakfast in America' story there's no reason she can't write about her babysitter and her waitress friend Leah. It's just the pretence that gets me. I mean, does she think I'm a chump? Does she think I don't know? Sometimes she tears neat strips out of the floral notepad and lets me see them. She pretends she doesn't want me to see them but I know she's just being tactical – so that I don't try to look at the ones that she writes and never burns.

I've tried to ignore the signs – the fact that the dream house in her head is a shambles, the fact that she's talking more and more about her useless mother and her bullying stepfather. The fact that she keeps going off for mysterious 'walks' and 'drives' on her own and you never know what mood she'll be in when she comes back. This morning, for instance, she told me she was going for a drive. At six twenty-five, she picked up her bag and the SUV keys, marched to the door and announced she needed some fresh air.

The rapid exit wasn't due to anything that happened between

us in the bed. The grand sharing-of-the-same-bed turned out to be a damp squib if ever there was one. We were both exhausted from the long drive and fell asleep quite early that evening. Then, in the early hours of the morning, I was woken by the violent rocking motion of Billie's disco damage, which seemed to be even worse than usual. I looked over at her, tossing and turning on damp pillows, but even then I couldn't work out what was going on. You couldn't tell if she was asleep or just pretending to be asleep. There was sweat all over her. I could feel it. Smell it. The fruity ashtray next to me. The sizzling sherbet. The sheets were drenched. She was moaning, and then I saw the hand under the blankets. Moving and rubbing. She was bloody wanking off! She was pounding and tossing and sniffing away ten to the dozen – with her eyes closed. But was it really wanking? Was it sleep-walker wanking? The grand conjunction of a nightmare and a king-size jerk-off? Did she know what she was doing? Did she want me to join in?

I moved closer to the dampness just in case she did. I didn't care. I was going to burst if something didn't happen soon and this seemed as good a time as any to consummate our relation-ship. So I got closer and closer and as I got closer I heard her muttering, 'No! Put out the fire! Stop the fire!'

That was encouragement enough for me. I'd put her fire out all right! And so I put my arm under the blankets and touched her. Fuck! I touched her leg and it was sopping wet – bad dream wet, not wet dream bad. But it was also soft and hot and my hand seemed to melt into the slippery flesh. The puppet-on-a-string thing happened. The wetness made my nipples harden, the heat from her skin set my crotch on fire.

It was perverse of me, I admit it. I knew very well that what-ever was going on in the house in her head, it wasn't pleasant. I could smell the fear – it was being whisked up under the bedclothes – some sort of cold fry-up. Raw kidneys. A butcher's shop mixed with the cement dust. And the sherbet coming through her skin. Some sort of trauma smell in any case. We'd already had a conversation about fear, about how it's less of a burning smell than pain and more of an acrid smell than sex. She said that fear had the icy, synthetic taste of a prepacked sandwich bought at three in the morning in a gas station as a break from a night of selling cocaine.

And yet still I kept contact with the slippery leg. My body slipped over hers by dint of my hand and a desperate imagination. I was gazing down at her face, at her delectable, troubled face. My own face was centimetres from hers, I wanted to breathe her in, breathe in everything about her – her fear, her sweat, her dream place, her pain – and then, all of a sudden, her eyes snapped open. She wasn't properly awake, though. Her eyes were bulging out of her head like the shrieking black train tunnel in Van Horn. Except that in Van Horn you knew that the train would re-emerge and normality would resume but with Billie, right then, you couldn't be sure that normality would ever resume.

She sat bolt upright. Her face was pale and drenched. She couldn't speak, only hyperventilate. There was just the frightened black eyes and the panic breathing and the sound in the background of a woman on TV gabbling hysterically, 'He called me from the hundred and fourth floor and then the line went dead . . . I know that with God's help I'm going to find him alive . . .'

And then Billie started to speak. Once she started, she couldn't stop. 'It was terrible. There was this war going on in my dream place. There were these men with knives cutting off children's heads and pulling out old ladies' fingernails and people were screaming and there was smoke and gunfire and at the transport dock people were trying to get on a train but it was burning down. And the sky was filled with German shepherd dogs with lizard faces. And then there were all these gayboys putting on their makeup ready to go to a party. And I was saying, "But you can't go to a party, something terrible is happening." And they were just like, "Relax, girl, you can't miss a party!" and I was just screaming at them. Screaming and screaming.'

When I told her that it was probably noise from the TV that had affected her sleep, she became furious. She stormed out of bed, went to her pile of clothes and pulled them on. She snatched up the gold bag and went to the door. She was going for a drive, she announced. She said something about needing some space to think. She said that she'd see me the next afternoon in the Thunderbird. Then the door slammed and there was just the sound of the TV. 'We got into the street and when I turned round he was gone. I was, like, "Did he really exist? Was he, like, a guardian angel or something?"'

Vera points a waggling finger at Bud. She tells him off about some other chore he hasn't done so I leave her before she starts informing me about any other unexpected Billie sightings. I concentrate on my mission to pick up our passports for Clara, although I can't stop a voice coming into my head saying, 'Something's going on with Billie, Mo Snow, and what are you going to do about it?'

But by the time I get back to the room, I've made up my mind. I decide to let it go – Billie and her secret writings. She can write what she wants. It's probably good for her to get it out of her system. The big sink bonfire is sure to come soon. It will all go up in a mass of flames and, as usual, I'll be the one to clean up the smuts the next morning.

So I pick up the passports and as I walk back to the Thunderbird I also resolve to put a stop to the jealousy I some-times feel about her. After all, it's inevitable that people will be dazzled by her. Actually, I don't think it is jealousy. I think it's more like envy. That I want to be like Billie, have her charisma. Yes, I think this is the best tack to take: concentrate on how other people react to Billie – to Ruby Rose, to be precise – be proud of that and concentrate on the imminent 'trick' in Carlota.

When I get back to the table she looks straight through me as if she couldn't care whether I was there or not. Then Clara comes over and glances at the passports. 'One Rolling Rock coming up, you guys,' she says. She winks at Billie and says, 'You got this one well trained!' and I try my best not to feel like a lemon. When she's gone, Billie finally speaks. She says she reckons Clara's a Blue Book case.

'A what?'

'The Blue Book. You know. Alcoholics Anonymous?'

'What's the Blue Book?'

'Like the Bible,' she says. 'It's the book you have to follow for the Twelve Steps.'

'But why do you think she's one of them?'

She shrugs. 'They get kind of prudish, ex-alcoholics.'

'Maybe she's just being a good waitress,' I suggest.

'Yeah, what do I know?' Billie snaps, scraping her chair back suddenly, saying that she needs to be alone.

When Clara comes back with the beer and our food – two plates of chicken burrito with refried beans – she asks where Billie's gone and I tell her that she's just gone for a sleep. 'Can't take the pace!' I say, with what I hope is a beam, but I don't think Clara gets my sense of humour. She looks over to the door and says she hopes Billie's OK.

I decide to be relieved that Billie's gone off. I transform her into the two burritos on my plate that I push disconsolately around wondering what to do about the food and money wastage.

My thoughts are interrupted by a twangy voice, saying, 'You an outta-towner?' It's coming from a young girl with cow eyes and milky skin sitting at the next table, holding a plump baby. She has a sweet smile and I invite her to join me at my table, thinking that it's time for me to make some friends independently of Billie. Her conversation is bland – 'Yeah, it's real beautiful round here, huh? Me and my husband, we come whenever we can' – and we're soon joined by another woman, a divorcée who introduces herself as Diane. She wears denim shorts with hemmed bottoms, white socks and trainers and one of the poodle haircuts. 'Hey there, y'all,' she says, coming over. 'Clara tells me you're from London, England.'

Diane is about as interesting as Jackie but, nevertheless, I try to appear enthusiastic. She says that she came to Lariat with her alimony money. 'Sold my house in Austin, Texas, bought a red setter and a global positioning system and moved right on out here. It was Clara turned me on to the place. We went to school together.'

'Did you really?'

'Sure. I count myself as blessed. I spend my days hiking. You been to the waterfall yet?'

I shake my head.

'Oh, you gotta go to the waterfall. There's kind of like a suspension bridge that runs over some rapids.'

'Really! We're heading to Carlota.'

'You be careful of the Barnard road,' she warns. 'Not one of the switchbacks has guard rails.'

She adds that she hopes I'm not scared of heights because Carlota is located nearly seven thousand feet up in the air. 'Still,' she says, 'it's worth the ride. You'll be able to see the Wilderness.'

'What's the Wilderness?'

'It's five hundred thousand acres of prehistoric forest.'

'I see.'

'Carlota is just incredible. During the heyday of the mines, the population was estimated at two thousand people. There were seven saloons and two red-light districts for starters!'

'You don't say.'

'Geronimo roamed there too.'

'Yes, I—'

'It's kind of quiet now. I wouldn't go without my GPS.'

When I ask her why she looks at me, incredulous.

'Sweetheart! A global positioning system is a worldwide radio-navigation system formed from a constellation of twenty-four satellites and their ground stations. A GPS can calculate positions accurate to a matter of meters!'

'I see.'

'You know where you are in the world with a GPS.'

'I'm sure.'

'In fact, with advanced forms of GPS you can make measurements to better than a centimetre!'

'Never go off the rails with a global positioning system, then!' I say to Diane, trying to inject some levity into proceedings.

She gives me a blank look.

'Never find yourself in the dark night of the soul . . .'

'Pardon me?'

'"The Cloud of Unknowing."'

'You've lost me, hon.'

'People like the idea of knowing where they are—'

She cuts me off with a 'Mo, sweetheart, these critters are serious things. Knowing the precise location of something, or someone, is especially critical when the consequences of inaccurate data are measured in human terms.'

'I see.'

I can't work out if everyone is incredibly dull or if it's just that Billie isn't there. When I go back to our room there's a note saying, 'Taken car, back later,' but I can't be bothered to get worked up. I lie down on the bed and decide that I'm exhausted from the long-term effects of driving from New Orleans and that's the reason I've been obsessing so much about her.

I'm not a lesbian, if that's what you're thinking. I just like Billie, that's all. Do you see a blazer with brass buttons? No, you don't. Do you see a Martina Navratilova haircut? No, you don't. You see before you a scruffy woman in jeans and a lumberjack shirt and . . . Let's call it a crush.

I can't deny that I have had sexual fantasies about women in the past. I think most women have. My fantasies are usually headless, although the hair is usually blonde and the bodies all have big breasts. Sometimes I get a bit disturbed about this. I worry I'm approaching the whole issue like a man.

I've often wondered what it would be like to do it with a friend. There are times when you leave a party and the girls you're with are drunk and they kiss you goodbye on the lips. Sometimes they've got their eyes open and they'll be looking at you when they kiss you. But the next day, if they touch on it at all, they'll just say something like, 'Funny when you're drunk. You'll snog anything – you'd chew off your dog's ear!'

I snogged Muriel.

I know.

A proper snog it was as well. I thought it would be better to do it with her. I thought it'd be easier than to go to a gay bar and chat up a lesbian. From scratch. I didn't even know of any gay bars. There was just Duncan and his cronies. And 'the parties' that they were always giggling about. I'm not even sure I want to do it with a lesbian anyway. I'd rather have one of those women who got married by mistake. Or one of those sexual tourists. I wouldn't mind trying out one of them.

So far, all I've managed is Muriel.

I ended up seeing a fair amount of her. She was only too pleased to give me some journalism coaching – for what it was worth. I can't deny that I liked her perversity. It interested me how quickly she could switch from talking her nonsense ('Happy as a pig in shit, you are, when you've come up with a good stand-first!') to grabbing my leg under the table and hissing in my ear, 'Animal, vegetable or mineral. That's me!'

I'd leave her hand there for a while, looking over the notes I'd written in my exercise book, pretending I hadn't noticed anything, and she'd wrinkle her nose in a way she thought fetching. She wasn't fetching at all – so it was strange how I often got the urge to claw her breasts like a sixteen-year-old virgin man or jump on her body and ride her like a bucking bronco.

I made her wait, though.

One day she asked me if I'd like to go for a drive with her to Castle Howard in North Yorkshire – the place where they made *Brideshead Revisited*. She was over the moon when I said yes, and when she arrived to pick me up she'd obviously picked a scab off the side of her mouth especially for the occasion. You could see it had bled a bit. There was still some tissue on the ripped skin where she must have dabbed it with a Kleenex. I didn't say anything, though, and we set off on a journey punctuated with her gasping, 'Blinding day, we're going to have! Blinding!' Her self-belief was incredible. She squeezed my knee. 'Happy as a pig in shit, I am!' she said. I winced then. I know it was snobby of me, but I said that maybe she could think of some more choice phrases to use than 'happy as a pig in shit' all the time. I said, 'What about "happy as a lord" or "happy as – as a peacock"?'

She said, 'Bloody peacocks. There was an old peacock in the village. Beautiful he was. Some twat ran him over. Flat as a bloody pancake.'

You couldn't help but laugh. At least she was straightforward. At least she seemed to know what she wanted. Unlike Gary. The secret, though, with Muriel was not to get too much of her. That could seriously do your head in and, unfortunately, I hadn't reckoned on how long the trip to Castle Howard would take. I was ready to wallop her one by the end of it. Everything she did, everything she saw, she kept saying it felt like she was 'having an orgasm'. She was still screeching in her broken-glass voice about how she was 'having an orgasm' as we walked into this posh restaurant she'd reserved for lunch. Well, I say posh. The place was just like the Bateau Ivre – all cheap balsamic vinegar and 'exotic' lettuce leaves that don't taste any better than the stuff you get in bags from Sainsbury's. If you were lucky one of the snooty gayboy waiters would take a shine to you; if not, you never got the bread roll you asked for.

We didn't get any bread because the waiters didn't take a shine to Muriel. Not that she seemed to notice. She was in her element. 'I don't normally eat properly,' she squawked. 'I starve myself and then stuff myself. Could transport myself round Scarborough on farts!'

We ended up with two plates of warm *foie gras* for starters –

over-rich and cloying as Muriel's attentions. She said some good things, like 'You're gorgeous,' and 'You're perfect for me,' but it's funny how adulation can make you feel lonely. You're overflowing with being loved, you're being given so much worship and attention, but all you can think is how depressing it feels to sit in a muggy restaurant watching a woman with dead eyes dying for a shag with you.

She started saying all those things that drunk people say: 'I'm so happy' (deep sigh) or 'Wow, I'm so lucky . . .' (deep sigh). And I just sat there looking at her crispy hair and her glinting glasses and her eyes the colour of clouded water. I was looking for some kind of life in them and maybe she thought it was a significant stare. She suddenly said, 'I love you, Mo.'

'I love you, Mo.' In that terrible voice. 'I love you, Mo' from Muriel was even worse than another helping of *foie gras*. I speared the remains of my liver and smeared it round my plate, pretending I hadn't heard. She carried on smiling but the bottom of her left cheek was twitching so you knew that she didn't want to smile at all. She had no idea how ridiculous she looked. It was almost fascinating. She was like that sad woman from *Jaws* – the mother of the first little boy to be killed by the shark. First you see blood in the water, then everyone begins to scream and run around the beach looking for their loved ones. But gradually the camera focuses on the sad woman, on her pitiful plain head, bobbing round the beach like a nodding dog in the back of a car. You just knew that the goner was going to be her son because she was a bit overweight and a bit ugly and even her ridiculous sunhat made you want to cry as she rushed hopelessly into the water awash with bits and bobs from her son's mulched-up body. That was the last thing she needed, you thought, as sadness slithered down all over you.

Muriel's phoney smile twitched away. I wondered how long before it dropped off, like a slit throat with all the blood drained out. Suddenly I wondered what she'd look like if I told her that she was pathetic, that I found her a joke. I felt like saying it. It was a rush. I thought of all the things I could say to her right then, to crush her, to turn her face into a shattered mirror along with that stupid voice of hers. I wondered what I could do to make her go home that night and crouch down in a ball and shut her eyes tight and cry so much that her eyes would be red instead of dead. It was like the rush I get when, for the thrill of a split second, I want to jump off the top of a building, or chuck a boat of hot gravy over one of my nicest customers at the Sceptre or pull Billie to my breasts and dissolve into her lips as a thousand towers come crashing down on our heads.

CHAPTER THIRTEEN

Doris Day Throws One

The door slams and Billie breezes in.

'Wake up, Peachy Peach!' she says, bouncing on to the bed. 'Plenty of time to sleep when you're dead!'

I rub my eyes. 'What put you in such a good mood?'

'Friends!' she says.

'Friends?'

'Friends!'

'Are you OK?'

She strides over to the TV and picks up the zapper. 'The new fall schedules. They start tonight. *Ally McBeal* should be on later too.'

But there are no sitcoms anywhere. Every channel is filled with Twin Towers coverage. Billie flicks from one channel to the next. From crashing planes and fireballs to decimated skyscapes to ant-sized people jumping from burning towers, to dazed anchormen talking of heroes and freedom and evil, to Twin Towers workers covered in grey snow saying, in dazed voices, 'Someone lifted me out like Superman.'

'Fuck this,' she says.

I rather like the story of the Twin Towers worker who managed to run from the building and was saved from blindness by having a can of iced tea in his briefcase that he washed over the burning ashes. (He'd bought it that morning in Staten Island because it was cheaper there than in Manhattan.) Billie's not impressed, though, so we walk over to the Thunderbird. Inside, Vera is hunched on a stool behind the bar, smoking a cigarette and holding a shot of something. In front of the bar are Clara the waitress and her friend, Diane, and beside them is Vera's husband, cradling a plump baby. The mother, the bland woman, sits huddled in a corner of the room weeping into her striped red pyjamas.

Vera looks pleased to see us. 'Good to see you girls made it!' she says, thumping the bar. She asks us what we'd like to drink and Billie orders tequila for both of us. Diane starts to regale Billie with tales of her GPS while I ask Vera if the crying woman is OK. Vera rolls her eyes and says, 'Same old, same old,' and then Billie turns back from Diane and whispers, 'Another freak with a global positioning system. As if that's going to put her somewhere in the world. Guess what, hon, you're out to lunch and there's no going home!'

We both snigger and I start to relax. The old Billie seems to have returned. It looks as though we're going to have a good night, after all.

'Let's get really hammered?' Billie says, to nobody in particular, slugging back her tequila.

'You go, girl!' Vera says, downing her whisky in a few gulps. 'They say that the beginning's one half of the deed.'

Clara prods Diane with her Diet Coke and tells her that Billie was the one who reminded her of her election as homecoming princess.

'Do you think we should tell her?' Diane winks at her friend.

Clara winks back. 'I think we should!'

So Diane turns to Billie and says, 'Well, prepare to turn green, but I was voted homecoming queen that very year!' Diane and Clara turn to each other and make one of those American-style whoops followed by a high five. As they dissolve in a haze of cackling and chortling and 'oh, my!', Billie turns to me and hisses, 'Oh, my God! They're *both* like my mother!' While Clara and Diane reminisce about their days as the chosen ones of their Texas high schools, Billie fills me in on how American schools work: you go to high school aged fourteen when you're known as a freshman; when you get to be fifteen you're a sophomore. When you're sixteen you're a junior, and

in your final year, aged seventeen, you're known as a 'senior'.
In May you have the prom where the class votes for 'the queen'
but the best party of all is in November to celebrate the end
of the football season. It's known as the Homecoming Ball and
it ends in a finale where the students get to vote for 'kings',
'queens', 'princes' and 'princesses'. The homecoming queen is
the most prestigious title. Usually the girls are good-looking
and the boys are sporty, but the most important thing is to be
popular.

The obsession with being popular doesn't stop there. The
students who go on to university will pass sleepless nights waiting
to be invited to join a variety of gangs or 'sororities' (for girls)
and 'fraternities' (for boys).

Billie tells Diane and Clara, 'My mom was always being voted
Queen this and Princess that. I was never good enough to be a
homecoming anything . . .'

Both of them cry, 'Shame!'

'Neither was I, Ruby Rose, hon,' Vera confides. 'You and me
are what they call "individuals".'

'Really? That wasn't the word they used for me at school.'

The women laugh and Clara urges Diane to tell us about when
she dated George W. Bush. Diane looks bewildered and says she
can't remember much about him. 'I seem to remember he was
gallant, though. He held doors open lots.'

'Diane was with me in Chi Omega,' says Clara. 'We got up
to some adventures, huh?'

'I even nearly got a job one time!' Diane exclaims, as though
this is something surprising. 'My friend's dad, Mr Johnson, was
head of an airline company. Her mom was the heiress of this
big Texas ranch. I mean, they were serious money.'

'Didn't they have a chapel in their house?' Clara asks, goading
her friend.

'Yeah but I don't think Mr Johnson ever used it.'

Chuckles.

I can see Billie's lips twitching and then she proposes a toast:

'To all cheer-leaders and homecoming queens: the royalty of America.'

Everyone chinks glasses.

'Shame how I ended up being a waitress.' Clara sighs, taking a sip of her Diet Coke. (It seems that Billie was right about the Blue Book.)

'Nothing wrong with being a waitress,' Billie tells her.

'I guess not,' Clara sighs.

'Waitressing, stripping, acting,' Billie says. 'It's all the same.'

'All the same?' Clara looks puzzled.

'Yeah. Hooking too. It's all the same.'

'How do you mean?'

'It's all make-believe.'

'Will someone tell me what in hell we're talking about?' Clara frowns.

Billie smiles. 'They all provide people with false pleasure, Clara. Pleasure that doesn't come from the heart.'

'Ain't that the truth?' Vera says, knocking back her shot.

When Clara asks her what her job is, Billie hesitates for a moment. Then she replies, 'I'm a dominatrix.'

Silence.

Diane's face tightens. 'Well . . .'

Clara's crow's feet deepen.

'You are . . .?'

Billie bursts out laughing. 'Not really,' she says.

'I was going to say . . .' You can hear the relief in Clara's voice.

'Yeah,' Diane says. 'That'd be pretty bad!'

'I'm sorry, you guys,' Billie says. 'Didn't want to shock you.'

'What do you do really?' Clara persists.

Billie tells them that she's a nanny. They seem to swallow that one, although Clara wants to know, 'How comes you know about . . . all that stuff?'

'I did this dance course once,' Billie tells her. I try to keep a straight face. 'I met a lot of interesting people.'

'You mean lap-dancing?' Diane asks, her eyes shining.

'Yeah.' Billie shrugs.

'Shoot!' Diane exclaims. 'That's like me. I did one of those courses too.'

'She sure did!' Clara says, looking proudly at her friend.

'I read it in one of the papers,' Diane pants. 'About pole-dancing and lap-dancing being the new form of exercise?'

'Well, I'll be . . .' says Billie, getting down from the bar stool and moving to the sound of Elvis on the juke-box. 'How's about we start a bordello?'

Vera, Diane and Clara stare at her as though they haven't quite heard her right.

'We gotta beat the market, though,' Billie goes on. 'We gotta have different things to offer. Like lesbian virgins.'

'What's that?'

'Lesbians that never slept with a man.'

'Men'd like that?'

'Sure they would.'

'What else?'

'I once knew a man who paid to watch girls get their hair shaved off.'

'Get outta here, Ruby Rose!'

'He tipped them extra if they cried.'

A rumpled chorus of 'Sheee-it' and 'Maaan!'

Billie knocks back another tequila. 'Then we'd start with a little dancing for the gents.'

Her hips start to sway.

'Go on, hon.' Diane nods. 'You show me what they taught you.' She turns to Clara. 'Reckon she'll be able to show me some new moves.'

'Reckon she will,' Clara agrees.

'You gonna put some more music on?' Diane asks. 'How about "Erotica" by Madonna? That's the one we do in class.'

'"Erotica" is such a great turning tune,' Billie says. 'I don't know what we did before it came out. Oh, there was Roxy Music, of course. Avalon was big . . .'

'How about "Slave To Love"?' Clara chips in.

Billie wrinkles her nose. 'That's for those cheesy love-sex things. When they want you to be all pretty.' The hips turn on a wider and wider circle. 'Uuugh, I don't want to think about that,' she says, closing her eyes.

Billie is pretty wasted by this time. I think she's probably forgotten where she is. Clara and Diane look puzzled by the references to 'turning tunes' and 'cheesy love-sex things'. But Billie just looks at me and asks me to put some better music on the juke-box. '"Personal Jesus" by Depeche Mode if they got it,' she says, turning back to the audience of Vera, Diane, Clara and Vera's husband (who has been dumbstruck for a while now). 'I call this one the "Nanny Wind",' she says, revolving round harder. 'Nanny's your kooch . . . so my teacher told me. Idea is to twist round and round so you draw a circle with your pussy.'

I'm standing by the juke-box now. I watch her bum, her fantastically obscene bum.

'I always liked "You Can Keep Your Hat On",' Vera's husband murmurs over the plump baby's shoulder.

'Oh, shame on you!' Billie coos, sending a red rash into his cheeks. 'That is *such* a strippergram song.'

Billie's swaying is becoming more interesting. Vera's husband shoves the baby to one side to get a better view.

'Holy shit,' he says, his mouth wide open. 'That's an evil thing to do to an old man.'

Billie stares at him, and he responds by jogging the baby up and down on his lap very fast.

'If you can look into the eyes of someone in the audience then you don't have to do too much dancing,' she tells us. 'Also, you have to make sure you do it real slow. My first strip, I went on stage and I'd done all my tricks in forty-five seconds. I still had four minutes left. There are about ten stripper tricks and you only need to do about five in the course of one show.'

She starts off on another Nanny Wind.

'Maybe I'm gonna take some of those classes of yours,' Clara says, mesmerised.

Billie slurs, 'Why, thanks, Mom,' then stops dead. Confusion floods into her eyes.

'Mom?' Diane chuckles, looking at Clara. 'She look that old!'

'Sorry,' Billie mumbles. She frowns and returns quickly to the bar stool.

'You forget guys' names as quick as that too?' Clara snaps.

But I can see that Billie isn't joking any more. She sits on the bar stool clutching her tequila glass. Clara starts to look concerned and goes to put her arm round Billie's shoulders. 'You OK, Ruby Rose, hon?' she asks.

'Aw, c'mon sweetheart,' Vera says, topping up Billie's glass. 'You can call that there Clara anything you like. She's not as good as she might be neither!'

Billie looks shy now. She knocks back the tequila shot, then shoves her hand forward for another. 'Sorry, Clara,' she says quietly. 'I was forgetting myself there. The guys in my amateur-dramatics group are always bagging on me for that.'

Clara raises an eyebrow. 'You do acting classes, too?'

'Oh, she's good,' I tell them. I'm pretty drunk myself. 'You really should see her up on stage.'

'On stage!' Diane and Clara chorus.

'Performing in public is the greatest high in the word,' Billie says, warming up again.

Clara and Diane look impressed.

'It's the hugest drug I ever had in my life. It's like the ego boost of meeting a guy and digging him and then actually scoring with him. It's like that but times a thousand.'

There's a murmur of approval. Clara asks her how she first knew she liked to perform.

'Show off, you mean?' she says, with a smile. 'I was telling Mo about this book I read as a kid. About a nineteenth-century French courtesan called Nana.'

'A what?'

'A hooker.'

'Nineteenth-century, huh?' Diane puts a hand on a hip.

'The point about Nana is that she had no talent but it didn't matter. She got up on stage and threw her arms out and did her thing. It's the same with me.'

'You should get her to do her Christmas show,' I say, enjoying it when Billie gives me a double-take.

'Christmas show?' Vera squints through her glasses. She chucks back another shot.

'For her children . . . her nanny charges, you know.'

'What kind of show?'

I try to get it right: 'A Doris Day-Courtney Love schizophrenic striptease!'

'Say what?' Diane splutters into her gin and tonic.

'Sounds weird for kids,' says Clara.

'Sounds good to me,' Vera says.

Billie picks up her glass and struts over to the pool table. She slots some coins into the side and a line of coloured balls comes tumbling out. She settles herself into position. She must know we're all watching her. She spreads her legs wide apart, sticks her bum out and takes picturesque aim with the cue.

'You want to do your show for us, then, Ruby Rose?' Vera asks.

'Yeah, come on,' Clara and Diane chime in. 'Do us your show!'

Billie shoots and the triangle of coloured balls ricochets over the table. Then the bar door bursts open and a man with a beer gut wearing a Stetson staggers in, yelling, 'I want him back! I want ma boy back!' He lunges at Bud, who whips the plump baby back from his clutches as the weeping mother in pyjamas starts to whimper.

'You're an unfit mother!' the man shouts at her.

Whimper.

'Look at her there, unfit mother!'

Sob.

'Gimme back ma boy!'

While Vera, Clara and Diane get caught up in the kerfuffle at the bar I stagger over to the pool table to remind Billie about the Carlota trick.

'You still on about that?' she says, taking aim.

'Of course.'

She looks so great sprawled all over the table. She hits a purple ball into a pocket. Everything she does is effortless.

'C'mon, then,' she says. She stands back from the table, leaning on her cue.

'What?'

'Let's call the freak up.'

'Are you serious?'

She doesn't even bother replying.

'But what about the number?'

She taps an index finger to her forehead.

'You remembered it!' I'm ridiculously over-excited by this time.

She raises an eyebrow. 'Like Vera said, "The beginning is one half of the deed."'

We go over to the pay-phone and Billie starts to dial the number. She stops and hangs up. She turns to me with a frown and says, 'I'm only doing light BDSM, you know.'

'And . . . that is?'

She makes an exasperated sigh. 'Bondage, discipline, sado-masochism.'

'Oh, right.'

She picks up the phone again.

'And what's the difference between discipline and sadism?'

'You can discipline someone without being sadistic about it,' she mutters, preparing to dial. 'Discipline's not always about pain.'

'What's it about, then?'

'Obedience. You do what I tell you and you say, "Yes, ma'am."' She hesitates before touching the keys on the phone. 'He's probably going to be a fucking masochist.'

'What's wrong with masochism?'

'It's about people getting off on being called a worthless piece of shit. Not my kink, personally.'

The light in the bar by this time is just a blur of red and green and I can feel the Midas touch flowing back into me. Fuck 'Breakfast in America!' Fuck bacon and grits and *chorizo con huevos*! Fuck journalism! Fuck writing! Fuck everything and live for the moment!

Over at the bar they're going at it hammer and tongs. The beer-gut man is still hollering, 'Gimme ma boy!' but even louder now, while the mother in pyjamas whimpers away and the baby, caught in a tussle between Vera, Vera's husband and the beer-gut man, screams the house down.

Billie takes a deep breath and starts to dial. 'You'd better fucking appreciate this,' she says. She sounds almost sober, and when she glances at me quickly, she suddenly seems very young.

I'm not sure what I'm supposed to say. 'Just be Ruby Rose,' I tell her.

She turns sharply away as if I've disappointed her again. 'You know what I think, Mo?' she says. 'I think you're a latent sadist.'

I hear the phone ringing in Carlota. Her mouth hardens as it continues to ring. 'He'd better not ask me for Greek either,' she mumbles.

'Greek?'

'Catholics think they haven't cheated on their wives if they do it up the ass.'

'Really?'

'Whatever.'

She says this with a cynical emphasis on the *ever*. The transformation is complete. Ruby Rose has returned.

The phone clicks. Silence. Then a man's voice saying, 'Hello?'

'Hello. My name's Ruby Rose. I read your ad in the *Explorer* and thought you might want to play.'

She's off. Her Ruby Rose voice sounds so bizarre now that I know her. It sounds so fake. So sexy fake. I nearly laugh. I nuzzle nearer to her ear. I pretend I can't hear anything so I have to get even closer. The tequila has more than done the work on me by now. I grab her thighs, paw her shoulders, dribble nonsense into her ear: 'Fuck breakfast! Ruby Rose is worth more than twenty plates of refried beans!'

'Why, yes . . . yes, I do remember an ad I placed in that paper.' His voice sounds old on the other end of the line.

She's smiling now. She's pushing me from her. I can tell she doesn't want to, though. For a dominatrix, she's giving me wimpy little shoves.

'Ruby Rose is worth fifty rounds of toast! She's worth sixty-eight and a half tubs of complementary maple syrup . . .'

And then, finally, I can't help it. A guffaw flies from my mouth and I'm punished with a firm shove that sends me skidding across the floor. It's fantastic, though, it's funny. I put my arms out like I'm flying and then I turn the move into a dance by the pool table. All I'm aware of now is low light and red and green flashes and being invincible to everything, to pain and love and light and hurt, and everyone adores me and I know that Billie will do anything for me – I saw that look in her face, it came to me in a flash, I have power, too, she will do this thing for me. The night in Van Horn flashes before my eyes again. The pussy, the gnarled joint of beef, the stings on the back of my hand, the flesh zip over my body.

I skid back a bit closer to the phone and hear her talking slowly and calmly, in hushed, velvety tones – a cross between a stern waitress and strict nanny.

'. . . that depends what kind of scene you're interested in.'

She is even standing differently now that she's Ruby Rose again. She's taller, more confident. As she listens to 'the freak', her lips become taut and her jaw sturdy. The conversation seems to go on for a while. Long silences are punctuated by Billie going, 'Yes, that will be extra,' and 'OK, that can be arranged,' and 'Do you have your own cleaning materials?'

The tussle at the bar is entering orbit. A sheriff has now come into the premises. He's trying to put handcuffs on the beer-gut man as the beer-gut man hollers, 'Gimme back ma boy!' and the woman in pyjamas whimpers and the plump baby screams and they're all ineffectual, so ineffectual; nobody knows how to do anything right in the whole world apart from Ruby Rose.

'You are drunk and disorderly,' the sheriff puffs. 'You will come with me.'

'What kind a mother you think she is? Comin' to a joint like this with a baby!'

'He bin drinkin' all night. I had come out find him!'

'You are drunk and disorderly! You will come with me!'

Then everything is a blur. The Thunderbird is a smudged blur of lipstick and I am on the verge of going over to the phone and putting my hand up Billie's skirt when I hear Diane calling to me. She's saying, 'Mo, hon, why don't you go get Ruby Rose her cabaret costume so she can do that show of hers?'

And it's me she's asking for this favour. I am a cog in the wheel, I am needed after all, and everything is perfect.

Outside there is deep silence accompanied by cicadas, the occasional cat on a corrugated-iron roof and the buzzing of the electric wires above. The fresh air clears my head a little and when I get back to the room I pour myself a glass of warm tap water, sit on the bed and try to gather my thoughts. My eyes fix on the drag bag, the open drag bag. I go over to it and rummage around, trying to remember what accessories Billie told me she needed for this act. I locate a corner of the pink gingham dress, some laces from a black corset, some trailer-trash cut-offs, some fishnets, the fanged head of the Devil Barbie. I pull them all out. It takes me a while to locate the bottle of stage Valium because there are several plastic pill containers in the bag. There are a few small filled envelopes, too, that I come across before finding the larger envelope filled with what I presume is Sweet and Lo and marked 'Cocaine'.

I don't have much time to ponder the significance of these finds because, next to the doll's severed body, I see something that sets my heart racing: Billie's gold bag. Billie has never left this bag unattended, apart from that time in Dougal's Smokehouse, and yet now here it is inside the drag bag. Inside the gold bag is something I know I should leave well alone.

I try to ignore it. I concentrate on a three-inch cockroach crouched on the cheap brown carpet by a piece of half-chewed teriyaki jerky next to the Roach Motel. It's rubbing its feelers together, chafing its hairy thorax, thrilling to the smells of mucus and rotting organs and green cheese that waft enticingly through the garage doors as it prepares to walk unsuspectingly to a dark and sticky death.

The gold bag smells tempting too. I peek inside and there it is: the floral cover stares up at me, inviting me to look and feel. I know it'll be bad if I touch it and yet I want so much to touch it. I want to open it and look inside and see what she's been writing in it so manically and so secretively these past few days. Then I think of Vera, who says that the beginning is one half of the deed, and I do touch it. I put my hand inside the gold bag and I take it out. I open it and it is bad. There's a humming in my head.

'You're under arrest, buddy!'

Things have moved on in the Battle of the Thunderbird. The sheriff has placed cuffs on the beer-gut man and now he's trying to push him out of the door as the man shouts, 'Gimme back ma boy!' one last time.

Billie's off the phone. I'm worried she's going to ask me why I've been gone for so long. She doesn't, though. She's in eager conversation with Vera. 'You know the curtains in our room?' she's saying.

'Those chintzy old things?'

'Those are the ones.'

'What about 'em?'

'I need the gold braid.'

'Huh?'

'Don't worry. You'll have it back by nightfall.'

Billie winks when she sees me behind her. 'Think the sheriff'd lend me his cuffs too, Mo?'

'I—'

'What have you been up to!' she demands, suddenly. 'Don't think you can get away with it!'

I freeze in my tracks until Clara whoops, 'Look at that face! Now, there's a guilty conscience!'

Everyone laughs and I realise they're just drunk and being silly. The others have obviously convinced Billie to do the Doris Day-Courtney Love striptease (and topped her up on the Dutch-courage front, judging by a half-empty tumbler of tequila in her hand) because she grabs the bundle of things from under my arm and plants a kiss on my cheek. 'Thanks, Peachy,' she says. 'You're sweet!' She turns to the line of women at the bar and hisses, almost hysterically, 'How sweet is this girl!' whereupon Vera, Clara and Diane all start doing the American whoop thing and cheering and saying that, yes, I certainly am sweet and fantastic.

And, of course, now is completely the wrong time to be nice to me because I feel shabby. Like I've had a peek at the Christmas presents before the big day and everything's gone stale. More to the point, I realise I'm surrounded by strangers and Billie is the biggest stranger of all.

When it starts, it frightens me. She walks out from the restroom dressed in the pink gingham frock and the bobbed blonde wig. She looks so suburban and mumsy that it's eerie. She mounts an upturned wooden crate that Vera has turned into a makeshift podium, taking care not to knock over the vodka bottle at her feet that's been filled with water. At a nod, Vera sets the CD mix in motion. Billie smiles sweetly, swaying from side to side in her Doris Day persona, lip-synching to a cosy version of 'Que Sera, Sera'. For a moment it seems as if this is going to be a run-of-the-mill drag show. The sheriff and his assistant have come back for a nightcap beer after the excitement of the domestic dispute, and they beam as they watch her mouth the cute words about how, when she was a little child, she asked her mother what her future would be.

They tap their fingers in time to the music as mumsy old Doris Day croons on, and then suddenly the track cuts sharply into raucous Courtney Love yelling furious, love-lorn lyrics, shrieking at someone to take everything, to steal everything away from her, daring them to leave her with nothing. Billie rips open the gingham dress to reveal the hooker fishnets and the black corset; she grabs hold of the bottle of vodka and starts chucking it down her throat in tune to a violent tirade, screaming the desperate command to take everything from her, to go on, take everything, to leave her with nothing. Then the music switches and the tormented Ruby Rose stops, looking shiftily at the audience as though she's been caught in the act of illicit masturbation. She wraps the pink dress around her hurriedly and carries on lip-synching 'Que Sera, Sera', mouthing sweetly about what she's going to do when she grows up. And then it comes again: the music rips savagely into Courtney Love and the deranged, twisted Doris comes back to life. She gulps down the rest of the vodka, she chucks a handful of Valium down her neck, she tears open the cocaine envelope, throws the contents all over her face and cleavage, then rips off the doll's head and pulls out the day-glo red and blue brains with such frenzy that I'm not sure this is play-acting any more. I think that maybe she's gone completely off the rails and as the Love music becomes slower she takes the vodka bottle and licks the rim suggestively, ominously. She trails it slowly over her breasts, her belly, her crotch. She thrusts against it as if she hates it, as if she couldn't care if she lived or died, as if she wants to die and yet she is still being sexual.

And then, with an almighty scratch, the music skips back to Doris Day – although Doris has obviously not fully recovered from her Courtney Love trip. Her eyes are wild as she wraps her dress round her and looks shiftily from side to side as if she's just been ravaged, although she ends the number with a cheesy smile, swaying from side to side with outstretched arms, singing the final line of 'Que Sera, Sera' for the grotesque finale.

Clara's mouth hangs to the ground. Diane starts fumbling in her bag as if her GPS might be able to explain what on earth is going on. The sheriff and his assistant seem unsure as to whether what they've just witnessed is an arrestable offence. Only Vera is bright-eyed. She shuffles over to the sweating, dazed Billie to congratulate her on whatever it was she just saw. Billie smiles weakly past her. She's looking over at me. Her eyes are young again. She wants something from me, I know that now, yet I can't give her anything. I'm still frozen from what I just read in her diary. The only thing that keeps coming through to me is the line from the Doris Day song when the little girl asks her mother what the future holds.

And I want to cry but I can't do that or I'll give the game away. So I drink. I drink and drink.

CHAPTER FOURTEEN

Dammed

Everything was in my mind but it was held in ice. And when the words started to burn their way through the ice I just drank more tequila and it stopped the ice from melting. The tequila kept most of it frozen and the yellow snake did the rest.

Besides, by the time we'd staggered out of the Thunderbird, what I'd read in the floral notebook didn't even seem real any more.

We were roaring drunk by then. In stitches, we were – about the beer-gut man and the sheriff, about Diane and her global positioning system and then about the Carlota trick with the retired sea captain. To start with, Billie was cagey about what had gone on in the phone conversation, but by the time we got back to our room she'd informed me that a limo would be coming to pick us up the next afternoon. When I asked what kind of trick it would be, she said, 'Bor-ing!' like a little kid might. She wouldn't stop being a kid. She was wild, utterly hyper, bouncing up and down on the bed.

'Wass bori'g?' (I could barely speak by that point.)

'Cleaning tricks!' she said, exasperated.

'Cleani' trick?'

'Yeah,' she said, still bouncing. 'You're, like, "Wash the floor with your tongue and mop it up with a Q-Tip or you'll get a heel in the chest!" And then you spit in his face and go, "And if it's not done properly you'll get a hiding you'll never forget!" And you come back in five minutes and he hasn't done it properly because he wants a hiding he'll never forget.'

She jumped down from the bed and from a pile of her rubble scattered over the brown carpet – makeup, Reese's Peanut Butter Cups, piles of frothy fabric, the ever-ripening pomegranate – she pulled out a white doctor's coat and a black whip with long thick strands of leather attached to a plaited handle. She started flicking it at the wall on the other side of the room: schlack! It came curling back to heel like a black lizard's tongue. Then she produced Clara's waitressing badge from her pocket and threw it up and down in the air. When I asked her why she'd got Clara's badge she just raised one eyebrow and said, 'Ask me no more questions, I'll tell you no more lies . . .' which was part of a rendition of a song she kept singing about Miss Suzy and her steamboat:

'Miss Suzy had a steamboat,
The steamboat had a bell,
Miss Suzy went to heaven,
The steamboat went to hell-o, operator, please give me
    number nine
And if you disconnect me I'll kick you in the behi-nd the
    'frigerator there is a piece of glass,
And if you don't believe you I'll kick you in the assss-k
    me no more questions,
I'll tell you no more lies . . .'

She collapsed on the floor in a burst of laughter as I slouched in a drunken stupor, my back propped up against the wall, staring at the Roach Motel, which kept going in and out of focus.

'Wha' makeup you g'n'wear?'

'My God, you're, like, so wasted!' She giggled, leaping to her feet. 'Oh, you know, something severe. I like the idea of some badly applied rouge, actually.'

She grabbed hold of the doctor's coat and slipped into it, stretching it tight over her breasts, then thrusting her chest forward. When she told me to come and pin her up I hardly noticed the effort of standing up, although as I held the pins I saw that my hands were shaking. When she leaned past me to grab the curtains and rip gold braid from the cheap brown fabric there were two warm breasts dangling in my face. Warm musky apples hanging from a tree – although it felt more like my nose was buried in a bag of glue, apple glue or a vat of synthetic perfume. Somehow I managed to carry on pinning as she stopped ripping and moved to a new position: bum stuck out, churning round and round in freestyle Nanny Winds as she shortened the coat with the scissor attachment of her penknife. She then took off the coat and cut open the side seams, lacing them together with gold braid, which could be pulled tighter. As she said, 'It's more Janet Jackson than admiral of the realm but it works.'

She put on the finished article and pranced round the room, occasionally stopping to admire herself in front of the mirror and sing a line of her song: 'And if you don't believe you I'll kick you in the asss-k me no more questions . . .'

Suddenly I remembered why the words sounded familiar. The ice in my head started to overheat. There was no tequila in the room and the tip of the iceberg began to trickle. And then, as if by magic, the joint came my way. I took it from between her fingers and it made things much better. My thoughts dispersed and, the next thing, I heard myself laughing because she'd jumped up on the bed, tossed the DIY admiral's jacket to the ground and I was grabbing at her legs as she bounced up and down, singing:

> 'Hell-o operator, please give me number nine,
> And if you disconnect me I'll kick you in the behi-nd the
>   'frigerator . . .'

And then she passed out. The only reason I didn't pass out, too, was that I was feeling so horny – although my head was spinning round like mad at this point and I was having trouble gathering the right pieces for the jigsaw of my wank fantasy. I couldn't decide if I'd take her over the pool table and do it with a snooker cue or if she'd do it to me. And then there was the question: would anyone be watching? Would that be a good or bad thing? Who could possibly be watching? Clara? The sheriff? The story board was looking promising: there were handcuffs and a mound of pomegranate seeds – wet and red and scarab-bright – and the American flag and her big thighs and bum as she posed over the pool table.

And then the flames.

The flames rose up out of nowhere. In the flick of an eyelash there was a downpour and everything melted. A flood of emotion filled the room.

Billie hadn't burned her words at all, had she? She'd left them there for me to see. She was asking for it. She'd left her floral book in the drag bag and she knew I was nosy – didn't she? Didn't she know I was nosy and sadistic? She told me I was a latent sadist.

I crawled out of the bed. I sat flopped on the brown carpet and looked at her as she slept. I sometimes think that people look dead when they're asleep. But Billie didn't look dead. She looked like she was drowning. Drowning or receiving electro-convulsive therapy. ECT. It was what they gave Sylvia Plath. Plugged her in, wired her up and shot fireworks into her brain with the flick of a switch.

I could see the floral diary peeking from the gold bag. The silk flowers were staring up at me, beckoning me. She hadn't made any effort to hide it. I was still awash with tequila and marijuana. I couldn't even properly remember what I'd read three hours ago when I came back for the costume. Something about hair gel, I seemed to remember. Something rude about my hair gel.

I hardly even felt guilty as I picked up the book. I was sort of used to the routine now. I undid the cord and some loose pages fell out. Yes, I remembered them now. They were some loose strips of paper she'd shoved inside. One of them had something about me on it. Yes, here it was:

Why will she persist in using hair gel that smells of vomit? (Coconut flavor apparently from a British health-store chain.)

The cheek! What did she think *she* smelt of? 'You smell of pub grub right now, actually,' I mouthed at her, as I watched her tossing and turning in the bed. 'That's what an unwashed body smells of – cottage pie and warm gravy.'

I put the floral notebook down and held just the loose sheets.

She reminds me of the geeky surfer boy I always wanted as a boyfriend when I was a kid. Now, there's a fish who's always gonna be out of water. My Little White Sambo. Wouldn't mind a bite of her butt.

She started thrashing around in the bed and my heart thumped away but I couldn't stop reading. On the next series of charred strips it said:

She looks like she's been dragged through a hedge backwards but it kind of works.

She has the awkward bravado of someone who has never been loved.

She has no idea that I am watching her.

So far so good-ish. I carried on to the next strip:

It was weird when Shana said she thought Mo was stiff and not very sexy because I suppose that she's not very sexy, in spite of her great rack. So why do I like her so much? Because she gives me back my confidence? Because she sees good in me when nobody else does? She's so obsessed with Ruby Rose but she doesn't know that she's helping bring Billie back when I thought that Billie was dead.

I'm not sure if it's the right time to bring Billie back.

We'll see.

One larger scrap of paper had scribbles down the side made with coloured crayons:

I don't think in straight lines. I think in colors and shapes. The curl of a wave, the twist of a flame. I like to color. This is the color of Mo when I set fire to the bedroom at the Cosy Inn. This is the color of Mo the evening at the Van Horn motel. And if I spanked her just how I think she'd like it, this is the color she'd be.

Colors and shapes come even better with drugs. Colors and shapes and fire are less tiring than words. Words tire you out so much. They hold you to ransom.

Then, on the last strip:

Human passion can reach a pitch where it combusts and morphs into an experience of the supernatural.

There was just the floral notebook now. It was thicker than it had been the first time I went inside. The ink from the silver pen had puffed up the pages – every one of which was filled with writing I saw as I opened it. I went carefully, in an orderly fashion, taking care not to flick to the middle or the end of the book before I had to. The first page began as I'd seen it the first time in Dougal's Smokehouse:

There is never enough food. I am always starving. Mom says that eight-year-old-kids don't need much food but when I come back from school I've always burned up a ton of calories.

I turned over a few pages and saw mentions of things I was familiar with: eight-year-old Billie, Mrs Harrison's flight school, Reba the babysitter, the Bible room, William the son, the purple frosting, the Tabasco sauce . . .

I went back to the word 'William'. I knew there was something significant about it. William, the babysitter's son whom Billie had trusted. Sure enough, there was his name again on a fresh page in a new entry:

There is someone else who understands me. William understands me.

Then I remembered. Dirty grey slush burst through the dam and everything came back. My insides were scraped out. I didn't know what to do next. But, of course, it was obvious what I did next.

CHAPTER FIFTEEN

Dear Diary

There is someone else who understands me. William understands me.

He is seventeen years old and sometimes when Reba has to go out to one of her church meetings, he babysits for me and Ned. William doesn't let me go hungry. He brings me pieces of cold chicken that they didn't sell in the diner where he works. Also, he brings some of the onion loaf and the Idaho potato French fries that still have skin on – not like the fries you get from Arby's or McDonald's. Sometimes I bring him some green cough syrup from Mom's medicine cabinet – where she also keeps her secret chocolate – because he says that it tastes real good.

William tells me that he works *como un negro*. That means 'like a black man'. It's Spanish. Reba doesn't like him to speak Spanish because she says he'll never get a good job unless he speaks English. But when she's not there he teaches me stuff in Mexican. He says that Granada Hills – the place in the valley where we live – means pomegranate hills in Spanish. We live in pomegranate hills! It sounds better than it is in real life. In real life we live in a big old apartment complex filled with divorced moms and their kids. There is lime-green carpet and we eat off of a white table with a lemon wedge carved in the middle and lemon-yellow chairs around it. There is a gold bar with padded leather stuff covering it that goes all the way round the apartment. Me and Ned use it as a ballet bar to practise moves on and sometimes as a tightrope.

William teaches me lots of things. He tells me about the Americans' obsession with *cleanería*. 'Always the white folks they mow the lawn, clean the car. I like to be *tranquilo*.'

He tells me about his job at the diner where he works as a chef.

212

He shows me with his hands how he peels and chops the onions to the right width and how he picks the greenest leaves of lettuce. The lettuce comes in crates from California where it is grown by Mexicans working in huge fields called 'agribusiness enterprises'. William writes down the word and shows me. He says that white Americans have relied on Mexicans for over a century.

The other things he teaches me are practical things that will be useful to me in later life. He taught me how to pick open a lock with a penknife and he also taught me how to hotwire cars. All you have to do is break the steering lock and enter the steering column from below. Then you take the ignition wire out and touch it to another live wire.

William has lots of good ideas but Reba is mean to him. She says he is a good-for-nothing slaving for the gringos. She said that he wasn't even a chef, he was a kitchen boy who spent his days scrubbing floors and being ordered around. She said she hadn't christened him William for nothing. She hadn't christened him Pedro or José, she'd christened him with a good American name so he would make progress in life just as she had made progress in life, thanks to the help of God.

Me and William, we don't care about Reba when we're together. He says that his boss has promised to make him a waiter soon. He shows me how the waiters carry big trays filled with plates on their shoulders. One time, the tray fell and a couple of the glasses on it broke and William looked worried. I told him that I'd tell Reba it was me who did it. So I did and I got beaten with a wooden spoon over Reba's knee, but it was OK because I could see William. He winked at me like he does when we play together.

William is like my big brother. If he wasn't at Reba's I don't know what I'd do. Sometimes we play snap with Reba's Plants of the Bible playing-cards. Sometimes we play chase and 'It' and trampolining on William's stomach. He has big hands with hair on the back like a man and he has zits and a harmonica. He plays 'Oh My Darling Clementine' and I clap and laugh and he lets me keep my shoes on in the house. Sometimes I show him a selection of my cheer-leader routines. I've told him that when I get to junior high I'm going to be a cheer-leader. I can nearly do the splits already.

My favourite dance is the Cookie Monster one. It goes:

> The Cookie Monster says the Centurions are
> The great big cookies at the top of the jar!
> The Cookie Monster says the Cowboys are
> The itty-bitty crumbles at the bottom of the jar!

William likes to watch me doing my cheer-leader dances. Sometimes he lifts me up over his head even though I am five foot four. After the day of the broken glasses he bought me some wool for a present and I made pompoms for my shoes. Another time he bought me ribbons — pink and red and blue ribbons — and another time, when he hurt me when we were playing our secret game, he bought me perfume, Loves Baby Soft, which smells like peppermints and cotton candy. And then one day he bought me a cheer-leader outfit. A cheer-leader outfit that must have cost a lot of money! It's for basketball games because the sweater is form-fitting with no sleeves and it has a zip-front — not like the ones for football games, which are tight but without a zipper. And there's a pleated skirt too. Mom never lets me wear skirts. I like skirts and pretty dresses. Mom makes me wear pants. Sometimes I try to wear shorts to school, real short ones that ride up my ass but Mom finds out and then it's back to long pants again.

Once I said that Reba had a monkey face and William laughed. Then he brought out the Blue Book to show me. He spoke to me just like I was a real grown-up. He told me that the blue book is for people who belong to Alcoholics Anonymous. He says that they should stick to liquor because when they give up drink they turn to God and that's even worse. At least when they're drunk they're in a good mood some days, he says.

I know William doesn't like Reba. He came in at the end bit of the Tabasco-sauce day. He saw her. He saw what she did. He let me go up to his room and he played 'Oh My Darling Clementine', just for me and then he twirled me around over his head. William is as good as a climbing frame. He let me climb all over him and bounce on him as I said the Cookie Monster cheer. It was fun. We were twirling and laughing and then I was trampolining and it was squidgy at first and then it suddenly wasn't squidgy. A Peter, it's called. Like in the Judy Bloom books me and Marnie have read. It was hard and warm. And soft like velvet tips on pussy-willow that Mom has in her flower-decoration vase at home. Pussy-willow. 'Not pussy-willow,' he said. 'Ain't no pussy.' 'OK,' I said. 'Like a tulip, then.' It was real funny. It was funny and we laughed. I screamed and laughed at the same time and then I felt sick. The room smelt of fried bacon and dog fur. It hurt a lot but he was kind, he wasn't mean. He was better than Reba. Reba shook Tabasco sauce down my throat the day my mouth was purple.

I told Marnie about Reba. She said I should tell my mom. I told her I couldn't tell Mom because Mom would stick up for Reba. She'd say, 'Life isn't fair, Billie,' in a wobbly voice with the fire breath she has when she parties at the flight school. You never know what's going to happen next when she's got her fire breath. Sometimes I do my TV thing, which means switching off and pretending that all the bad stuff is happening on a TV screen in my head. But sometimes, when I go to bed, I can't pretend it's TV any more. My face gets all hot like the burning pit of sulphur and I cry and wonder where the place for me to go is if Mom thinks I'm bad and Reba thinks I'm evil and William says I'm not to tell anyone about us playing together or they'll call me devil spawn and beat it out of me.

One day I went to pick up Ned from the playground. Marnie was there, too, and we stopped off on the way home to play Red Indians. Red Indians have way better outfits than cowboys – little skirts and bra things – plus they're much cooler in the hot weather. Marnie was already wearing hers but I have to pack mine in my backpack in secret because of Mom and her no-skirts rule.

First we made perfume from green peaches and squashed oleander flowers and twigs. I put mine on my wrists and behind my earlobes because that is what William says you do with Loves Baby Soft. Then Marnie found a rainpipe gully that ran all the way down the hill from the new apartments. She said that if we smeared ice plant on the gully we could go really fast. Ice plant is like a cactus full of sticky stuff that's even slippier than the strawberry ice-skating rink me and Ned made in Sambo's the day when Leah spilt shake all over the floor. So we went over to the gully and we rubbed ice-plant leaves all over the concrete. Then we got a piece of cardboard box and we used it as a sled to go down the slope and it turned out to be bitchin'. It was even better than the flight simulator in Mom's office when you set the dial to crash mode and everything jiggles around and all the alarms go off. It felt like your belly was flying up through your mouth and it felt like there were two Billies – one Billie sitting on the flying ice carpet and the other Billie thirty feet down the bottom of the hillside, a ghost Billie who'd whizzed out of her body and was waiting for her at the bottom of the hill among all the juniper trees and the scrub.

At the start, I didn't let Ned go down the slide because I didn't want him to hurt himself. I was about to say, 'Well, life isn't fair, Ned,' just like Mom. But then I thought, Why does life have to be not fair all the time? I told Ned he could go down the slide because me and Marnie would wait at the bottom to catch him. He got on the cardboard. And the next thing I know he's flying through the air, shrieking like me the day Casey took me up in his plane and put us in a nose-dive spin and the plane plunged towards the ground like a stone while Casey punched the air going, 'Yeee-haaa!' in his beer breath, and I screamed and laughed at the same time.

Then Ned stops shrieking because he's landed in a clump of euca-lyptus trees. Thump! He's not moving a muscle and my belly, my heart, my soul, my everything flies out of my mouth because if Ned dies I don't know what I'll do. I slide down the hill on my ass, screaming out, 'Ned! Ned! It's OK, Ned!' But I don't think it will be OK because Ned is lying there like a dead body and I'm crying and panting and shaking and I'm wondering how much more I'll be crying and shaking if he really is dead. And then I reach him. I put my hand on his body and there's some shaking and I think that maybe an earthquake is happening. Maybe this is the big earthquake when California falls into the ocean and then I realise it's Ned! He's shaking like a laughing earthquake. He's laughing so hard he can't turn over. He's just lying there, face in the dirt, coughing his gut out! And when he finally raises his head there's dirt stuck all over his teeth and he chuckles, 'Wow, Billie, I was laughing so hard I couldn't move!' And then I start laughing too. Because Ned is alive and it is sunny and it proves that you can be nice to people and nothing bad will happen.

And then, suddenly, I do die. Very briefly. I see what time it is. Me and Ned were supposed to be home an hour ago. I hardly have time to say goodbye to Marnie before I'm grabbing Ned by the hand and running back to Reba's. And then the trouble comes. The shadow comes again. She's there, shouting, her face like a smashed plate, like a dirty, greasy plate of refried beans covered with spiders' webs. And she has the spoon.

It was pink icing that day. It was fresh, dripping off the spoon. There were spots on the spoon. Pink spots like William's zits. She said I was late. She kept screaming, she wouldn't stop screaming. It was a long twisty sentence that never came to an end: Evil, evil, evil, girl, never trust again girl, good-for-nothing insanity girl, disgusting polluted death girl, loathsome pestilence Jezebel girl. She said that hell was just crying out for the rotten souls of the likes of me, that deep down under the earth there were reeking pools of boiling sulphur that flowed into a burning lake filled with misery and poverty and low, filthy prostitutes and cut-throats and murderers and that I was going down into that lake, down, down, down into the lake, that hell was yawning to receive the putrid masses such as me.

She came closer and closer, waving the spoon in my face. Why was I late, she wanted to know, why was I late bringing Ned back, why had I taken two hours when I should have taken thirty minutes, why was Ned covered in dirt and why was I wearing a mini-skirt and smelling like the whore of Babylon, the triple-breasted whore of Babylon, and why and why and why and why?

And mainly I was thinking about the nice evening it had been — flying through the air on the ice-plant slope — and I wished there was a way I could get her to understand. I wished what I was feeling could soak out of my brain and just fall down over her like a mist, like the Loves Baby Soft in the spray bottle that William bought me.

I say, 'Sorry, Reba, but we were Red Indians making puddle perfume and then we got on this ski slope . . .'

I don't know why I even bother trying to explain because she wrenches me by the arm. If I was a doll my arm would definitely have come out of my socket. I'd have been broken by now.

But she doesn't care about breaking me. She just cares about the spoon, the pink spoon she's sending down after me. Down on to my butt it comes, down on to the butt of my Red Indian skirt, and I wonder if I'll have to have an extra beating at the end because now my Red Indian skirt is going to get all dirty, all covered in pink frosting, and then I can't think any more. I just see pink being hit harder and harder and harder like a metal horseshoe being hit by a hammer on one of those metal things they use to make horseshoes called an anvil, and I know about anvils because I saw one on a TV show on PBS and anvil reminds me of 'anthill'. On the TV, they hit harder and harder to make the metal as thin as they could and the longer they hit it the more it changed color. Maybe it's the same with my butt. The pink frosting must be red now, my ass must be red by now, the spoon's hitting me so hard. And maybe it'll be like on the TV when the metal burns so hot that it goes from orange to white and they have to put the horseshoe into a bucket of water that sends up clouds of steam and, oh, boy, I wish I was in the bucket too, not just my ass but my whole body. Reba has pulled down my panties and now the spoon is slamming down right on my naked butt and I wish I could just dive into a bucket and lose myself in the clouds of steam. I try to make myself forget the wooden spoon with the pink

frosting. I do the patty-cake rhyme that me and Marnie play at school.
It's a good rhyme because you almost get to say rude stuff:

> *Miss Suzy had a steamboat,*
> *The steamboat had a bell,*
> *Miss Suzy went to heaven,*
> *The steamboat went to hell-o operator please give me*
> *   number nine*
> *And if you disconnect me I'll kick you in the behi-nd the*
> *   'frigerator there is a piece of glass,*
> *And if you don't believe you I'll kick you in the assss . . . k*
> *   me no more questions,*
> *I'll tell you no more lies . . .*

And then I stop because the steam is just getting hotter and I
don't want to think about hell and lying because I am a liar and I
am going to hell. I close my eyes because I can't look at the floorboards any more with all the bugs down the sides and because they
remind me of the bubbling lake of sulphur. I just dissolve into the
cool, cool steam, all white and cool that cuddles round you. And then
everything stops. The spoon stops. And that is worse. Because now
everything's going backwards. At least the white heat was numb. You
couldn't feel it too bad. But now the spoon's stopped it's not white
any more. It's going back to orange and orange isn't really that hot
at all so that makes my butt sting. Probably the burning lake of hell
will be white so it'll be better than this. Better then this horrible pain
like Little Black Sambo when the tigers got him by the butt.

And when she starts again the beating is different. It's not on my
ass now, it's going all the way up my back, like she's thumping away
at a xylophone, ruining the keys of a xylophone, just hitting them and
clanging them. Except the keys on a xylophone are normally red and
orange and blue and yellow and green and I bet the keys on my back
will be black and blue and purple. But, no, that's another lie. I'm an
expert on bruises. The blows are coming so strong that at first they
won't color at all. They'll be numb for a day and then they'll go deep
black like a storm sky and then purple and then, last of all, pea-green.

And then they'll be gone. So, you see, I can be colorful too, I can be like a xylophone. I can be good, I can do the right thing, I can be well behaved. I can be trusted. I'll never do anything again, I'll never do anything bad again, I'll never play Indians or make perfume or eat frosting. I'll stay in my room and I'll just breathe, I won't move – not even an inch – and then I won't be able to do anything bad and then the devil won't get me and I won't get thrown into a reeking pool of sulphur and it'll be all right.

The floorboards stare back at me like the sulphur lakes waiting for me, just like Reba said. They're sticky and black and maybe that's what the devil will do to me. He'll turn me into a speck of greasy dust and he'll stick me in a crack in the floorboards of someone's house and one day a dog's claw will come and step on me and I'll be spiked through the heart and who will help me then? Who will help me now? I know that life isn't fair like Mama says but who will help me now?

'Mama! Mama!' And then there's too much pain. 'Aaaaaaaaaaaa!' I can't even sound like a xylophone. Xylophones make chimes, little chimes, but I'm just big and ugly and I just yell, yell like a hellcat, that's what Reba says, 'You take your punishment, hellcat. Your mama knows you're bad too.'

Wham! Wham! she goes on my backbone. Slap! Slap! she goes on my hellcat hide. She's a useless xylophone player, she can't even get a nice sound out of me, she just makes me sound ugly. She's stupid, she's a stupid monkey, stupid Reba monkey face! I should have eaten more frosting, I should have stolen more cake, then I'd be fat and then my back would be like my ass, it'd have flesh on and it wouldn't hurt, it wouldn't hurt . . . hurt so much . . . I think I might be about to die . . . It feels like ghost Billie shooting down the slide before the real Billie and I'll end up like Ned, lying in the dirt by the juniper trees only I won't be not moving cuz I'm laughing so much, I'll be not moving because I'm dead, because all the music's been beaten out of me. And then I hear some music . . . real music . . . and I think it might be because I've arrived in heaven and that means that maybe I'm not going to hell at all because I bet the devil doesn't play such soft tunes that help to soothe a ripped-up back like mine. I can hear it properly now. 'Oh My Darling Clementine'. It's him! William is here! William is going to save me! He's going to help me, he's the one who loves me, I'm his special cheer-leader. He told me I'm his special cheer-leader. He bought me a basketball cheer-leader outfit with a zip, even though I am too tall and skinny to be a cheer-leader, and he likes to zip it up and down. He zips it up and down like one of our hot-wire cars, he likes that, he likes me because I am special and now he is going to save me.

I look up from the anvil, from the burning lake. I know I shouldn't because normally I don't say anything but this time I can't help it. I call out, 'William! William!' and the blows come even harder then and I can't make a sentence come out, I can just sob and squeeze a word out: 'Perfume.'

'Perfume . . . William . . .' And again I say it. 'Perfume . . . Will . . .' I can hardly speak. I just need a bit of him and I will feel better. Just a wink maybe and the wooden spoon will not be so bad. But the harmonica stops. I can see his eyes. He's glaring at me. It's a mean look. He wants to make me vanish just with his eyes. I know it was bad of me to say, 'Perfume,' because that is just between him and me. It's our secret. Part of our big secret. But it's too late. He stands up and hurls his harmonica to the floor. It smashes into the burning lake and then there is another sound. A sharp crack. A tree falling. The wooden spoon breaking. My back has split the wooden spoon. It must be true. I must be the devil. I can never be trusted ever again and William will never speak to me ever again and it's all because I am evil.

And then I don't care any more. I just run. I don't wait for Mom to come pick us up, I run off into the evening. I run to start with and then I just walk slowly because there's no point in getting home. Home just means another telling-off and I can't walk very fast anyway. My back hurts. My back and my legs and my head. I don't make any noise, though. There is just the sound of trudging through dust and over dirty stones and then a car screeching to a halt. I look up. There's a man in a blue car. He opens the door. His zipper's

221

open. He beckons me over and I know that when a naked man wants you then you go over to him. So I go over and I watch him jack off. There is a purple spot on the end of his thing. I'm scared. I don't know this man. I know William and he's nice to me and it doesn't always make me feel sick but then I remember that William won't be nice to me ever again and I start to cry.

The man drives off and a cop comes. He takes me to the police station. It's like a gnarly Mexican bandit movie inside. There are some small jail cells in front of the police desks and there are some men inside kicking the walls and some are sitting with their heads in their hands. A lady takes me into a room. She's nice to me. I know she wouldn't be so nice to me if she knew how bad I really am but she doesn't have to find out everything. She gives me a glass of milk and some Oreo cookies and it tastes so nice that I start to cry. She asks me where my parents live. I don't tell her about Reba. I tell her that my mom and me and my brother live in Rose Avenue in Granada Hills. I know that Mom will be real mad to be called up by the cops but I don't care any more.

Mom and Ned come into the interrogation room just as the lady cop is asking me to describe what the man in the blue car was doing with his Peter.

Nice things that Mom does:

1. When we drive in the car we sing to songs. Our favorites are 'Here Comes the Sun', 'Sunshine On My Shoulders' and 'Fifty Ways To Leave Your Lover'.

2. Sometimes, when I can't go to sleep, Mom will let me come in the living room and put my head on her lap and she strokes my hair until I get tired.

3. After we go out in the rain Mom makes us sit by the fire and then take a warm bath. I never get that because why would Mom want us to go in inside water if she was scared of outside water? But the point is that she is worried about us. This is the proof.

CHAPTER SIXTEEN

Jezebel Girl

The family groups in cagoules and pastels who are packing up their cars in front of the Buffalo motel in preparation for a day's picnicking seem slightly bamboozled by the spectacle emerging from room number four.

When, at two p.m., we make it into the daylight, Billie is dressed in a *décolleté* admiral's jacket (worn over a straining black-leather catsuit), black-patent spike-heeled ankle boots, an East German military cap, and she is already sweating profusely through her very severe makeup.

Even though she has an immense hangover (I presume) she is holding everything together very convincingly. She hardly seems to notice the embarrassed parents and the impressed children into whom she strikes the same awe that the huge black bird flying in from the land beyond the setting sun struck into the Navajo Indians.

As usual, reality feels slightly out of focus. When we heard the knocks on our door we couldn't believe it. Actually, I was the only one to hear them. There were these short, sharp raps and then silence. Then some more raps and then more silence. I've no idea how long the sequence went on but the whole thing was becoming increasingly annoying and as Billie was making no effort to get up – she was still in the thrall of another of her baroque nightmares – Muggins, whose hangover was a bit of a stunner too thank you very much, staggered to the door to do the honours.

There was a man with a bushy beard, a chauffeur's cap and a cheap grey suit who said, 'Morning, ma'am. Mr Maddox sent me to collect you.'

I was wondering whether I should be flattered about being mistaken for a dominatrix when a loud groan erupted from the bed followed by a voice going, 'Fuck . . . I don't fucking believe this.'

It isn't even a proper limo. It's a cheap limo. When we get inside there's nothing in the back. No alcohol, no TV, no nothing. There is a glass door between us and the driver and the only noise in the car is the sound of the Moonlight Sonata from the tape deck and the creak of the chauffeur's dandruffy shoulders as he moves his neck to look in the mirrors every once in a while.

Billie is in a very odd mood. She says she feels as if she hasn't woken up from her dream house yet. That in her dream house last night all the floors were falling out and she was going down with them. She hunts in the drag bag for a new packet of Advil, and when she remembers that the only things in the drag bag are a broom, a feather duster, a packet of floor-cleaner, several lengths of washing-line, a pair of pink rubber gloves, a leather belt, a bull whip and a gold bag, she starts throwing herself about. She says that the 'fucking music' reminds her of her mother and that the driver reminds her of someone else and she's pissed off because she can't remember who.

I'm silently cursing my tequila hangover and the fact that Billie has run out of the yellow snake again just when I need it most. The steep climb up the hill to Carlota isn't making matters any easier. The countryside is picturesque to start with: about five minutes out of Lariat we pass through a plateau – the prairie location of Clara's ranch where acres of tiny yellow sunflowers sprout up through swathes of sunburned green weeds and sway against a backdrop of blurry blue mountains. And then reality changes. We leave the desert heat of the San Francisco Valley and gradually ascend into a cold, sharp, alpine zone of aspen and fir. It feels as if we've passed through another time zone. The road twists and turns and even if we wanted to return to the security of Lariat it seems doubtful that we could physically turn round on such vertiginous terrain. Round some corners, embedded in the soil, are rusty old hulks of cars like the ones from the Wacky Races, abandoned for decades by time and the pioneers. At one point we nearly crash into a man driving a car who suddenly appears round a corner – a battered old Cadillac about as impractical as our limo on this tightrope of a road.

And then, out of the blue, everything seems absurd. Here I am on a flimsy roller-coaster road nearly seven thousand feet above sea level with a total stranger on my way to a rendezvous with a 'retired sea captain' who could be a complete bloody psycho. The higher we go, the twistier the road gets and the more my palms sweat. I wonder what would happen if the limo fell off this huge height – if anyone would know I'd fallen, if anyone would care. My mother? Gary? Acid Sarah? Muriel?

I feel dizzy. I try to find something to fix my brain on to stop it blowing away altogether. I can't go over the various items of my breakfast story because the thought of food makes me feel sick. So I think back to my cockroach article, I turn it into a mantra.

Cockroaches bleed white blood.

Cockroaches have claws on their feet.

The cockroach eye is made up of two thousand individual lenses.

The cockroach brain is spread throughout its body.

There are five thousand species of cockroaches worldwide.

Cockroaches fried in oil and garlic can be used as a cure for indigestion.

Cockroach droppings may look like grains of pepper.

Cockroach kidneys look like a bunch of writhing snakes . . .

But 'writhing snakes' is wrong. When I think of writhing snakes I think of pestilence and death and that makes me think of 'evil evil evil girl, never trust again girl, good-for-nothing insanity girl, disgusting polluted death girl, loathsome pestilence Jezebel girl'. The leather knot bracelet tightens on my wrist. My body tightens. I try to to grab hold of the concept of 'home'. I chew my gum methodically and think of Scarborough. I think of me and Gary lying up on the roof of the Sceptre with the greasy old extractor going at full blast and the smell of crispy duck from the Chinese restaurant next door wafting under our noses. We used to lie on that roof and look up at the sky – white and grey and cloudy – and now I try to make myself understand that this ominous El Greco New Mexico sky is the same sky that hangs over the Sceptre. That maybe, if they took away the roofs and the TV aerials and the drunks in the streets, then the Scarborough sky would be frightening too.

But everything seems to loom above and loom below and I think of Geronimo who used to hunt here and the ghosts of pioneers who came here for the gold and died on the way. And then I think of ghost towns. Of the ones on TV westerns – burnt-out house husks with tattered 'Welcome' signs flapping in the breeze, eerie noises of wind howling through broken windows and dust blowing fiercely all around, like the tormented souls of the inhabitants of the place who probably all came to grisly deaths.

Suddenly, there's a hand on my bracelet. Billie's. I flinch. She says, 'It's OK, babe, I think it's the height. Altitude sickness. It's freaking us both out.'

And that frightens me even more. She knows exactly what I'm feeling. I wonder if she can read my mind. I wonder if she knows what I've done.

Human passion can reach a pitch where it combusts and morphs into an experience of the supernatural.

That was what she wrote. That was one of her lines. I start to fiddle around with my bracelet toggle, gabbling, 'When you're sometimes in a high-up place do you ever get the urge to push people over the edge?'

It's a silly thing to say. I don't know where it came from. But I suddenly see myself pushing her off a cliff. There'd be a moment when it was fun. The pushing moment. The thrill of the shove, the exhilarating, taboo-smashing rush of pushing her off the top of a monumental height just for the hell of it.

She turns to me and narrows her eyes. 'Pushing people off of cliffs, conning roaches into eating plaster of paris . . .' She smiles. 'Like I said, Mo, I think you might be some kind of a latent sadist.'

I turn to her, relieved. She smiles at me. I even start to laugh. She's right. The height is doing the strangest things to my head. Everything is fine. All I've done is come on a bit of a wacky holiday and last night I read a small part of a diary belonging to a woman with a vivid imagination. I laugh again. I say, 'Maybe we should have brought Diane's GPS with us!'

She smiles again and says that she's going to show me something that will cheer me up. She pulls out a crumpled brown envelope from the drag bag and hands it to me. Inside is a newspaper cutting showing a photograph of a little girl smiling coquettishly as she sits on the steps of a church. Below her, the caption reads: Saugus resident Billie Harrison will be taking part in St Jerome's Easter pageant. 'I can hardly wait!' Billie exclaimed.

Billie starts to poke around in the thick black rope of hair coiled under her military cap. 'I was nine,' she says, pushing a red-beaded pin into the shiny black bun. 'It's the first time I had my picture in the paper.'

I can't think what to say. 'You look . . . like . . .'

'Like a big old flirt, is what I look like!' she says, her mouth full of pins. She takes the picture back and looks at it again. 'I wanted so bad to be beautiful that day, I remember.'

My throat becomes a rotten apple filled with crawling ants swarming round in a brown mush. I'm sitting there in the back of the limo feeling them all fuzz round, wondering when the crying will come and if I can make it go away if it does. This must be her, then: the 'loathsome pestilence Jezebel girl'. How much she must have known about life when that picture was taken.

She puts the cutting back in the envelope. 'Funny,' she goes, taking a slug from the never-empty Jack Daniel's bottle. 'I've been thinking a lot about my family since the terrorist thing. About my childhood and shit. Sorry if I've been acting a bit weird.'

'That's OK,' I say quickly. Maybe she'll make mention of the diary stuff she's written in her floral notebook. Oh, please mention the diary and then everything will be all right. But she sinks back into silence, the exuberance of last night all gone. I know she doesn't really want to do the trick any more. I know now that her mind's not in that place any more.

She says, 'How's your writing going, Mo?'

I jump in my seat. 'Writing? What writing?'

'What do you mean, "What writing"? I thought you were trying to be a journalist.'

We hurtle into another hairpin bend. 'Oh, yes, it's going fine, thanks. I'm just waiting for the California breakfast and then it'll be finished . . .'

She thumps the side of the car and I jump out of my skin for the second time. 'What the hell are you doing?'

'I know who he is now!'

'Who?'

'The driver.' She lowers her voice. 'I told you, he reminds me of someone.'

'Who?' The cloak-and-dagger stuff is irritating me now.

'This punter in New Orleans.' She frowns. 'Sweet guy. Mr Eggmont. His wife was very ill.'

And then it clicks that maybe Mr Eggmont was the one whose wife had died of leukaemia. The one who liked Billie to pee into his rubber suit.

'He was the one into sensory deprivation, then.' I say it as though I'm certain what I'm talking about.

'It was his drug.' She shrugs, putting her feet up on the scratched black leatherette opposite. 'He wanted to dissolve for a little while.'

'You two had a bit in common, then.' I can't help saying this. 'He wanted to dissolve his life and you want to dissolve yours.'

'Excuse me?'

'By burning everything you write.'

A twitch of something passes over Billie's mouth. I can't say it doesn't give me pleasure. Maybe she's right, after all. Maybe I am a latent sadist. Or maybe I'm just pissed off. How come it's all right for her to ask me about my writing? I want her to do something about what I read. To blot it all out. To tell me it's not true or at least to explain it. Most of all, though, I want to read some more.

My eyes dart down to the opened drag bag. I know it's in there. I can see the raspberry threads and the black flowers. I start looking at Billie out of the corner of my eye because it feels as though I've never really seen her before. She catches me doing this and snaps, 'What the hell is wrong with you today? I told you, it's the altitude. Everything's going to be fine.'

And she's right. I see a group of trees – not scrub or weird yellow flowers or cacti or shards of burning rock – but real trees that look like the smily green oaks you see in England. Constables conquering El Greco, for a minute at least. And then we arrive in Carlota and the ghost town's not scary at all. There are flowers and wooden houses and a main street that looks like a set from *Little House on the Prairie*. More to the point, there are ordinary modern cars parked – like the cars you have in towns that aren't ghost towns – and there are colourful Charlie Brown mailboxes in front of houses with rocking-chairs on the porches.

We pull up in front of one wooden house with a sticker on the mailbox saying, 'Hug a tree!'

The driver gets out, saying, 'If you'll excuse me one moment, ladies.'

CHAPTER SEVENTEEN

Did She Come This Way?

What is left of you when you are standing on a stone surrounded by five hundred thousand acres of prehistoric forest? How do you feel when all your previous life is washed away, all your worries and cares and interests – jealousy, guilt, libido – when everything floats away, sucked up into the powerful skies above by the ghosts of Geronimo and the wild animals and the white settlers foolish enough to try to wrench gold from the bowels of a land that was never theirs in the first place?

Is it silly to think that spirits hang in this place and in the valleys and in the air around the mountains – humorous at one moment, cruel and mocking at the next? Is it death you can taste in your mouth like a sticky skin of jasmine that coats the back of your throat before you see it with your eyes or smell it with your nose? And what is the feeling that weighs you down? Is it fear entering your stomach or is it a restless spirit blown in from the ancient air?

The population of Carlota was decimated by an influenza outbreak between 1916 and 1918. Corpses – many of them Hispanic – were buried in a small plot of land at the entrance to the prehistoric forest. It's a modest place. Most of the head-stones were tinkered together from a variety of cheap materials now wonky and rusty with age: wrought-iron bedsteads, scraps of sheet iron suspended from bent nails, pieces of scaffolding and plumbing pipe bound with rope into crosses. The graveyard is abandoned now. Lizards scuttle under stones, wild rabbits dart from behind wind-scoured animal skulls, ancient shrubs rustle, and through the tangled branches you glimpse the sloe-black eyes, the caramel skin, the alluring smile, the coiled serpent.

* * *

Under the circumstances, Billie is on pretty good form. Here we are, seven thousand feet in the air in a strange, run-down cemetery, and from the way she's acting you'd have thought we were in K-Mart on a day when they'd run out of Easy Cheese.

'You know,' she sighs, stretching out on a shady slab of granite – trust her to find the ritziest grave in the cemetery, 'when my time comes, I want a hell of a lot more razzmatazz than this.'

'Personally, I find the simplicity very tasteful.'

'Simplicity! I want marble pillars and fire and reflecting pools. Oh, and everyone gets to snort my ashes up with a fifty-dollar bill.'

'Beautiful.'

'You're right,' she says, flopping back on the gravestone. 'Snorting powder's nasty. Maybe everyone just has to put me in a joint and smoke me.'

I wonder how much longer we have to stay here. When the driver came back from the house he told us that 'Mr Maddox' was running a little late and could we come back in three hours? Three hours! I couldn't believe it. What were we supposed to do for three hours? Once we'd been round Carlota's take on K-Mart – a spooky Aladdin's cave filled with deer skulls, Rita Hayworth posters, sachets marked, 'rattlesnake eggs', replica six-shooters and packets of Chee-tos – it seemed that we'd exhausted the town's sightseeing possibilities.

A grey-skinned Mexican woman emerged from the back of the shop. She didn't say anything. Not even 'How y'all doing?' She just stared at us like the mad old man's wife from *Scooby-Doo*. I wondered momentarily if she was anything like Reba, and then Billie asked her if she could suggest how we might kill three hours. The woman grunted something about the cemetery.

That was our initial wrong move – apart from coming to Carlota in the first place, of course. The woman didn't tell us how long it would take to walk to the cemetery – three-quarters of an hour, as it turned out, and that felt even longer in the baking heat of the late afternoon. There we were, traipsing up a shadeless dirt track lined with withered wood houses and hot clumps of fir trees – me in my usual jeans and T-shirt, Billie head to tail in black leather and a hacked-up doctor's coat because she hadn't brought anything else to change into.

She'd removed her spike heels and was off on one of her things about how good it felt to press her feet into hot, crumbling earth while I, of course, was the one elected to lug the drag bag. I started off trying to be all jolly, but suddenly I couldn't be arsed. I launched into a rant about what a stupid idea it was to come and see the freak and how it was so predictable that this was going to happen – even though I knew very well that I was the one who'd wanted to do the trick in the first place.

So there she lies on the granite headstone, irritating me by being so calm. Actually, I don't think she's feeling *that* calm. I think she's just relieved that the trick's been put back for a few hours. She sits up and fiddles around with the zip on her catsuit. She claims she can't decide if she looks more ridiculous with the admiral's jacket over the catsuit or with just the straight catsuit. She finally decides to remove the white jacket and put the black boots back on. While she does this, I stomp around in the snarled undergrowth, pointing out in no uncertain terms how fed up to the back teeth I am. (I want to see if I can get away with throwing a fit, and also I think that if I throw a fit then maybe the cemetery won't feel quite so spooky.)

'This is a complete bummer!' goes echoing round the canyon.

'Poor baby.'

'Plus I'm the one who's been carrying your bloody drag bag round all morning!'

'Baby,' she says gently. 'Don't say "plus". It's bad grammar.'

That sets me off even worse. 'What have you got in there, anyway?' I snap. She just smiles and blows me a kiss as she squeezes her feet into the black stiletto boots and I think, I don't care, I know exactly what's in there. I know more about you than you think.

My having-a-fit theory seems to work. My rage seems to chase away the bad spirits. I know I should feel bad about being so mardy – especially since it's my fault that we're here and I've betrayed her and everything – but I think that the hot afternoon and the infuriating situation must have burned all guilt out of me. It seems to have burned out all that tedious sexual tension, anyway. Thank God! Perhaps if you fantasise about people for too long without doing anything about it, they go stale in your head. When they're ready for the plucking they're like stale chocolate. Obviously you're not going to turn it down, but it's still stale.

I walk back towards her granite bed. She doesn't seem to even notice my mood. She laughs and says, 'You know, hon, one of my all-time fantasies was to get my ass beaten in a cemetery.' She crosses her legs and turns her ankle from side to side, admiring her heels. 'And then afterwards, I'd cool it off by sitting on a slab of cool marble.'

I stand next to her, looking down at her. I can't believe she just said that. A rabbit leaps out from behind the headstone and I read the inscription:

Ignacio Sanchez
Died 1918
26 yrs of age

Poor Ignacio didn't even get to have 'years' written out in full on his miserable grave and now Billie wants to use it as a sex toy.

'Maybe I'll be lucky one of these days,' she says.

She's got her play voice on but I'm not even going to comment. I turn my back on her and ask if she isn't scared of having sex in a cemetery.

'Oh, no,' she says. 'Dead people are nice and quiet.'

There's something in the tone of her voice that makes me turn round and look at her. It's then that she unzips the catsuit. Slowly, the leather skin peels open, tooth by tooth by tooth. When the zip reaches her belly-button she stops and slides her arms free of the sleeves, wriggling the suit down to her waist.

Her eyes are the beginning of the deed. When I look into them I melt. I become hot wax waiting to be moulded into anything she wants. Damn it.

Her body sparkles with sweat and the precious stones from the jewelled body harness she's wearing under the leather. It rubs against her breasts, making her nipples hard. She walks away from me.

Damn and blast.

She turns round and beckons me to follow her. My mouth is dry, my body's on fire.

Bloody bloody hell.

She's standing under a tree. She grabs hold of me by the arms and pushes me front-first against the trunk. I'm just wondering if this isn't a little over-brusque when she suddenly starts taking chunks out of my neck. One minute it's nibbling and the next thing it's gouging and then suddenly there's this liposuction nozzle. There's a bloody liposuction pipe on my neck and there's a swarming clump of ants on the bark with black beady bodies and then she's ripped my jeans undone and she's trying to put her fist up me.

'Ow!'

'You little pussy,' she sneers, 'come on. Take that!' and she lashes my bum with her open hand.

Having sex in a graveyard has absolutely never been on my list of fantasies. And now here I am in a graveyard being ravished and it's still not on my list of fantasies. I'm thinking that maybe it's the shock – of the lash, of the fist, of the graveyard? I'm worrying about why I'm not enjoying it more. Is it the ants? The heat? Is Geronimo sticking his oar in? Maybe she really is a Satanist and what am I going to do then?

I keep waiting for the supreme-focus eyelash thing to happen, for the grain of sand to be as big as the whole world, but it doesn't come. All I'm aware of is a fire. A fire that is essentially situated in my groin but that keeps darting all over my body. It feels as if I've got a candle and it's reached the stem of the wick and it's really burning my fingers and I really want to put the thing down – somewhere, anywhere. But all around there's fire too so there's nowhere to put the bloody thing down and I can't bear it any more. I don't know how to get rid of the fire and I'm moaning with some sort of pleasure but the hand-lashing business is starting to piss me off. Did she never hear of foreplay?

'Ouch!'

If she thinks a gravestone's going to take the sting away from my bottom she's got another think coming! Maybe if she lashed me in a slightly different place it would work better.

'No, not there, there!' I pant. 'No, a bit softer!'

'Shut your mouth, you little whore! I'm going to use you.'

Ah, that's a little better. I quite like that. Use me. Yes, let her use me. I push my bum up into the air, but then she starts going too fast again. It's too hard, it's painful, and now she's pushed me over to a grave with a rusty coat-hanger for a cross and a tatty wooden plaque saying, 'Gone but not forgotten'. But I notice that they *have* been forgotten because you can't even read the name of the person on the plaque any more – there's just a huge green cricket thing perched on the coat-hanger, rubbing its hairy legs together and sucking its feelers as if it's having a leisurely wank session. It's having a better time than me.

And all the while, the firecracker darting over my body is dying for a bucket of water to put itself out but it has no idea where the water is located. It's certainly not in my bottom, thank you very much, Billie Harrison. She's just irritating me more and more with the slapping while the non-specific fire in my body grows bigger and bigger. And then her voice starts saying, 'I'm doing this because I love you,' and I wonder what that might mean because I thought she was going to use me. I don't want her to do it because she loves me, I want her to treat me like an object. That's all I want from her – to treat me like an object. She seems like a bomb that's about to explode and finally she does explode: 'Stop thinking!' she roars in panic. 'Close off your mind!'

But I can't close off my mind. There's smacking and the ants and the scary masturbating cricket. 'Ow!'

'Don't tease me! Stop it!'

'No!'

'I'm doing this because I love you!'

The wavering voice, the dam that's about to burst at any minute.

'I'm not a bloody turkey to be stuffed, you know!'

Then I really get a thump. There's a heel in my rump and I find myself lying on my back in the dust with a load of stones and spiky grass digging into me.

'You fucking jerk!' she yells. She storms off to one of the wrought-iron bedsteads.

I feel ridiculous, an utter failure.

I heave myself up from the ground, rubbing my behind. I walk towards her. 'I'm sorry,' I say. I try to touch her shoulder. 'Maybe it's because it was my first time . . .'

She flings my hand away from her. 'Be honest, Mo. You're not into this kind of sex. You don't like pain and you don't like discipline!' Beads of sweat drip down her delectable breasts. 'What kind of useless sub are you!'

'But – but maybe we could try again?'

'Face it, you're a big vanilla chicken shit.'

'What?'

'You're from the fluffy-handcuff school of SM. You're like those couples who tie each other up in bed at the weekend.'

'That's unfair, Billie.'

'Yeah,' she goes, tearing up handfuls of weeds and throwing them to the ground. 'Big Red chewing-gum's the most painful thing you can deal with . . .'

That does it. 'Shut the fuck up! Just because you've got a fantasy about shagging in a graveyard and I haven't doesn't mean that I'm – that I'm . . .'

'Frigid?'

'Shut up!' I'm screaming at her now. 'Maybe you didn't want it either!'

'What?'

'Maybe you're using sex as a kind of – medication!'

'Medication?'

'I mean . . . maybe you've got a lot of things on your mind at the moment . . .'

'How the fuck do you know what's on my mind?'

I can feel myself blushing. I change tack. 'What are we even doing, anyway? We're two women. I mean, are you a lesbian or something?'

Billie just raises her eyebrows. With an irritating dignity in her voice, she says, 'Go fuck beer-gut man if you're so worried about being a lesbian.' She begins to walk towards the granite grave.

'I never said I was worried about being a lesbian!'

'What is your problem?' she says wearily. 'You've been gagging for it all the way from New Orleans. And actually you've pretty much already had sex with me – bits and pieces of your kind of wimpy sex.'

'Shut up!' I don't know what to say. 'Just . . . shut up!'

'What*ever*.'

When she reaches the granite grave, she stands on the stone and kicks off her boots. She peels off the rest of the black catsuit and throws it dramatically on to one of the adjacent graves. Then she just stands there – her flesh oily with sweat, her body adorned in nothing more than a jewelled body harness and a small black thong, her eyes hidden in the shadow of the visor of the black leather military cap. She takes a deep breath and raises her face to the sky.

She turns her back to me. She turns to the setting sun and, for what seems like an age, she stands motionless, just breathing in and breathing out.

I want to see her face. I'm wondering what kind of new game this can be. I creep up behind her and there it is: the rouge on her cheeks is smudged into warpaint and bathed in a soft orange glow. She's let go: she breathes in the ancient mountain air, deeply and serenely. She starts to sway to the sound of the trees, to the chirping of the crickets, the whirring of the cicadas. Gradually her eyes open. They fix me to the spot. Her hands pass over her body: the reckless breasts, the nipples, then sliding down the belly, touching and brushing and lingering, lower and lower she goes. She dances to the sound of the air – grave-top lap-top dancer – real-life Salome right before your eyes: moist flesh gleaming, hot thighs dripping, nipples hard, cap severe, paint and perfume, beads and crystal, peacock green, ocean blue, cherry red, superhuman, sacrilegious.

I moan. I start to moan.

The devil has sugary red lips and when you kiss them they melt like a hot knife through butter. Hot buttered sugar lips, suck me down, draw me in. The devil does cartwheels and high jumps. Her teeth are sparkling white. Her skin is rough and mottled. I will murder and lie for her, I will give her a head on a plate.

She turns her back to me, bends over, defiant. She caresses her feet, then slowly surfaces, her hands sliding up the oily legs. So close, you can smell her – unwashed sweat on burning skin streaming down a writhing back – dirty, oily, muddy holes round and round in salty circles.

A black creature jumps in the grass. A black shadow. And then a gasp. A gasp and a whimper but not from me. She falls to her knees, my tongue drips, the black creature has its wings ripped off – its wings ripped and its legs torn – and the tongue goes in deeper and there it is, the whimper, 'Mo! Stop it! Stop!' and I know she wants some more. Picking her ass, busting her ass, suing her ass, kissing her ass, and then she wants some work between her thighs, like licking ashtrays and dried leaves. She turns everything she touches vaguely stale and bent at the edges with her dirty nails, her dirty body, the devil with a forked tail and a huge butt who takes you to the burning lakes: *Evil, evil,*

evil, girl, never trust again girl, good-for-nothing insanity girl, disgusting polluted death girl, loathsome pestilence Jezebel girl. Oh. Oh. A flash of fantastic vertigo and then I lose consciousness of everything around.

The cap falls to the ground, a hand appears to shield the ravished butt, the sweating and straining and longing butt. 'No!' she moans again. 'No!' And then I know what I have to do: crush the black creature, stun it dead.

The belt unbuckles. Gasps again. And now the world has disappeared, now there is nothing on earth but power and sweat and devil tail. She pleads, she begs, she kisses the tomb of Ignacio Sanchez. She takes the first scourge, and then the second. I know how to do it, I know how to do everything. I strike her on the most fleshy part, little by little, harder and harder and then, just as it seems to be more than she can bear, it stops. It stops for so long – for hours and hours, days and days – and she wants more, her red skin pleads for more, begs for more and so there is more, harder and harder, swifter and swifter, spreading her legs, kissing the stone, bowing to shadows in a field of ripped black creatures.

A groan and then a pant – a plea – then the tingle of laughter, then tears and sobs and 'Please!' and 'Please!' and 'Please!' and then the fall, the collapse of the Ruby Rose colossus. She falls forward, she tosses and turns, 'No! No . . .' but that just beckons me in, into the mouth of the cave, the warm blue shelter where the sea comes in and out with jewels and gems caught up among the sand and the shingle. And all the time I hear something in my head, a backbeat wave, something far away that says, 'Look after Billie . . . Billie was dead . . . you brought her back to life . . . Look after Billie.' I want that noise to stop. I want to put a stop to her American schmaltz. So I give her what she's really waiting for and then she starts to whimper, 'Oh! Oh!' and she thrashes around on the front of the tomb. She writhes and twists and little by little she changes. Some other form of life comes into her, some other life force. Ruby Rose leaves, Ruby Rose has long gone, and in her place is this roaring giant, this roaring gentle flower.

She writhes and coils before me on the plate of granite. Her eyes are wild and frenzied and it feels too private, as if I shouldn't be in this secret place, seeing all these secret things. She turns towards me. She pulls me towards her. She wants to take me down to the fiery lake of burning sulphur and it's not what I expected. It's a different lake altogether. I didn't expect such an immersion. Not the first time. I didn't expect this at all.

A violent slash of orange bleeds into the evening sky. And then they come over the hill – the riders with the breastplates of fire and sapphire and sulphur and the horses with the heads like lions. I know that they're there – if only I could take my hands from my eyes but I can't take my hands away, I can only squint through clenched fingers. And I know it's ridiculous because here at last is real life – raw life on the bone – which is what I've been after all along. I should be lapping it up. Taking it all in. But I can't because it's too much. It's too much emotion for six o'clock on a Tuesday afternoon when all I was doing in the first place was taking a Thomas Cook break to get away from my bloody gay husband. I want to be doing macramé and swotting up on journalistic facts and serving sole *meunière* to customers with no teeth and having a laugh with Acid Sarah in the pub after work even though I hate the pub and I hate Scarborough and, actually, macramé is completely boring but it's a sight more normal than the horsemen of the bloody apocalypse in an abandoned graveyard in America seven thousand feet in the air.

I say I've got my hands up against my eyes to shield me from the terrifying vision of Billie scarfing and barfing passion and subterranean fury, but of course I haven't got my hands free at all. My hands are plunged inside her, in a place I don't even dare imagine. And then everything is madness. Billie's been felled. A cataclysmic power-cut, a scythe with flashing teeth hacks and severs through red and green and blue cables sending gashed wires and copper filaments into spasms of electro-convulsive energy. And then, like the eerie chiming of the Mass bells to alert you that bread and wine is changing into flesh and blood, a warm flush of perspiration comes between her shoulder-blades – pinpricks of water on her spine, a dusting of salty glitter, a path of coming.

It seems as though nothing will ever be normal again. It's a new world. As if you've walked through a mirror into another place, another state. All the lines are down. And I almost falter, I almost topple. There's a strange silence and you notice things for the first time – things that you never notice when the power is up – the mystic rushing sound that could be traffic or water-falls or roaring lakes of sulphur if you let yourself believe. But I don't let myself believe, I put a stop to it. I can see the precipice – I'm on the very edge – I could tumble irresistibly, go and listen to the chiming of the mast tops by night in a deserted marina. Is it the wind or is it something else? I can see the fall, the plunge. But I resist. The roaring lakes are just wind in the trees. My panic dies down.

Billie's gone, though. She's floated away somewhere or fallen somewhere like the man in the cartoon who plunges from the sky, crashes through a roof and passes slap-bang through a bed – leaving only a cut-out silhouette as he carries on falling to who knows where. A trick of the eye, though, would have you believe that she's still here, lying on a granite tomb in an abandoned grave-yard. There she lies on the stone: silent, drenched. An immense arm clings tight to my body and I want to run as far as my legs will carry me. I don't know who I'm lying with any more. I just know that Ruby Rose has gone and some other creature – compli-cated, needy, possibly in love – has come in her place.

I wish there was a safe word. I wish I could say 'peanut butter' and it would all change. She'd go back to being Ruby Rose, the dominatrix with good one-liners who'd make a good story for when I get back home.

The stream of sweat on her back feels so delicate. Delicate and innocent. And I want nothing to do with it. I want to wrench myself away from her but I don't dare. Fucking love. Hookers are stupid. Hookers are sentimental. They spend all their life fucking because they have to and it takes the pleasure out of it. They think there is more to life beyond the fucking. They think that real life lies beyond the fucking. But that's not true. Life's not so much better beyond the fucking. People are just as shit when they don't fuck as when they do. Fuck fuck fuck.

Then she rolls over on to her back. Another ejaculation as butt finally hits stone.

'Oh . . . my . . . God!' She says it slowly, savouring every word and presumably every atom of cool granite crystal on her flayed skin. Slowly she hoists herself up and looks at me. 'Where the fuck did you learn to do that?'

I still can't see too clearly. I tell her I've no idea where I learned to do that.

She doesn't care about the answer. She lies back down on the tombstone, murmuring, 'I was going to do a big number on you.'

'Oh, yeah?' I say weakly.

'Yeah. I was going to leave instructions for you. The morning after the night in Van Horn? Written instructions. I was going to say for you to be in the room at a certain time. And you'd have to have twine and a chair and . . .'

'Oh . . . right . . .'

'Yeah, but I decided that I didn't want to be Ruby Rose for you . . . I didn't know what I wanted at that point. Nor did you. You know what I'm saying?'

'Yeah . . . I know what you're saying.'

'I was going to leave notes for you. Like an Easter-egg hunt.' She makes a sigh of deep peace. She lifts her head slightly. 'Hey,' she goes, 'are you OK? Your face looks like a corset that's been done up too tight.'

'I'm fine.' I smile. 'Just a bit exhausted, I think.'

Just terrified, I think.

'Little wimp.' Her head flops down again. 'You didn't even come.'

I wonder momentarily if I should deny it. But then, momentarily, I forget how to lie. 'Maybe another time.' I shrug.

'Get over yourself, girlfriend, who says there's going to be another time?'

I relax then. I start feeling better. I say, 'You've got to write me that note next time.'

'Yeah, well,' she says, propping herself up, 'I'm not sure written instructions are a good thing. I don't like to write stuff down unless I'm going to burn it.'

'Apart from your diary!'

I'm not even aware I've said it. To start with, I'm just waiting for her to tell me the exact instructions she's going to write down for my special Ruby Rose SM night. But suddenly there's silence. And then I see her eyes.

It's horrible what's happening to her eyes. In each one there's a three-days-dead cockroach. Desiccated and disintegrating – a leg here, a mandible there, everything floating around in a yellow puddle. An old roach from an old Roach Motel. When her voice finally comes, it's pocket-size. A voice shrunken to the size of a doll.

'You . . . you read my diary?'

'You lied to me!' I fight for my life. 'You lied about the burning! You said you burned everything you wrote!'

And now what am I supposed to say? The truth? Maybe that's what I will do. I'll take a risk and go for the truth and maybe that will work.

'I'm sorry, Billie. I – I only read a bit.'

'Don't lie!'

'I did! I—'

'You read my diary! You went to my secret place!'

The ants in my throat have shifted to my head. My head's overrun.

'I'm sorry, Billie . . . I'm so sorry.'

'I finally felt safe with you, Mo!' She leaps up. 'For a moment there I thought that maybe the world wasn't full of people who suck you dry. I thought maybe there was a ray of hope in the world. But it turns out that there's not.' She wrenches the catsuit back on.

'Billie!'

'You want to ruin it just like everyone else!' Her hands tremble on the zip.

'Maybe you *wanted* me to read your diary!' A new tack. Aggression when the truth doesn't work. Didn't she like me being a sadist just now? A latent sadist I am, that's what she said.

'*Wanted* you to read it?' There's contempt in her voice.

I know I'm being an idiot. A coward. 'Look, Billie—'

'OK, man! Yeah, let's let it all hang out! Why don't you, like, write home to your mama about how you're hanging out with this bulimic, coke-snorting, weed-smoking, mental case with a pervy stepdad and a suicidal mother? That'd take her mind off international terrorism, don't you think!'

She raves on for a bit longer, and all the while I'm thinking, Coke snorting? Pervy stepdad? Suicidal mother? I don't remember reading that. Is she a coke addict? Is that the concrete smell then? The night sweats? Is it the drugs or is it an overactive mind? A crazy mind? I look down at the doctor-cum-admiral jacket. Where did she get a genuine doctor's coat from anyway? From a hospital? Did she steal it or was she a patient? What kind of hospital was she in? Maybe she's not charismatic at all, maybe she's just mental. And if I am attracted to her charisma and her charisma is actually madness, does it mean that I'm not all there myself?

Then a spine-chilling noise blocks out all the other sounds in the canyon. A raw cry of passion and pain all at once. 'No!'

She squints at the sunset as if the amber glow hurts her eyes. 'Billie has to die. I killed Billie once and nobody was supposed to see her ever again. You brought her back, Mo. You brought her back before she was ready.'

'Please listen! I didn't—'

'Now you've done this. She can't come back again. She can't

ever come back. It's not safe for her to come back. She has to die!'

It's the end. The petals close over her face, she closes down. She runs off down the dirt path. I'm left shouting stupidly after her, 'Your shoes! Your shoes!' She hasn't just forgotten her shoes. There's the admiral top, the cap and, more importantly, her bag. I'm in a complete panic. It's the first time I've seen her out of control. I don't like it when she's not in charge. I'm rushing to put all the things in the bag because even now, at this desperate second, I'm worrying about leaving this wastage up here in the cemetery. I'm folding stuff up and shoving it into the drag bag thinking about how I'm going to tell her that I didn't read all of her diary. I'm trying to collect myself, work out what I'm going to say to her. I'm going to say that I just read the stuff about me, and something about the devil and some mad babysitter and her fucked-up son William, because that's the truth. And then other thoughts come in – I wonder, for instance, if we'd have had sex like that if I hadn't read the diary and I wonder if that was even me who just had sex with her. But, most of all, I don't want her to be hurt, I really don't want her to be hurt, and I wasn't just using her. And then, as I'm picking up the East German military cap from down between two rusty headstones, the badge chinks on a bent nail. And when I hear the chime – the sound of the Mass bells ringing, the magic chime of a Significant Ring tossed on to a sleazy pool table – it's then that I realise. I freeze in my tracks under the orange sky, standing on the baking earth. I stop fiddling with the drag bag. I scream into the prehistoric trees, 'Billie! Billie!'

Tears are streaming down my face. I do love her. Fuck it, I do love her! But all the rusty crosses in the cemetery are rising up over my head, enclosing me in a tangle of cheap graves and laughing at me for letting the only bit of passion ever to come into my life – sex and affection all in one fantastic package – laughing at me for letting it get away. Suddenly I want her to know that I love her. I don't care that I'm using up my three wishes from the genie all at once – I realise that this moment is what genies were made for: 'I love you, you fucking idiot! I love you!'

The words echo round the canyon – but not for very long. They get eaten up, shrivelled and massacred in Geronimo's savage stomping ground. Geronimo and all his tribe are laughing at me for making light of love, and without her here I don't feel so safe. She's gone and the spirits are tumbling on top of me again – an avalanche of mocking souls – and the only escape is to find her.

But she's gone. By the time I stop blubbering and get my act together to rush off down the dirt track there's no sign of her. I'm useless. I drop the bag a couple of times and items come rolling out – envelopes, a pink rubber glove, the floral bloody diary.

Half an hour later when I come limping into Carlota town, the limo's still there. The chauffeur's standing in front of the retired sea captain's wooden house. I hobble up to him. He must have seen her go past. 'Did you see her? Did she come this way?'

He just stares at me with his cold blue eyes. He turns and looks over to the door of the house. It opens and I see a long grey beard and a glittering eye. Then a skinny hand appears – ancient as a strip of withered wood, weatherbeaten as a piece of old rope. I'm about to smile politely and say, 'Sorry, I'm in a bit of a rush, actually,' but a bold new voice comes into my head. It whispers, 'Fuck it, Mo. A bit of free money wouldn't go amiss.' So I take out the East German military cap and I wedge it firmly down on top of my head.

CHAPTER EIGHTEEN

Oh Dear Diary . . .

At one in the morning, when I arrived back in Lariat, the SUV was still there. So was the pigsty inside – the handles, the melted Reese's Peanut Butter Cups, the spilled-over cups of root beer, the marijuana Roach Motel, the stray lighters, the skeleton necklace. The road map was still on the window-ledge, opened to the New Mexico page with Carlota circled in silver marker pen. Billie hadn't taken anything.

She hadn't been back to our room either. The place was just as we'd left it – various pieces of costume were strewn over the floor along with scissors, bits of gold curtain braid and scraps of white doctor's coat stuck to the carpet. The pomegranate had rolled up against the Perspex heels of the silver stripper stilettos, which were capsized next to the bed.

The presence of all Billie's things in the room and the huge lack of Billie herself suddenly felt overwhelming and the ants stomped their way back into my throat turning my glands into an over-stuffed settee about to split at the seams. I dropped the drag bag to the floor, grabbed the pomegranate and, with the scissors, I hacked into its skin. But it had turned into a shrunken skull: the rind had wizened into hard plastic and inside it was brown like fermented soil jelly. I looked at the abandoned stripper shoes and I saw Billie prising them on to her hot feet, wobbling to an upright position, brows knitted in concentration, tongue clenched between teeth, a look on her face that said, 'Stupid pesky shoes!' and then, suddenly, triumph in her eyes and a face that lit up and said, 'Ha! There ya go! All done!' A sweet face, a kid's face that had nothing to do with sex or domination or imprisonment in a deep black hole.

I'd hoped I might find her in some way up at the freak's house in Carlota. But, of course, I hadn't found her there at all: I'd found something entirely different. Waves of panic and exhilaration were still rushing through me from that encounter and more surges were coming on at the thought of reading the next section of the diary. I still wasn't sure what it was, this diary – some way of dealing with her past, some way of beginning 'the deed' that Vera kept talking about? And if it was the beginning of the deed, then what was the end?

I collapsed on the bed, floral notebook in hand. I stroked the raspberry-coloured threads on the cover, traced the shapes of the embroidered black flowers and then started to play with the green and yellow cord – feeling out the shape of the knot that locked the silk front door. I hesitated about prying into her soul again but then I reasoned that if Billie had gone for ever the nearest I was going to get to being with her again was among those thick cream pages.

The cord was tied in a bowline, one of the best-known loop knots – a cinch to undo. Once I was through that I turned to where I'd left off, deciding to work systematically through – to soak everything up, take everything in, throw nothing away.

God is someone I apologise to a lot, although I think that maybe when the sulphur lake part is over then being dead wouldn't be so bad. You could sit and dry off on a cloud and you'd be everywhere at once. I could look down on Mom and Ned and Leah and my dad (and I'd know where he was because I'd be dead).

You can never be sure of anything, of course. That's why I like Mr Harper's science classes. There are answers to everything in science. Also, you don't have to sit still all the time – you can run around the classroom looking at different samples Mr Harper brings in to show us. One day I asked him about why sulphur was bad – because I want to get prepared for what's coming to me. He said there was nothing bad about sulphur. He said that sulphur is the stuff on the end of matches and that it smells of rotten eggs and armpits but, apart from that, there's nothing bad about it. He said that it was once used as an ingredient in explosives but that now two-thirds of the world's consumption of elemental sulphur was in fertiliser.

'You're not scared of fertiliser, are you?' he said.

I said that of course I wasn't scared of fertiliser, but I wanted to know what would happen if someone threw you into a sulphur lake.

He said I shouldn't worry. He said that hot springs are filled with sulphur, that people pay good money these days to be thrown into sulphur lakes.

'Take Palm Springs,' he goes. 'That's a town founded on a bunch of hot sulphur water.'

That makes sense because Reba calls Palm Springs 'Devil's Town'.

Sometimes when we're in Sambo's, Mom asks me what I did at school and I want so bad to impress her. I think about my day: the pledge of allegiance at nine followed by history class, science class, lunch (taco day with any luck), sprinting, picking up Ned, getting beaten at Reba's, doing stuff with William, bed at eleven or twelve or one or whenever Mom remembers to pick us up. It's safe for me to tell Mom about Mr Harper's science class. This semester we learned about black holes. We were in Sambo's when I told Mom about the black-holes class. I said, 'Mom, did you know that black holes are stars that die? They die and there's a vacuum in space and so they turn into the deepest, darkest place in the universe with no bottom.'

'Is that so?' Mom says. She sounds a bit impressed.

'Yeah, it's pretty wild, huh? Mr Harper says that if something goes into a black hole it never comes out. Not ever again.'

'Uh-huh.' She signals for Leah to bring her some more coffee.

'Yeah, Mom, and I was thinking . . . you know the sun?'

'Yeah, I know the sun, baby.'

'Well, it's a star, right?'

'I guess.'

'Yeah, so what if the sun died one day? I mean, if the sun died one day it might suck our whole universe into it and then we'd be trapped in a big black hole for ever and ever!'

'That's a cheerful thought,' Mom says, leaning back so that Leah can top up her mug. It sounds like she's not impressed at all by what I have to say about black holes.

'What's that, Mrs Harrison?' Leah says. 'This here little kiddiewink trying to cheer you up?'

'She says we're all going to die,' Mom says, with a smile, but it's a phoney smile.

I've made her sad, I can tell. I want to let her know that Mr Harper didn't say any of that stuff about the sun. I want to let her know that I thought of it and so I've probably got it all wrong and there's nothing to worry about (even though I'm not sure there isn't anything to worry about). I say, 'Probably the sun isn't a black-hole kind of star, Mom. Probably the sun won't ever die.' But Mom's stirring Sweet and Lo into her coffee so I look up at Leah to see if she believes me.

Leah's holding the coffee-pot. She says, 'Child, don't you worry about that old sun. That old sun ain't gonna stop working if I got anything to do with it. I wouldn't be busting my ass in Sambo's every day if I didn't know the sun was going to shine tomorrow.'

A man with triangle eyes from another table shouts over, 'Leah, honey, can I get another cup of coffee?'

Leah raises her eyebrows as she looks over at the man with triangle eyes. 'Sure, Arnold,' she says. Then she leans closer and whispers me a secret. 'If you wanna see a black hole for free, kiddiewink, then just you look at this here coffee-pot. Talk about a black bottomless pit!'

She smiles at me. A nicer smile than the one she gave the triangle-eyes man. I feel a bit better but, even so, I wish I could make Mom love me by telling her about black holes rather than making her love me by being quiet.

Mom never eats anything in Sambo's. Just the coffee. She is always saying that money is tight and that is why we split the Blue Plate Special and the girl-cheese or boy-cheese sandwich. But when

I offer her something off of my plate she just says, 'Billie, for God's sake, will you please eat your food? You're trying my patience!' Mostly she tells me off because she says I'm drawing attention to myself. Sometimes men stare at our table and it's me that they're staring at. I don't mind men staring at me. Not if they're nice men. I just smile politely back and that's when Mom tells me off. So I concentrate on the Sambo pictures, although sometimes I sneak a look at the men when she goes to the restroom or when she goes off to make a call. I like to make people smile.

Sometimes Leah gives us free pieces of pie from the pie box with the mirror on top. And it kind hurts in a way — to be offered one choice out of twenty kinds. To only be allowed one kind of pie. I guess my heart hurts too because Mom doesn't like us to get stuff for free. She tells me off afterwards even though I tell her I didn't mean for Leah to offer me the pie.

One day Leah gave me and Ned free soda and Mom didn't know about it. She gave me a root beer and Ned a Coke because she knows that's what we like. It was the day when Mom had a really bad headache and Tommy Rice read my diary because I had a messy desk.

Mom went outside to make a phone call. I knew she wasn't happy. She'd started forgetting to pick us up from Reba's again and Reba would lock us out in the dog yard until dark or whenever Mom showed. And then last week, when we got back home at about midnight, I had to call up her boyfriend, Ron, and tell him on the phone that she didn't want to see him any more. Mom came into my bedroom and her face looked kind of tweaked. She was holding a bottle of the green cough syrup and the phone. She gave me the phone and told me to call him.

When I spoke to Ron, it reminded me of 'Fifty Ways To Leave Your Lover' by Paul Simon. I was very polite, though. I said that my mother would no longer be able to see him and I hoped he had better luck next time. He got mad and said a bunch of bad swear words and told me to put Mom on the line but she refused to speak to him. Later in the evening he came round to the apartment and they had a big fight. I listened from my bedroom and thought that Paul Simon should have said that the fifty-first way to leave your lover is to get your nine-year-old daughter to do it for you.

In Sambo's that day, Mom had already drunk five mugs of coffee and her headache was so bad that she couldn't even walk in a straight line to go to the phone booth. When she was gone, Leah came over and sat with me and Ned. Usually Leah doesn't sit at our table. It was cool. I pretended she was our mom. She asked us if everything was OK with Mom and we said yes, and then I told Leah about Miss Baker. I told her how she opened my desk up and tipped it upside-down on the floor because she said it was so messy. It wasn't that messy. There was a bag of melted Reese's Peanut Butter Cups and my books were in a kind of swirly arrangement. I try to keep them in neat rows but after a couple of hours of going in and out of my desk, the swirly thing just happens.

'She tipped up my desk in front of the whole class, Leah.'

Leah opened her eyes wide. 'Well, I'll be . . .' she said. She thought Miss Baker was a crazy woman, you could tell.

I wouldn't have minded about the desk. Not really. It looked kind of pretty when everything came spilling out. Like a waterfall of pencils and books and melted candy and cheer-leader ribbons. Only my diary was inside. My totally top-secret diary that nobody in the whole world is allowed to read, not even Marnie. And Tommy Rice got a hold of it. He grabbed it from the pile while Miss Baker was giving me a lecture on lying. She asked me why hadn't I tidied my desk and when I told her that I had cleaned it up she didn't believe me.

'I had tidied it, Leah. But then it got all swirly inside when I had to pull out my science books really fast.'

'I know what you're saying, hon. Things do get swirly before you know it.'

I knew that Leah would understand. I wondered if I should tell her about the diary. Or about what happened at recess when everyone was crowded around Tommy in the playground. I could hear him reading out these sentences that I knew from somewhere. 'Treat me like a princess and I'll treat you like a king.' Tommy can't even read very well but everyone was laughing. And then I suddenly realised he was reading my diary. My secret diary! So I pushed everyone out of the way and I told him to give me back my diary or I'd give him a fucking black eye.

I said 'fucking' and all the kids started jumping up and down and getting excited so I had to go in and take him out. In the middle of the fight — I was definitely winning — Miss Baker comes out and pulls us apart and me and Tommy had to go see the principal. Of course, I never told the principal about the diary because I didn't want anyone else to know about it, and Tommy got off scot-free and the principal told me I was a trouble-maker with a 'dirty mouth'. On the good side, though, I got the diary back. While the scuffle was going on, Marnie snuck in and got it for me.

I can't tell Leah that, though. I'm not sure if I can tell Leah my deep secrets or she might not like me any more. But I decide to risk it. I say, 'There was a diary, Leah. A boy found my diary and I had to burn it because he read it and there was bad stuff inside.'

She looked totally impressed by my secret. She was so impressed that she went off and fetched me and Ned the free sodas.

She told us to drink them quick before Mom came back. She looked over at the phone box where Mom was talking and these big-ass lines went into the place between her eyes. She must have guessed that Mom gets mad if we get stuff for free. So we drank the sodas quick and she told me that Tommy Rice sounded like a bad boy. She told me that I mustn't stop writing my diary, just that I must keep it hidden better next time.

Then we see Mom come back from the phone box. She's still not walking in a straight line. A man calls out from the next table, 'Leah, sweetheart, that coffee coming any time soon?'

Leah stands up and takes our free soda glasses off of the table. 'Any more secrets you guys want to share, old Leah's always here.' She looks at me and her eyes are not like normal Leah eyes. They're serious eyes. Like teacher eyes. Like Leah teacher eyes.

When Mom gets to the table she looks real tired. 'Will you kizz keep the noise down?' she says. She's speaking in the slippery voice she has when she gets real bad headaches.

When Leah comes over with the check, Mom says, 'Leah, have these kizz been ginvig you trouble?'

The wrinkles groove back into Leah's place between the eyes. 'Trouble, Mrs Harrison? You got yourself a couple of the best-behaved kids in Granada Hills.'

My heart swells up then because I think Mom's going to be pleased with what Leah's said about us. But she just rummages in her purse, looking for money to pay the check. When she's paying Leah I wonder if giving someone free soda is a sort of a lie. Then I see that Mom's only left a fifty-cent tip even though it's for Leah. That's a shame, that's a real shame, because if you don't get a lot of tips you might think that nobody loves you. So I make it into a special fifty-cent tip by tucking it away in some secret places: one quarter under the Sweet and Lo box and one quarter under Mom's coffee mug so that when Leah finally finds it she'll be totally stoked.

We get up from our seats and go out to the parking lot. When we get to the car Mom asks Ned if he's been to the restroom. 'Have you gone big potty, Ned?' she goes, in her slippery voice, and he stretches out his arms like he's just caught a big fish. 'Yeah, Mom. It was this big!' Me and Ned giggle in the back seat of the car while Mom mumbles, '*Quieta la boca*,' but in the rear-view mirror I can see that she's smiling.

I have a new babysitter. She is called Mystic Mountain. During the summer vacation I spend all day, every day with her. For thirty dollars you can get a pass for a whole year, which means it's free every time you go in. I've convinced Mom that now I am eleven years old it's educational and economical for me to spend the day at Mystic Mountain. One of the single moms in our complex works there as a cleaner and she drives me over in the morning and brings me home at night so I get to stay from ten in the morning until twelve at night, six days of the week!

Mystic Mountain is thirty-five miles north of Santa Monica in Saugus, which is the dry area before the beginning of the Mojave desert. Mystic Mountain is where they filmed the movie *Roller-Coaster* so obviously it's the coolest place and the rides are totally gnarly. My favorite is the Colossus, the world's largest roller-coaster. You travel slowly up this big white arc — really, really slowly — until you're so high up in the air that all you can see are fields and mountains and you feel nearer to the sky than you are to the ground and you can hardly bear the suspense.

It's really quiet as you travel up to the top of the arc. That's part of the thrill. All you can hear is the oily creak of the steel wheels and the sound of your heart beating faster and faster and your breath getting shorter and shorter as you approach the point of no return when gravity takes hold of you and throws you down the deep ravine on the other side. You wonder if you might die because that's what happened last year when a fat lady was thrown out of the Revolution — the first roller-coaster in the world where the cars do a total upside-down loop. The attendant asked her if the bar was down and she was too embarrassed to say that it wouldn't fit over her belly so when the car turned upside-down, she fell out and when they found her body on the concrete it was just a heap of blood-stained blubber. Me and Marnie, we were there that day and we saw it. Well, I tell Marnie that we were there that day but I don't actually think we were.

But, anyway, when the Colossus throws you down the other side of the big ravine it's as exciting as catching on fire. The air shoots past you like a knife and you push your face into the knife. You're going up and down and up and down and the people in the cars are screaming, and the people in the cars on the parallel track are screaming and the ones who think they're brave are throwing their arms up in the air but they're not brave — not like me and Marnie. Putting your arms up in the air is OK for beginners because you feel like you're flying out of your seat, but the most bitchin' thing of all is to put your arms out to the side so you can feel what it's like to be a bird. The other bitchin' thing to do is to sprawl around in the carriage like you're sitting on the couch at home. Me and Marnie sometimes just sit there looking tough and blowing bubbles with gum and all the couples and the families get freaked out. I put a bored expression on my face and I look at the backs of my nails or something and I say to Marnie, 'So, what did you think of that bikini in Chacha's, dude?' and Marnie goes, 'I thought the top was kind of big, dude. Like, a bad tan situation?' And it's hysterical because we're acting just like Valley Girls and all the time the cars are rumbling and vibrating like jack-hammers and everyone thinks they're going to die and we're just there being, like, totally laid-back, looking like we're cruising along in a Cadillac.

The most times I've ever ridden the Colossus in a row is twenty-five, which isn't as amazing as it sounds because the whole ride only lasts for two and a half minutes. The only thing that I don't like so much – but of course I don't tell Marnie about this – is the bit when you reach the bottom of the ravine and the car jerks back up the loop really quickly so that your stomach feels like it's being ripped out. But the good thing about this jerking is that I don't feel like eating afterwards. This is just as well because Mom never gives me lunch money for Mystic Mountain. She tells me to take something from home and carry it in a backpack but naturally I don't want to go round all day looking like a dork so I just go hungry. Sometimes, when she's in a good mood, she'll give me a dollar and I'll spend it on candy – probably salt-water taffy or Reese's Peanut Butter Cups.

The best ride for making you lose your appetite is the Cage. You get in the Cage and you basically free-fall for ten storeys. When you get to the bottom you're lying on your back and you feel incredible. You can't speak and you get up and your knees buckle and then you can't stop laughing for half an hour. The Cage totally rocks. If you were to set it on fire and drop it, all at the same time, then that would be my number-one most exciting thing that could ever happen to me.

Marnie doesn't really like the gnarly rides so for her sake we get on the funicular and go up to the Japanese garden. It's really neat there, actually. The only noises are of the waterfall running under the little bridge and recordings of frogs and cricket sounds. The Japanese garden is a good place to go to watch the night-time fireworks display and it's also a good place to get high. Getting high and watching fireworks is totally gnarly. There are the little wiggly fireworks like the sperm in our science books at school and the ones that go bang in your ears and the bigger ones that go bang in your throat. There are the big-ass ones that spiral up like airplanes made of glitter and then explode silently in a huge spray of fire. They come sprinkling down from the sky like pinches of silver salt and you think it's all over but it isn't all over at all because there's a huge, gigantic bang at the last minute, a bang so loud it feels like a cannon blowing through your stomach.

I like to get high and watch the firework display at Mystic Mountain and it doesn't even matter if someone catches you smoking because all you have to do is run down the hill as fast as your legs can carry you. You have to go so fast you think your heels are going to catch up with your ears but there's nothing to worry about because you always make it to the bottom. You collapse in a heap of laughter and it feels like the Miss Mary Mack patty-cake rhyme about when she jumped so high she reached the sky and she didn't come down 'till the fourth of July.

She didn't look like Mom that day. Her head was back, like when you go to the hairdresser's and they wash your hair in the basin. Sometimes I'm allowed to go to the hair salon with her if I sit real quiet and don't get excited. I told a friendly man there that I wanted to be Lucille Ball or a hairdresser when I grew up and he said he'd wash my hair for free to give me some training. He was nice. At first the cold of the basin stings the back of your neck but you soon get used to it. They rub on the suds and then they massage your head and that's real nice. If they like you, they massage it for a long time.

I think the hairdresser liked me so I told him about the cheerleader try-outs. About how they didn't call my name at the end. I told him that I didn't cry but I didn't tell him about the bad thing.

About how Jody Delagringa told Marnie that I didn't get chosen because my impro dance was too 'suggestive'. Jody Delagringa's dad is one of the coaches. Marnie said that Jody Delagringa is ugly. She said she looks like a green apple and that's true because she's sour and fat. Mom was nice too. She said she was sorry I didn't pass the trials and she made me a huge bowl of ambrosia that I ate all up. It made me forget for a while, but then the bad feeling came back. I wondered what I'd done that had been wrong. I wondered what Jody Delagringa's dad meant by 'suggestive'. Mom said that I must have been too tall to be chosen and that we can't afford for me to have another try-out because if you're a cheer-leader you have to pay for camp, which is eight hundred dollars, and for cheer-leader outfits, which are five hundred dollars, and for meals before games and stuff like that.

I'm not going to give up, though. I told the hairdresser man that one day I was going to get elected as school mascot. School mascots get to go to cheer-leader conventions and travel all over the state of California meeting people and carrying a sword and wearing this neat Zena Warrior Princess outfit that's like the breastplates of fire and sapphire and sulphur that the apocalypse riders got to wear.

When I told the nice hairdresser man that school mascot is the biggest show-off thing you could do – that it was even better than being a homecoming queen – he said, 'You go, girl! You *take* to that stage! You *hog* that limelight!' and he patted me on the shoulders like I'd done something good.

When I told him about my black-hole theory, he said, 'Ain't that just the truth? Dying stars are nothing but trouble. They don't just go off quietly. Oh, no! They gotta have lights, they gotta have music, they gotta be found lying in their beds with chignons and an empty bottle of Valium!'

I wasn't sure what he was talking about. Maybe I didn't explain my black-hole thing properly. He was funny, though. He made me laugh. The water was warm and his fingers massaged my head. My eyes were closed and inside it looked like outer space with slow-motion fireworks.

I told him that my favorite star was Lucille Ball. I said that I liked her hair and that I wished I had perfect hair like Lucille Ball. He said that perfect hair was boring but I guess that he was just trying to be nice to me because I'm messy and not neat like my mom.

He told me to tip my head even further back so I did and I could feel all the shampoo rinsing off the top of my head and down my neck. It was funny, it tickled. I said, 'Your head has a special treat on the day it goes to the hairdresser's,' and he said that it was nice to be appreciated. 'It's good to meet a polite young lady,' he said. 'When you become the next Lucille Ball make sure you don't become one of those black-hole kind of stars.'

On the day they carried her out on the hair-washing chair I was playing funeral with my Barbies. I was at the bit where they get to clean up and go home and drink martini cocktails when Mom came in and said, 'I love you, Billie. Remember that I love you very much.' She definitely said it. She looked kind of sleepy. And then she hung around by the door, staring at me. I didn't look up but I could feel that she was staring at me. After a bit she said, 'OK, then, I'll be up in a little while.'

It wasn't until she went out of the room that I let myself think about what she'd just said. She said, 'I love you,' and it felt like I'd suddenly been told I could be a cheer-leader, or like the chores chart had been rearranged and it didn't say, 'Monday, wax floors; Tuesday, wash clothes; Wednesday vacuum carpets.' It said, 'Monday, let's play skipping rope together; Tuesday, I love you; Wednesday, I never want to let you out of my sight for ever and ever.'

And the next thing I remember, Mom was back in the room. Only she didn't look like she loved me this time. She looked totally grey – like she was a sick old lady. She asked where Ned was and I told her that he was playing at Greg's house. Ned always goes to play at Greg's house on Saturday afternoons. She looked at me like she couldn't see me properly. She had a weird voice. She said, 'Mrs James wants to talk to you on the phone.' Then she went out again and she didn't say anything about getting up in a little while.

I was nervous to talk to Mrs James on the phone. She's one of Mom's friends. She comes round and they get the silver cocktail-shaker out and they start doing stupid things like patting our heads a lot and sometimes they'll shout at us to clear off, and me and Ned scram like rabbits. On those days, we don't get any dinner. Not even lettuce and Jell-O.

But on the phone Mrs James said, 'You know how to make black coffee, Billie?'

I said, 'Well, Mrs James, I'm not sure,' because I'm not allowed in the kitchen so how should I know how to make black coffee?

She didn't say anything like 'Quit whining!' like she sometimes does. She said, 'OK, hon, you just go in the kitchen and I'll tell you what to do.' It was awesome. It was like in the movies when a normal person has to land a plane because although they've killed off all the hijackers the pilot good-guy is too injured to sit in the cockpit and he has to tell the normal person how to do it. Mrs James told me where to find the coffee. She said to put in two heaped teaspoons and then to pour on boiling water.

So I did all that and then I took it into Mom. All the curtains were drawn in her room and it smelt like sleepy bedclothes skin. I put the cup on her side table and I said, 'Here's some black coffee, Mom. I made it myself.'

She must have been asleep because she didn't reply. So I went out, and the next thing I know, Mrs James is in the house and then there's a loud noise and an ambulance is there. Mrs James didn't tell me what the ambulance was for. She just said that Mama had to go to hospital real quick.

That's when I saw them take her out in the hair-wash chair. They loaded her into the back of the ambulance and then the ambulance drove down the driveway real fast, like in a movie. It was gnarly. A man with a moustache came and gave me a Malibu Beach Barbie because it was a special day. Mrs James and the man with the mous-tache went to the kitchen to talk grown-up stuff and I went to Mom's room to see if I could work out why she disappeared in an ambu-lance. There was no blood, just the cup of coffee untouched by her bed. I was worried then. I wondered what I'd done wrong. I wanted to tell her that I made it just like Mrs James told me to – that I'd followed the instructions and there was no reason why it should have come out wrong. Then the man and Mrs James came into the bedroom. The man had a happy voice on. He said, 'Let's go have Chinese.'

Usually we never get to have Chinese but today we do because today is a special day. Today Mom was carried out like a lady at the hairdresser's.

The Chinese restaurant was neat. Our table was on a dance-floor and behind us there was a stage with red velvet curtains and the waiter put the food on a metal thing that he said was called a lazy-susan. He showed me how you spun it round to get what you wanted. My favorite thing was this weird crunchy watery stuff that the waiter told me was called water-chestnut. He was very nice to me. He said he liked my Malibu Beach Barbie and I said that I got it because my mom went to hospital today.

When the meal was over, the waiter gave us all some things in tiny plastic bags called fortune cookies, and the man with the moustache said that everyone got those at Chinese restaurants. Fortune cookies are cool. You get a cookie to eat, plus you get a prophecy inside. My prophecy said, 'To climb a mountain you must start at the bottom.' Mrs James's said, 'Don't worry about money. The best things in life are free,' and the man's said, 'Anticipate a rainy day.'

I wondered if Mom knew what fortune cookies and water-chestnuts were and then I remembered that she wasn't there.

I need some air. I leave the notebook on the bed and get up to go and open the door. But the muggy night brings no relief. All I can see is a red neon blur from the Thunderbird and all I can hear are the sounds of chirping cicadas and yowling cats.

And then something else comes. Some other voices start to speak:

– Have we got 'chopper' yet, Mum?

– Didn't we think 'cleaver'?

– Doesn't fit.

– It's not cryptic, is it, Mo love? I can't do cryptic.

– I can't either.

– 'Beach peril – roar out and you can't be blamed!'

– 'Foreigner coming up to see a fixer at one!'

Chuckles.

– Hang on, Mum. 'Throttle'. Something T, something A, something something something something. What do you reckon?

– Strangle?

– Wait, what have you put here? 'Gloria' ends in *a*.

– Does it, love?

– Course it does, you daft thing!

– They're devious, these people.

– What could 'Spectrum' be – in five letters?

– Spectrum?

– Prism!

– Come again, love?

– 'Spectrum', Mum. It could be 'prism.'

– Oh, well done.

– What have you put here, Mum? That's not how you spell 'liaise'.

– It's not?

– No, idiot! It's L-I-A-I-S-E!

It's starting to sink in. How I don't know I'm born, how, if you've got a mother, you've got everything. It makes you feel safe. It's a place you can go to in your head and I know that Billie doesn't have a place like that. What do I have to moan about?

She was right.

I'm just a bore who wants to be a whore.

I'm pathetic.

I slam the door shut and go over to my rucksack. I fetch out the last of my emergency candles and then take the Gideon Bible from the drawer of the bedside table. I arrange the candles on top of that, then light them. As I watch the flames I remember a flaming strip of paper floating up into the air and a tiny ear of it not burning and Billie saying, 'You see, Mo, the words that stay could be the important ones.'

The words that stay could be the important ones.

I pick up the book again.

I've just turned fifteen. Reba's has stopped. Quite a lot else has stopped. Pomegranate Hills has stopped, Sambo's has stopped, Leah has stopped. A moustachioed black hole came and swallowed us all up and then I didn't give a shit any more.

Mom got the Blue Book. After the suicide attempt she stopped drinking. She went the way of Reba. She didn't get the religious thing. Something worse happened. She met the Creep.

It was so predictable. They met at an AA meeting. They promised each other they were going to help clean up each other's lives. Me and Ned were going to be cleaned up too. We moved from the apartment complex in Granada Hills to a home in Saugus. Saugus! I mean, Saugus is OK for going to visit Mystic Mountain but it's the furthest east you can go and still be in LA county. I'm nearly not even a Californian any more!

The funny thing is that when I met him aged twelve I liked him OK. I always wanted Mom to be happy. I knew she deserved to find a nice man. At the Chinese restaurant he was just the nice man with the moustache who gave me a Barbie doll. A few months later when he came round to our house I was still really impressed. He was big as a bear and he had cool swept-back hair like Andy Williams and eyeglasses like I saw Rock Hudson wear one time. Mom was wearing her white tuxedo pants that make her look like Bianca Jagger and her gold halterneck top that she made from a Vogue pattern that she gave to Mrs James afterwards to use. I was really rooting for her. When they went off for their date, I said, 'Go for it, Mom!'

He was clever. He'd majored in science and, for a twelve-year-old, I had a lot of questions. He told me why the sky was blue, why the ocean was green, why waves came in three sets of three. He told me funny thing, too, like how the word 'hooker' comes from the women who used to tag along after the soldiers during the civil war.

They got married and I got to wear a peach and green-striped boob tube dress with butterfly sleeves and have my hair all feathered. And the house wasn't so bad; it might have been a way out but it was much bigger than the one in Granada Hills. It had its own swimming-pool and my new stepdad helped me and Ned with our swimming. Soon I got better at butterfly stroke and Ned didn't belly-flop so much.

He was adventurous and fun. He took us sailing in his dinghy and he taught us about wind direction and how to tie knots. On a hiking trip, he'd suddenly stop and go, 'OK, guys, we're going off track now. Let's figure our way down this waterfall!' And sometimes he'd stop the car in the middle of a bridge and say, 'OK, kids, why don't you jump off into the river?'

He didn't even mind me arguing. In fact, he seemed to appreciate it. On one of our first camping trips, I said that the gas smelt bad when he got the calor stove out to cook the wieners. He explained that the smell was sulphur and I told him that I was going to die in a lake of burning sulphur – just to see what he'd say. I said that I didn't see why the devil should like swimming around in sulphur more than, say, gold or diamonds. And he didn't tell me I was a dumb ass. On the contrary, he said that I'd raised a very interesting point. He said that in the Greek translation of the Bible, *theion* is the word for both 'brimstone' and 'divinity'. In a poem called *The Iliad* by Homer, written seven hundred years before Jesus Christ was even born, sulphur is considered as something that purifies because the man in the poem purifies a goblet with fire and brimstone. Brimstone, apparently, is the same thing as sulphur. It comes from the German word for 'amber' because when you grow a crystal out of a bag of yellow sulphur granules the crystal is orangy red in color. He said that when they came to translate the Bible from Greek to English, they really dumbed it down and in the end it only had a vocabulary of eight thousand words (and Shakespeare used thirty thousand!). That's why there are so many mistranslations in the

Bible, he said. Like 'sulphur' being something bad and associated with the devil.

By the time he'd finished, I'd forgotten about campfire dinner. It felt like a weight had been lifted from my chest. He cracked eggs into the pan and the air began to sizzle. He said, 'You should never accept things on face value, Billie. Did you know, for instance, that the Greek Bible has twenty-seven different words for "love" but the Gideon only has one?'

I asked him what different kinds of love there could be and he said that there was love of God, love of one's neighbour, love of one's brethren, love of one's parents and kin. 'Love was once a many-splendoured thing,' he said, nudging me in the ribs. 'And then sex got involved and everything turned bad!'

When I was thirteen, I made them dinner for their first wedding anniversary. I wrote up a menu, I dressed up as a waitress in a pink gingham overall lent to me by Leah that I cinched in at the waist and wore with shiny tan pantyhose and high heels. I brought in the different courses: Lipton's onion soup mixed into sour cream, for a dip, followed by Campbell's cream of mushroom soup mixed up with ground beef, followed by raw Pilsbury cookie dough.

Ned was the Mexican bus-boy, and when he'd cleared away, we brought in a cake with sparklers in (it was just a chocolate muffin piled high with three containers of Betty Crocker frosting) and we sang 'Happy Anniversary' to the tune of 'Happy Birthday'.

That was the first night he was different. He looked at me in a weird way. He didn't say anything about the food or the menu that I'd spent hours drawing mini Little Black Sambos on. He looked worried or something. Finally, he asked me where I'd gotten the high heels from. I thought he was joking. Then he said, 'I'm waiting for an answer, Billie.' I said that Summer Lopez from school lent them to me. That was true: they were espadrilles with woven wedge heels. He glanced at Mom and then turned back to me. He made me feel stupid. He said, 'Heels that high are not good for children's soft bones.' I just nodded like I didn't care, but this stupid gulp noise came out of my throat and when I got to my bedroom I burst out crying.

Things changed after that. I worked out that he was only pretending to show an interest in me because he wanted to impress Mom. Then he realised there was no point in trying to impress Mom because like, she could give a shit about me.

I didn't get any more attention from her now that she was sober. She'd dropped the Lutherans and gotten into meditation tapes and yoga instead. Her private living room was filled with conch shells and self-help books and she'd started hanging wind-chimes and drift-wood mobiles all around the house and playing weird-ass music like 'Greensleeves' and 'The Battle Hymn of the Republic'. Everything had to be pure and wholesome (although, for some reason, eating crappy food was OK), and as usual I was too untidy, too gangly, too messy to have any real pride in.

She started throwing AA meetings at the house and all these freaks came round. Then she gave up the flight school. She said she wanted to but I knew it was the Creep who made her do it. She said that there was too much liquor around the airport, too much bad energy, although for some reason there was good energy working as office manager in the Saugus branch of a major chemical fertiliser company.

The Creep soon thought up other ways of impressing her. New rules started appearing. Suddenly there was no more staying out late at Mystic Mountain. 'Stay at Mystic Mountain until midnight?' he'd splutter, and there'd be globs of spit all over his gross ginger moustache. (That was when I noticed that he was a redhead. I also noticed that he didn't look like Andy Williams or Rock Hudson at all. His hair was swept back because it was thinning on top and Rock Hudson would never have had his glasses smeared with greasy thumbprints.)

'Are you crazy, Billie?' he'd go, his red complexion turning even redder. (He was always asking me if I thought I was crazy.) 'No thirteen-year-old of mine is staying out until midnight.'

Since when was I his?

He decided that we needed to be a proper family. There were to be no more diners, no more babysitters. He and my mother were going to ensure that we had a good upbringing. He was going to bring back discipline to the house. It was 'Yes, sir', and 'Yes, ma'am,' from now on. We were all going to be one happy family. There was going to be no more TV. We were going to sit around the table together and discuss issues of the day — like regular families did, apparently. I wondered if regular families were served up evening meals consisting entirely of cottage cheese topped with tinned fruit salad or orange-flavored Jell-O with grated carrots inside.

Now at every dinner-time, instead of the familiar hiss of the Sambo's coffee machine and the friendly yammer from Leah, there was the blare of Beethoven's Ninth or the tinkle of the Moonlight Sonata accompanied by the *chink chink, clink clink* of silverware on china plates, followed by the Creep barking, 'So, Billie, how's the reading going?' followed by silence. It was enough to drive anyone to an eating disorder.

'The reading' was a reference to my latest babysitter: novels. Not even regular American novels but weird French ones. The Creep had taken a course in French literature and he said he thought I might appreciate a bit of advanced reading. 'You really are very advanced for your age,' he said one night, appearing from nowhere when I was sprawled out on the white suede couch in my new K-Mart bikini (still wet from the pool), flicking through one of his *American Science* magazines that he got on subscription. He was always doing that. Coming home early from work. Appearing from nowhere. Making me feel weird.

I didn't just have to read the books, I had to write papers on them. I was supposed to write them when I got home from school — during the two hours before he got in from work. But he was always surprising me just when I thought I was alone and I never knew how he'd react. Some days he'd say weird things, like about me being advanced for my age, and other times he'd go crazy if I went near the couch wearing anything wet or if he caught me slouching around doing nothing. I was never allowed to just do nothing. That scared the living daylights out of him.

So, there we'd be: another *chink chink, clink clink* dinner session with the Creep asking me about another fucking French novel and I'd feel the pool of slimy Jell-O I'd hidden in my pocket and think about throwing a bunch of it into his slimy face but I knew that the time wasn't right yet.

The thing about the Creep was that he could out-smart me like nobody else could. And even though I hated being out-smarted by him, the fact was that I also couldn't help being interested in what he said. One day I was trying to piss him off. I said that his mind had been taken over by the Communists. (At school, being called a Communist is as bad as being called a lesbian or a faggot.) But the Creep just said, 'And what's wrong with being a Communist, Billie?'

I hesitated. For a few seconds I wasn't sure which way to tread. Then I blurted out, 'You're talking propaganda!'

He pulled on one of the skinny ends of his gross moustache. I knew I'd said a dumb thing. I was waiting for his smart-ass retaliation.

'Did I hear the Great Brain talking?' He looked around the room like a retard, as if some ghost was flitting about. 'Oh, no!' He looked me right in the eye. 'I think a bimbo just took over Billie's body!'

I could feel myself start to shake but I didn't want him to see that he could make me shake. There was something creepy about the way he said, 'Billie's body', and then looked at my breasts. It weirded me out. I couldn't think of anything clever to say. I just opened my mouth and stupid stuff came out, 'I'm not a bimbo! Plus it's not . . .'

His knife and fork dropped down on his plate.

The Creep is a nut for grammar. He has a thing about double negatives and starting sentences with 'plus' or 'and'. He said, 'We don't start sentences with "and". Nor do we start sentences with "plus".'

For some stupid reason, I looked over to Mom for support but, of course, she was just sitting there with that glazed look in her eyes.

He wasn't done with me yet, though. 'You don't believe all that propaganda, do you, Billie?' he snapped. 'About America being the land of freedom?'

I was stuck again. I realised that, yes, I did actually believe all that stuff. I still got a lump in my throat sometimes during the pledge of allegiance that we said every morning at school, hand over heart.

'Do you think a black guy born to a heroin-addicted mother on a project in Compton has freedom, Billie?'

'I—'

'I'll tell you what's liberty, Billie. If that black baby had been born in Russia, at least he'd have had the same chance as the white daughter of a doctor. Now what do you think of "propaganda"?'

I felt that tingle that you get when new ideas take root in you. But I still hated him for telling me. He didn't tell me because he wanted to refresh my mind, he told me because he wanted to humiliate me.

So I go wary now. I try to be polite at all times. I know I have to bite my tongue for a bit longer. One day he went, 'So, Billie, how's *The Stranger* going?' and I shrugged and said, 'I'll let you know when I've finished the paper.'

'C'mon, smart ass,' he said, goading me. 'You must have some views on one of France's most famous novels.'

Fucking asshole, I thought, sitting there, biting my tongue. 'It's OK, I guess,' I said, with a smile.

And he raised an eyebrow, which meant I had to correct my sentence to, 'It's OK, I guess, sir.'

But even that wasn't good enough. He went, 'Are you crazy, Billie? One of the premier works of French literature of the twentieth century and that's all you have to say?'

I made a deep sigh and said, 'I don't know. I found it kind of annoying. I'm, like, "Get off the beach, dude. Get away from that gun."'

Then the Creep's mouth couldn't decide where it wanted to set itself and his skin went bright red, like he was a weight-lifter lifting up twice his bodyweight. He was about to say something real mean about my 'use of colloquialism', as he calls it. I knew he was about to bite my head off because my mother intervened. Not that she wanted to come to my defence. She just wanted a quiet life.

'So, how was school today, Billie?' she said, nibbling on a piece of iceberg lettuce smeared in orange Jell-O.

'Oh, you know,' I mumbled, thinking it was a pity she wasn't interested five years ago.

Silence. *Chink chink, clink clink.*

'You know, Billie,' Mom said, 'if you want to bring any of your boyfriends home then that's fine by us, isn't it, John?'

'Sure is fine by us, sweetheart,' the Creep said, sipping at a glass of Diet Rite cola and wishing it was a triple bourbon on the rocks.

Ned said, with a smirk, 'Billie ain't got no boyfriends. When we go to Mystic Mountain she—'

But he didn't have time to elaborate on what I do at Mystic Mountain because the Creep dived in with '*Doesn't have* any boyfriends, Ned. "Billie *doesn't have* any boyfriends."'

'I guess it must be her height,' my mother said, with her new Stepford wife smile that she never had before. 'Boys must find her kind of intimidating.'

Do you see what I have to put up with? Am I getting through to you, O floral-covered diary to whom I am pouring out my fucking heart? Mo told me to write a diary that I didn't burn because it might be a way to 'work things out' but maybe the best thing is just to forget this shit. My old shrink used to talk about expressing my inner child – writing a diary to express my inner child – but the thing is that my inner child never took up residence. My mother took my inner child, she took it and ripped it to shreds, and then she didn't know what to do with the ikky mess. Rock on, Courtney Love. '*Boys must find her kind of intimidating.*' '*Billie doesn't have any boyfriends.*' I felt like shouting at them all that I didn't give a shit that I didn't have any boyfriends, that the tourists at Mystic Mountain didn't find me intimidating, that the tourists at Mystic Mountain couldn't get enough of me as a matter of fact. And, anyway, if the Creep wanted me to be a better person, why was he giving me books about hookers who make good? I hadn't told him, but I totally liked that *Nana* book he gave me to read. Nana is this high-class hooker who's like a French version of Rizzo – the bad-ass leader of the Pink Ladies in *Grease* – only Nana's from the nineteenth century. She has sex with ugly guys who are rich and then they give her castles and nice clothes and she gets to party a lot. In France this is called being a courtesan. It seems a pretty good set-up because the courtesan gets to fall in love for real sometimes. She can afford to fall in love for real, thanks to the money of the rich ugly man. Basically, the money of the rich ugly man enables her to have her cake and eat it.

Sometimes there's a whole bunch of men waiting in different rooms of her house for her and her maid's getting totally pissed off and stressed out because Nana hasn't even come home yet and then she'll just cruise in and tell the maid she can't be bothered to see any of them.

In the end Nana dies all alone in a ritzy hotel with weeping pustules all over her face – but in those days you had to have come-uppance endings for women who had too much of a good time. And we don't get smallpox in America anyway.

So I did hold my tongue, and now that I've turned fifteen I've learned how to handle him better. Thanks to a series of new papers I've written on Cyrano de Bergerac and yet another one on *Nana*, the Creep has finally agreed that I can stay at Mystic Mountain until eleven o'clock on Friday and Saturday nights. Every Friday morning at ten, when the Creep drops me off outside Mystic Mountain I turn into a California-style courtesan.

As soon as his car is out of sight, I take off my cut-offs and T-shirt and underneath there's my really hot Bo Derek white suede bikini. This bikini is the best thing Chacha's has come up with in ages. Actually, the Bo Derek bikini is something the Creep came up with. He's normally as tight about money as my mother is (my bikinis usually come from K-Mart) but he went out and bought me the Bo Derek one from Chacha's. It wasn't even my birthday. He said it was a reward for improvement in my diving technique. I know. He's a freak, right?

Meanwhile the bikini is so hot. It has hardly any top and the bottom has this kind of Tarzan vibe. Summer Lopez and Karen Schwartz were totally jealous. They're my new friends from my new school – Montana Blanca Junior High. They were the ones who told me about the roller-skate cheesecake scam.

They soon come over to join me because you totally can't miss me in my bikini and my roller-skates (I wear my Dolphin nylon running shorts over the bikini bottoms for modesty's sake – although only because the shorts show the bottom of my butt cheeks). Summer and Karen have their roller-skates on also, and Marnie trails along behind us with her dorky backpack that she has to put all our stuff in. Marnie has turned into a dork. She's not really interested in wearing cool bikinis and roller-skates and making money from taking pictures with the tourists. I think she'd rather be back skiing on ice plant and making perfume out of flowers and twigs even though we've just turned fifteen years old.

Still, she has her uses. She doesn't seem to mind carrying our clothes. I told her that she can be my maid. Nana had a maid to do the practical things she didn't have time for, like wash the sheets and sort out her schedule and get rid of creditors.

Sometimes, me and Summer and Karen can make five dollars each in a day posing with the tourists while Marnie takes the pictures. You can make more if you do more than cheesecake, which means going on the wet rides and then waiting outside the exit for over-excited tourists.

It started one day when a man said to me, 'You wanna earn some extra money?' I'd been giving guys at school blow-jobs for a while now so it was no big deal. Plus Karen and Summer do it too, even though Karen's dad gives her a ton of pocket money and she doesn't even need the extra. Another guy said, 'Can I see you later?' I took one look at him: lank hair, knee-length denim shorts with factory-machined hems, white socks with 'sport' written on the ankles and a red top saying, 'My kids went to Chicago and all they brought me back was this lousy T-shirt!' I said, 'You can see me later but it'll cost you.'

You have to be careful that the Mystic Mountain guards don't see you cruising around on roller-skates because you're not allowed to wear them. Not because they don't want you to hurt yourself but because they're scared you're gonna sue their ass if you hurt yourself. 'That's America,' as the Creep would say. The only people allowed to wear roller-skates are the cleaners who go around sweeping and picking up trash all day in polyester uniforms.

It's OK, though. We have the joint pretty much cased by now. We're friends with lots of the guards and, more importantly, with a bunch of the people who work on the rides. We hardly ever have to get in line to go on a ride. Plus Summer Lopez knows Tony Carrara who has embezzled twenty-five thousand dollars. He works at the cash-up place. His job is to count out all the coins from the arcade games. They never know how much money there is in the first place so it's pretty easy to steal. Once he lent us his credit card and we went to stay at the Motel 7.

We ordered up room service and we jumped around on the beds but they'd taken all of the liquor out of the mini-bar and we got bored and went back to Mystic Mountain. Tony and me got kind of friendly. He's got the most beautiful cock I've ever seen. Most dicks are pretty gross to look at, but his is like sculpture. Like Michelangelo's *David* only bigger. We haven't had sex or anything. I'm still, like, a virgin. I tell him he's my Count Moffat, the guy Nana was a courtesan to, only the Count Moffat was gross and ugly and Tony's cute and laid-back. One time I told him that I wanted to go to Paris so he dug into one of the fruit-machine cash bags and took out a couple of handfuls of quarters that he put into a brown-paper bag. He handed it to me and told me to go treat myself at the Swiss place. How cool was that!

The Swiss place is another part of Mystic Mountain. It's a Swiss-themed restaurant that I'd never been to before. Unfortunately it turned out to be pretty lame. The waiters were wearing those leather shorts like they wear in *Heidi* and they were singing, like, *The Sound of Music* shit. The chick who came over to serve us was wearing this wench outfit, though, and I really dug it. It was a scoop-necked frilly blouse with a piece of black velvet ribbon threaded through the hem and pulled tight so your boobs were really on display. She gave us menus and put four glasses of iced water down on the table and I told her that I liked her *décolleté* (because that's what they call it in *Nana*). She just wrinkled her nose and went, 'Excuse me?' Summer and Karen sniggered. I was pretty pissed at the waitress so I just ordered a round of root-beer floats because that doesn't cost much and the waitress probably thought she'd get a really bad tip from us.

When she schlepped off back to the kitchen I said to the others, 'She thinks she's so cool but she has to work in this dumb restaurant all day wearing that stupid *Heidi* outfit.'

Everyone said, 'Yeah,' in agreement. Summer said that if she worked at Mystic Mountain she wouldn't work at the dumb Swiss restaurant. She said that next year she was going to get a job on the Log Jammer. The Log Jammer is a gnarly water ride. You sit in a hollowed-out log and you go through a forest and a dark tunnel and down this gigantic hill and then a huge wave comes and gets you, unless you know the trick. The trick is to sit in the middle of the log then crouch down, throw your arms round the back of the person in front and hide in their shadow.

The Log Jammer is a cushy job because it gets up to 130° in the shade in Saugus in the summer. Plus we know people who work on the Log Jammer. They don't do much apart from making sure nobody drowns in the splash fights. Most of the day they just kick back and get high. Plus the uniforms they wear aren't so bad. All the uniforms at Mystic Mountain are made from polyester but the Log Jammer people have lumberjack shirts and they get to wear jeans.

I wish I could work at Mystic Mountain but, of course, the Creep has already outlawed this. He thinks the place is full of gangs and underage sex. 'No kid of mine is going to work at Mystic Mountain,' he goes, whenever I broach the subject.

'Since when have I been his kid?' I ask my mother, but she just comes back with 'Don't upset the applecart, honey,' which has taken over from 'Life isn't fair, Billie,' as her mantra of the moment.

Before we left the Swiss place, I had to pay back the waitress for being shitty. So I dropped four dollars in quarters into my water-glass, saying, 'Who'd want to be a waitress? What a dorky job!' The coins pushed the water nearly up to the top of the glass. Then I got a paper napkin, and I spread it over the top of the glass. I turned the glass upside down, slammed it on the table and pulled the soggy napkin out from underneath. A four-dollar tip is a good one. It's seventy-five per cent of our six-dollar root-beer-float check. But the waitress would have to mess up her table with a tidal wave of water before she could get at it. Everyone laughed and thought it was a totally cool trick.

Then I caught Marnie's eye and I felt bad. I wondered why I'd gotten so mean lately. I thought of Leah and I felt sad. I wondered if people did that kind of stuff to her and if Leah was still at Sambo's. I remember her eyes when we said goodbye to her. Her crow's feet dug in and she said, 'You make sure you come back and visit old Leah once in a while. Huh, kiddiewink?'

I nearly cried. She gave me and Ned a free soda and a plate each of Curly Q Cajun French Fries. Then she said she had a special treat for me. She went out the back and she brought in two things wrapped up in pink tissue paper and covered with a pink ribbon. I could hardly believe it. I ripped open the first one and inside there was a plastic window with Sambo on – a Sambo that had never been on the wall before! 'Kitchen boy found it in the back room when they were having a clear-out,' she said. In the new Sambo picture, Sambo was walking along in his purple shoes with crimson soles holding a green umbrella over his head to protect him from the sun. The second present was even more special. It felt a bit like a book, but the covers were padded and there was something hard in the middle like a metal belly-button. I ripped off the pink tissue paper and inside there was a sky-blue book – a special book to write in with 'Diary' in curly gold letters on the front. But, most importantly, there was a key. You could write and then lock the diary up and nobody would ever be able to read your secrets. I loved the Sambo picture but I loved the sky-blue diary with the lock and key more than anything else I'd ever had – apart from my roller-skates and my chemistry set and my Red Indian outfit.

I looked at Leah with my mouth open and I was nearly crying. Leah understood. She knew about the importance of secrets. She said, 'I didn't sign inside, of course. That's no place for me to be going.'

My sky-blue diary has become my secret place. I write everything in it – past, present, future. I write about people I know, people I imagine, things I think of doing, good thoughts, bad thoughts, mad thoughts. I wrote about the rest of that night in the sky-blue diary. About the Log Jammer and the open-air disco that goes on after the fireworks. We always end up at the open-air disco after the fireworks. We point and laugh and giggle like fifteen-year-olds are supposed to and sometimes we all wear our T-shirts saying 'Super Freak' because that is a song that we like Mystic Mountain's resident cover band, Three Stripes, to play. Summer says that Super Freak means you're a slut when you have sex. She's researched it because she's obsessed with the band's lead singer.

There's no alcohol allowed at Mystic Mountain since the Mormons bought it, but that's OK because we bring oranges injected with Jack Daniel's with us (Karen's dad's a veterinarian and she steals syringes from him). Normally I'm careful about how much I drink, because of the Creep. But the night after the Swiss place it was different. I suddenly didn't care any more. Summer was making a joke about slutty sex and that made me think about what happened with the principal at school. About how the principal called me into his office and said that he was pleased with my work as student leader – that, in fact, Mr Harper had especially commended my work – but that he didn't think it would be 'appropriate' for me to be school mascot because of my 'reputation'.

I couldn't believe it. I was so embarrassed that he was even saying this to me! What was he talking about – my 'reputation'? He said he thought I'd be a good politician but not a school mascot. When he said that Jody Delagringa was going to be school mascot this year I nearly died. Just because she's a fucking cheer-leader! Everyone knows that the jocks only like cheer-leaders because they go on the bus with them to games and they fool around with them in the back seats. Oh, but, of course, that's different, right? Because cheer-leaders usually have steady boyfriends and people like Billie Harrison only have guys who want them to suck their dicks after school.

Everything was a blur. I looked up and saw Tony Carrara making out with some tourist chick, and Summer in hysterics because she'd managed to get the phone number of the lead singer of Three Stripes. She'd called him up and got a date with him because Summer knows no fear. And I was sucking more and more oranges and the lights were bulging in and out and I kept seeing Leah's face and then Sambo's, and then Donna Summer came on with 'Last Dance', which is all about how you have to dance right now because this may be the last chance you'll ever get. But where were all the men of my dreams? Why did nobody want me to be their girlfriend or their cheer-leader or their school mascot? What did I do wrong? How come I suddenly became a Super Freak?

And then I heard Marnie saying to Summer, 'But how did you do it? How did you get the lead singer's number?' and 'But, Summer, what are you going to do when he finds out you're only fifteen?' and I suddenly heard this voice and it was me, shouting, 'Marnie! We're young! We're young! We can do whatever the fuck we want!'

And the next thing I knew I was in the front seat of the Creep's car and I was going off about the rides, about how some people were scared of the rides, and what was the fucking point? I said that they were stupid because nobody was going to die on those rides and if they were scared of a fucking roller-coaster then what chance did they ever have in fucking life? I said that I didn't care about authority anyway because one day I was going to roller-skate through fucking Mystic Mountain because I wasn't scared and I didn't care about anything.

And then I was flying into the windshield. My head smashed against the windshield because we'd arrived home and the Creep had slammed his foot on the brake when we'd got into the driveway. He did it on purpose. I came to then. I remembered where I was. I realised I hadn't put my safety-belt on but the Creep hadn't said anything. I heard the crack on my forehead and then I felt the pain and then I heard the Creep say the first thing he'd said all night. He said, 'Liquor's not good for a girl's figure, Billie. Makes her fat.' And then there was a slamming door and that was it. He didn't even ground me or yell at me. See what I mean when I say that he was smart? He was real smart. I sat there in my seat, wiping the blood from my cut eye, looking down at my big fat belly, and then I didn't want to look at it any more. I felt totally humiliated. I felt ashamed and dirty.

I held it all in, though — my pork belly, my throbbing head, the strange sick sensation that was located in my throat — I managed to hold it all in while I got into bed and wrote up my diary. I wrote about how I hate anyone to laugh at me, about how it's my worst ever thing and in the background there was the sound of Mom and the Creep screaming at each other downstairs. It was only when I turned the lights out that I started to cry. I hugged the pillow, I hugged it over my fat stomach and I scrunched my face into it and soon it got wet. I pretended I was on the Log Jammer, on the middle seat with my face squashed into somebody's back so I wouldn't get any water on me. I imagined crouching, throwing my arms round someone's back and hiding in their shadow. I thought of curling up to a warm back and closing my eyes and not thinking about what I'd do when I opened them.

CHAPTER NINETEEN

Oh, Dear Dear Diary . . .

Apart from the flickering night-light candles, the motel room is in blackness. It's as if I'm surrounded by a big shadow, a big, dancing shadow – only before, there were drips of amber nectar rolling down the lid of the maple-syrup jug and now there are just tears pouring unstoppably down the sides of a vessel that's scratched and chipped and doesn't want to be used any more.

I look at the rotten pomegranate lying split and stabbed on the carpet and in spite of the spoiled juice and the mouldy seeds, I can imagine her – spinning round and round on the counter stools at Sambo's or climbing up the Colossus at Mystic Mountain preparing to touch the sky. But that's all gone now. Just like Billie's gone now. All that's left is silver chicken-scratch writing on thick sheets of creamy paper.

Part of me feels frozen yet the silk covers burn in my hands.

Tony got caught. They only got him for ten thousand dollars. It was pretty hard to pin anything on him. Luckily he'd bought me the 1966 purple Mustang convertible before that. I had a tent, too, for when the back seat got too cramped.

This is the part where I run away from home.

It was a weird summer.

Turned out that the Bo Derek bikini was just the beginning.

Things began to mount up.

He took to walking around the house with no clothes on after a shower, roaring about the stench of my pot when even a shower couldn't rid him of the stench of bourbon that came endlessly through his skin. My mother might be saying nothing but I knew what was going on. I knew he'd hit the bottle again. I couldn't work out what planet Mom was on. You couldn't tell if she was back on vodka tonics or if she'd just gone hippie-dippie.

Poor Mom. I hate having to hate my mother. She shouldn't be so worried about me getting high. It makes me think better of her. I know she's not in love with him. In my better moments I think that she married him because she thought she'd be a better mother, that we'd have a better life. She always worried that she wasn't a good mother. She wasn't a good mother. She didn't really want us. It was the thing to do in those days. To have kids even though you really wanted to fly planes. She loved us but she didn't show us love. She treated us like dolls, like one of our limbs might fall off if she held us too tight. So she didn't hold us at all. And we didn't have a better life when she married the Creep. At least before she was all ours and we didn't have to share her with a creepy stranger who wanted to control us.

It became worse the older I got. I felt I was being watched all the time. I started going into the kitchen in the morning when I knew he'd left for work, when I knew he wouldn't make comments about what I was eating for breakfast or give me a sticky lip kiss and a smack on my ass before he went off.

Mom seemed in league with him. She'd say stuff like 'Honey, why don't you put your hair up this evening? John likes it when you put your hair up.' I didn't even bother telling her about how he'd started sneaking into my room at night, stinking of liquor and trying to climb into my bed.

And then there was the day I put the makeup on. I was about to turn seventeen. I'd spent the morning experimenting with a new blue eyeshadow. I wanted to try putting it on with a brush like the professionals do, according to Summer Lopez, instead of with my fingers. It was an OK job. I could have done it better but I suddenly realised that it was twelve thirty and I hadn't even started my chores yet. There was the usual list of vacuuming, polishing and dusting to do and I had to leave in an hour to go to Summer's house. I didn't panic, though. I figured I could do everything in an hour and then go back and finish the makeup job in time for going out. My mother and the Creep were so drunk, these days, that they wouldn't notice if I'd cleaned or not.

So I started to relax a little. I told myself to enjoy having the house to myself. I dressed up in my cool outfit of skin-tight jeans with bandannas tied around the ankles and seven-inch stiletto heels, and then I strolled into the living room and put on 'Personal Jesus' by Depeche Mode. I started the vacuuming session, wondering what color I was going to put on my lips.

There was the sound of a briefcase falling to the floor and a voice saying, 'Take that crap off your face.'

I didn't even know he was there. I felt sick. I ran to my room. I wanted to cry but I didn't. I'd given up crying. My new tactic was to stand up to the asshole and console myself with the thought of 'Summer's house'. 'Summer's house' is a code word for my new job. My and Summer's new job. Even though I am going on seventeen, the Creep still refuses to let me earn my own money. But, thanks to a connection we made through Three Stripes, the resident Mystic Mountain band, we work for a company that designs bomber-style tour jackets and embroiders names and logos on the back. The best part is that Summer and I get to go measure up the rock stars themselves. I mean, we actually go in there and measure their inner arms and their waists and talk to them about logos and designs. Other people we know have measured up the Shadows, Van Halen and Shirley MacLaine for her one-woman show.

Whenever I'm off working for the jacket people, I tell the Creep that I'm going to 'Summer's house'. This works out OK because Summer's dad, Randy, sympathises with my problems at home. Randy's from San Francisco and he's a real hippie. Not an incense-burning, self-help junkie like my mom's become. He's a good guy. He brought Summer up after her mom died of breast cancer when she was six. He has killer weed, too. A lot of the time I really do go to Summer's house and we all smoke pot together. But when I'm not there and my dad calls to check up where I am, Randy lies for me. He thinks it's hysterical that the Creep makes me read about French hookers.

So, anyway, as I marched past him, a packed overnight bag in my hand, 'the crap' all over my face, he barked, 'And where do you think you're going?'

'To Summer's house,' I said, without looking at him.

'I don't think so.'

'What?' I stopped in my tracks. It was a seriously big drag if he was going to stop believing the Summer ploy. Or worse still if he was going to ground me. Then I'd have to run away and I didn't want to do that just yet.

'Why would you want to make up like a whore to go to Summer's house?'

'What?'

'Getting it on with that hippie, huh?'

I saw red. I just saw fucking red. I wanted to leap at his throat. I screamed at him, 'What did you say? What did you fucking say to me?'

How dared he talk about Randy like that when all Randy had ever done was be nice to me and give me some space? Randy had never embarrassed me by walking around with no clothes on. He'd never made comments about the size of my breasts or told me that I should walk in a more 'ladylike' fashion or put my hair up just so because he liked it that way or bust into my bedroom in the dead of night and start groping me.

The Creep could see he'd gotten to me, gotten me all worked up. 'Been going on long?' he said, with one of his thin, mean smiles. 'Your thing with the hippie been going on long?'

Then I realised. He expected me to scream back. So I didn't. I stopped still and just stared at him. I realised that he'd lost it, and when I realised that, I wasn't scared of him any more. A wave of calm washed over me. I opened my mouth and I said coldly, 'Pissed off cos you can't get *me* to be your little whore?'

Of course, it was a dumb thing to say. Actually, I was quite surprised myself when it came out of my mouth. I should have stuck to my regular tactics of being meek in public and hating him in my head. But I guess I couldn't keep all that stuff inside any more.

I thought he was going to smack me in the face because, of course, I'd totally hit the nail on the head. His pupils went like pins and his body was shaking, 'You little bitch . . .'

He was lost for words. He was going redder and redder, his body was trembling. 'You're not going anywhere, you—'

'Yes, I fucking am!' I said, running for the door.

I started to laugh. Some weird, manic laugh. The Creep had finally got his comeuppance. I was making him look stupid, I was humili-ating him. I'd gotten to him and I wouldn't come back and take my punishment. It felt great. Like going fast, going very, very fast down the Colossus, the tracks spread with grade-A ice plant.

I didn't care what was going to happen later. I forgot about every-thing as soon as I was out of the house, out of Saugus, speeding along the highway in my purple Mustang convertible on my way to El Fresno. Back on with Depeche Mode, back into 'Summer's house' mode, back into the next 7/11 to pick up a bottle of makeup remover, back to the world of Zach Blaze and his inky blue eyes.

I looked at my watch. I hoped I wasn't going to be late. You could say I was working overtime at 'Summer's house'. In the back of the car I had a bunch of jackets to deliver to the El Fresno Hilton — a three-hour drive from Saugus. This isn't the norm, of course. The norm is that you chuck the jackets in a truck and some dork delivers them to whatever hotel they're supposed to be at. But when Zach Blaze, lead singer of Come Together asks if you would personally deliver his jacket then you go do it.

I love hesher music — Def Leppard, Van Halen, that kind of shit. Come Together are the kings of hesher. They wear tight jeans with bandannas round the ankle and open shirts and checked Vans and they have long, feathered hair. Summer was so fucking pissed when she heard I'd got the job to go measure the band. She'd been assigned that day to the most boring job in the world — tracing over letters in a calligraphy book, pinning them on the front of the jackets and then sending the results up to the Mexican boys in the embroidery room.

Poor Summer. Zach Blaze is her favorite ever pop star. She has posters of him all over her bedroom wall. She was screaming at me down the phone. 'Shut up!' she was going. 'You have to go measure *who*? You are fucking kidding me!'

She was devastated when I told her about how I'd finished up the jacket-measuring session with him fucking me monkey style as he squatted on the floor, balancing himself by grabbing my knees. He was short. He only came up to my tits. It was a shame that I couldn't go into these details with Summer, but I obviously couldn't. She was having a seizure at the other end of the phone. She's going, 'Fuck you! I hate you! I saw him first!' She sounded more pissed off than if I'd slept with her boyfriend. (Later, I did sleep with her boyfriend and she didn't get half as mad.) So when, after the initial fitting, Zach said he wanted to see me again, I thought I'd try to make things better by bringing Summer along.

When I finally make it to the El Fresno Hilton, there she is at the door, wearing her best heels and jeans and a ton of red lipstick. She's totally nervous. She starts yammering about how I'm late and what a total drag it is that I'm late. So I tell her briefly about the fight with the Creep. But she still doesn't quiet down. She's convinced that they're going to throw us out of the Hilton. She keeps going, 'They're going to find out! They're going to find out!' And I'm saying to her, 'What do you mean, they're going to find out? Find out what?'

It was *so* not a problem going into that hotel. The bottom line was that we had money. Zach had given me the number of one of his credit cards and he was expecting me in his room at three thirty. I'd just given the jackets to one of the bell-boys to deliver to the Come Together suite. (There was no way I was going to ruin my entrance by hauling thirty polythene-wrapped bomber jackets through the Hilton lobby.) But Summer was still convinced we were about to be arrested.

'We're not allowed,' she kept hissing. From the corner of her eye she was checking out the marble and the chandeliers, the Tiffany and Cartier showcases, the Tammy and Jim Baker lookalikes – the fake hair, the shoulder-pads, the glittery appliqué shit on the lapels. 'I'm telling you, Billie, we are not allowed in here!'

I stopped and took her by the shoulders. 'Summer, man,' I said, 'for the thousandth time, we are *so* totally allowed here. We have money. And if you have money you're allowed to do anything.'

Then I just strode up to the front desk and I said: 'We are the guests of Mr Peter Movie. Would you please say that Miss Billie Harrison has arrived.'

I've seen them do this on TV and, right on cue, the guy goes, 'Certainly, ma'am.'

He calls the number of Peter Movie (Zach's name for the front desk) and announces that I've arrived. The guy puts the phone down, looks me in the eye. (He can't help switching into flirty mode when he looks at me, most guys can't.) He says, 'Mr Movie says to go right up.'

He casts a sneaky glance at Summer and I wonder if I should say something. I didn't mention anything about going up with another chick. Zach doesn't know I'm with a friend. But it'll be fine.

'She's with me,' I tell the reception dude. I turn on my heels, link my arm into Summer's and pull her down the corridor. 'How d'you get to be so cool?' she says. She sounds genuinely impressed. I'm feeling pretty pleased with myself, too, and then I remember that I don't know what room Zach is in. But it's OK because there's suddenly a voice behind me, the voice of the receptionist going, 'Um . . . Room 1004, ma'am.' I know he's talking to me. I turn round and look at him. He gives me a wink, then points subtly in the other direction, mouthing, 'Elevators.'

I don't wink back. I just raise my head even higher. I say to Summer, 'Know what? I don't think the elevators are this way.'

Anyone would think I owned the place. I feel as if I own the place because this is where Zach Blaze is staying. This is where Zach Blaze is staying and he has invited me up to his room.

When he opens the door, he looks at Summer and his face falls. 'You brought a friend with you?'

I'm pissed off when he says this. How would he like it if he just met his dream god and the dream god's face fell? I walk into the room. Fucking five-foot-nothing geek. 'Come on in, Summer,' I say.

I know my power. Zach's mumbling something at the door and I guess it's about the other people in the room because when I get to the bed area there's a bunch of people lying there, a couple of other groupies, two more band members and some rank guys — roadies, I guess.

Zach comes over to the bed. 'So, um, this is Billie. She brought us the tour jackets,' he tells everyone.

'So, like, where are they?' one of the groupies on the bed says. Her gum bubble bursts with a loud bang.

I'm momentarily thrown — until I remember that Summer thinks I can handle the situation. So I handle it. I turn back to the groupie and look her right in the eye. I say, 'Bell-boys, dude. I just make the things. I don't do manual work.'

Zach laughs. He thinks I'm cool. So I turn to him and say, 'This is my friend Summer. She's a big fan of yours.'

And Zach is polite this time. He says, 'Nice to meet you, Summer. We're going out in a little while. Band practice. You're welcome to join us.'

Summer's ears turn pink. She says, 'Oh,' about ten times. Finally she gives up and just says, 'Thanks, Zach, I'd love to come.'

There's a snigger from one of the guys on the bed. 'You can come right here with me, babe.' He burps. 'You wanna beer?'

Summer says to him, 'If you want what I think you want, it's gonna take more than a beer.'

And then all the guys on the bed snigger and the mean groupie looks pissed off, although the other one giggles and moves over to make space for Summer.

It turns out to be a totally sweet afternoon. We smoke pot and drink beers on the bed like we're all on a big boat, and then Zach takes me into his private room and he does the monkey thing again. Except afterwards we get into his bed and he takes all my clothes off — he keeps his T-shirt on — and he does it properly with him lying on top of me and then he tells me nice stuff. About how I've got amazing eyes, like liquid black, and how I've got a great ass and how he likes my attitude. He starts to tell me about what it's like travelling in Europe, and I tell him what I know about Paris from the French novels I've read and he says he likes the idea of courtesans and we laugh and it's totally bitchin'. I stroke his feather hair, and for a moment I lay my head on his belly and I hug him and he hugs me. I close my eyes and I don't want to open them again. Then he goes, 'Hey, what are you doing down there, you crazy thing?' (I wonder why everybody always calls me crazy.) He kisses my forehead and rips back the covers. 'Sound-check time, baby,' he says, jumping back into his jeans and sliding his feet into his Vans.

I feel like a mouse who gets woken up too soon from hibernation. But I soon snap out of it. We walk together over to the concert hall and Summer is already there, lounging all over the sound desk. She's got friendly with one of the roadies and she's totally loaded. She dribbles into my ear about what an amazing guy her roadie is and how he's going to take her to a hotel where they have a happy hour that lasts for five hours and an all-day free buffet. 'I mean, y'could eat, like, two hundred dollars in free food alone . . .'

But I'm not really listening. I'm watching Zach on stage doing his sound check and I don't even notice that he's five foot nothing any more. I think about the soft white skin on his hip bones and I imagine it right now, hitting up against the back of his guitar and I hope it doesn't get bruised. And then there's a loud thud and it's Summer hitting the floor. One of the guys has pushed her off the sound desk because she's just thrown up. She groans. 'Billie, dude, I think I need to go home.'

It's OK, though. I'm still feeling good about the day. I can still smell Zach on me and Zach says I have eyes like liquid black. Poor Summer looks bad. I figure I'll drive her home to Saugus and then I'll come back later. I go tell Zach that I'll be back for the concert just as soon as I've got Summer home and he says, 'Sure,' because mainly he's concentrating on the music rehearsal.

So I get on the freeway and drive to Saugus with Summer passed out on the seat next to me. Three hours later, when we make it to Randy's house he's cool about everything. He thinks it's hilarious that Summer has rocked up at home all green. I'm about to drive all the way back to El Fresno but then, at the last minute, I decide I need to freshen up and pick up some more clothes from home because I want to look nice in Zach's bed.

The evening sky is beautiful tonight. A tint of a sunset rose on the crest of a milk-white wave. I rock up at home, and when I stop the engine I just sit there for a while, grinning at the sky. 'Just like a courtesan!' I say to the sunset, because I'm pretty drunk myself. 'Pretty for now, but you'd better make the most of it cos it won't last!'

And then it's the beginning of the end.

I know this as soon as I go into the kitchen. There's not even any pretence now. It is six thirty in the evening and there are bottles on the table – vodka, beer, gin, an empty tonic bottle lying on its side. My mother is smoking, dragging desperately on a cigarette as she flicks through the pages of a book. She doesn't even look up when I come in. She carries on flicking and trembling and dragging away. The one who is looking at me is the Creep. He's sitting there, staring right at me with something in his eyes like malice and triumph and caffeine. He's drinking coffee. He picks the mug up from the table and takes a slurp, then bangs it down with a smack of the lips. The coffee machine hisses behind me. Those are the only sounds: the hissing of the coffee machine, the flicking of pages and my mother breathing in short, panicked breaths.

And then I know why I'm dizzy. I knew it all along, but it becomes clear when she starts saying, 'Oh, my God. Oh, my God, Billie,' as she rifles through the book, a sky-blue book. She rifles through the sky-blue book and the grin on his face gets wider and wider.

They're reading my book, my words – they're reading my secrets, my ideas. They're stealing everything I've felt and thought and done: they know about how I want to kill the Creep and my nightmares about German shepherd dogs with lizard heads that pick my mom up by the scruff of the neck and take her over to the piece of ground where I have been fucking with Tony Carrara. They know my stupid stuff about being a Californian courtesan and about cruising round Mystic Mountain on roller-skates. My sky-blue book is filled with secret stuff, stuff and nonsense and not even all of my nonsense, but that is not the point. The sky-blue book was mine and they had no right to go there. They had no right to go to a private place and break everything. They kicked in the doors and they broke into my house. They smashed the windows and sprayed graffiti on the walls and spat at my pictures and pissed in my bed and now my house is dirty and defiled.

He pulls on one side of his ginger moustache. He looks at me with the caffeine eyes. He slurs, 'German shepherds with lizard heads, huh?' He twists the knife. And then I know that there's more. I know that he hasn't stopped there. I catch his eye and a spear runs through me. I turn, I run off down the hall to my room.

But that's not mine any more. He's defiled that too. My soul is ripped out, my life is spilling out all over the floor — my Red Indian outfit, my sprint certificates, my makeup bag, my cheer-leader clothes, my papers, my letters, the plastic Sambo window — they're all lying in a pile in the middle of my room, in the middle of a room that no longer has anything to do with me. He's there, again, behind me. He never leaves me alone. He spears me in the eye again. 'You thought you could get away with it?'

That's all he says before he snatches up a bundle of more of my things and runs off down the hall.

I'm ready to run off down the hall too. To go after him, to chase him. And then I stop. I see my father. The only memory of my father comes back to me. Running behind him as he plods down the hall holding my flaming mattress aloft, my daddy saving me from the flaming mattress when I burned it with fire. My daddy who loved me and then left me. I fall into a trance. I walk slowly down the hall and when I reach the kitchen I stop. There's no more point. There's no more point in struggling. Everything's lost, nobody cares.

I watch him take a can of gas. He pours fire on my dreams. He takes them all and he burns them all, not just my clothes and my makeup but my memories, my thoughts, my things that have nothing to do with him. He burns the happy times, the things I got at a happy time before Mom tried to kill herself, before she got saved by the

Creep and everything changed. I watch him in the backyard setting fire to my things to hurt me, just like my real daddy put out the flames to save me, and I wonder what it means. I wonder what I've done wrong. And all the while my mother's face is a blank. She just sits stiff in her seat at the kitchen table, petrified into stone like an angel on a tomb.

I want her to do something. Why doesn't she do something? I turn to her. Everything is being sucked out, sucked away from me, the floor is made of sea, the floors are falling out of the house, dropping down like a stone, all of them — one, two, three, four, five, six, seven, eight, nine, ten — all of them falling down a big black hole, like in the Cage, free-fall for ten storeys, like in a sunset, the color being sucked from the day, everything being sucked from the day. Why doesn't she stop it, why doesn't she do something?

'Mama! Mama! Stop him, Mama!'

I fall to the ground, I bang my head on the floor, bang, bang, bang, screeches ripping through the house. Fists pummelling the floor then a wildcat, hellcat cry for help: 'No more "*quieta la boca*," Mama! No more! You're supposed to love me! You're my mama and you're supposed to love me!'

But she stills her mouth. Her tongue is still so I cry: 'What did I do wrong, Mama? What did I do wrong?'

And still she sits there, silent as a stone, so I drench her in a wild howl of pain, the bad dreams of my childhood made inarticulate flesh. Because words have let me down again, words have gotten me nowhere again, and they always will get me nowhere, which is why fire and brimstone and gnashing of teeth are the only ways to go. Because they at last are familiar to me, they're what I've known, every day of my childhood when they came to haunt me, a squalling tangle of fear that haunted me for every day of my childhood, a niggling doubt I could never put into words but which came to me in sleep every night as a house with collapsible walls and floors made of sea and beds that were always damp and strangers who were always messing around with my things and nothing was ever quite right.

There are twenty-seven different words for love in the Greek Bible, but in my life there's never even been one. There was never enough love to go round. There were only scrapings of love. Like the crusty layer of frosting all stuck with crumbs that you had to chip off the side of Reba's frosting bowls. Dregs of the frosting. It wasn't enough. There was never enough. Why not? Why do adults do that? Why are people mean to children? Why were they mean to me? What did I do wrong? Nobody's ever told me the answer to that. None of them ever wanted to look that in the face. There has only ever been silence, the hissing of the coffee machine and the crackle of the flames.

I close my eyes and there is a swirling catherine wheel made from a slice of four-hundred-year-old oak, a slice of trunk so old and thin it has the lines and creases of a leaf skeleton. And then I see a dark hole with egg-timer-quick sand streaming into it. Hungrier and hungrier, the sand is sucked unstoppably down, everything slithering into the black hole, everything just going, disappearing, sliding under, never to return. And then I see a flash of white light and then blue and yellow melting into orange and then floor and table leg and then day, and then my eyes open up and the world is here again. The fucking world is still here, the world and black smoke and the smell of melting plastic and the hissing and belching of the sulphur lake, the kitchen-coffee sulphur lake, spluttering and gurgling and drawing me in, into the hot mouth of the devil, the black mouth of nothingness, the pit with no end. When I stagger to my feet, the sunset has bleached the color from the day, there is nothing left, just the flames burning up my things, things that are not part of me any more, husks of my old self, old skins burning up in the same old flames, the roaring flames that will always be there.

I slam the book shut. I want her back. I wish the door would burst open and she'd come roller-skating in, shrieking, 'Mo! We're young! We're young! We can do whatever the fuck we want!'

But there's only the shadow in the room and the flickering candles that throw light on to the plates on the wall, illuminating the hieroglyphics and the wholesome faces of John and Jackie Kennedy and the stiff smile of Queen Elizabeth II. And that's when I think it. That's when I think I have to get out. I have to get back in the car and get back to England. I'll drop the car off and get my deposit back and then I'll change my ticket and get the hell out of here. I'll go back to Scarborough, go back to the Sceptre and lose myself in silver service – in thin ears of overcooked beef seamed with thin rinds of yellow fat and served up with lukewarm gravy on cold plates. My mission has been accomplished in America: my breakfast story is more or less ready for the *Evening Post*, Gary has all but disappeared from my head and I've got lots of good adventures to tell. And Billie will be fine. She obviously wants to be left on her own so I'm going to do the decent thing and leave her to it. I'll look upon her as my holiday romance. My Spanish waiter, my Greek fisherman, my . . .

'Mo! We're young! We're young! We can do whatever the fuck we want!'

I can hear her. I can bloody hear her calling out from the shadows. I can't help opening the book again. The silver words. They sparkle up at me, glittering and rotten at the same time. Who am I kidding? I can't leave them now. I can't start the deed without finishing it.

I drove to Sambo's because I needed someone I could trust. Every mile of the drive I thought of Leah and her smile and the way she always used to make me feel good. I drove and I drove, and at last I saw the eucalyptus trees and the orange and yellow building and the expanse of windows and the pictures of Sambo with his jewelled turban and his purple slippers with crimson soles. I got out of the car and I ran inside looking for her. And then there's a sob, a snivel, a howl, and it's me, it's me howling for Leah. And I must be making a huge noise because one of the waitresses comes up and frowns and I know she doesn't want to deal with me and I know that my makeup must be looking really bad by this time. I tell her I'm sorry,

I tell her I'm real sorry, and then I start to blubber about Leah, I say I need Leah. The waitress says that Leah is out back but now's not a real good time to go see her. But I can't wait. I break away. I know where Leah goes for her cigarette breaks: out by the empty lettuce crates, out at the back by the flies and the air-con units. Her safe place. I smooth my hair down so I don't look too scuzzy and as I walk along the dusty path I can hear her voice. I can hear her! It's a different voice from the one in Sambo's: 'That's right,' she's saying. 'That's right.' She sounds sad, as if she's burying one of her Barbies in the back garden: 'Malibu Beach Barbie was a good doll. She was loved by her mistress.'

And then a man's voice comes. It keeps going, 'Just get rid of it, hon,' over and over again.

And Leah is saying in her sad voice, 'Is that all you got to say?'

'Sure that's all I got to say, hon. You know it was a no-strings thing.'

'That's not what you said all these months . . .'

'I never meant to . . . to get your hopes up.'

'So you was doing me a favour, then, all those nights . . .'

'Now just calm yourself down, hon—'

'Don't you call me hon!'

'Come on, babe. You know I feel for you real deep.'

'Pity you don't feel real deep for what's inside of me!'

'Come on, babe—'

'Fuck you, Arnold!'

Leah's voice digs deeper and deeper into sadness. I hardly recognise her. Leah saying 'fuck!' Leah talking about a baby being inside of her — from the man with the triangle eyes! My legs just keep walking, though, they keep on going. I just need to see Leah and I will help her. I will help her with her baby, I won't tell her to get rid of it like stupid Triangle Eyes. I will help her.

I look at Leah looking at me. Looking through me. She looks as though she can't quite remember who I am, but at the bottom I can see that she knows very well who I am. She knows it's me, Billie. I know she wants me to get the fuck out of there. She shakes her head. 'Hey there,' she says, wiping her hands down her greasy apron. She doesn't call me kiddiewink like she used to inside of Sambo's. But then again, outside of Sambo's nothing is real.

The truth comes to me in a flash: it's *inside* of Sambo's that nothing is real. Outside is the real world and outside nobody is paid to be nice to you. Sambo's is just a pretend place and waitresses are only nice to you because they don't know you. Once you leave the diner world it's back to reality where people don't have wise things to say, where guardian angels shrivel up and die, where pink gingham uniforms turn to greasy rags.

'Billie,' she finally stammers, 'now's not a real good time.'

She doesn't want to talk to me. She wants me to go.

'I'm sorry,' she says. 'Another time, hon.'

Sometimes I spend the night at Summer's house back in Saugus. It's the only time I get to see her now that I quit school. She and Randy are nice to me. On my eighteenth birthday they invited round Karen Schwartz and Marnie, and we had a barbecue with dips and ambrosia and macaroni salad and afterwards they let off fireworks.

But it wasn't the same. It isn't the same, and I can't really hang out with those guys right now. Even when I see Zach I don't stay in his hotel room any more. For his last tour I had to make him two miniature jackets. It turned out they were for his kids. I said, 'Kids? You didn't tell me you had kids,' and he said, 'You never asked.'

I said that it wasn't right doing what we were doing if he had kids and he just said, 'OK.'

I guess we'd come to the end of the groupie thing by that stage.

My one ray of light is my car. My home. My purple 1966 Mustang convertible. I feel safe in my car. I've been driving, getting to know new areas. I like Venice a lot. Summer's dad says that Venice is like New York on sea. It's full of freaks. Super Freaks like me. You can hide yourself away among the freaks. Lots of people in Venice wear black clothes, like me. Like they do in New York, like the New York Dolls wear. It's hard to wear black clothes in California because it's so hot. You need to wear makeup with black, but as soon as you put on foundation, it gets sticky and runs down your face and you look gross.

I like to be on my own now. Just me and my car. Safe in my car in my black clothes where no one can get me. A car is a good place to live. My favorite thing is to wake up in the morning all alone. To wake up really early before all the tourists get to Venice, when there's just you and the freaks and the new day's ocean ready to give you another chance. I get out of my car and go to a café called the Tree House where I buy a glass of orange juice and a piece of coffee cake and I pretend I'm in New York.

One evening I have to go to San Bernardino to drop off a consignment of jackets. San Bernardino is known as a place filled with white speed freaks and when I come back to my car the ground is all crunchy. I think it's gravel that I didn't notice before but then I look and I see that it's glass: shattered glass from my car window that's been smashed by some kid.

I hear myself breathe quickly, panting like I've run a long race — a race that I lost — and then I start to feel weird. My hands are in my pockets and my body's spinning around as I stare at the tiny piranhas of broken glass all swirling round at my feet and the ribbons of jagged lace blowing from the window rim like a tattered cobweb in a haunted house. There are sharp splinters everywhere — on my boots, on the car seat, on the sidewalk — and then there's a soft thud and then a crunch and I'm splintering up too. Except my broken body doesn't just fall down into a neat pile of fragments on the sidewalk. Bits of me start spinning all over the parking lot and flying up over San Bernardino — pulled up into the skies and then turned into poison gas like mustard gas or sulphur gas. I've become a lethal air that won't stop but at least I'm far away in the clouds where I can't harm anyone.

A tiny piece of paper in the pocket of my jeans brings me back down to the crunchy sidewalk. The corner of an acid tab. Zach must have given me that tab months ago. I put it on my tongue and when it's melted I know that everything will be cool. Acid is gnarly. It makes you calm. It makes you laugh, and I guess it will stop me floating out of my body. I only have to wait for a bit and then, yeah, the cavalry rides in. My breathing gets slower and slower. I feel calm and then I feel numb. Novocaine numb. Just more crunching under my feet. A nice crunch now. A glittery noise, like raking around in a jewellery box. I paddle around in the glass some more. I bend my knees like a dork and pretend I'm walking round the North Pole wearing big snowboots treading on crunchy white snow and crackly blue ice filled with strands of silver chain. And then the giggling comes. It's pretty funny, really – the broken blue ice and the noisy flakes of snow on this hot orange evening. The pieces of ice scattered over the driver's seat are spiky ice cubes in a cooler. I brush some of them on to the ground with my hands and then I sit on the car seat and I laugh because I'm a dead fish perched on a bed of crushed ice. A lucky dead fish in a chilled purple cooler. And when I put my hands on the steering-wheel I see that I'm not really a dead fish at all because there's blood in me. Bright red blood that's oozing out of my fingers on to the steering-wheel. It feels like I haven't seen anything this bright in a long time. It's beautiful. It's not cold fish water blood it's the real human McCoy. Funny how it's smooth and red. Diner blood Heinz red. Funny how it's not black and icky and filled with spiders' legs. I smear it into the steering-wheel and I smear some on to the windshield because I am sick and weird. I am a very sick fish or I am a very real human being.

The engine starts slowly, ever so slowly, and when it's up and running I rest my elbow on the jagged lace cobweb to my left. The beautiful red's on my arm now and red drips are running down the side of the purple fish. Cool. It's all coming out now, all the bad is coming out of me, and as it does, it pulls me back down from the skies where I nearly vanished. I watch the blood drip out and it brings me back to earth and back to life. I push down on the jagged lace curtain some more so it purges and cleanses some more – like purging the goblet with fire and brimstone so it'll be fresh and clean to use again.

When I turn back on to the freeway, a long stream of red is

trickling down my arm. Real fast it's going. Whizzing away like red-water rapids. I shout out of the window, 'Go on the cavalry! Bring out the hostages! Bright red cushions down the ice-plant slope! Yaaaaay!'

I'm having a totally cool time and there's this beautiful bright sunset up ahead and a trippy stream of ocean breeze coming in through the eye in the left window. I'm really in the mood for some music now so I lean over to put a tape in the machine. But there is no machine any more because someone broke into my car and stole it.

And then the breathing comes back. The tightness in the chest. The walls of the world breathe in and out, sticky and slimy, and words have clotted and tears are dammed up so there's nowhere to go, no room to unravel the ball of anger all knotted up inside of me. There's only the blood. Only it isn't smooth and warm any more. It's jagged rocks scraping and scratching their way out of my body and so even that's not enough.

But then, at the lights, I see a white boy. White boy speed trash. I pull over. He looks like he's got stuff to sell. Looks like the type to have stolen a stereo or two. He's perfect for the story. A story I need to tell. I look at him, suck up just enough of him for the fantasy to work. I breathe deep and close my eyes and wait for the violence to begin. Yes, I can see it now, coming into focus, coming closer and closer. There I go: I smash his neck, I mush his nose and break some ribs and boot his chin (omitting the head in case he dies). Then I kick his balls — his soft little balls — I kick him and kick him and kick him until he curls up on one side and spews up a wheezy puddle of green puke, until he's got less strength than an old grandma, until he looks at me and pleads for mercy and I make him shout: 'I am a worthless piece of shit! My mother is a drunk! My father fucks me up the ass!' And I pretend I can't hear him so he shouts again, in his pathetic cracked voice: 'I am a worthless piece of shit! My mother is a drunk! My father fucks me up the ass!'

Red-hot boulders shoot through my veins as the show goes on behind my closed eyelids. I grip hold of the ragged glass eye of the window as I decide what should happen next. Soon it becomes clear what should happen next: I rip more glass from the broken eye and I carve into his forehead — his forehead or his belly — words like T-H-I-E-F or S-I-N-N-E-R or L-O-S-E-R. And then he can't see any more because blood is streaming into his eyes. This is a good twist to the tale — it makes my body twitch and jerk around in my car seat like some crazy robot whose head's blown off but sparks are still pouring out of the smoking wires in its neck.

And the fantasy can't end until I've burned him — stuffed his pockets with tour-jacket order forms and doused him with gas as he sobs — hoarsely now, like a little boy, because there's hardly anything left to him, he sobs, 'Please, oh, no! Oh, please! I beg of you!' Sweat pricks out through my skin and my heart gets ripped from my body and left on a summer lawn to turn leathery under the sun, to turn to heart jerky and get pecked up by hungry crows. And even though for a split second I almost feel sorry for him — his pleading eyes and his quivering shoulders — I have to remember that he's not a little boy, that he's getting what he deserves. And then I throw the match.

The acid is strong. The sky looks calm, though. Silver pink dusted with white powdered sugar. I sit in the Tree House and look at my awesome red arm tattoo. It says, 'G-O-D H-A-T-E-S Y-O-U.'

The waitress chick comes over with my order. She's hot. She's got backcombed disco bangs and a mini-skirt and black pantyhose with ripped-up stockings over the top and the black dancing boots from Madonna's 'Borderline' video with scrunchy pink socks inside. When she sees my arm she stops chewing her gum for a second and then she goes, 'Cool.'

She puts the orange juice and the cake on the table and says, 'That'll be three fifty. You wanna pay now? I'm cashing up.'

Funny how I still like cake. Coffee cake is my favorite.

CHAPTER TWENTY

Bacon and Grits

My gullet splits and a noise comes out of my throat – a strange, inhuman noise, like a stray dog or a monkey. I can't work out what the sound is because I'm just aware of a fleshy hand clamping round my chest, squeezing me in, trying to squash me up and turn me into a mush of sludge, chugging slowly to the edge of a craggy cliff, and once I fall over I know there's no going back. I'm holding back, though, I'm damming it all up and then, just when it seems that I might break, I hear the voice of the guardian angel. 'There's a pony in this shit somewhere.'

The voice digs through again, louder this time. 'Yes, siree, there's a pony in this shit somewhere!'

I turn round and it's Vera, illuminated from behind by the light from the Thunderbird. She's standing there in her slippers, head sticking out of the front of her chest, a cigarette poised between two sepia-stained fingers. Her presence makes me start and sets me off on a ramble of 'Gosh, I'm so sorry,' and 'Goodness, apologies for the terrible mess!' until Vera breaks in with, 'Now don't you start all that goshing and goodnessing again, girl!'

So I stop. I stop everything and drop down on to the bed. I put my face in my hands and concentrate on the Roach Motel on the carpet through the gaps in my fingers. Vera's voice says, 'What do you need?'

I can't think what I need.

'She take the map with her?'

It takes a while for me to understand what this means. Is it a riddle? A test?

'Vera, I don't—'

'The map's still in the car, right? So she must know where she's headed. And where's the only place she knows how to head?'

'I don't—'

'California, girl!'

'But how would she get there without a car?'

Vera turns to face the Thunderbird. 'See those guys?' She points to a crowd of men huddled together in front of the bar, swigging beer. 'They got a part to play in all of this.'

She steps outside the room and I walk, too, into the blackness, following the shuffle of her slipper and the glow of her cigarette. When it stops I become aware of a voice. Beer-gut's voice. He's standing in the middle of the group of men. 'I been thinking of getting one for a while,' he's shouting.

'You crazy, Joe! You not even calling in the cops?'

'Cops! Ain't going to dirty my hands with no cops!'

'What you gonna get, then?'

'Gonna get me a Camero. Or one of them new Dodges.'

'You was insured on the stolen one, Joe?'

'Who cares if I was insured or not? You telling me I'm not man enough to buy a new Dodge?'

'No, Joe, man! I ain't saying that!'

'You drinking my beer and telling me—'

Vera pulls me away from the scene. 'She sure had a lot of tricks up her sleeve, your Ruby Rose.'

'You mean she stole . . .?'

'Hotwired his beat-up old Dodge!' She chuckles.

'She—'

'Never seen nobody do it so quick. And, believe you me, I seen some varmints in my time.'

When we're back in the room I ask her if she spoke to Billie. 'Did she tell you where she was heading?'

Vera removes her glasses and wipes the lenses with the bottom of her T-shirt. 'Like I said' – she squints, her face turned away from mine – 'she left you the map.'

'Yes, but—'

'Mo, hon.' She meets my gaze at last. 'You done the beginning. And you can't stop at the beginning, right?'

'Right. "The beginning is one half of the deed."'

'Sure is.'

'But what *is* the deed, Vera?'

She takes the remains of the cigarette from her mouth and
stubs it in an ashtray filled with Billie's joint butts.

'You better get some sleep,' she says. 'Tomorrow morning you
gonna get back on the 10 and head west.'

'But how will I know—'

'You want that pony bad enough, you'll find it.'

Finding the pony wasn't so straightforward, though. I found
myself on a wild-goose chase along a thousand miles of
American countryside – I don't think Vera realised how bad my
sense of direction was and how blurry my eyesight without
contact lenses. It took me two and a half days to reach California.
(This included a day's delay due to a flat battery from a night
spent sleeping in the SUV because I was trying to save money.
Typical. It felt so terrifying, being there all alone, that I left the
headlights on all night.)

I hardly noticed the rest of the drive. Arizona seemed similar
to New Mexico only less dramatic, and then suddenly there were
all these dinosaur heads on hills, pecking at the ground, and
these rows of huge white arms reaching up to the sky and I
realised I was in the Californian desert passing oil refiners and
wind-power machines. Then the 10 started breaking up and there
were massive posters erected high in the air above eight-laned
freeways advertising real estate and enhanced bodies: 'Brenda
Swanson Sells Homes' (with a picture of Brenda) and 'Safe
Liposuction ("as featured on ABC's 20/20")'.

Then the air temperature dropped by about ten degrees and
I smelt the salt and began to feel better. The roaring desert air
began to give way to cool, sticky sea air, and when I drove through
a long black underpass, I finally saw the Pacific Ocean which,

as Billie had promised, looked sporty and clean-living and had beautiful blue eyes.

It felt as though I'd come through a black hole and arrived on the other side. Everyone on the other side was young and thin and tanned and relaxed – as I discovered when I took a wrong turn and found myself in the serene car park of a shop called Fred Segal. There were waves of beautiful people – whose age was hard to determine – all heading towards the fancy-looking store. So I followed them and went inside, telling myself that the experience might make an interesting colour piece for the *Scarborough Evening Post*.

I felt much better when I came out again. I felt like a new woman. I was feeling so confident that I even 'flipped a bitch' to get back on the right road to take me to Venice Beach. I remembered how Billie had once said that Leah used to live by an old lingerie store called Flambée, near the centre of town. So I followed the signposts until I arrived in a place where there were skinny boys with golden curls cruising along on skateboards long as beds and tanned girls with arms like fingers in the rest of the country and thighs like wrists, walking along holding yoga mats. I spotted a panting woman jogger in a pink designer track-suit – an old lady where I come from – clutching a huge poly-styrene cup saying 'Jamba juice'. I pulled up alongside her, noting as I lowered my window that she was wiping her brow with a hand wrapped in a pink cotton weight-lifting glove. Our eyes met. 'Liver spots,' she said, reading my mind. 'Avoidance of.'

'Flambée?' I said, hopefully. 'Directions to?'

She shook her head wistfully. 'Hoo-eee,' she whistled. 'You'll have trouble getting a négligé there.'

This was because Flambée had had a makeover. When I drove to Rose and Main it turned out that the place was still called Flambée and the building looked turn-of-the-century, as Billie had described it, except now there was a neon martini in the window because the place had become a diner. I went in and ordered the $6.50 Body Builder Combo breakfast (five egg whites scrambled with six ounces of chicken breast and a carbo side order of your choice). It didn't seem the kind of place frequented by regulars. There was a bony old woman with hair dyed shoe-polish black asking a waitress with a thin body and thin eyebrows whether she should have the baked yam or the cottage cheese as the 'carbo choice' for her Body Builder Combo. The waitress snapped, 'I can't manage your life for you!' and that made me think of Leah who can manage your life for you.

Then it struck me that Leah must have moved out of Venice years ago and this was just another part of the wild-goose chase. The egg-white omelette sort of stuck in my throat too. This was it, then: my end-of-the-line breakfast. Now that I'd eaten my way across the whole of America what was I supposed to do next?

I left Flambée and walked aimlessly down some small pedestrian walkways lined with old wooden beach-houses painted in pastel colours. I wandered there for a while, trying to focus on the different décors and trying to come up with a structure, a plan. The houses were nice enough. Some of them had gardens with weeping willows and eucalyptus trees. Some houses had the front door open and you could see inside – mattresses thrown on the floor, scattered skateboards and clothes, fuddy-duddy bits of furniture, shelves filled with a lifetime's collection of corny mementoes. On some of the porches groups of older people were talking about the candlelit vigils they were preparing to commemorate 9/11 as they're calling it. (The attacks happened on September 11 and 911 is the American 999 equivalent.) On other porches groups of golden-haired surfer boys were hanging out on battered settees, smoking pot, listening to jangly grunge music and sporting a variety of T-shirt messages: 'Suicidal Tendencies', '420' and 'Good Bush, Bad Bush' (under pictures of a vagina and a president, respectively).

And then I saw Vera through a window. Vera in Venice! This particular beach hut looked like an old-fashioned American school-house. A line of red geraniums on the porch was the

only concession to frivolity and inside there were only wooden
floorboards and a few austere pieces of furniture. My contact
lenses might not have been in but I was almost certain it was
Vera: there was the hunched back, the plumes of smoke rising
from the chain-smoking fingers, the fuzzy perm all squashed
down at the back from a lifetime of leaning on headrests to
watch TV.

She had a whole TV-watching concept going on: in her cigarette-
free hand she gripped a TV guide with pegs on various pages
to remind her of what was on. There was a clipboard on the
arm of the chair along with a TV control, a video control and
a pile of *Globe*s and *National Enquirer*s. In the unlikely event
that these precautions might fail to alert her that one of her
programmes was about to begin, she had an alarm clock on the
other armrest.

A battle of wills was going on between Vera and a woman in
the kitchen. You couldn't see the woman. You could just see a
pair of hands chopping red peppers or possibly chillies.

The windows of the house were wide open and words floated
out on to the porch. The kitchen voice was saying something
about 'seriousness' and 'George Bush' and then you saw her –
she was a fat blonde – storming into the sitting room. She
snatched the TV control from Vera's hand. Channels were flicked,
sounds passed from canned laughter to jingle music to hand-
clapping to the doomy voice of George Bush snarling, 'There's
a saying out West: wanted, dead or alive . . .'

Vera grabbed the control back from the blonde. She turned to
the Shopping Channel but was greeted by the sight of a man
with a square jaw holding a sculpture of an aeroplane, going:
'Throughout history, by sea and by air, the US armed forces have
answered duty's call. Working together to defend freedom wherever it may be challenged . . .'

The serious nature of the shopping seemed to placate the fat
blonde. She went back to the kitchen as Vera threw the TV
control to the ground, sprang up from her seat and began a

protest of 'Nine eleven, twenty-four seven! Nine eleven, twenty-four seven!'

It soon became clear that this wasn't Vera at all. This woman sounded as though she had a clothes-peg nipped over her nose, and when she turned to the window you saw that instead of a mouth she had a small black hole at the bottom of her face the size of a button. Her shrivelled lips quivered involuntarily like a giraffe nibbling at a morsel of greenery located high in a tree. In spite of this, there was a slash of bright red lipstick daubed over what used to be her mouth. When she saw me looking into the house, she started up again with her protest of 'Nine eleven, twenty-four seven! Nine eleven, twenty-four seven!' breaking into an infectious chuckle until the fat blonde yelled out from the kitchen, 'For heaven's sake, Marlene, will you shut the fuck up?'

'This side view shows the remarkable sculptural craftsmanship of this unique fighter jet. And it can be yours by sending just $39.95 plus a total of $5.99 postage and handling. Illinois residents must add state sales tax . . .'

I wondered if I should feel nervous at having been spotted by Marlene but then I forgot everything because a deep, rumbling laugh suddenly filled the house. A large hand located at floor level grabbed the TV control and the screen flicked back on to the canned-laughter channel. There was an exclamation of 'Shut up! That's too funny!' and a pair of grubby feet waggled contentedly, sending waves of rippling pleasure through legs, up thighs and into buttocks barely covered by a pair of denim cut-offs.

She looked the same as she did on our first night: hand propping up chin, brown legs waving in the air, snacking untidily on a pile of Mexican food. She tugged on a piece of soft tortilla, chewed ravenously, licked her lips, sucked her fingers. I imagined the grubby grass muck beneath her nails, the piece of lettuce between her teeth.

Then a bird's claw grabbed hold of my wrist through the window. It was the woman with the funny lips. 'So, sweetie,' she yelled, her cigarette hanging from the small black hole in her lower face, 'do you think it's true that Whitney's on crack? I mean, I know she's an anorexic. That's for sure, right?'

Then Billie appeared at the window. She looked furious. 'What do you want?' she said.

There was a piece of lettuce between her teeth.

'Why did you run off?' I asked.

'Because I hated myself.'

'Why did you hate yourself?'

'Makes me feel at home.'

'What home?'

She looked at me as if she was about to punch my lights out. 'The house in my fucking head,' she hissed, drumming her temple with an angry finger.

'But that's not the whole of your home, Billie!' I pleaded with her. 'Your dream house is a big place, remember?'

'My dream place got taken over. It got invaded.'

She slammed the window shut in my face.

My heart missed a beat. Was that it? Was that the end of me and Billie? Then I heard her shouting something towards the kitchen and soon the front door opened and she appeared on the porch holding a couple of *National Enquirer* magazines.

A voice shouted sharply from the kitchen, 'Don't be late for the soup!' and Billie called back, 'Sure thing!'

She shut the door behind her. She wouldn't look at me. She flicked through one of the magazines. 'We'll go to the beach,' she said. She sounded bored. 'You'll feel at home there.'

'At home?'

We looked at each other then. We couldn't do it for long, though. She turned back to the *National Enquirer*. 'You took your time getting here,' she said.

'Were you hoping I'd come?'

'I was hoping I'd left my gear in your car.'

'Oh.'

'Did I?'

I'd never heard such coldness in her voice. 'I . . . thought we'd run out.'

'*You* might have run out. I had a secret supply.'

'Oh.'

'Another of my tricks.'

I felt crushed.

'So?' she insisted. 'Did I leave it there?'

'Sorry?'

'The pot.' She sounded impatient.

'I don't know if it's there. I . . . didn't look.'

Her eyebrows rose dramatically and a pregnant pause ensued before she said, 'Funny. I thought you looked at everything.'

I started walking towards the car. I heard her follow behind. Not for me, of course. For the drugs. I did my best to sound cheerful.

'So . . . so what kind of soup are you having?'

'Chilli.'

'Chilli soup?' I turned round. 'But I thought—'

'You thought I hated hot food. You think you know everything about me now, right?'

We reached the car. I unlocked the back doors and she started rummaging through the drag bag in search of the lost pot. I fiddled nervously with the knots on my wrist and wondered if we were going to pretend we didn't spend an incredible week together. I wondered what would happen to us now.

It was odd to see her in such a familiar pose. Now that everything had changed. She smelt different, though. Scrubbed worktops, scrubbed skin, formaldehyde. She smelt different now she didn't sit next to me in a car all day. Her eyes looked tired too, as if someone had come along with a cloth and scraped all the sheen away from the blackness.

'I do like it,' she said. 'But I can't eat it.'

'Sorry?'

'The chilli soup.'

'So why did that woman . . .'

'Leah.'

'That was Leah!'

'The one and only.'

'But I thought that Leah . . .'

'You thought that Leah was sweet and kind.'

'I . . .' I suddenly had a vision of hours and hours of having to eat humble pie with Billie. I didn't know if I could stand the strain. 'Look, Billie, I'm incredibly sorry for reading your diary. I know that—'

'Yeah, well. You should be sorry because it's ruined everything.'

She zipped up the drag bag, slammed the back door shut and then, the red spotted *papier-mâché* codpiece in hand, moved to the passenger side of the car. 'You think you know me now, right? You think that I hate hot food and that Leah's a cute little waitress and that because I had an alcoholic mother and an abusive babysitter I became a kooky sex worker. That's what you think, right?'

She settled herself into the passenger seat as I reflected that, well, yes, that was pretty much what I had been thinking, actually. I watched her remove a red cardboard bung from the codpiece and pull out a handful of ready-rolled joints. She lit one, inhaled deeply, exhaled, and said, with a wheeze, 'Let's just say that someone mollycoddled probably wouldn't grow up to be a dominatrix.'

She smoked the joint as though she was famished. When two or three inches had burned away, her face relaxed and her breathing calmed down. She started checking out the inside of the car. She saw the Fred Segal carrier-bag and soon noticed my new key-ring decorated with what looks like a silver Medusa head. Then she examined a pink leather sports bag I'd bought with a couple of interlinked gold Cs on the handle. 'Looks like you've been doing some sensible shopping at last,' she said, the ironic eyebrow raised. She began to loosen up and when the car was once more filled with a screen of yellow smoke she even made a joke. 'I knew you'd been in my notebook, anyway,' she said.

'What?'

'I knew you'd been in my notebook. The cord was done up in some kind of fancy knot.' She blew smoke into my face. 'Dork.'

And then there's the sound of parrots and reggae music, and this means that we've entered the hectic circus of the Venice Beach boardwalk. We're up and strolling along and Billie's pointing out the fire-dancers, the toe-ring sellers, the fortune-tellers, the spray-painters ('getting high on the fumes'), the Thai men who paint your name on a grain of rice for ten dollars, the Mexican maids with white toddlers in pushchairs, the Europeans looking down their noses at the Americans, the amateur artists selling pictures of girls in white petticoats on bicycles (and I don't even flinch), the skaters and joggers, the bum with a dirty tan and a pile of grubby possessions strapped to his bike, the bum dragging three soda-can-filled shopping carts tied together like a condominium house, the skateboard boy wearing a T-shirt saying '420' ('The police code word for a marijuana offence. At four twenty in the afternoon, you're supposed to smoke a joint'), the single men hanging out with young children ('Divorced fathers get to take their kids out on Saturdays'), the Maharishi on roller-blades wearing a white turban and golf visor playing Jimi Hendrix on an electric guitar ('Don't look him in the eye'), the tambourine-banging old white lady with yellow hair and a froth of pink tutu and a younger gospel-singing black man in a huge glittery green jockstrap playing a synthesiser. She keeps shouting, 'We're married! We're married!' ('So you forget about the terrible music and just think of his huge glittery dick.') There aren't many black people on the beach but there are groups of white people in black clothes who, Billie tells me, are posh Californians. Their clothes have that odd cut and startling appearance – like the stuff in Fred Segal's – that mark them out as designer apparel: jackets with three lapels, skirts that turn out to be trousers – that sort of thing.

It turns out that this is the scene Billie thought would make me feel at home. It doesn't, of course. It's Billie who makes me feel at home.

We go and sit on the beach and watch a Mexican family frolic around in their clothes in the foamy white water of the shallows. 'The Mexican washing-machine,' Billie says, reading my mind. 'That's what they call it. Mexicans don't feel the need to conquer the waves on surfboards, I guess.'

Billie was right about the Pacific being like a Californian teenage boy but the fact that California is obsessed with not being sleazy just makes the place more pervy as far as I'm concerned. (Lying next to us are a couple of girls sunbathing in bikinis with the top parts the size of ten-pence pieces because topless bathing is forbidden in America.) That's why I like America – there's so much you can be told off about. Americans are always talking about freedom and liberty but the place isn't free or liberated at all. Hardly anything is allowed: there's no jay-walking, no open liquor containers in cars, no liquor under twenty-one, no smoking in most areas and no topless sunbathing on the beach because California is filled with people with bodies like Brad Pitt and minds like Benny Hill. They say that California is like the Garden of Eden and it is because it's beautiful and fig leaves are mandatory.

Suddenly there's the sound of Billie in a panic. 'What the hell are you doing?'

'I'm sunbathing.'

'Not in your bra, you're not!'

'Why not?'

'You can get in trouble for that in California, you can . . .'

I start laughing.

'What's your problem?'

'You.'

'Huh?'

'How come you started out in New Orleans as the devil and ended up in California as Julie Andrews?'

She can't help smiling then. 'Yeah, well. California girls still talk about the day Brigitte Neilson came out of Patrick's Roadhouse on to the beach and stripped down naked before sliding into her bikini. Like they do in Europe.'

'So?'

'Californian girls thought she was just trying to get attention.'

'It does seem a bit funny.'

'What does?'

'Californian women paying a fortune to have plastic surgery because they want to be noticed. They might as well have saved their money and just sat on a beach in a grubby bra.'

'What-*ever*.' Billie gives up with a sigh. 'You're turning into a bit of a Californian girl yourself, Miss Jackie O Shades.'

My hand goes up to my head and touches the new sunglasses that are perched there.

'Hope you're not too high and mighty now,' she teases, fishing in her pocket. She pulls out a new, oddly shaped stone. 'For you,' she mutters, handing it to me. 'Nearest thing I could find to a heart.'

The stone is grey-white in colour and it does look quite like a heart, apart from the left lobe, which has the texture of a sinewy piece of tuna ripped in half.

She starts flicking through the *National Enquirer*. 'OK. Here we go: "She is depressed and humiliated by two failed marriages by the age of twenty-six and as a result is turning to fatty foods for consolation." Guess who.'

'Winona Ryder?'

'Nearly.'

'Drew Barrymore?'

Three spotty adolescent boys walk past. They look at Billie and one says awkwardly, 'Nice ass.'

Billie raises a weary eyebrow. '"Nice ass, ma'am," thank you very much,' and we watch the boys increase their pace over the sand.

311

'See, Mo,' she sighs, 'I've always attracted attention. According to my mother I'd be in a diner, aged three, and men would stare at me. You know, those decent kind of men that don't rape kids? They couldn't take their eyes off me. They didn't know what they were attracted to.'

I hesitate. I don't want to say the wrong thing. 'Billie, I'm so sorry that—'

She turns to me. 'Don't you dare feel fucking sorry for me. You can fuck right off if you're going to feel sorry for me. I've always known how to work people. I'm not in this line of business because I got beaten as a child. That's got nothing to do with it. Discipline isn't about getting off on fear.'

'OK.'

'All that shit could not have happened in my childhood and I'd probably still be into rough sex – only I wouldn't have done it for money.' She starts flicking through the *National Enquirer* again. 'And I wouldn't have been so good at it,' she adds, with a wry smile. 'I had a sucky childhood,' she says, 'but, hey, let's look on the bright side: I'm a big mess but at least it made me into a strong person.'

'So, being a dominatrix is like going on an assault course.'

She looks up, surprised. 'An assault course?' She smiles. 'Maybe. Although I don't know if I came out the other side yet.'

'How do you mean?'

She throws the magazine to one side and starts playing with the sand. 'That evening after the cemetery,' she says, 'I didn't exactly drive off into the sunset.'

'I know. You hot-wired Beer-gut's car!'

'That wasn't the only thing I did.' Her face is serious. 'Naturally, I had to do something utterly self-loathing.'

'What did you do?'

'Oh . . . I don't know.' She looks out to the ocean. There are angels tap-dancing far out on the horizon. 'I stopped off at the Thunderbird,' she says, quietly.

'And?'

312

'I pick up Beer-gut and I go back to his room and I let him fuck me.'

A fist smashes into my chest.

'And the thing is that he's got this tiny dick. I mean, like, four inches when erect? It barely grazes the inside of my thigh. I'm just aware of a slight movement in the cunt area but, of course, he thinks we've had great sex. He's, like, "Yeah, you want it, I know you want it, baby." It was my triumphal fuck to spite you and . . . well, actually I'm not sure who the hell I was trying to spite.'

I feel sick. I sit up and grab my T-shirt and pull it on.

'I wasn't really there.' Billie looks at me, concerned. 'When I was doing it . . . you know?'

I see the San Bernardino boy in the diary having his forehead carved up with a broken shard of glass. I can see the glass in my mind. I push it into the fat gut of the fat man. I kick him in the head until his skull collapses and his brains ooze out on the pavement like a two-minute egg. How could she? How could she do this to herself? To us? It's hopeless. She doesn't want to give me her heart. She gives me stones and pretends they're the real thing. She gives me substitutes for her heart. I've had enough.

'You can be sadistic when you choose!'

'Excuse me?'

'That boy you set fire to in San Bernardino.'

She looks sulky. She reminds me that it was only a fantasy of violence. 'That diary was a crazy thing to write. You don't begrudge me a little fun, do you?'

When I ask how she'd imagined the fantasy episode ending she says that fantasies don't have to have a beginning, a middle and an end. 'I'm not like you,' she says. 'I can jerk off without having the plot all sorted out in my head.'

Another mini-conflagration springs up in my chest. I'm wondering how on earth she knows about my masturbation failures when she says, 'Actually, there was an ending, but I only came up with it yesterday.'

She starts to dig a hole in the sand.

'The boy who smashed my car – in real life I wouldn't bother kicking him or setting him on fire.' She looks up. 'I'd ask him where his mom was.'

'What?'

'His mother. That's what kids are all scared of, right? Not punches or the police. I'd force him to his knees and grab him by his ear and say, "Where does your mama live? Does your mama know what you're up to? Does your mama know you go stealing people's things? Is that how she raised her boy?" And I'd watch the tears run down his face. I'd watch him snivel like a baby, going, "No, don't tell my mom!" That's better than the bruising and the battering: "You're a worthless piece of trash and you're going to make your mama sad."' A streak of pain shoots through her eyes.

'Do you feel better now?' I ask. 'Now that you've written about what happened to you as a kid?'

She looks bored. 'I had a therapist, way back, who told me I should connect with my "inner child". Try finding that voice again. I thought that was a lot of crap. But things changed when we started the drive. Like I told you, the further on we drove the further I was going back in my head. And then there was you . . .'

'Me?'

'You told me I should try again. Try writing again. Remember telling me that back at that dumb motel with the receptionist on amphetamines?'

I can feel the blush coming. I ask her if she ever thought of re-establishing contact with her mother. 'Why not put *all* the old ghosts to rest?'

This, apparently, is the most gauche thing I have said all day.

'My mother!' she screams.

The girls in the ten-pence-piece bikini tops sit up.

'What the hell do you know about my mother?'

'Billie, I'm sorry . . . I'm sorry I keep saying the wrong thing.'

'You think there's some kind of neat order to life, Mo, and it pisses me off! You think your curse is that everything you see turns to sex. The truth is that you turn everything you see into sausages and knots and stories because that's your way of controlling life. Well, I don't do that. I'm living the real thing and there's no "cut" and "paste" keys where I'm standing from!'

I can't believe I'm hearing this. How on earth does she know about the Midas touch? And how dare she tell me I'm running away from life? I'm not falling for that. It's not the truth, it's just that she's clever. She's the one who's good at knots. She can twist any argument into a knot.

'Mo, you think that there's only one key to unlock a heart. But you know what? A heart's got more locks than one.'

'Oh, yes, you know everything. I forgot that!'

'And even if someone gives you the key, you might enter the front door and find that you need a whole bunch of other keys even to make it to the next room.'

'But what about—'

'You've never even been in love before!'

'Now just stop right there—'

'Face it, Mo. You don't know jack!'

That does it. I've taken about as much as I want to.

'Now, just you listen to me, Billie Harrison. I didn't read your bloody diary because I was a voyeur – well, all right, part of me read it because I'm a voyeur, but mainly I read it because . . . well, you interest me, I like you . . . I mean, I . . . Well, whatever there is between us, it's been so hothoused and twisted up and neglected that I don't know what remains of it, to be quite honest. And you're right, it probably is too late. You're probably right about me not knowing what day it is when it comes to emotion and you're right about me trying to protect myself from pain but . . . well, that's just the way it is. And now, Billie Harrison, it's been great knowing you, it really has. You're the most amazing woman but I think it's best for both our sakes that we part now before we rip each other's throats out.'

I can't talk any more because I'm too choked up. I start stomping up to the boardwalk, pinching and tugging and rubbing away at the stupid knots on my stupid bracelet, wondering what I've just been talking about if I told Billie in the graveyard that I loved her – 'I love you, you fucking idiot! I love you!' – wishing that the genie of the bloody lamp would make an appearance so he could tell me what I really feel. I'm vaguely aware of a round of applause from the bikini girls and a comment of 'lesbian freaks' from some gay man standing under a palm tree dressed up like a merry-go-round but I don't care any more. They can bloody bog off. It's all become too much. All I want to do is get back to the Sceptre – to boredom and predictability. Except I'm only too glad when I hear a shout behind me saying, 'I found my dream place!'

I stop in my tracks.

'Mo, I found my dream place!'

I turn round. She's there behind me.

'What do you mean you found it?'

'I found it.'

'And where is it?'

'My mother built it for me.'

'What?'

'My mother built the dream house.'

'Are you serious?'

'I'm totally serious,' she says helplessly.

A sigh of exasperation erupts from my chest. 'So don't tell me: you've got the keys to the house of your dreams and now that you're inside you need even more keys?'

She shrugs shyly. 'Something like that.'

I plonk myself down in the sand. 'Oh, for goodness' sake!'

'Sorry, Mo.' She makes a lop-sided smile and sits down next to me. She holds my hand.

'That's as may be,' I snap. Her hand's hot. Suffocating.

'Excuse me?'

'Never mind. Expression.' I pull my hand free and sift sand through my fingers. 'Like finding a pony in the shit.'

'That'd be good.'

*　　*　　*

She starts to tells me about a fortune-teller. A fortune-teller on the boardwalk when she arrived two days ago when she was 'jonesing for some drugs' – some coke, some grass, anything. She was going up to strangers in the street and asking if they had any stuff on them. She got to the point when she wondered if getting a grain of rice painted with her name on might help matters when she saw the fortune-teller. She was sitting in front of a white Formica table. No big advert. Just some 'big old grandma with tattoos'. Billie couldn't pinpoint what it was about her.

'Maybe she reminded me of myself. Of how I'm going to look in a few years' time. Whatever it was, I sat down in front of her and she wrote something on a piece of paper and passed it to me. Inside, it said, "Fifty Dollars." I handed over the money and she just stared at me. She didn't bother telling me shit about how my life was going to get better or how it was going to get worse. She just looked at me and said, "Your mother is dead." I looked right back at her. I couldn't believe what she'd just told me. I was furious. I said to her, "What fucking palm-reading school did you go to?" And meanwhile I was thinking about how I'd spent the past fifteen years of my life hating my mother. Hating her and trying to forget her. But the thing was, I always knew I had a line to her if I wanted one. Through Leah. Leah knew me all through the time when I'd been living in the car. She helped me through breakdowns and shit, got me to see therapists. She was kind of heavy-handed, though. She insisted on sitting in on my therapy sessions. She got to know a lot about me that maybe she didn't want to know. After a couple of years it got to be too much. I needed some air. I needed to get away from LA, from Leah. Start over. I went to Europe for a stretch, then New York. Then New Orleans. I was out of contact with Leah for a while. I think she got hurt. At least, that's what I figured. It was the only way I could explain her hooking up with my mom. They bumped into each other at AA, of course.'

Billie rolls her eyes to the sky. 'I know. Misery loves company, right? Turned out that Leah'd had a rough ride of it too. Arnold, the guy who got her pregnant, made her have an abortion. So she did and they lived together for a couple of years. Then he ran off with another woman, leaving her to look after his mother. Leah's not as hard-hearted as all that. She's been looking after Marlene for nearly fifteen years now.'

'What's with Marlene's lips?'

'Mouth cancer. She only has a third of a tongue and no palate. Leah has to mash up all her food.'

'Poor Marlene.'

'Poor Leah too.'

'How do you mean?'

'After Arnold left, Leah got another boyfriend. Reckoned he was the love of her life. Marlene had an affair with him.'

'You're joking!'

'Marlene was hot property in her time. She was a singer with some 1940s swing band.'

'Really?'

'Apparently she used to have this amazing gospel voice. That's how she started out.'

'What does she sound like now?'

Billie shrugs. 'Never heard her sing. Guess she can't any more.' She smiles. 'Leah says her mouth cancer's God's punishment.' She turns to the ocean. 'What do you say, Peach? You always want to read. To unwrap.'

'Sorry?'

'You think the world's full of Christmas presents waiting to be unwrapped. It's nice to be able to think that.'

'And what do you believe?'

'Oh, I think a lot of Christmas presents don't have anything inside even if you bother to unwrap them.'

'Maybe you've got a point.'

She looks surprised. 'You think so?'

'Maybe it's best not to go near any suspicious-looking parcels.'

I'm only being facetious but a shadow crosses her face. She starts to chuck sand at her feet.

'Maybe you're right.'

'What?'

'Maybe you're right. Maybe you should just go away and maybe I should just forget about my mother and my crappy past and start over.'

'Billie . . .'

'I mean, when the fortune-teller told me my mom was dead, it just felt stupid. All those years when she'd been alive and I could have asked questions and now it was too late. I could have asked her why she didn't notice that I always had bruises all over me, or – or something.'

She takes a deep breath and exhales slowly. Her breathing gradually calms down. 'Stupid things I could have asked her. Could have asked her if she had bad period pains, like me. Could have shown her how to make a salad without Jell-O or marsh-mallows in.'

Her shoulders start to shake. Oh, poor Billie. 'I'm sorry . . . Oh, I'm so sorry your mother died. And, yes, of course you wanted to ask her all those questions . . . It would have been useful—'

'No, it wouldn't.'

'What do you mean?'

'Because I asked her and afterwards I might as well not have bothered.'

'You asked her? But I thought you said—'

'That she was dead? Yeah.' More sand flies to her feet. 'That's the first thing the fortune-teller told me.'

'What was the second thing?'

'She gets me to pay her twenty more dollars and tells me I should go see her.'

'Who?'

'My mother.'

'But I thought she said your mother was dead!'

'That was a metaphor, apparently.'

'You're joking.'

'I think the grandma chick was trying to spin out the session.

319

She's, like, "The seed corn must descend into the earth so that from the seeming death new life may germinate." Something like that.'

'Wow. That must have been strange for you.'

'What? That my mother's become a piece of popcorn? Not really. Being an insane cripple is my mom's dream come true. She can just sit there and have no more responsibilities for ever and ever.'

'She's a cripple?'

She puts her chin on her knees and stares at her buried feet. 'She was getting bad when I left home. She fucked up her back from years of wearing heels. Then I think she started sleeping on the couch while we were still with the Creep . . .' She takes a deep toke of the joint. 'She started slipping discs. She took more and more tranquillisers for the pain. She's pretty bad now. So she says . . .'

'You went to see her, then.'

'After I left the fortune-teller I couldn't stop thinking, like, What if World War Three breaks out and I'll never be able to see my mother again?' She smiles. 'I guess the diary was just the beginning.'

'Of the fucking deed.'

She lies back in the sand and stares up at the sky through the visor of her hands.

'Except I might as well not have bothered with the ending.'

'Why?'

'Because nothing's changed.'

'What happened when you went to visit her?'

'Nothing. She's still dedicating herself to the cult of suffering. Except instead of sitting in a wimple under the shade of a yew tree, she sits in this rocking-chair looking at walls covered with pictures of Helen Keller and the Cessna and me and Ned as kids . . .' She lights another joint. 'She spends all day in this house she had built with my stepdad's life-insurance money.'

'He died?'

'Yeah, he really did die. Heart-attack. Fucking good riddance.'
She sucks deeply on the joint. 'So it turns out she built this house
– and it's pretty much how I imagined my dream place to be:
huge doors so nobody would ever feel too tall, curved walls so
nobody would ever feel unloved . . .'

'And how did you feel when you got there?'

She buries her head in her hands. I know I must be sounding
like a therapist. I'm searching for some way to ask the question
in a different way when she unburies her head and says, 'I felt
sick, of course.'

She asks if I mind going back to the car so we start to walk
through the sand towards the boardwalk. 'Her face was new,'
she says suddenly. 'It was still kind of blank but some new pious
thing was going on. She apologised for being so out of breath.
Said it was her illness. She talked a lot about her illness. I listened.
I didn't stay long. She said it was the best day of her life.'

'That was good, no?'

'The best day of *her* life? It was all about her again. Just like
it always was. I was thinking, Fuck you.'

She stops suddenly. She says it was strange when she left. That
her mother hauled herself up from her rocking-chair and kissed
her forehead, just like she used to. 'And then she said, "I love
you, Billie."'

'And what did it feel like?'

She shrugs. 'Felt like bacon and grits kind of "I love you".'

'Meaning?'

'Meaning it went down OK and kind of hit the spot. And
then afterwards I was, like, "What*ever*."'

'Did you say, "I love you," back?'

'Yeah.'

'And what was that like?'

'Like a stale Danish.'

'I'm sorry.'

She squidges her nose up. 'She probably didn't even notice it
was stale. She eats any old crap.'

We start to walk again. I'm trying to come up with something positive. So I say, 'You thought, Fuck you! though.'

'What?' She looks puzzled.

'I mean that sometimes "Fuck you" can mean "I love you", and sometimes "I love you" can mean "Have a nice day."'

She eyes me suspiciously. I plough on: 'And you can have, "Fuck you!" or "Fuck off!" or "Fuuuuuck!" when someone's touched you in just the right spot, or "Fuck me!" when something nice happens or "Fucking no way!" when you're a child and you get taken to the beach and you get to ride on a donkey.'

'A donkey?' A smile breaks through.

'All right, then, a llama. And "I love you" can mean "I love you heart and soul every breathing, waking minute of the day . . ."'

'Or it can mean "I'll be back in ten hours, kids, mind you behave with the babysitter."'

'It can mean "My life suddenly slotted into place."'

'Or it can mean "Don't you dare tell anyone about what we're doing."'

'It can mean "I love that pair of shoes"!'

'Or it can mean "I love my child like I love that pair of shoes . . ."'

The bitterness has returned to her voice and silence falls again. We reach the boardwalk and make our way through the rollerbladers and the disco music and the shrieks of laughter and the smells of hot dogs and jasmine. I ask her what would be the ideal thing her mother could say to her.

She thinks for a while. 'She could say, "I was a shit mom, I didn't want to be a mom in the first place but I was and I fucked up and now I'm willing to move on."'

'Maybe with time she will say that.'

'Oh, no. She loves playing the victim. She loves having been a bad mother. She gets up on stage at AA and she's got a full hour out of that alone.'

I can't help smiling. The shine comes back to Billie's face too. She tells me that I can share the spare room with Marlene tonight if I want. 'You'll get on fine. Just read up on Whitney Houston. And Sting. She loves Sting.'

I say that maybe the first visit with her mother was just bad luck. That maybe she just needs to have another go. 'I think you should go back, Billie. I really do.'

She gives me a weird smile. She's silent for a while and then she says, 'You and your happy endings.' Before I can reply, she grabs me gently by the scruff of the neck and whispers into my ear, 'I've got a present for you.'

My ear is tingling. 'What is it?' I screw my face up. My ear is damp and warm, like a home for me and Billie to live in.

'It's going to be painful,' she hisses. 'Really painful.'

I pull away. 'Billie, I . . .'

'The worst punishment of all!'

'Now, look here, Billie . . .'

'I'm going to take you to meet my mother.'

CHAPTER TWENTY-ONE

Home Sweet Home

Marlene is still having trouble finding a channel without any 9/11 coverage. She finally locates a rerun of a talk show whose topic is adopted kids reunited with birth parents. The abandoned kids are all fat and they all seem to think that if they hadn't been adopted they would somehow have been more complete human beings.

'So,' the hostess asks one of them, 'how do you think your life would have been if your biological mother had kept you?'

'Well, I think I'd have been more, like, whole?'

'Whole lotta crap!' Billie spits.

'You're in for a surprise, honey!' Marlene shouts at the screen, squirting a mixture of Kahlua, vodka and milk into her mouth from a plastic squeezy bottle. (Marlene might have mouth cancer, no palate and only a third of a tongue but somehow she also has a voice like a foghorn.)

'Yeah, right!' she whoops, when the mother finally makes her entrance on to the set. 'First time in your life *you* ever wore a dress and a cardigan!'

'Yeah!' Billie shouts. 'And check that big old watch they've made her wear to cover up the biker tattoo on her wrist!'

When the spruced-up mother runs over and hugs the daughter, gushing, 'It's like the sky opened up and a thousand rainbows came pouring out!' Billie and Marlene both make a big 'puh!' of disgust.

'Someone never came down off their acid trip.' Billie groans.

'What a phoney,' comes the foghorn. 'She's just in it for the free hotel room!'

Marlene turns round from her seat smack in front of the TV

set. 'Can you see OK, hon?' she asks me, waving the squeezy bottle in the air. This means she wants a refill of the White Russian. I get up and take the bottle from her. I don't mind. It gives me a better chance to listen to the show going on in the next room. It's pretty similar to the one going on here in the kitchen, although next door nobody is allowed to jeer at any of the people on stage.

'My name is Sandy and I am an alcoholic.'

'Hi, Sandy.'

'My name is Brian and I am an alcoholic.'

'Hi, Brian.'

I met all the AA guests earlier on and they seemed nice enough. There's a woman called Willa who smokes cigars and wears a Stetson, a gay hairdresser called Brian in a leopardprint shirt and blue John Lennon shades, and a yoga teacher called Sandy. It's Brian and Sandy's first time here. Sandy is sweet but a bit dull. When it's her turn to testify, she talks in general terms about the 'degradation' and 'unmentionable suffering' she experienced during her days on the 'liquor'. Willa, on the other hand, is very specific. She begins her tale of degradation by telling the room that she used to have a relationship with a woman who beat her up and then she met a man who ended up having his legs cut off. After this, she got married to a man who was actually quite nice but then the liquor made her start going off with women again.

'I'd be going off to meet Lowanda at this joint in Santa Monica and I'd lie to my husband that I was going to see my grandmother in a coma – she was ninety-five per cent brain dead but I spoke to her anyway because the doctors told me she might be able to hear what I was saying. So, anyway, sometimes I'd go to the hospital and chew the fat with my grandmother but usually I'd go off to that joint in Santa Monica to see Lowanda and we'd dance and canoodle until three or four in the morning. We'd be drinking root-beer schnapps with beer chasers and then we'd go to the bathroom to snort coke and smoke pot. Man, it was crazy! Plus we'd get guys queuing up to buy us more liquor and then they'd start hitting on us. This one time a guy comes up to me, asks how comes I always turned up with cute women.'

Willa adjusts the brim of her Stetson to a rakish angle and pauses for dramatic effect. 'I told him. I said, "Go home, buddy. Get a shave and change your shirt. When you come back you go buy a woman a drink. You go buy a woman a drink and you talk to her. It's cheaper than going to a hooker."'

Willa smells of fried food and cigar smoke and she's not very attractive. After the AA meeting, when people start coming into the kitchen looking for more coffee, she comes over to the table where I'm helping to prepare dinner. Following Leah's orders, I'm cutting up carrot and orange Jell-O salad and placing it on iceberg lettuce leaves in a green Tupperware bowl the size of Billie's butt. Willa introduces herself by saying, 'You're thirty-four, right?'

'Sorry?'

'Your chest. It's thirty-four. Feel my calves. I'm strong.'

I glance over at Billie, who is still slumped in front of the TV making no sign of coming to my rescue. Luckily my waitress training has prepared me for encounters such as these: I smile politely, try out my new old-wine laugh and carry on chopping.

Billie is not taking much care of me at her mother's house. When I asked her if I could have a beer she snapped, 'You know where the fridge is!' It's not been an easy day for her, though. To start with, her mother's house was a nightmare to get to. We drove for ages – up a long cliff-face followed by miles down an overgrown dirt track dotted with various dilapidated signs pointing to 'Bellevue'. And then, when we finally arrived at Bellevue, it turned out that Mrs Harrison was sick. Leah got out of the car and went inside the house only to emerge a few minutes later to announce, 'Your mom's in bed. She says she'll be up in a couple of hours.'

Her thin, pursed lips looked faintly smug. She whistled at Marlene as if Marlene was a cross between a dog and a child in disgrace. 'You! In here!'

Marlene finished applying some powder to her jerky-textured skin and some smears of red lipstick to her pieces of lip. 'Can't go to a party without a party face,' she buzzed happily, in her clothes-peg voice. Then she gathered together all her prepared odds and ends – her magazines, her plastic bags, her alarm clock, her pegs, her tissues, her spittoon – and started shuffling towards the house, adding, with a chuckle, 'Don't you girls get up to no mischief now!'

Billie sat in silence. I asked her what she thought was wrong with her mother. She muttered, 'Nothing.'

I knew she regretted her decision to come and visit her mother as soon as she'd made it. It was me who pushed her. She agreed to go to the house but only if Leah came too, and Leah – who bears a frightening resemblance to the old trout landlady from the Maples Guest House in Scabs – claimed she could only go on Thursday, the day of Mrs Harrison's monthly Alcoholics Anonymous meetings. At the time, Billie thought it'd be fun to take me to an AA meeting. But when I persuaded her to get out of the car and go and face the music, she took one look at the motley crew gathered in the living room gripping their Blue Books, and marched aggressively into the kitchen.

'Nothing's changed,' she snarled. 'I used to think that if Mom was going to have an AA meeting in her house then at least she could get some famous people up from Hollywood. And hey! She's still dishing up the same old freaks.'

We could hear Leah banging about next door, a jug of coffee in her hand, welcoming newcomers with bursts of fake laughter. I'm still unsettled by Leah – the way she rarely looks me in the eye, her fake jollity. I think she's jealous of Billie because Billie managed to escape and she didn't. I think she's decided that if she can't get pleasure out of life from being nice then she's going to get pleasure from being nasty and Marlene is an easy target.

Billie started settling Marlene into her chair in front of the TV.

'Are you worried about your mother being ill?' I asked her.

She handed Marlene her plastic bags and her pegs. 'Worried about my mother? Give me a break. There's nothing wrong with her.'

'But she's in bed.'

'She loves to be centre stage,' she said, balancing the alarm clock on one of the chair arms. 'She figures her entrance will be better if she comes on late.'

Even though the AA meeting is now over, the cigar-smoking woman seems unable to stop the stream of personal confession. She comes into the kitchen and sits down next to me at the table. She removes her Stetson and tries to brush her hair into some sort of normality. 'I like your lumberjack shirt,' she says, clenching the cigar between her teeth. 'And that weird accent of yours.'

'Thank you.'

'Willard was my dead husband's second name. That's why I'm known as Willa.'

'Your husband died?'

'Murdered.' Her eyes well up. 'And a better man never walked God's earth.' She pulls a Kleenex from her back pocket.

'I'm sorry.'

She nods and blows her nose.

'Did you ever kiss a woman before?' she asks, from the folds of her tissue.

'Pardon?'

'It's real soft,' she explains, her voice turning thick with longing.

In the end it's Marlene who rescues me. She comes up to the table, gobbing into her spittoon. 'Looks like your charms failed on the British chick,' she says.

'She spoken for, then?' Willa looks disappointed.

'She don't know it yet.' Marlene wipes her chin.

'Oh, well.' Willa shrugs. 'I never did have much luck. I was born on Friday the thirteenth. Guess I was asking for trouble.'

Marlene gazes into her spittoon, swirling it round and round in her bird's claw. 'Can I ask you a personal question, Willa?' she says.

'Sure, hon.'

'Even the girls in the band didn't know the answer to this one.'

'You ask away, sweetheart.'

'Is it possible for two women to have a simultaneous orgasm?'

Willa removes the cigar from her mouth and contemplates the soggy end as she ponders the question. Meanwhile, Marlene gets impatient and blurts out, 'My best way to come's taking the shower head off the shower and spurting warm water on my clit!'

Willa is about to comment on this method when Leah swoops over and says, 'For heaven's sake, Marlene. Go see if the shrimp are cooked!'

Then the timorous yoga teacher approaches and starts trying to join in the conversation. She talks about my foreign accent, saying that she once went to an AA meeting in Glasgow. 'I couldn't understand anything of what they were saying, but that didn't matter none.'

She looks slightly overawed at the sight of Leah commandeering her way round the kitchen. 'I never been to Carrie's house before. I heard it was kind of non-conventional, though.' She looks at Marlene's squeezy bottle and bites her lip. 'I never went to an AA meeting where there was, like, liquor.'

Marlene thrusts the bottle into her face. 'Here, hon,' she booms, 'you wanna taste?'

The yoga teacher recoils in horror.

'Marlene!' Leah stands towering above her. 'Will you get up off of your ass?' She gives her a vicious dig in the arm and Marlene responds with a very loud burp.

'Well, excuuuuuuuuuse me!' she whoops. She turns to Billie and asks, 'Did you set my clock for eleven?'

'What's at eleven o'clock?' I ask.

'*Night of Heroes*,' Leah says stiffly. 'It's a tribute to the people who died in the attacks.'

'Goldie Hawn and George Clooney!' Marlene fizzes.

'Down, Marlene! Down!' Billie's face loosens at last. 'Your clock's set for eleven.'

'There's going to be famous people manning the phones,' Marlene explains to me, 'taking in donations. You never know who you might get to talk to.'

'Yeah, right,' Leah sneers. 'I'm sure George Clooney's going to drop his St Tropez babe when he sees you!'

'Don't you worry!' Marlene says, giving me a wink. 'I'll tell him some of my tales. Tell him what we got up to after gospel-choir practice back in Arkansas. Make that broad run for the hills!'

Leah digs deeper. 'Your gospel-singing days are over. He'd run for the hills when he got a look at your shipwreck of a face!'

She laughs her horrible laugh, her eyes looking at nothing and nobody in particular. Marlene starts gazing into her spittoon again, tapping the side and shaking it back and forth as if there's something wrong with it. She mumbles a few agitated words although you can't tell what they are. They clump together into a manic buzz noise so that as she struggles to get out of the chair she sounds like a bluebottle that flew by mistake into a very large and sticky spider's web, and it is only by the greatest of wills that she manages to fly out of it.

I follow her to the patio where twelve enormous prawns are cooking on an enormous barbecue (with no smell and no smoke) that looks like some ancient console from Cape Canaveral. The ground is a mass of white marble slabs – thick and chunky just like the architecture in the rest of the house.

I look up at the house – Billie's dream house. It's even bigger than I expected, with balconies and balustrades and beams on the ceiling as big as pylons and doors that could frame a giant. It's true that all the walls are curved and there are no edges or spikes, and yet while the place might make you feel thin it certainly doesn't make you feel loved. The outside walls are covered in a mesh of apple-green and apple-red ivy leaves – the kind of apples so shiny and beautiful that you know they're poisoned – with suckers that cling to the house like tiny insect legs. And inside everything is too soft. Mattresses are flabby as the Pilsbury dough-boy's stomach, and there is such waste. The thickness of the toilet paper is beyond belief. And the bad taste. The bookshelf, for instance, is a mass of self-help, hippie-dippy and just plain boring, with titles including *The Celestine Prophecy*, *Coping With Anxiety*, *Healing Yoga in New Mexico*, *The Power of Now*, and some bound tomes of *Reader's Digest*. The air inside the house is cold as opposed to refreshingly cool. It smells of stale cellar mixed with the ghost of old junk food. It feels as though this house was built for parties and then nobody ever came to the parties and now there are just occasional AA meetings where second-rate hairdressers and yoga teachers gather together to bemoan the death of the good old drinking days.

Round the corner from the Cape Canaveral barbecue console is a stretch of untended garden overgrown with weeds and matted scrub. The chipped swimming-pool is filled with green water and surrounded by an array of faded deck furniture blighted with mildew and rust. There is one place that is still splendid, though. Breathtaking, even. Through a wide gap in a tangle of euca-lyptus trees it becomes clear that Bellevue is built on the edge of a cliff. The view over the Pacific is incredible, as is the view to the east where you can see all of downtown LA – the huge skyscrapers and the towers and the tall buildings made of glass.

I look at the horizon and remember Billie telling me about how our trip was going to smell of neon and hot pomegranates and sunsets. There's a touch on my back and when I turn round it's her. She's got a beer and a caffeine-free Diet Coke in her hands. 'For you,' she says, handing me the beer. 'Sorry I've been such a pain.' She sounds sheepish. She says that the Coke's for her mother – that the kitchen scene has become so unbearable that she's going to go and hang out with her mother. She asks if I want to join her.

A vision of a woman with claws and fangs and green scales

growing over her skin from years of self-loathing and alcohol abuse and neglect of her children flashes across the bay. I imagine a monster with a jutting-out jaw and shifty eyes and veins standing out in her neck like whipcords.

'Let's go,' I say, a bit too enthusiastically.

CHAPTER TWENTY-TWO

Turn on, Tune in, Drop Out

Billie takes a deep breath and knocks on the door. 'Mom?' No reply. Just faint strains of flute music. She knocks again. 'Mom? I brought you a Diet Coke.'

A shaky voice: 'Caffeine-free?'

'Sure, Mom.'

Some coughing and wheezing, the sound of a creaking chair and then a half-whisper: 'I guess you'd better come in.'

When I see Billie's mother, my heart skips a beat. Mrs Harrison is the spitting image of her daughter as Doris Day in the schizophrenic striptease. You notice first the honey-blonde bob (although this one doesn't appear to be a wig) and then the smooth smile. Then you see the sparkling black eyes and the air of serenity, and you realise that Mrs Harrison is much less of an ogre than her daughter's cabaret portrait suggests.

Instead of the prissy pink gingham frock she wears a white cotton blouse and skirt – like the outfits you imagine angels wearing when they sit on clouds. She holds a staff – a walking-stick – and in her lap she protects a pool of photographs with a small, elegant hand.

Billie was right about the terrible new-age music (a version of 'Greensleeves' is playing on the stereo) and about the photos on the wall – her and Ned as kids, Helen Keller, a twenty-something Mrs Harrison patting the belly of an aeroplane. But at least there's some character to this room. There's a bed forged from curly spirals of wrought iron, and hanging over the rocking-chair where Mrs Harrison sits is a mobile made from seashells and driftwood that chinks and clinks softly in the breeze from the open window.

Mrs Harrison (Billie's told me that her mother reverted back to her maiden name several years ago) puts out her hand and soon it's holding mine in a warm grasp. 'I'm very pleased to meet you,' she says, with a friendly smile. 'I'm sorry I couldn't hang out with you guys. I don't know if Billie told you but I'm a little out of sorts at the moment.'

She might be out of sorts but she looks fantastic for fifty-five. My mother never looked like her at that age. The ocean breeze coming in through the window makes the thin fabric of her white clothes ripple gently over her body so that she seems to be covered with a extra layer of life.

I tell her that I hope she feels better soon and that it's very nice to meet her. She says she hopes the AA meeting wasn't too boring.

'It wasn't boring at all,' I tell her truthfully.

'Willa was there, huh?' she says, with another glint. 'I guess she was delighted to meet you!'

'Well . . .'

'Willa says she chased girls becuase she was drunk. But you know what? I'm not so sure.' I feel slightly awkward when she says this but when she sees that she's embarrassed me, she has the courtesy to change the subject. 'Did you meet Billie at the makeup school?' she asks.

'Sorry?'

'The makeup school where she works?'

There's a glow in her eyes that looks like hope or hunger. You can see that she's suffered a lot. Billie was right about that. And yet right now she really does look like a repentant woman sitting humbly under the shade of a yew tree in her wooden rocking-chair. She looks as though she's dedicated her life to repentance and that's surely not such a bad thing. It's strange. I expected to hate this woman, despise her for what she did to Billie, for what she failed to do. Yet she seems to be trying so hard to make up for her mistakes. For some reason it makes me sad that Billie told her she was a makeup artist and Mrs Harrison believed her and was happy for her. I glance over at Billie – who's scowling.

I smile at Mrs Harrison and tell her that I didn't meet Billie at the makeup school. That we had friends in common.

'That's nice.' She beams over at Billie. 'I guess that time she went to England to be a nanny she must have met a lot of people.'

'You seem to have been following my career path, Mom.'

Mrs Harrison fails to detect the sarcasm in her daughter's voice. 'Oh, Leah keeps me updated.'

Billie mumbles, under her breath, 'Yeah, and Leah *really* knows what's going on in my life . . .'

Suddenly Mrs Harrison gasps as if she's skidded unexpectedly down an icy path. She clutches the side of her rocking-chair to steady herself and squeezes her eyes shut. She stays motionless until the painful moment has passed and her breathing has become slower and more rhythmic. 'I'm sorry,' she apologises. 'I guess I shouldn't have brought all those boxes up from the cellar.'

'You lifted these boxes?' Billie says, exasperated. She glances at the series of crates dotted round the room, overflowing with books, photos and bric-à-brac.

'Oh, it's fine,' Mrs Harrison says. 'It's kind of damp down there but . . . well, I just wanted to make sure everything was perfect.'

Billie turns away and Mrs Harrison tries to bring her back into the conversation. 'Do you remember our arts and crafts afternoons, Billie?'

'Potato printing,' Billie says quietly. 'I remember that.'

Mrs Harrison turns to me. 'She and Ned loved potato printing!' She slaps the side of the chair. 'Hey, I forgot!' she says, looking down into her white-skirted lap. 'I got some pictures out to show you.'

The chair starts rocking as she sifts through the pile. 'It's a shame Ned's off on tour,' she adds. 'We could have looked at them together.'

'That's the life of the roadie, I guess,' Billie says.

'Yes,' Mrs Harrison adds. 'I guess life on the road suits him.'

She passes Billie a picture, looking at her face eagerly for a reaction. The reaction is a grin. A spontaneous one. Billie passes the picture to me. 'I was dive-bombing from a rock into the water at Castaic Lake.'

'Look at that grin on her face,' Mrs Harrison says, leaning forward. 'Actually, Billie, you were in a bad mood that day because you'd just had your wisdom teeth out.'

She rummages some more among the photos in the hollow of her skirt. She says, 'Dang it, I can't seem to find the one . . .' She takes hold of her walking-stick and heaves herself up out of the chair. 'Just a second,' she pants, hobbling over to the door. 'Maybe Leah knows where I put them. Some special ones I prepared for you.'

She strokes the top of Billie's hair as she goes towards the door. Billie is poking around in the bottom of one of the cardboard boxes and doesn't seem to notice her mother's gesture. Then Mrs Harrison touches my shoulder. I look up into her black eyes and she says softly, 'Mo, thank you for bringing Billie to me.'

I start to protest, 'I—'

'No,' she says, with another squeeze on my shoulder. 'Thank you. You've made me very happy.'

I'm aware of some gooeyness in my stomach and then a vague feeling of self-righteousness, although this stops as soon as the door closes and Billie looks up from the cardboard box, saying, 'So, she won you over too.'

I try to tread carefully. 'She seems . . . sweet.'

'Yeah,' Billie says grimly, delving back into the box. 'Everyone loves my mother.' Her hand comes to rest on something in the box and a smile creeps on to her lips. 'You're right, Mo. You can't read people.'

'What?'

'You can't read to save your life.'

She brings her hand out of the box, examining a tiny piece of paper between her thumb and forefinger.

I can feel myself go hot. 'Actually, I think I'm a pretty good reader,' I snap, thinking of the diary.

But she doesn't retaliate. Not even a dirty look. Her smile's turned into a smug grin.

'What are you planning, Billie?'

She holds up the square of paper the size of a small fingernail. 'I think Summer's dad gave this to me, back in the early eighties.'

'Billie, is that an—'

'Acid tab? Sure is!'

She takes the Diet Coke can and snaps open the ring pull. She rips the square of paper in half and drops one piece inside.

I'm speechless. Which I suppose is just as well because what am I supposed to say when Billie's mother comes back into the room — 'Excuse me, Mrs Harrison, but your daughter just put an acid tab in your can of Diet Coke – but, then, I guess you did give her a pretty bad start in life, even though you might sit here now with your white clothes and your shell mobiles and your "Greensleeves" soundtrack'?

The look on my face makes Billie laugh. She tells me to relax. She says acid'll be the best thing that ever happened in her relationship with her mother. I'm thinking of Acid Sarah seeing Siamese cats with blue heads coming out of the walls. But mostly I'm thinking how putting acid in your mother's drink is one of those exhilarating, pushing-an-innocent-person-off-a-cliff moments.

The door opens and Mrs Harrison appears. She eases herself back into the rocking-chair, her face flushed with exercise and excitement. 'Here we are,' she pants. 'I'd given them to Leah to look after. I swear, my head's like a sieve these days!'

'Hey there, Mom. You look pretty hot and bothered. Why don't you have a drink?'

'Thanks, Billie,' Mrs Harrison says, delighted by the gesture. She takes the can of Diet Coke and has a big swig. 'I can't drink caffeine,' she confides to me. 'My doctor took me off it a few months ago.'

She passes the can back to Billie, who takes a smaller swig. Knowing Billie's constitution, I imagine she could drink the whole can and remain pretty unaffected. She smacks her lips and passes the can back to Mrs Harrison before rushing over to me with a tome that says '*Yearbook*'. She kneels down and flicks through it as Mrs Harrison watches over us. What we see are black-and-white pages of white girls with bouffanted hair flicked at the ends and white boys with chiselled jawlines wearing baseball jackets. Near the middle there's a bookmark in a section that begins, 'In every group there are the outstanding, the different, the ones who shine above the others . . .' followed by pictures of boys and girls under headings that say, 'Most popular couple', 'Most witty couple', 'Most representative'. On another page there are girls standing alone above captions that say, 'Homecoming Queen' and 'Homecoming Princess', followed by their names.

The name of the princess is Carrie Clare Harrison.

Mrs Harrison says, 'I wasn't voted the queen that year. That was a blow.'

It must have been a blow to her because, when she hands over some more books and pamphlets, it seems that every year she was the queen of something. Over the years she was a cheer-leader, a head cheer-leader, a homecoming queen and a prom queen. Even though she couldn't afford to go to college, she was chosen as one of the pin-up girls for the calendar of the Sigma Nu fraternity of Santa Clara University. This she proves by unearthing a black-and-white calendar and passing it to me. 'I was December,' she says, with a small laugh. And there she is, sitting on the front of a Cadillac in a 1960s bikini, leaning back on her arms as a shapely leg in a tasselled cowboy boot kicks cutely up into the air thanks to a graceful cheer-leader thigh muscle.

'Mom, you look so great!' Billie says, looking genuinely impressed.

'My top's all stuffed with socks. Can you see?'

We look and have a laugh.

'Those Sigma Nu boys had the best parties. That was why we hung out with the best fraternities.'

'You scarlet woman, Mom!'

'There was this one party, everyone was 'gatering on the floor . . .'

''Gatering?'

'Oh, that means getting down on the floor like you're fucking it.' She puts her hand over her mouth. 'Oh, my! Where did that come from?'

Billie starts rocking her mother's chair playfully. 'Wash your mouth out, Mom!'

'I wasn't cheap by any means,' she says, leaning over and pulling another album from a box.

'No?'

'No! I kept my virginity till I was twenty-three!'

'She made up for it afterwards!'

'Now, you hush your mouth, Billie Harrison,' she says, with a smile. 'Let me show you something.'

She opens the new album and it's filled with small square photos from the sixties with white borders and soft colours. Mrs Harrison still looks like the most popular girl of her year. Her long honey hair cascades on to her shoulders and no matter who else she is photographed with – other cheer-leaders, boyfriends, female friends – her aura seems to shine above all the others. All the photos of her show gleaming cheeks, a flash of perfect white teeth, a glinting circle of white light in her pupils.

She points to a man with a moustache in flared beige trousers standing on a tropical beach with his arm round a beautiful girl in a red striped halter-neck top and a perfectly flattering pair of denim shorts and honey tanned legs. 'Jerry,' she says, with a whistle. 'That was when I discovered what Quaaludes were.'

'Mom!' Billie exclaims.

Mrs Harrison smiles. 'He went crazy one night in Acapulco. Too much tequila.'

She turns some more pages, then stops at a photo of a group of white-toothed, tanned young people gathered on a porch. She points to a wide-eyed boy. 'That's Denis, the disc jockey. I thought he was the hottest thing. One of his friends wanted to meet me one night so he went up to Denis at the music booth and he said, "Where is she?" Denis said, "She's the prettiest thing on the dance-floor." Next thing I know, there's a tap on my shoulder and there's a guy standing there going, "Are you Carrie Clare?"'

'He picked you out?'

She nods. 'There must have been two hundred people on the dance-floor that night.'

It's interesting how she doesn't come across as boastful. It's as if she's never questioned that she was picked out as the prettiest girl in the room or that she had rich men queuing up to date her or that the frat boys voted her sweetheart of the year. She doesn't mention Billie's dad. What he was like. Where he fitted in. And she doesn't say what it felt like later. When her life started going downhill.

'Denis stopped being a disc jockey and started to do the weather on CPTV.' She frowns. 'He wasn't so cool after that.'

Billie seems to be finding the photo collection fascinating. She picks another picture out. 'Hey, look!' she exclaims.

Mrs Harrison leans over Billie's shoulder. 'Centurions game!' she says.

'Centurions versus Cowboys!' says Billie. 'Me and Ned called it the toenail picture.'

Mrs Harrison chuckles. 'Yes, siree, I was at the front of that parade, twirling that baton around like there was no tomorrow.'

There's a humming sound in the room competing with the sound of 'Greensleeves'. Mrs Harrison is mumbling something.

'Mom?' Billie enquires innocently. 'Are you OK?'

Mrs Harrison looks up from the picture with an odd smile on her face. 'You know, Billie,' she says, 'I'm feeling a little . . . weird.'

'Oh, look, there are the cowboy boots!' Billie says quickly, showing her the picture.

Mrs Harrison grins. '"I was marching so hard . . ."'

The two catch each other's eye and chime, '"That all my toenails came off!"'

'Look at all that red lipstick you're wearing, Mom.'

'You and Ned used to say I had a cheesy grin.' She takes another swig of the Coke.

'You do!'

'Well, you know what my cheer-leader coach used to say: "Look 'yes', say 'no'!"'

Mrs Harrison touches her lips and starts giggling. Not just ordinary giggling but the sort of uncontrollable, over-excited laughter that takes hold of you when you're shooting down the slope of a roller-coaster.

'Will you look at that?' she says to Billie, prodding her lips some more. 'Jell-O! Bouncing Jell-O mellow face!'

That sets Billie off, and when the two finally pull themselves together they just sit there in silence smiling at each other. I think they might need to be brought back to reality so I say to Mrs Harrison, 'Um . . . what did you like best about cheer-leading?'

She turns to me, her eyes now bouncing around like plates of Jell-O. 'I guess it was a good way of keeping fit,' she says, in a tone that suggests she has made some profound discovery.

'Come on, Mom,' Billie bursts in. 'You loved the attention!'

'OK, then,' she says, with a chuckle. 'I admit it, I fucking loved the attention!'

The two of them catch each other's eye again and give each other a high five.

'Kinda cool,' Mrs Harrison says.

'Excuse me?' says Billie.

Something strange has happened to Mrs Harrison's voice. She sounds like a teenager. 'Yeah, way cool,' she's saying. She leaps up from the rocking-chair, sending her walking-stick flying and a shower of photographs cascading to the ground. She starts doing high kicks and simulated pompom twirling accompanied by a cheer-leader chant of: 'Go! Bananas! B-A-N-A-N-A-S!'

She is oblivious to everyone else in the room. She's started parading round the room, cheering: 'Go! Bananas! B-A-N-A-N-A-S!'

Billie finds the whole thing hilarious. She starts clapping and yelling, 'You go, girl!'

I can't tell what's Billie and what's the acid.

Mrs Harrison, meanwhile, encouraged by the applause launches into another version of the chant, this one: 'Be! Aggressive! A-G-G-R-E-S-S-I-V-E!'

Billie whoops. She goes over to her mother and hugs her. 'Not bad!' she says.

Mrs Harrison looks at her daughter as if someone in the playground is trying to pick a fight with her. 'You trying to tell me I'm not cool?' Mrs Harrison has started to chew invisible gum.

Billie chuckles. She turns to me and says, 'So much for the bad back!' Then she asks her spaced-out mother what she's called.

'Carrie Clare,' Mrs Harrison goes. 'That's two names. Not just one. So don't you forget it!'

'Ooooh! You *are* aggressive!'

Still chewing her non-existent gum, the fifteen-year-old Mrs Harrison segues seamlessly into a baboon impersonation. She stoops forward, droops her hands to the floor and starts stomping round the room in a lumpen fashion, roaring, 'Cookie Monster!' then, 'Cooo-keee!'

Billie cracks up. She goes and stands next to her mother and both of them start shaking imaginary pompoms and cheering:

'The Cookie Monster says the Centurions are . . .
The great big cookies at the top of the jar!
The Cookie Monster says the Cowboys are . . .
The itty-bitty crumbles at the bottom of the jar!'

They collapse on to the carpet, laughing at first, and then they just lie there – head to head on the floor – listening to the peaceful sounds of the room, the flutes and the bells, the tinkling shells and the pieces of driftwood knocking together in the breeze from the open window.

Suddenly Billie sits up. She stares at the mobile, confused. She stands up and touches one of the pink shells. 'You used to be magic, Mom,' she says, letting go of the shell. 'And then you lost your magic.' The mobile swings back and forth on its translucent thread. 'Where'd it go, Mom?' Her voice cracks. 'Where'd the magic go?'

Mrs Harrison sits up. 'One day at a time, girlfriend,' she says, still in gung-ho teenage mode.

'Stop speaking in car-bumper stickers, Mom. You weren't there for me.'

'Like, relax, dude!' Mrs Harrison's eyes look like they are swinging on threads at this point.

'You made me do my hair nice for the Creep . . .'

'I was sick!' Carrie Clare retorts as if this is the most obvious thing in the world. 'I wasn't well, honey. I didn't know what was going on.' She pulls out her lower lip and observes it with interest, as if it doesn't belong to her.

'Oh, yeah!' Billie turns vicious now. 'That's always been your excuse, hasn't it?'

'Billie, I was sick.' Mrs Harrison's a bit huffy now, speaking as if Billie has accusing her of putting too much Jell-O salad on her plate.

'Here we go again,' Billie explodes, leaping to her feet. 'Victim, victim, victim. You couldn't do anything, the drink came and made you drink it, everyone took advantage of you. That's it, huh, Mom?'

As Billie paces round the room, Mrs Harrison, still splurged all over the floor, stares intently at one of the shells on the mobile. She seems oblivious of what's happening around her, and then suddenly she starts quivering like one of the folds of her blouse flapping too fast in the breeze. Dark shadows flood into her eyes and horror seeps into her face, gradually turning her into the disturbed Doris Day from Billie's show. With a sharp intake of breath she turns away from the shells, looking as though she just staggered from a horrific car wreck. Like a blind woman, she feels her way along the floor, and when she finds the rocking-chair, she clambers into it, muttering words under her breath until her voice builds up into an audible sound: 'I'm sorry, Billie,' she's whimpering. 'I'm so very sorry.'

Billie stops pacing the room. She strides over to confront her mother in the rocking-chair, looming over her – a huge, angry figure to Mrs Harrison's shrunken, trembling form. 'You know what, Mom?' she says, her voice cracking with emotion. 'I thought for a minute that I might want to get to know you. I thought I'd make a joke about your salads or I'd ask you how it used to be working in the flight school. But you know what? I don't want to know anything about you. I don't want to know about salads or the flight school. I don't even want to know what you felt when you read my diary that day. And I certainly don't want you to tell me what *I* was feeling the day I jumped into Castaic Lake! What the hell do you know about how I was feeling? Whatever you say, whatever you do, you can never give me back what you took away. I've tried to forgive you but I can't.'

'I'm so sorry . . .' Mrs Harrison is shaking her head from side to side.

'I don't want you to say you're sorry! I want you to *be* sorry. But you won't because you're still too wrapped up in yourself to care about me even now!'

'I'll make it better, Billie.' She grips the side of her chair, hauls herself to her feet and walks over to Billie, her arms outstretched.

Billie turns away. 'You fucked up! You can't make it any better. Stop trying to be my mother.'

Mrs Harrison screams suddenly, tearing at the air, her arms clawing the room as if she's being attacked by imaginary insects. 'But that's the point! That's the whole point, Billie! I never did want to be your mother in the first place!'

She freezes. Her eyes dart round the room as if someone just said a terrible thing and she's trying to find out where they're hiding. Then she closes down. Her head drops, her shoulders stoop, she struggles to pump out breath. She hobbles to the bed, bends down and crawls underneath. She lies there, curled into a ball, hugging her body for dear life, only occasionally unclenching to stare in disbelief at her hands as if, any minute, they might run off and commit some dire act.

Billie grabs the can of Coke and takes a big drink. She looks at her mother hunched there under the bed, trembling and mumbling and flexing her hands open and closed. She swallows audibly and then, finally, she goes to the bed and kneels down. She takes her mother's hand and when their eyes meet, Mrs Harrison crawls out slightly and lays her head on Billie's lap. Billie strokes her mother's hair, lightly at first, and then she releases a deep, deep breath and says quietly, 'Oh, Mom,' as if her mother has still insisted on the large helping of Jell-O salad on her dinner plate, in spite of her wishes. She coaxes her back to the rocking-chair. 'Come on,' she says. 'It's OK.'

Eventually she lowers a bewildered-looking Mrs Harrison into the rocking-chair. Mrs Harrison frowns, rocking quietly for a while and then she flinches as if a memory has just returned. 'Billie,' she gasps, 'what did I just . . .'

'It's OK,' Billie says softly.

'Billie, I don't know what I just . . . I feel . . . so strange . . .'

'It's all right,' Billie says. 'I think we might be finally moving on.'

'You think so?' Mrs Harrison brightens.

Billie nods. 'If you're not my mother do you think you can be Carrie Clare?'

Mrs Harrison looks surprised. 'But I am Carrie Clare,' she tells Billie. 'The one and only, truly invincible . . .' She makes a doo-lally wink, then closes her eyes, her head flopping on to her shoulder. Her lips twitch as she sinks into some kind of half-remembered bliss. 'Remember the home movies, Billie?' she mutters, eyes still closed.

Billie looks towards the window, blinking as if the light hurts her eyes. 'The home movies?'

'Disneyland, Billie. Santa Monica pier. Going out in the rowboat Grandpa Jo built. Footage of flying into Vegas . . .'

'The shots Grandma took from the plane are amazing,' Billie says, as if she can see something.

'Shots at the beach, Billie.'

'Shots of you as a kid, Mom. Thick blonde hair to the waist. My twelve-year-old mom-to-be with the womanly walk of a twenty-year-old.'

'Your grandma was an artist, Billie. My mother had that talent for capturing the perfect expression in the perfect lighting.'

'She was glamorous as well, right? In all the pictures she's got a cigarette permanently perched between two upright fingers and a perfect figure cinched in at the waist.'

'Yeah.' Mrs Harrison sighs. 'We looked like the perfect family.'

'Tell me about when Grandma met Grandpa!' Billie hugs her knees. 'Go on, tell the story.'

'You mean how they met in Vegas?'

'Yeah! In the war, when Grandma had just given birth to you and she was working at the hospital as a nurse's aide.'

Mrs Harrison puts her small hands on her lap. 'Well' – she takes a deep breath – 'one day your grandma walked through the emergency room – her uniform all splattered with blood from the baby she'd just delivered and her chest huge from the breast-feeding she was still doing with me – and she saw this twenty-two-year-old drunken sailor on leave.

'And Grandma said, "He took one look at me, went, 'Wowee,' and slurred, 'I'm gonna see you again!'"

'And, boy, he did! Three days later he took Grandma on her first date and before the night was over he'd asked her to marry him.' Mrs Harrison shakes her head from side to side.

'And what did she reply, Mom?'

'She said OK, but that they'd have to wait until her divorce came through and she'd bought a crib and a high chair.'

'Do you remember your real dad?'

'He was marching in Paris when I was born and he never tried to see me. Grandpa Jo was the one I called Daddy.'

She rocks back and forth for a while, staring at the carpet. 'He wasn't a good daddy. He was bitter. He was a frustrated inventor. Their home was filled with things, which, in their day, had been the top of the range. In 1966 they had a microwave oven – the first of anyone in their street.'

'I think I remember that.'

'Yeah, it was still there in 1976, all five feet square of it. Sitting there like some goddam rabbit hutch.' Mrs Harrison puts a hand in the pocket of her white skirt and takes out a packet of Virginia Slims and a lighter. 'As for the perfect family, Grandpa Jo went on to beat his wife and drive me into a marriage I didn't want.'

She lights a cigarette and sucks deeply on the end. 'Her friends all hated his guts. That used to upset my mother. "I wish they could remember how good he was once," she used to say. "He didn't mean to become a monster. He was just too smart."' She stares Billie firmly in the eye. 'There speaks a lifelong victim.'

She takes a deep drag on the cigarette, looks into space for a while and then she eases herself up from the chair. 'Grandpa Jo didn't let her work once they got married.' She takes the stick and walks to the window. 'Although one time she got a gig at the local magnesium factory. She said, "Some guy just picked me off the street. Said there was something about my face. I posed with a cheese-shaped slice of magnesium in my hand. Load of French guys came in a big bus and took my picture."'

Mrs Harrison leans on the window-ledge and looks out into the overgrown garden. 'She paid for her moment of glory later that night. Dad was drunk as a skunk, as usual. He wasn't mad that she'd been posing with a lump of magnesium that was probably soon going to end up in some bomb. but that men had been taking her picture. It was the usual stuff. He called her a whore. Slap across the head. Boot in the belly.' She shivers as she closes the window. 'Mom never let on anything was wrong. That was the worst of it. She always made out everything was fine.'

'But they stayed together?' Billie wants a happy end.

'Oh, sure.' Mrs Harrison looks baffled. 'They lived in that house for near on forty years, chainsmoking Camel non-filters until the walls turned sticky brown and Grandpa Jo died in his sleep holding Grandma's hand.'

She moves away from the window, back to the rocking-chair. 'Is it me,' she says, still looking genuinely puzzled, 'or have all the women in my family gone from independent, strong fighters to self-made victims?' She slumps down in the rocking-chair, staring at me. 'Please, someone, save me,' she says, rocking harder and harder.

My mouth opens but only nonsense comes out. 'You – you've got an amazing oral history.' I start to pull on my bracelet. 'My family doesn't know anything about its past . . .'

Mrs Harrison stops rocking. 'You know, honey,' she says, in a daze, 'this family's great with the past. It's the present it can't cope with.'

CHAPTER TWENTY-THREE

Cessna Stiletto ... Crash and Burn

Night of Heroes hasn't yet begun. The TV screen is still covered with more distressing scenes from the day of September 11.

'Those poor families,' the yoga teacher is saying. 'They don't even have the remains of their loved ones.'

'Can't even give them a proper burial,' Willa adds, through a puff of cigar smoke.

'Yeah, and it's important to give your loved ones a good farewell,' says Brian the hairdresser, in a meek voice.

'Amen.' The yoga teacher nods.

'When my grandmother died, we buried her at sea,' Willa informs them.

'Oh, my goodness! How beautiful!' The yoga teacher's eyes well up.

'Yuk!' Marlene growls. 'I ain't going swimming no more.'

Brian moves on swiftly: 'It makes economical sense too. A land funeral with casket, urn and interment can run to five thousand dollars compared to a thousand for disposal at sea.'

'That cute John-John Kennedy was buried at sea,' Marlene slurs, with a squirt of White Russian and a cheery lipless smile.

'I believe the Neptune Society has some good deals.' Brian turns to the yoga teacher for support. 'And, of course, these days, they can use the latest global positioning satellite technology to record the precise co-ordinates of scattering.'

'Wow!' the yoga teacher says, all fluttering eyelashes. 'There's something real comforting in that.'

'Sure is, Brian,' Willa says, chomping at the cigar. 'I got a certificate of scattering details.'

'Phooey!' blows the foghorn. 'Who the hell cares where you are when you're dead?'

'Well, you can rest assured that nobody's going to care about you, Marlene!' Leah breaks in, with one of her fake laughs.

Brian and the yoga teacher huddle closer together on their adjacent chairs in this room full of crazy people.

'There are some companies that operate planes to drop the ashes,' Brian ploughs on.

'Really, Brian?' says the yoga teacher, wiggling in her seat.

'Yes. And under federal aviation regulations, planes and pilots are qualified to carry family members if so desired.'

'Wow, Brian!' the yoga teacher gushes. 'You sure seem to know a lot about this subject.'

'Oh, yes,' Brian says, with a nod. 'When my mother died we had a choice of a single engine Cessna 172 Skyhawk or a twin engine 414 Chancellor . . .'

This is when Mrs Harrison dive-bombs into the room, borne up on the Indian summer of her acid trip. Everyone turns round to see her – arms stretched out on either side of her body, impersonating a pair of aeroplane wings.

The change of scenery seems to have done her some good. She launches into an excited monologue about the Burbank flight school and the good old days of the beer and the boys and her own Cessna 172 Skyhawk.

The yoga teacher is obviously miffed to be so rudely interrupted in the middle of her intimate moment with Brian, although Brian is doing his best to follow his hostess's train of thought: 'Oh, yeah . . . back in those days . . . so cool . . . you're flying on this bird – whiz, whiz, whiz – and there's just this patchwork down there, you know . . . kind of like cheesecloth, like that waistcoat from that . . . Billie knows the one . . . I mean, there's cherries and plums, and white mice . . . and then, of course, you've got the seals . . . the blue ones . . . You know what I'm saying, Bud?'

'Um, my name's Brian.'

'Yeah, Brian, but what I'm saying, Bud, is that you can't just have the cheesecloth – you need a white pant suit.'

'And a gold halter-neck top, Mom,' Billie chips in, with a snigger. She leads me and Mrs Harrison to the TV area. She sits on the couch with her mother on one side and me on the other.

'Yeah, Bud,' Mrs Harrison continues, undeterred. 'You need that halter-neck. And you gotta remember that a halter-neck is like those wind tunnels . . . you know . . . and when you get in one of those, it's like . . . some kind of crazy . . .'

'Stiletto.'

'Yeah!' Mrs Harrison exclaims, looking approvingly at her daughter. 'The stiletto!' She wiggles a finger at Brian. 'You know what, Bud?' she says, licking her lips.

'Er . . . Brian, Mrs Harrison. My name is Brian?'

'You ever tried that, Bud?'

'Tried – tried what?' Brian looks helplessly at the yoga teacher, who is only too pleased to give him the reassurance of a hand on his knee. He flinches at her touch.

'You ever landed a stiletto shoe?'

'I think – I think maybe this would be a good time for me to leave,' he says primly. He stands up, smoothing a shaky hand over his thinning thatch.

Leah looks daggers at Billie. 'Don't think I don't know what you've done,' she hisses. 'I can't believe . . .'

But she has to interrupt the telling-off by jumping up and prising Mrs Harrison off Brian's leopardskin shoulder. 'You gonna take me on safari, big boy? You ever been dated by a homecoming queen?' She breaks into another interlude of uncontrollable laughter.

The yoga teacher can restrain herself no longer. 'Carrie,' she says, 'are you sure you're OK to be out of bed?'

'Carrie Clare, you mean!'

The yoga teacher flushes scarlet.

'Stupid booby!' Carrie Clare glares at her with her freaked-out face.

'Well, I'm sure I was only—'

'Get the hell out of my house!'

'Now, calm down, Carrie Clare.' Leah grasps hold of her arm, but Mrs Harrison shakes it off and stands up.

'You're all just a bunch of losers. Next time I'm going to invite some famous people to my AA meeting!' She starts flying round the room again, her arms outstretched, as Billie and Marlene clap and whoop.

'But we didn't eat the shrimp yet!' Willa points out.

'You know what, Willa?' Mrs Harrison drawls. 'Why don't you just grab all of those shrimp and take them home with you? Put them in your bath. I bet that'll be the best fun you had in years!'

Willa thinks about this for a few seconds, then nods and says, 'You got a point there, Carrie Clare.'

She takes the plastic bag Marlene is holding out to her and hurries off towards the patio.

Leah shows the yoga teacher and Brian to the door as a chuckling Billie observes her mother's Cessna Skyhawk impersonation round the sitting room. ('Whizzy! Whiz! Whiz! Hey, look at me, everyone!')

Marlene turns to Billie and says, 'You know what I want for when I die?' A stream of White Russian misses the target of her mouth.

'What's that, Marlene?' Billie asks.

'I want them to put my ashes in a firework.' She dabs at her chin with a tissue. 'I want them to light the touch-paper and watch me dart up into the sky.'

Billie chuckles and Marlene, straining in her chair to catch Mrs Harrison's attention as she cruises round the room, slurs, 'Shoot! This daughter of yours is a bundle of joy.' She prods me. 'What do you say, Brit? You think she's fantastic or what?'

I can't help laughing. I look at Billie and she looks at me. And then the alarm clock goes off and Marlene shouts, 'Whoopee!' because *Night of Heroes* has just begun.

Willa stomps through the room with her bag of shrimp. 'See y'all later,' she says, patting her Stetson. 'Thanks again for a great evening, Carrie Clare. You sure know how to throw a party!'

And then there's a damp hiss of sugar-coated steel in my ear, saying, 'Go to hell!' I jump, and it's Mrs Harrison, sitting next to me. Her eyes are still Jell-O bouncy, although you can see that she's coming back slowly to earth from her acid trip. Her jaw is grinding and I can see flickers of irritation in her eyes. 'People can out-stay their welcome, don't you find?'

'If you want me to go, Mrs Harrison . . .'

'Oh, no!' She looks alarmed. 'Oh, no, I don't want *you* to leave. I want you to tell me!'

'Tell you . . . what?'

'About Billie, of course. About what's so fantastic about her.' Her hands are back in her lap, all small and poised, like before.

I don't know what to say. 'Maybe . . . maybe it was the fire thing.' She's making me nervous. 'I remember when I first met her she told me about how she liked burning words.'

'She did?'

'Yes. I thought that was very strange.'

'Oh, yes,' she says, with a smile, 'when they made Billie they sure broke the—' She starts to wheeze. She clutches her chest. Billie jumps up but Mrs Harrison pushes her away with a feeble hand. 'Go on, Mo, sweetheart. I want to hear what you've got to say about Billie.'

'Well, she's just really . . . unpredictable.'

'Oh, yes,' Mrs Harrison is saying, in this weird voice, 'Billie was always a fire-cracker. She set her bed on fire when she was five.'

'I know.'

'Pardon me?'

'She told me. And her dad carried it through the yard . . .'

'Oh, yes. Her dad.' She takes a deep breath and exhales very slowly.

'It was her first memory, apparently.'

'Really?' Mrs Harrison glances over at Billie. Her eyes look anxious, her jaws grinding again.

'That, and a pair of high-heeled shoes.' Billie smiles, snatching Marlene's bottle from her and taking a squeeze.

'I didn't know you remembered so well,' Mrs Harrison says, in a low voice.

Billie shrugs.

Mrs Harrison turns back to me. 'And what did she say about me?'

'Sorry?'

'Did I have a role in this burning-bed episode?' There's sarcasm in her voice.

'I – I can't remember. I think you were shocked or something. Yes' – I look over to Billie for back-up – 'I think you stood there watching her dad put the fire out . . . looking shocked.'

Billie wrinkles her nose. 'You know,' she says, 'do we really need to go through all this?'

'Oh, we do, Billie!' A gust of energy seizes Mrs Harrison. 'Gimme some water.' She clicks her fingers impatiently at Billie, who hands over a glass, and Mrs Harrison drinks, fixing me with black eyes that become beadier by the minute. She slams the empty glass down on the coffee-table. 'You're right, Mo,' she says, getting her breath back.

'About what, Mrs Harrison?'

'I was shocked that day of the burning mattress. You have no idea.' She stares at me gleefully.

It makes me nervous. I decide to move on to another memory. I tell her about the day that Billie set fire to three acres of hill-side.

'Oh, I remember that day, too,' Mrs Harrison says, her jaw grinding away. 'Billie was a spitfire, all right!'

'I wish I'd been there,' I say.

'Do you?'

'Gosh, I—'

'Would that have impressed you? Seeing her set a field on fire?'

'Well . . . it must have been amazing.'

'What must have been amazing?'

'You know, a fire in a three-acre field. It must have looked incredible.'

'Smelt of burned hair, if I remember right.' Mrs Harrison fumbles in her pocket for the packet of cigarettes.

'Burned hair?'

'She was hopeless at lying.'

'Well . . . but even so . . .'

Leah sees Mrs Harrison getting out the pack of cigarettes and reprimands her. But Mrs Harrison just winks. 'Oh, darling Leah,' she cajoles, 'it's my special day! Look, the fatted calf came home.'

I'm wondering if this is a sensitive expression for Mrs Harrison to use in relation to her daughter. But she doesn't stop to apologise and the acid seems to make Billie oblivious to what her mother's just said.

'That fire stuff impresses you, does it, Mo?' Mrs Harrison goes on.

'I'd never dare do it myself.'

'But you're impressed by the kind of people who do?'

'I—'

'It gives you a big old leap in the belly, does it, Mo?'

I want her to be quiet now. I don't know what she's driving at but I sense that something is about to come leaping out of *her* belly. I look over at Marlene, but she's glued to the TV screen, lip pieces twitching as she watches famous people pay tribute to firemen. 'It's a shame they all got black clothes on,' she murmurs.

'What?' Leah snaps.

'What's the point in a Hollywood star with no sequins?'

'Do you have no respect?'

'Course I got respect, Leah.'

'Those people were heroes!' Leah growls, trying to draw Marlene into a fight.

'Being in the wrong place at the wrong time don't make you no hero, Leah. Makes you unfortunate.'

'You are sick!'

Mrs Harrison snatches a cigarette from her packet and lights it with a trembling hand. She puts it into her mouth, then stares at the flame from the lighter. She becomes increasingly fascinated with the flame. She moves it in a line from left to right. She draws lines in the air, then squiggles and circles and waves. She makes a strange smile, then raises her arm above her head as if she's at a pop concert, as if she's watching Barry Manilow on stage and she's waving her arm from side to side in adoration. Except she's turned towards Billie. She stands up, facing Billie, waving the torch above her head in honour of Billie. Obviously her trip isn't totally over. Nor is Billie's – at least, that's the only way I can account for her good mood.

'Mom?' she says, with a chuckle. 'Mom, what are you doing?'

Mrs Harrison carries on waving the flame at Billie. 'I'm just being impressed, baby. I'm just showing you that I'm so impressed.'

Billie grins. 'Mom, you sure you don't want to go take a nap?'

Mrs Harrison starts to walk round the room. 'Oh, but, Billie, I've never felt better.' She heads towards the kitchen.

'Mom?' Billie says. 'Where are you going?'

A thin voice calls back, 'I'm going to the garden.' And then, coquettish, 'Are you coming, Mo? I'm going to impress you. Come to the garden and you can tell me who's best at fire – if it's me or Billie.'

I look over to Leah and Marlene for some help, but it becomes obvious that no help will be coming from that direction: Leah is intent on drawing Marlene into her spider's web. 'You are sick,' she snarls, poking Marlene in the arm, 'talking about sequins. Daring to say they're not heroes.'

Marlene is trying to watch the TV. 'Maybe it was a big high,' she buzzes, moving her arm.

'What?'

'The ones that jumped. I guess they must have produced a bunch of that feel-good hormone as they fell. Serotonin.'

'What?'

'You get it in pig's gut. Counteracts pain.'

'What are you talking about?'

'Or maybe they felt like in a Superman movie.' She's going for it now.

'Superman?' Leah splutters.

'If nine-eleven had been a Superman episode, he'd have swooped down and plucked all those people from the air just in the nick of time.'

'You are so sick!'

'Maybe that's what they thought was going to happen.'

'Huh?'

'That Superman was going to come and pick 'em all up.'

'Silence!'

'No, Leah!' Marlene turns to face her. 'What I'm saying is that there was a moment of hope. The people who jumped took their fate into their own hands. They didn't just hide behind no filing cabinet or look for the stairs.'

'You need help!'

'I'm saying that for a few seconds maybe they felt happy when they were falling from that building.'

'How dare you tell me that those people died happy?'

'And maybe Superman did come. Maybe he came and picked up every last one of 'em but we just couldn't see him.'

'Have you lost your mind?'

'They didn't find any dead bodies!'

'They got vaporised in the heat!'

'Maybe not, maybe they escaped into thin air!'

'You live in a fantasy world!'

'So what if I do?'

A fist slams on to a glass-topped table. 'I've had enough!'

Marlene flinches back in her seat. The panicked bluebottle fizzes back into her voice. 'I'm just trying to make the best of things, Leah! You gotta try and make the best of things!'

'You have gone too far this time.'

'You gotta have hope, Leah!'

'You are going to the home.'

'Leah!'

Now Marlene's bluebottle buzz sounds as though it's been immersed under water. She sounds as if she's drowning, as if she's scared or sorry she ever dared to have hope. 'I'm sorry I spoke out of turn, Leah.'

'People who jumped from those towers didn't feel no happiness. People who worked in that place were a bunch of gung-ho bankers. Jumping out of windows is the kind of dumb shit they do.'

'Leah, I—'

'You treat me like shit. And after all I done for you.'

'I am grateful, I am!'

'After what your loser son did to me.'

'He's no good, I know that!' Saliva trickles down her chin.

'And after what *you* did to me!'

'Leah, I've tried to make it up to you.'

'At least God gave you cancer for your sins.'

When Marlene speaks again she sounds stronger, as if she doesn't care any more. 'Yeah, well, I sure got my comeuppance, right?'

'Yes, siree. That man loved me.'

'Phooey!' She's fighting back now. She wipes the dribble from her chin.

'What do you mean, "phooey"?' Leah has stumbled. She can't believe Marlene is daring to answer her back.

'How comes he jumped into my bed if he loved you?'

'He – he was drunk.'

'He sure was, Leah. He was always drunk. You're best off without him.'

'He said I was beautiful.'

The opportunity proves too much for Marlene to resist. 'Beautiful? Your head looks like someone stepped on a piece of sausage, then stuck it on a neck in the hope that it might end up looking like a face.' She slaps her thigh. She's getting into it now. 'Did nobody tell you, Leah? You look like something that was shit out of an old lady's butt!'

If Marlene had sunk an axe into the middle of her daughter-in-law's skull, Leah's eyes would not bulge out as much as they are doing now. There's the sound of scuffling, and 'You're hurting me, Leah!' and 'Deformed freak, Marlene!' and then frantic buzzing, a macabre laugh and 'We're going to settle this once and for all,' from Leah. And then the thread is spun. The fly is in the parlour, wrapped tight in the spider's sticky shroud, the desperate buzz has turned into a weakened drone. And then they're gone.

I hesitate. Billie has been watching Leah's Marlene massacre as if it's one of the best films she's ever seen. Then, as if an even more entertaining channel has just popped up outside on the patio – screams are raging in the garden – she starts to mosey on out to see what high jinks her mother's getting up to.

By the time we reach the patio, Mrs Harrison is brandishing a bottle of barbecue lighter fluid. In her other hand, the naked lighter flame sways agonisingly from side to side. She totters round the garden, squeezing the barbecue bottle at various plants and shrubs and mumbling about how she hates the Pacific Ocean because it makes her hair go flat. 'Hey, tell Marlene to get out here!' she shouts. 'She could do a bit of squeezing too!'

Billie laughs when she sees what her mother's up to. It's madness. I knew the acid was a ridiculous idea – for both of them. 'Mrs Harrison!' I shout. 'What are you doing?'

'I got a whole lot of fire in me too!'

'Mrs Harrison, please stop!'

'Wooo-hooo! I haven't had such a good time in years.'

'Mom, what are you doing?' Billie chuckles.

Maybe it's the tone of Billie's voice that makes Mrs Harrison stop and stare at her daughter. 'What did you say?'

'You're too much, Mom!' Billie says, beaming.

'You think I can't light a fire? You think you're the only one who can cause mischief? How dare you say I can't light a fire?'

'Mom—'

'I can do it! I can!'

It's not clear who she's talking to now. She's staggering round the garden, waving the lighter-fluid bottle and the lighter. Occasionally she jerks her hand to her chest to make a wince of pain. 'You think Billie's so clever,' she wheezes. 'You've no idea how clever I can be!'

Billie stops still. She seems stunned. She watches her mother pouring kerosene on the oleander bushes and she blinks as if she can't believe what she's seeing. Finally, she can't bear it any more. She turns away from her mother and looks out over the cliff towards the sunset – a beautiful sunset as perfect as the logo for the Cosy Inn. Her eyes move slowly to the east and she looks over LA, at the city with its columns and skyscrapers and towering walls of glass rising up into the sky, glowing with the luminous red of the setting sun.

A shudder passes through her body. Her face turns pale as if she can't believe what she's seeing. She looks at the towers and there's horror in her eyes. She looks at the sky and the twitch comes. The squeeze of a lemon on a very fresh oyster. Then she looks at her mother, squirting threads of kerosene into the air and flailing around to catch them with her lighter. Billie starts to moan. She wails quietly at first because it seems as if she can hardly breathe. 'What did I do?' she gasps. 'What did I do wrong?'

Then a helpless scream, a desperate cheer: 'What did I do wrong, Mama? What did I do wrong?'

Over and over again: 'What did I do wrong, Mama? What did I do wrong?'

CHAPTER TWENTY-FOUR

The Last Chapter?

There are many ways to try to make the world safe. If you are a jogger you will wear gloves in the sun to protect your hands from liver spots. If you are afraid of the ocean you will try to conquer it by balancing on a fibreglass plank. If you are lost you will buy a global positioning system. If you tend towards anxiety you will drink caffeine-free Diet Coke.

You will go to cheer-leader camp. You will be popular. You will be pretty and sporty, you will listen to songs by Simon and Garfunkel, you will not be a Communist. You will say, 'How y'all doing?' to ascertain the motives of strangers and you will chew gum in an exaggerated fashion if they seem suspicious. You will eat egg-white omelette and sushi, you will smoke little and drink only two beers a day. You will drive an SUV to give maximum protection in the unlikely event of a car crash, you will hang out a flag and you will always say your prayers. You will know the exact location of your bodily remains, you will buy chocolate in wrappers with American typeface, you will eat ambrosia, you will go to a diner where you will sit at the counter and listen to the waitress as she tells you that when life throws you lemons you make lemonade.

You will do your best to be good. You will wear your top on the beach, you will only cross when the light is green, you will not drink liquor in a stationary vehicle. If you are an office worker you will get to work early so you can finish sooner and come home to spend time with your family. You will bring up your children to believe that Shelley Winters will always do a heroic swim in case of emergency and that if they ever find themselves in a burning building there will always be Steve McQueen on hand to dangle them to safety on a swivel chair hung with pantyhose.

Some people, like Helen Keller, believe that avoiding danger is no safer in the long run than exposure – that life is an adventure or nothing. For this reason, Billie and I are doing spells on Venice Beach. We are playing because that is what we do best and playing is the best way to be free.

Everyone in America is doing a candlelit vigil tonight but ours is special. The spell we are doing is magic. It involves some nightlight candles, some paper, a lighter and lots of sand.

'Here's to you, Mr Eggmont,' Billie says, staring into the circle of flickering orange lights. 'May your mind be free and may your ass always burn!' Billie has a bottle of Jack Daniel's in her hand and a spliff hanging from her mouth. The whiff of cold concrete and sour plums hasn't entirely vanished. 'Sorry I didn't rise phoenix-like from the flames,' she says, looking up with a shy smile. 'I guess the damage took such a long time to do there's a lot of work ahead.'

She swoops down over the candles, which sizzle like bacon. 'Still,' she whispers, skimming her face dangerously near to the flames as she wafts her hands mysteriously over the plate, 'at least the fire's still burning.'

Her hand gets too close and one of her palms gets scorched. She snatches it back and puffs on it like it's burned toast.

'Darnation!'

'Silly Billie!'

'You hush your mouth!'

'But look!'

'At what?'

'Your eyebrows!'

She puts her hand up to her face and finds that her eyebrows and the ends of her eyelashes have been singed off.

'Oh, no!' She wrinkles her nose. She looks at me and we both giggle.

'Never mind,' she says, 'we're going to offer it up for Mr Eggmont!'

Billie killed Mr Eggmont.

It's true!

Mr Eggmont who liked sensory deprivation.

Mr Eggmont who didn't tell Billie that he had a bad heart.

It was funny at the hospital.

She took off his bondage suit and put him back in his pinstripe, but when the taxi dropped them off at the emergency room he was still wearing blue eyeshadow. She tried her best to smudge it off but she didn't have time because she had to leave. Who knows what the nurses made of a sweaty man in a pinstripe suit smelling of rubber and pee and Krispy Cremes and wearing blue eyeshadow?

Billie is philosophical. She says it was good to go to the funeral of someone who was old, of someone who was actually ready to die.

She picks a single candle from the plate, places it in her burned palm and holds it out as an offering towards the black ocean glinting with moonlight. The angels aren't tap-dancing any more. 'Here's to the disco angels,' she intones.

We giggle!

We bury everything!

Everything under the carpet! Everything into the sand!

Everything can disappear if you put your mind to it.

'Youch!'

'What, baby?' she asks.

'Some cinders came on me.'

'Poor baby. Did you get hurt?'

'Yes.'

She kisses it better and I pull my hand away. But I like it. It's soft. Willa was right.

She rips a handful of bound pages from the floral notebook – cream paper scrawled over with K-Mart silver marker pen. She throws them into the air and they flutter gracefully to the sand like silver leaves.

'Dance! Dance! Fly! Fly! Fall! Fall! Die! Die!'

Then she ruins everything. Her index finger is pressed into her chin like she's thinking too hard. She's staring into the flames and I know something's coming.

Being serious isn't part of the game.

'I know it's stupid, Mo, but I really thought the world was on fire for a moment there up at my mom's house. And there was so much of it. More fire even than when I torched the hillside or when my stepdad set fire to my things.'

Stop it!

'It was like a lake of fire, like a fire that you see in your dreams – scrub scorching, brush raging, trees and leaves and logs, matter pressed with energy, energy repressed for aeons, pain coiled up like a spring – a garden full of pain, a lake packed with badness, a prehistoric forest locked with ancient breath, and when it burns it dances and then it goes insane.'

Stop it!

'I guess it looked like I was just standing on the cliff looking at the sunset, but I thought the sky was on fire. The sky burst into flames, Mo, it really did! A sheet of fire ripped over LA, the skyscrapers ignited and there were these trapped faces howling inside and skin melting like – like cheese on a burger. I saw Post-it notes flying and coffee cups dissolving and singed people getting sucked out of burning towers and as they fell their flesh exploded and their fingernails flew off and the day went dark with blood . . .'

She swipes her fingers through the flames, back and forth, back and forth.

'Then I snapped out of it and I saw Mom on the ground. This twisted figure clutching a kerosene bottle. And there's a faint noise coming from the dirt track, going, 'I'm sorry, honey, I'm ill. I'm really very ill.'

Stop it! I don't want to hear!

'So I knelt down and touched her arm, you remember that? It was soft and warm under the thin fabric of her sleeve. Our eyes met, and for a second we shared this lunatic hope – like people feel in mid-air when they fall from a tower. And then the hope vanished.' She looks towards the disco angels. 'Maybe you're my lunatic hope, Mo.'

'Stop it, Billie! That's not part of the game.'

'Sorry.'

She turns back and grabs me with her lion paws. She is warm and furry and meat to maul. Her strength ripples though my body like a wave that builds up and up, and the thrill is that you never know when the wave is going to break. She is the roller-coaster that takes me to the top of the slope and I tingle as I wait for the gravity to come and pull me into the deep ravine.

But I don't want any of that. The glittery tingle is coming and I don't want any of that. I don't know.

She flops down in the sand with a sigh. 'But maybe you *are* my lunatic hope,' she says. 'I might live and I might die.'

'Stop being dramatic.'

'I *am* fucking dramatic!' She rears up. 'Didn't you read me right yet?'

Not answering. Not going to speak. Time to sift through the diary pages, put them in silver piles. Neat, regular piles. Symmetry and order. Pattern and precision.

I don't tell her about how I don't want to read anyone ever again.

I stare into the night-light flames and see Mrs Harrison's black eyes on the day that she tried to squirt kerosene threads on to the oleander bushes, and I certainly don't want to see them.

I start to undo the black leather bracelet around my wrist. When I pull it over my palm and twist it round my fingers, feeling each individual knot, the movement makes me feel better. I realise that there's always the sand. There is a lot of sand in the world and anything can be buried underneath.

She takes the joint back. She ruins it again. 'We're doomed, Mo! We are so doomed!'

'Why?'

'You won't let yourself go with me and I've let myself go too much with you.' She tugs at the pages of the diary, wrenching them out of the book, tossing them to me to collect as she does so. 'But, you know, Mo, there are moments when I feel a leap of faith. Like Marlene said – about jumping to your death but feeling hope for a few seconds? It only lasts for a few seconds but during those few seconds I believe in for ever and ever.'

'You're obsessed with for ever and ever,' I mumble. I touch her arm.

She pulls away. 'The thrill's in the chase, huh, Mo?'

'Sorry?'

'That's Courtney Love's take on life.'

'You think I just wanted your story?'

'I don't know.'

'Billie! How can you say that?' I exclaim, thinking that maybe she's right.

'It's OK. You wanted my story and I wanted your flesh. But you know what?'

'What?' I'm not sure I want to hear this.

'You're just like a pomegranate. Hard to get out, bitter when you get there.'

'Thanks.'

She looks at me tenderly. 'And the interesting thing is that you can't decide if you're a sadist or a masochist.'

'What?'

'Oh, you love to be in charge but you're also dying to let go. Dying to jump . . .' She shrugs. 'It doesn't matter. You're right to run away from me. I have to get back to the real world. I can't live on wieners even if you can.'

'We've got a lot of the money left from the rear-ending. I kept it safe.'

She raises an eyebrow. 'I'm a princess. Remember?'

'Yes.'

'Five thousand dollars is going to last me a month.'

'Yes.'

'So let's just forget it.'
'OK. Let's forget it.'

Billie seems to have her future mapped out anyway. Something about living with her mother. The acid did some good at least. After she'd recovered from the day of the Alcoholics Anonymous meeting when she'd tried to set her garden on fire, she told Billie that she couldn't cope with being alone any more. She asked Billie to sell Bellevue and put her in a home. Billie's not going to do that, though. She says she's going to buy somewhere where she can put her mother in an annexe. 'I'll give her a Spanish-style cottage with its own water feature and someone to order around. She'll love it.'

'You–think?'

'Sure. I'll hire her a maid who'll put her in the shade when she's hot and make sure her hair never goes flat and who'll talk to her when she's lonely and go away when she tells her to.'

'But I thought you hated your mother?'

The irritated look comes into her face. 'I'm a nurturer,' she huffs. 'I can't help it. You look after your own. You just do.'

I find myself undoing some of the knots in my bracelet. And then that's not enough so I unplait the thongs until the bracelet becomes two separate lengths of leather. I pull them taut, start work on them, twist them into elaborate shapes. Take it, use me, the New York strip, the raggedy roast.

It's funny how things work out. Funny how, after all, the best sex I ever had was with Muriel. Bag-over-the-head Muriel.

I thought she was joking when she offered to take me along to one of 'the parties', but I had time on my hands and she was addicted to my humiliating her by that point. Besides, I'd exhausted all the macramé classes that Scarborough and environs had to offer. It seemed a logical progression.

Clever people, the Japanese.

'*Unsui*'. Literally, 'cloud and water' or 'seeker of truth'. That was me. Muriel was my '*uke*', pronounced 'oo-keh', my passive partner in the demonstration of technique.

Japanese bondage wasn't so different from macramé. Muriel certainly liked it. 'Happy as a pig in shit, I am,' she wittered on, as I prepared a basic hitch knot to tie round her mouth and shut her up. The *Ebi-shibari*, or 'trussed shrimp'. That's what she liked best. I loved the marks it left behind. The roughness of the rope. James recommended silk scarves for beginners or mink oil to soften the weave, but I didn't care for either. Rough hemp rope was what she got. Splinters and all. He recommended pulling rope slowly and lovingly over nipples. But that was too time-consuming. I liked to get down to the business of technique. The trick is to start tying the big body parts so that the rope becomes shorter much faster. Most Japanese ropes tend to be seven metres long because the Japanese tend to have smaller bodies. Muriel's was an eight and a half.

The Samurai warriors trained in the art of Japanese bondage in order to capture prisoners without dishonour. My favourite trick is the *kataashi tsuri*. This is when your partner has her torso done up in *shinju* ('The Pearls', or breast bondage), her hands tied behind her back, her body bent forward, precariously balancing on one leg while the other leg is suspended behind and above her from a beam.

James favoured asymmetrical free-style bondage. I didn't, though. I strove for symmetry every time and never forgot the rule book once:

Watch for cutting off nerves.

Watch for slipping knots.

Always have a knife and scissors handy.

'Mo!'

'Yes?'

'What are you doing?'

I look down at my hands.

Drat.

'Sheet bend?' I say hopefully.

'What?'

'You use it to tie one rope to a different-sized rope. It's very strong and secure.'

She narrows her eyes. 'Why the fuck didn't you tell me that before?'

'Sorry?'

'You told me you didn't know anything about proper knots.'

I try and look innocent, taking the joint from her. 'Some of the Girl Guide stuff seems to have come back. Maybe I'm loosening up a bit.'

Billie gives me a look that says, 'You? Loosening up?' She snatches the leather thong from me and scrutinises the array of bowlines, sheet bends and lorry knots that she finds there. Then she looks at the expensive new Gucci shades perched on top of my head and folds her arms.

'Mo,' she says, sounding bemused and slightly jealous, 'is there anything you want to tell me about that Ancient Mariner dude in Carlota?'

Honesty is not always the best policy. I think that is my conclusion. There are many things that I, for one, could have lived without.

Oh, the truth, the truth.

And the sand, the sand.

It was a while before Mrs Harrison fell to the ground. The shock of what she'd done calmed her. She hadn't even done any damage. There was only a trickle of fluid left in barbecue lighter bottle and it's not an easy job setting fire to the leaves of evergreen trees.

Billie was gazing into the sunset and then all the screaming started. I wanted to rush over and help her, tell her that it was only the acid blowing everything out of proportion, making her think that the world was on fire. But Mrs Harrison grabbed my arm. 'Leave her!' she ordered.

I did what she said – but only because Billie wouldn't let me get near her. She pushed me away from her and ran to the patio to beat her hands on the white marble slabs, shouting, 'What did I do wrong, Mama? What did I do wrong?' Helplessly, she screamed until even that wasn't enough so she hurled a bottle of beer to the stone floor in a huge explosion of fizz and splintering glass. And you couldn't even begin to tell her what she'd done wrong, there was no way to even begin. You couldn't tell her that she wasn't bad because right then she was convinced that she was evil and stuffed full of lies and deceit and the foul energy of the foul people who have no right to call themselves decent human beings because they are not decent, they are foul and stained. And yet they must have been harmed, too, at some point. So where did all the blood come from? Whose fault was all the blood on the marble floor? Whose fault was it that I was huddled on the ground shielded by the sandbag of Mrs Harrison's body? Whose fault was it that Mrs Harrison had fallen to the ground in a sobbing mess or that her daughter was moaning like a monster with two of its heads cut off and the final one waiting to be severed, crying, 'What did I do wrong, Mama? What did I do wrong?'

The patio floor could have been a muddy ice-skating rink with footprints stomped over with Wellingtons. Only it was blood all over the white slabs and it had been stamped in with Billie's frantic naked feet and dripping arm torn with shards of glass. Some of the blood was in lacy droplets but most was in splodges – splodges and blodges and smears – like toddlers had rampaged through the house, potato printing as they went.

I thought about the neighbours, about if any neighbours would hear – just as I thought about the number of grains of rice I would allow myself for my next meal or the handfuls of dirty washing I would plunge into plastic buckets over the next few days to watch the dirt rise to the surface like gold dust. And then I saw that my hands were shaking. And my arms were shaking. The air was astringent and burning – that was the kind of air that was marinating my body, vinegar air that tore up my insides and I didn't have pig guts to save me from the pain. There was a shriek, a wailing shriek that only I could hear, the neighbours couldn't hear it, Billie and her mother couldn't hear it: it shot through me like the speed of light, a black shrieking sound, a shrieking car crash just out of sight round the corner that leaves people with mutilated limbs and decimated lives and it could have been you, it could have been you.

I hate to feel so much emotion, I can't bear it. It's too ugly. Too messy. I have a place in my head, that's what I do. I sweep, I rearrange. I fold and straighten. I pull down the blinds. That's what I do. I don't want to be this moved. I don't want to feel this tugging of the stitches, this plucking of the fabric, a sharp stone tossed into the millpond. I don't want to see the top of the ice rink – so nice and white and smooth – all scratched and scraped and ruined. And that's just the beginning.

It definitely did all happen. It was an open book, open and ready to be read. It was a talking book, I couldn't even close it. I try to believe that I could have misheard. That it might have been the acid in the Coke. The caffeine-free Diet Coke that Mrs Harrison thought such a safe choice of beverage. You never know where the boundaries are when you're dealing with drugs. The whole of my so-called relationship with Billie was based on the progression of the slinky yellow snake, ruining my order, nobbling my spring-cleaning.

'You know what?' Billie says, tearing the last few pages from the diary. 'I think you should forget journalism.'

'Sorry?'

'I think you should write novels instead.'

'Why?'

'People aren't interesting enough for you. You have to turn them into pieces of fiction. That's what you did with me.'

I don't know how to read Billie any more. Mrs Harrison told me that Billie's ill, just like her. That when she's at her most creative she's also at her maddest. Mrs Harrison told me a lot of things but I think I won't believe them. In any case I won't tell Billie about them. Fire, in spite of its poseurish qualities, is not so dangerous as smoke. It's the smoke that gets you in the end – the thick black fug that creeps into your lungs and gradually chokes you to death if you let it linger.

There's always the sand. There's an awful lot of sand. Anything can be buried on a beach.

Mrs Harrison sat there clutching the empty barbecue lighter bottle, mumbling like someone in a dream. At first, you couldn't hear what she was saying.

'Burning . . .'

She was sobbing but she wasn't making any noise. Her body rocked in spasms. She tried to keep it all inside but she couldn't.

'I burned it . . .'

I wasn't interested in her failed garden inferno. I wanted to run to Billie but Mrs Harrison's small hand gripped my arm. 'Don't worry, Mrs Harrison.' I tried to sound soothing. 'You hardly burned a thing. The kerosene bottle was empty.'

Her brow creased. Her face was troubled. She wanted to make me understand. 'But I burned it,' she said. 'It was me.'

'Mrs Harrison—'

'No!' She squirmed in the dirt. She started to hammer her head on the ground. 'Mo!' Bang! Bang! Bang! On the dirt track. When she looked up, her eyes were deranged. 'Billie didn't set fire to her bed!'

'Well, she seems to think she did.'

'I set fire to Billie's bed! When she was a baby. It was me!'

She collapsed into the dirt again. There was no more noise. That was finished. Only a pounding in my ears. A tightening of my skin. The ants.

Then she resurfaced. She wiped the stones and dust from her scratched forehead. Her cheeks were smeared with dirty water. She didn't look at me. She couldn't look at me. 'She used to fiddle with the gauze underneath the mattress. That's what gave me the idea . . . I was ill . . .'

'What . . .?'

'I came in when she was asleep. I set the bed on fire.'

Ripping down the curtains. Horrible hoodlums in the house. Get out, get out, get out of my house!

'My heels, though. The noise woke her up.' She wiped her eyes. 'Stilettos. Her first memory.'

She looked at me with something like triumph in her eyes. 'I was in a bad way,' she whispered. 'It runs in the family, you know.'

She threw herself down in the dirt and soon Billie was there, dripping with blood, looking down at her mother who lay twisted on the ground, clutching her back and moaning, 'I'm sorry, honey, I'm ill. I'm really very ill.'

And then came the sound from inside the house that made us all freeze. A sound that began with a deep fly buzzing, a gut-deep groan of a soul trapped under the earth – choking on poisoned gas, throttled by sinewy hands – but the soul rose higher and higher until it smashed through the crust of the ground, shooting up into the bright, the light, the unblemished blue sky. Up and up the note soared, clear and pure and easy on the ear, the voice of a gospel singer who hits the place, who gives it all up with nothing else to lose. The song of a sun angel perfect in body and face – a fearless arc of music flushing out all pain, all evil, uncontainable, indestructible. A bow of never-ending sound, a cry so moving, so full of hope that the air stopped burning, the chaos stopped turning, the spider's web dissolved and the day, for those few moments, was safe again.

The world is too confusing, the air is thick with pockets of smoke. I'm not going to read people any more. If you read people you'll probably get it wrong and, even worse, you might get it right.

The sand is the best thing. The ostrich and the sand.

✳   ✳   ✳

'No shit!' Billie cries suddenly, tossing the floral notebook to one side and slapping a page of her *National Enquirer*.

'What happened?'

'Drew Barrymore bought my dream house!'

'What?'

'Look, it's right here!' She passes me the magazine.

'Looks more jolly than your mother's version.'

'No kidding. Can you imagine what a great life you'd have if you lived there? A huge A-frame window that looks over the whole city of Los Angeles.'

'You'd think the world was on fire every time the sun went down.'

'I told you I'm not taking acid for a while.'

She's getting excited now. She jumps up and starts pacing round the candle plate, eyes glued to the *National Enquirer*, commenting on the huge fire-pit in the middle of the living room and the biggest refrigerator you ever saw in your life. And the pool! Imagine a pool like that! 'It goes all the way round the backyard! It's a wrap-around swimming-pool!'

'Gosh.'

'It's got a bridge over it!'

'Excellent!'

'Can you imagine the munchies you could have round that? Lipton's onion soup mixed with sour cream and served with extra thick Ruffles. You have to have extra thick Ruffles because they don't break.'

She says she bets there's a squishy red padded room right at the very top of the house where you can go and lie down when you don't want to think any more – a room of oblivion, a place where you can just be quiet and look up at the clouds bobbing along through the skylight.

She doesn't mention me there with her but she doesn't have to. As the spun-sugar devil lips talk away, she and I cartwheel off to a kingdom where we love each other more than anyone has ever loved in the history of the universe. Everyone believes that their love is the best, the most magic, but ours really will be. We will be invited on *The Jerry Springer Show* and they will send us out in flowery dresses and cardigans, and the audience will gasp in awe as we prove that our love is hotter than the hottest day and purer than the sweetest voice that ever sang on earth. And when we reveal that we haven't even kissed yet, the whole TV studio will be thrown into turmoil. The audience will rise to its feet and cry, 'No! It can't be so!' And when we finally kiss, the sun will turn blue and the black holes will end and pomegranate seeds will shower down from heaven.

I know she will take me there if I don't watch out. I know she has the power to pull me from my starchy white house into a play-den more colourful and sparkling than any room yet invented. An underworld dripping with crystals and honeycomb, strewn with presents and gold, limelit with dancing and cabaret that makes you sigh with desire and relief almost every night ('*Aaaaaaaah*'), but a world, none the less, also filled with ghosts and trap-doors and false mirrors and dangerous objects and beds that are some-times damp and strangers who are sometimes there and people who try to trick you and poison you and want to get your soul.

I don't want to go into that room and I do want to as well. And then it strikes me that maybe I'm in the room already, that maybe I've already taken up residence in Billie's dream house and it's too late to leave.

The silver pages are ready. They're waiting for the fire. Neat piles. Chapter by chapter. All sifted and proper. All about to be turned into ash. Billie holds open the diary before me. Only one page remains and it begs to be ripped from its floral prison. Already it's detaching itself from the frayed spine.

The moment came in the parking lot at Winn Dixie. My body felt like it was buzzing, as if a crushing weight had just landed on me. And then it registered that the feeling was happiness.

A plastic carrier-bag wrapping a sweaty sandwich. Her ridiculous

Brit packed lunch. She lowered the window. She was going to throw it out. She was ashamed of it because I laughed. She was embarrassed by the security of her sensible lunch but I saw worlds in it – an antidote to the taste of fear in an icy prepacked sandwich bought at three in the morning in a gas station on a night of selling cocaine.

The carrier-bag flapped in the breeze and the sound brought tears to my eyes. It felt like a perfect moment, like the pinprick of falling in love, a split second of eerie joy, like the sound of the mast tops chiming gently in the morning in a deserted marina. In the space of a few seconds, I spent the rest of my life with her.

'Billie!'
But she grabs the page from my hand. She's not weak. She's not going back. She holds one corner between thumb and forefinger. The flame licks up and the paper starts to burn.

The silver pen is magic, though. The paper chars but the silver words remain. They glow even brighter.